# HAVOC & MAYHEM

By Derrick A. Bonner

Check out: www.havocandmayhem.net and if you ever need a Trouble
Consultant, call 845-476-4678

1

 **WARNING**: THE AUTHOR IS NOT RESPONSIBLE IF YOUR BATHTUB OVERFLOWS, YOU MISS YOUR TRAIN OR BUS STOP, BURN YOUR DINNER, OR GET A BAD SUNBURN DUE TO YOUR INABILITY TO STOP PAGE TURNING. BECAUSE THIS BOOK IS THAT DAMN GOOD.

My advice to anyone who grew up during this era, the best way to read this dope time trip is the same way I wrote it. Pour yourself your favorite drink, mine is Hennessey. Put your favorite old school Hip Hop and R&B 80s classics on rotation. Let them play low in the background. Get comfortable. Now, let's go back, way back, back into time...ENJOY.

*'It is never too late to become what you might have been.'*

-Mrs. Charon L. Bonner

# THE DEFINITION OF A TROUBLE CONSULTANT

A TROUBLE CONSULTANT is the last resort when it comes to settling a major beef. When you can't squash it on your own and the police are basically waiting until somebody is outlined in chalk before they get involved, you hire The Trouble Consultant.

For a reasonable fee, he will put an end to whatever drama is consuming your life. But there are stipulations one should know before even approaching The Trouble Consultant such as: 1. He is not a hit-man, (it's one thing to kick somebody's ass, but killing is an entirely different matter). 2. He needs at least a week to check out your story, (this way he is not going into something blindly that could very well be the client's fault). 3. Half the payment is expected up front before anything goes down and is kept regardless if it does or does not (prices vary depending on the assignment). 4. He will not take a job against vicious-natured women and would never strike one, (cause his mama raised him right). 5. And lastly, some jobs may be flat-out refused depending on the risk factor, (for example, The Trouble Consultant will take out a small low-level drug dealer, but he's not single-handedly going up against a high-powered drug cartel).

Just because he can throw a punch, it doesn't make him a superhero. He's just an ordinary guy who can do extraordinary things.

# Chapter 1

*"What's up? You're listening to the super rocking sounds of pure hip hop on 98.7 kiss WRKSFM New York City's number one radio station. I'm your host, Kool DJ Red Alert going berserk spinning the phattest jams you wanna hear on the one's and two's. And as we bid a fond farewell to nineteen eight-seven, I'm gonna play a new joint from my man, Brooklyn's own, Big Daddy Kane. It's called Ain't no half stepping. Peace."*

*♫Aww yeah. I'm with this. I'm just gonna sit here laid back to this nice mellow beat you know. And drop some smooth lyrics. It's eighty-eight, time to set it straight kna' what I'm saying and ain't no half stepping-word! ♫*

Half way through the hot track, the Trouble Consultant muted his car stereo when the push button cigarette lighter popped out. He removed it and brought the orange glowing metal cylinder to the end of the blunt hanging from his mouth. Once it was lit, he took a deep pull then exhaled and leaned back comfortably behind the wheel with a Sony Watchman on his lap and the sizzling fat blunt between his thumb and trigger finger, stone cold lampin'. Thanks to the dark tinted windows, the car's interior was pitch black and the only sources of light came from the fiery glow of the burning blunt and the bluish haze that the watchman gave off. On the miniature screen the ageless avatar of American Bandstand's Dick Clark was dressed warmly on the streets of New York. In the background, countless vibrant screaming people wearing party hats and plastic glasses that blinked 'Happy New Year', shook noisemakers and blew into plastic horns to perform for the camera.

*"Welcome back to Times Square. It is now less than 3 minutes 'til midnight when the ball will drop and this crowd will go wild. For this very moment they have all gathered. They are ready, they are anxious and they've all got their eyes on that lighted ball atop a seventy-foot flagpole hoisted twenty-two stories up in the air. We are just moments away from the count down to the year nineteen-eighty-eight. The ball is in place and I have just gotten word that it's ready to drop!"* The Trouble Consultant watched through tight eyes as he took a long deep toke powerful enough to make a Rastafarian pass out. After exhaling he counted along as the famous apple shaped red ball of lights began its traditional year-end descent down the long pole to ring in the New Year.

"Ten-nine-eight-seven-six-five-four-three-two-one-HAPPY NEW YEAR! Different year, same bullshit!" he said in a voice of pure gravel made rougher from an endless stream of blunts and Newports. He switched off the miniature television then laid his head back on the headrest enjoying his buzz as the night came alive with drunken shouting and gunfire on the mean streets of East New York. It was New Years, Brooklyn style. Top of the motherfucking food chain.

The blunt had The Trouble Consultant feeling no pain, but he didn't want to get too lifted because he had a job to do, so he put it out in the ash tray for later then tilted back and put a couple of drops of Visine in each eye to get the red out. Now he was in the right frame of mind to work. He studied the intimidating-looking guard across the street standing outside of the dilapidated brownstone then cracked open a strawberry Calvin Cooler from the six pack on the floor. After emptying the bottle with one huge gulp to get rid of the dry mouth, he then fixed his stare into the rearview mirror and focused his attention on the passenger in the back seat.

"Aight partner listen up back there. This is a simple job, I'ma go in, get the goods, come back out. Piece of cake. I don't anticipate on needing any back up. So keep your overzealous ass in the car. If I need you, I'll call you. Are we clear?" he asked and a deep throaty grunt was heard indicating that while the message was received, it wasn't appreciated. "Cool!" he said and went to get out. He paused snapping his fingers and removed twin Glocks with pearl handles from behind his back and tossed them under the seat. He slid leather gloves over his sharp-scarred knuckles, a bell Kangol hat on his head and covered his eyes with a pair of Gazelles. Taking one last look in the mirror, he checked the pulse on his neck. It was beating like a racehorse. He exhaled. No matter how many consulting gigs he performed in the past, the minutes right before it went down was always a little stressful. He pulled back his sleeve. "Time to make the doughnuts."

The frosty temperature didn't faze The Trouble Consultant as a gust of wind escorted him across the street. He pulled his collar up just beneath his dark eyes and went to the pay phone on the corner then fed it some coins. After the third ring someone picked up.

"Hello?...Yes, it's taken care of. I'll stop by your restaurant around closing time to collect the other half of my fee." After hanging up he made a second call then turned his frown upside down when a familiar voice answered. "Hello?...Hey brat what are you still doing up?…Oh she did huh?…And Happy New Years to you too…Yeah I saw it drop…On that little TV set you and Mommy got me for Christmas…No you don't get any New Year gifts…Because…Just because…Wasn't Christmas last week?…And isn't your birthday next week?…Well okay then, stop being so greedy begging Billy…Okay we'll talk about it tomorrow. Now put mommy on the phone…I love you too…Mmmwwaa kiss-kiss…Okay bye…" The Trouble Consultant rolled his eyes at his sister's antics. "Tee-Tee, stop playing around and put Mommy on the phone before my money runs out…C'mon Tee-Tee quit play-heyyy Mommy-O, how're you doing?…Fine, I'm just calling to say Happy New Year, you know I can't start off the new year without speaking to you and the brat…So you're still coming over tomorrow?…Cool…No Ma I didn't forget…I'm headed over to see him as soon as I leave this party…Of course I'm in a safe neighborhood," he said surveying the area smack dab in the middle of a bad place to be even in the daytime. "…Nothing major. Just kicking it with some decent people to celebrate." As he noticed the tough looking guard outside the brownstone frisking a shyste looking man. "Yes, I promise to be careful…No, I won't be out too late. Stop worrying, I'll be fine. Listen, I'm about to head inside so I gotta go. See you mañana…I love you too Ma, bye."

The Trouble Consultant hung up feeling like a first–class heel for lying to his mother. But he knew she would sleep much easier thinking the worse that could happen to her precious baby boy was he'd wake up with a killer hangover from too much celebrating. He pushed the guilt out of his head as he approached the screw-faced guard eyeing him, while mumbling into a walkie-talkie and trying to keep warm in a red and black Lumberjack jacket, with the hat to match.

"The Hawk's out tonight huh Big Man?" the Trouble Consultant greeted cheerfully.

"Fuck you want?" the Lumberjack growled back sizing him up and down. He was so black the Vaseline on his face had him looking like a patent leather Easter shoe.

"Any action going on inside?" the Trouble Consultant inquired.

"It's a hoe house. There's always action going on inside."

7

"True dat!"

"So, you wastin' my time or what?"

"Neither yours, nor mines." the Trouble Consultant grinned then held out his arms to be frisked. As the Lumberjack started at his wrists and worked his way down to his ankles checking for weapons, he was glad he remembered to leave his guns in the car.

"Aight Money-grip, you straight." the Lumberjack said and swung the door open so he could enter the house of ill repute.

Making his way down the narrow hall, The Trouble Consultant could hear loud music coming from up ahead. Exiting through hanging beads in the doorway he paused taking in the scenery and muttered, "Never judge a book by its cover."

The brothel's interior was nothing like its exterior. It was an exotic refuge from the outside world. Luxurious, warm and clean, decorated nicely with hanging plants, colorful throw rugs, matching curtains, leather furniture and glass tables. A live Christmas tree patiently awaiting to be tossed stood in the corner and a few blinking decorations adorned the walls. Bikini and hot-pants-clad women were lounging on couches, laughing, smoking weed and sipping champagne as pioneer rap group, Funky Four plus One's song 'That's the Joint', played in the background courtesy of a huge JVC ghetto blaster boom box.

With stubble on his face and caution in his eyes, the Trouble Consultant flirted back with the bevy of beautiful women as he made his way towards a woman hairier than a Wookie and the size of Jabba the Hut, furiously twisting on a Rubik's Cube. Frustrated she couldn't solve the puzzle, she began peeling off the colored squares and putting them back on in the correct sequence. The Trouble Consultant pegged Jabba for the resident Madam and approached the disgusting example of womanhood gone wrong.

"Hello," he said.

The Madam glared and about sucked the filing out of her left rear molar, "So what chu want?" she growled.

"Well it's New Years, and I can't think of a better way to ring it in than with a woman who will, fuck for a buck, holler for a dollar, do something strange for a lil bit of change-Miss um?" he pried for her name.

"Bitsy. As in itsy," she said. The Trouble Consultant's amused expression asked, *'are you serious?'* as he eyed the woman who was so ugly if she went into a haunted house, she'd come out with a job application. "Look just go on over there and choose one of dem hoes. When you're ready come back to me for your room key. Rooms are twenty bucks an hour and whatever y'all do is between y'all. Oh, and before I forget here, you get a free bottle of Asti Spumante compliments of Diamond Ken. Happy New Year." Bitsy said unenthusiastically as she handed him a bottle of bottom shelf champagne from the milk crate at her feet.

The Trouble Consultant nodded thanks then glanced over his shoulder at the noisy ladies partying in the back. There was every type of woman for every type of preference. Thin, thick, short, tall, long hair, short hair, black, white, Spanish and Asian. Basically, the United Nation of hoes. The effects of the cheap champagne were beginning to take control as two of the friendlier girls began dancing seductively under the mistletoe, kissing and groping one another. Drunk and caught up in the moment, one of them snatched the mistletoe down and held it just below her navel as her giggling partner puckered up and buried her face beneath it. The lewd act started a quick trend that spread throughout the room like a venereal disease and it wasn't long before the other prostitutes were wiggling out of their clothes with no shame oblivious to the rest of the room.

The Trouble Consultant watched the rising orgy for a hot second then looked over at Bitsy and frowned. The chunky Madam was becoming aroused and licked her lips while rubbing on her cellulite marked thighs. "Hey Bitsy, wanna chill out with the self-love? You're gonna make me throw up, everything I've ever ate." he said then blocked her view with a picture. "This here is the girl I want." he said with an all-business intensity.

Bitsy rolled her eyes at him then snatched the picture and stared at the pretty black girl with long braids covered in white beads, Stevie Wonder style. Her eyes widened then she quickly regained her composure with an uninterested pout.

"And where'd you get the snapshot?"

"I'm a huge fan." he said unconvincingly.

"Is that right? Well sorry. She ain't here." she said.

"You sure about that?"

"Yeah I'm sure! What I gots ta lie to you fo'?" she snapped defensively then sipped some Asti and went back to working on her Rubik's Cube like she couldn't be bothered.

The Trouble Consultant could see the word 'LIAR' practically rise out of her forehead. He had been staking out the whorehouse for the past couple of hours and saw the girl in the picture come and go constantly with different men. He was about to cancel the job and settle for only half his consulting fee, because she obviously wanted to be there. Then ten minutes prior to Dick Clark's countdown things switched up when he saw her try to leave and get dragged back inside kicking and screaming by a large fat man and she hadn't come back out since.

"Hmm, now that's funny because I heard from a very reliable source that I could find her here." He said referring to himself.

"Well they can't be all that reliable, cause ya heard wrong. Now like I said either choose one of them or breakout."

"Nah I've got a better idea. How about I camp-out just in case she decides to come back." he said ignoring her attitude and got comfortable on the black leather sofa across the room.

Bitsy sucked her teeth at The Trouble Consultant then gave him her back and snatched the phone off the hook. From his past experience in dealing with situations of this type he knew she was calling whoever it was she answered to. No doubt Mister complimentary champagne himself, Diamond Ken.

"Hello, Faye? Put Diamond on the phone…Hello Diamond? There's some guy down here asking a whole bunch of questions about Mercedes. I think he's Five-O, cause he has a picture of her." Bitsy whispered into the receiver.

"Well whoever the fuck he is he ain't a cop. That's for damn sure. I paid them crooked bastards off yesterday. He's more than likely just some lonely trick that heard about her vertical skills. You tell his stalker ass she's not here and if he doesn't want one of them hoes you got down there, then he can take his business elsewhere." a stern voice said on the opposite end.

Bitsy glanced over at the man in question as he turned down a big-breasted woman's advances who playfully removed his Kangol. "I already told him that, but his bald headed ass won't leave."

There was a long pregnant pause on the other end. "…Did you say bald?"

"Yeah he's bald. Why?"

"…Describe this bald guy to me." Diamond Ken asked with concern in his voice.

Bitsy clocked him as he placed his Kangol back on his head, "Well he's a big guy, solid as a brick wall. Over six feet tall with a chest wide enough to play handball on. He looks to be in his early thirties. And his voice is crazy deep. Kinda like a cross between Barry White and Tone Loc."

"What else?" the voice on the opposite end asked.

"Um I dunno, he's brown skinned. He's got a moustache and a goatee anything else you want to know?"

"Just one more thing. And this is very-very-VERY important….is he dressed in all red?"

Becoming increasingly concerned, Bitsy inconspicuously glanced back over at the mystery man who in the blink of an eye graduated from a random John, to a person of interest and studied his sharp style of dress. Just as Diamond Ken feared, everything he wore was the same crimson complexion. He was cloaked in a ruby red leather trench coat, wine colored leather gloves, an open collared magenta silk shirt, sharply creased cinnamon slacks, a copper snakeskin belt and tomato red Clarks Wallabee suede shoes. Atop his dome was a rose colored Kangol, the Gazelle frames on his face and even his argyle socks were maroon.

"Hey how'd you know that?" she asked becoming concerned.

"Fuck! I hope I'm wrong, but I think that's Havoc." Diamond Ken said nervously.

"Havoc? As in Havoc and Mayhem? But I thought they was just some stupid ghetto rumor."

"Yeah, well that so-called rumor knocked the gold fronts down my homeboy Roc's throat so deep dat fool has to stick his toothbrush up his ass just so he can brush them. Buss it, keep him there, I'll handle this."

"No problem Dee. I got your back." Bitsy said picking up on the reverence and fear in Diamond Ken's voice. In all the years she had known the evil natured cold as ice drug-pushing pimp, she had never witnessed anyone or anything take him off of his game. Until now. Which led her to believe that the mysterious man dripping in red might very well be Satan himself, here to personally escort the diabolical pimp to Hell for his life of sin. Bitsy hung up and came over wearing a three-dollar bill smile. "So, how are we doing?" she asked cheerfully.

"Chillin' like Bob Dylan." The man in red answered drolly while mindlessly spinning a thin gold whistle on a medium sized rope chain around his finger. By the sudden metamorphosis in her attitude he anticipated something was about to go down. A second later, it did. The Lumberjack came in out of the cold and locked the door.

"Roaches check in, but they don't check out!" The Lumberjack hissed with an evil grin. At the same time a man larger than life came down the stairs shaking the entire structure with his weight and jingling from the 'Mister T.' starter kit around his neck.

"This oughta be fun!" Bitsy smiled anticipating a good show as she pumped up the volume on the boom box then tore into a bag of Doritos.

'Another One Bites the Dust' by Queen began to play. Rising from his seat, the man in red felt like he was in the middle of an action movie complete with soundtrack. He placed his chain and whistle back over his head and calmly removed his gloves with his teeth shaking his head with a sigh. The questions, the lies, the big tough guys. It had all become so boringly routine.

"Hey little red riding hood. Diamond Ken wants to see you." The Lumberjack said while walking up on the Trouble Consultant from behind, then put his hand on his shoulder.

The Trouble Consultant growled at the hand like a junkyard dog, "Yo Money-grip I should warn you that my patience is about as long as the hair on the top of my head."

"Ooh I'm shitting in my pants. Now move it tough guy!" The Lumberjack hissed unimpressed with a sharp shove.

Suddenly in a one handed move the man in red removed the Lumberjack's hand from his shoulder, twisting his arm behind his back bending it at an unnatural angle forcing him to drop to one knee.

"You're an eggshell," he said.

"Ow-shit! Huh-a what?" the Lumberjack asked cringing in pain.

"An eggshell my friend."

"What the hell are you talking about?"

"Oh, it's quite simple. A few pounds of applied pressure anywhere on the body and-Snap!" The Trouble Consultant said and with a gruesome popping sound he dislocated the Lumberjack's arm like a bread stick. "See, what'd I tell you? An eggshell."

The Lumberjack's shrieks blended with the prostitutes as a grotesque lump strained from his sleeve. The Trouble Consultant could no longer take his screaming and clubbed him over the head with his bottle of Asti Spumante then rolled his eyes frustrated, "I hate it when heads be frontin' like they're from Rikers Island, knowing Goddamn well they're from Fantasy Island."

Everything was happening so fast that Mister T. never had time to act. The man in red walked up on him with eyes so mean they had no room for fear in them whatsoever and said, "Either I'm going past you, or through you. But I am going up those stairs. Make a decision." The hired muscle paused for a second thinking over his options then went for his gun but before he could pull out, the Trouble Consultant landed a lead hook behind his ear and stretched him out like a rug. "Too late!"

"Rasheed!" Bitsy screamed when she saw her baby brother go down, then clambered out of her chair and stared down the man responsible with murder in her eyes. "Ooh you done fucked up now!"

"Come on Big Momma! Toro! Toro!" He goaded her flapping the tail of his coat like a matador. With a snarl and grunt Bitsy charged forward like a runaway bull.

The Trouble Consultant coolly waited for her to get closer then at the last possible second stepped to the side, yanked open the closet door behind him and slammed her inside then braced a chair up against the doorknob, barricading the hefty woman inside. He then hit the staircase and his adrenaline went from zero to one hundred in three seconds when a third man with dreadlocks appeared at the top clutching a Choo-Choo automatic and reminded him that this shit was real. Deadly real! Mechanically he reached behind his back for his own burners and swore loudly remembering that they were under his car seat. The dreadlocked gunman shouted, "Bon Fi-yah!" at the top of his lungs.

"Oh shit!" the Trouble Consultant yelled and dove over the banister as the Jamaican opened fire with a shower of hot steel. Meanwhile below the staircase amidst the panicked prostitutes running out the door screaming for their lives, Mister T. was regaining consciousness when a pair of size thirteen Wallabees dropped out of the sky and lullabied him back to sleep.

Relieving the pitiful fool of his weapon, the Trouble Consultant scrambled to his feet and fired up from below into the shooter's legs then stepped over him as he tumbled down the stairs.

Once he reached the top of the stairs, he faced down two more of Diamond Ken's goons. The bigger of the two grabbed him in a bear hug lifting him off the ground and squeezed until the man in red could hardly breathe and dropped his gun over the banister. The second rushed forward wildly swinging, burying his fists in his ribs and kidneys. Ignoring the pain, the Trouble Consultant kicked him in the chest knocking him down then slammed his head back breaking the nose of the man holding him as well as his bear hug. With the fight taken out of him, he was tossed over the banister. The second man climbed to his feet and tossed a few misguided punches that were no match for the Trouble Consultant's vicious street-fighter moves as he blocked them and sent him flying over the banister as well.

52

After taking out the trash, the man in red brushed his hands together then rolled his eyes as four more huge goons appeared.

"Aw geez fellas for crying out loud. Didn't you see what I just did to Kid and Play back there? I mean honestly, why would you wanna put yourselves through that?" Unfazed, the leering crew advanced forward, "All right. But for your sake, I hope you have good medical and dental." he said raising his hands defensively and switched to a South-Paw fighting stance. "Let's do this!" Then, using good footwork, sharp jabs, elbows, knees, clenches, his opponents as barriers against each other, all the while sticking and moving, he proceeded to tear through the motley crew like a tornado. Once they were down for the count he called out for Mercedes down the long brown-carpeted hall.

Muffled cries and the sounds of someone being abused came from behind the first door on his right and he violently kicked it off its hinges to discover an androgynous pale-faced man on all fours getting spanked by a shapely dominatrix in a leather corset, nipple rings, 6-inch spikes and panties to hide her modesty.

"Oops my bad. Carry on," the Trouble Consultant frowned. A woman's sudden screams for help snatched his head alert and he took off. He knocked down the door where the screams came from and discovered a naked woman with her back facing him. She wore her hair in long braids with white beads, Stevie Wonder style. "Mercedes?" he asked unsure and she shook her braids yes. He was immediately suspicious. A 'trouble consulting' gig was never this easy. But then again, there's a first time for everything. "Throw something on, time to leave!"

"Maybe it's you who should leave." the naked woman said and turned around in slow motion with her hands wrapped around a shiny silver nickel-plated 22. and a wide smile across her face. "In a pine box!"

"Shit!" it was the right hairstyle, but the wrong girl.

"Hands behind your head handsome. Now! Do it!" the naked imposter barked. The Trouble Consultant reluctantly obeyed. "Diamond I found him. He's out here baby." she yelled.

"Trifling bitch!" he hissed.

"Oh I gots yo' bitch right here." she retorted and cocked her gun.

The door behind him snatched open and someone stepped out holding a double-barreled shotgun. Covered in sparkling jewelry Diamond Ken was as clichéd as the cocked fedora he sported. In his left ear he wore a large diamond stud. All the fingers of both hands were covered in sparkling diamond rings. On one wrist was a diamond bracelet and on the other a glistening diamond faced nugget watch. Even the Gazelle shades he sported were diamond laden along the top of the frames. For a brief second, the man in red's riveting appearance left the iced-out pimp frozen but he quickly shook it off and the Trouble Consultant heard the all-too-familiar *Cha-chink* of a loading shotgun.

"Havoc!"

Spinning around when he heard his street moniker called, Havoc brazenly seized Diamond Ken's wrist. As the two struggled over the shotgun a misdirected shot fired blowing the naked woman back into the room.

"Faye!" the pimp called out visibly upset over all the revenue he saw flying out of the window.

In the blink of an eye Havoc head-butted the pimp to the floor then spun on his heels and zig-zagged down the opposite end of the hall as shotgun blasts chased after him tearing huge chunks into the walls. He came upon another flight of stairs and looked back to see Diamond Ken gun in tow, coming for him then bolted up another flight of steps. The third floor was dimly lit and every door he tried was locked. He put his hand on the last doorknob at the end of the hall when Diamond Ken entered the floor.

"You ain't gonna MacGuyver your way outta this one motherfucker!" Diamond Ken promised with a bead on Havoc.

Havoc clenched his teeth and twisted the knob. To his surprise it opened and he burst inside as the pimp fired a missed shot and cursed up a storm. Once inside he caught his breath and locked the door behind him. There was a large dresser in the corner and he pushed it in front of the door as a barricade, then backed away awaiting the pimp's forced entry when something moved behind him. He spun around with his fists raised to find a girl in bra and panties gagged with duct tape and handcuffed to an iron ring bolted to the wall. She too had white beaded braids like the girl from the picture but the room was dimly lit and her face was swollen, so Havoc was not one hundred percent certain if it was her or not. He checked himself for the photo and remembered Bitsy never returned it.

"Mercedes?" he asked unsure. Shaking uncontrollably with fear the girl managed a nod but that wasn't good enough for the Trouble Consultant. Moments ago, Faye claimed to be Mercedes too. He removed the tape from her mouth and asked in a stern voice, "What's your mother's middle name?"

"Huh?" she asked not sure if she heard him correctly.

Havoc clamped his hand around her chin, "If you're planning something sneaky, we ain't the two and I ain't the one. Now tell me your mother's middle name!"

"It's Jean. Barbara Jean Holiday." she replied meekly.

Havoc glared at the girl then let go of her face hoping that an impostor wouldn't know something as personal as the middle name for the mother of the person they were impersonating. Now that he located the goods all he had to do was figure out a way to get them both out alive. Piece of cake.

A toilet flushed.

"Somebody in there?" Havoc asked gesturing towards the bathroom door.

Mercedes nodded with wide frightened eyes and whispered, "Big Fella."

Havoc shook his head and sucked his teeth. "I swear this place is like Christmas, full of surprises."

The bathroom door creaked open and the room instantly became infected with a funky combination of shit and Lysol. Standing in the doorway naked and stretching was a horribly fat pear-shaped black man, twice the size of Mount Fuji, with thighs the size of infants. The obese man fanned the air and grimaced rubbing his stretch marked belly that hung so low it hid his dick.

"Coming out feeling 'bout ten pounds lighter. Okay baby let's do this-Nigga where in da fuck did you come from?" Big Fella demanded when he saw Havoc.

"What did you just call me?" Havoc asked through clenched teeth.

Big Fella waddled over shaking the claustrophobic small, room with each step. "What iz you deaf?" The obese man snarled but Havoc did not answer, "I said Nigga where...hold up...wait a second. It's you-" a choke gurgled in his throat as he locked on Havoc allowing his eyes to travel over his signature red attire and trademark Kangol. He nervously took a step back as if he'd just seen his own death. "The one who whooped Roc's ass."

Havoc pushed his Gazelles back on his nose and smiled. It was nice to be recognized for his work.

Outside the door Diamond Ken listened with a confident grin certain that his huge friend would make quick work of the smaller Trouble Consultant. Havoc set it off and hit Big Fella in his large belly that jiggled like jello with no real effect. Big Fella looked down at his sloppy gut unphased by the punch. He patted his belly then wiggled his eyebrows at Havoc. With a smirk he lifted Havoc and put him on his back across the room with a hard uppercut punch.

The nude obese man waddled over and stood over Havoc smiling victoriously. Havoc rubbed his jaw repulsed by the view. He climbed to one knee eyeing Big Fella through dark slits. Every fiber of his being accusing him with absolute rage. Then, without warning he planted his fist hard in the center of the fat man's crotch. The pain forced Big Fella's eyes to roll up in his head and he doubled over in pain holding himself. Havoc rose to his feet and dug into his coat pocket and pulled out a massive four-fingered ring that spelled out 'HAVOC' in big bold block letters which doubled as a pair of brass knuckles and slid it on his left hand.

"A-yo fat ass, wanna know why I wear all red?" Havoc asked in a voice that sounded like boulders crashing. Unable to answer, Big Fella meekly shook his head. "Well aside from the fact I look flyy as hell, it's because it hides the bloodstains!" he said then twisted back and landed a tremendous blow exploding Big Fella's face and sending blood spraying like a broken water main.

With one hand protecting his face Big fella tried to fight back and Havoc went to work, working the fat man like a punching bag landing solid blows until his legs gave out from under him and he came crashing to the ground like a ton of bricks.

Once Big Fella was down for the count Havoc immediately began searching for a way to free Mercedes. On the nightstand next to a hot plate keeping Big Fella's pot of chilli steaming hot was a set of keys. He scooped them up and smiled when they fit Mercedes' shackles.

The doorknob twisted back and forth wildly. "Hey what the hell's going on in there? Yo Big Fella is everything aight?...Big? Nigga you good?" Diamond Ken called out trying to Humphrey Bogart his way into the room. After no response it was obvious what had happened to his fat homeboy. "Havoc listen up, I don't know how the fuck you managed to take out Big, but the only way out of here is past me so open up and make it easier on yourself." he reasoned from the opposite side of the door.

"Yeah, picture that!" Havoc retorted then looked around the room for something to defend himself with but there wasn't anything. Frustrated he ripped the newspaper from the window and looked out then got an idea.

"I want to go home!" Mercedes cried frantically.

"Chill. I got this." Havoc said as he forced the window open and let in a surge of freezing air. Suddenly a loud shotgun blast ripped through the door and removed a chunk of the dresser. Mercedes screamed when she saw Diamond Ken's angry face peek through the hole. After blowing off the lock he still could not push open the door because of the heavy dresser and Big Fella's unconscious torso in the way.

"Fella, get yo family-sized ass up! Mercedes get over here and help me!" he ordered.

The sound of glass breaking startled Mercedes as Havoc shoved a twin sized mattress out the window. "Time to go!... Out the window!" he said sharply.

Mercedes looked up from sliding into her clothes, "Out the window?" she said feeling nauseous from fear.

Havoc grabbed her by the hand and pointed out the window. "Look, down there. See? Try to aim yourself right there," he said referring to the mattress he dropped onto a pile of garbage below the window. "I know it's not much but if you land on it it'll absorb some of the impact from the fall."

Mercedes was scared and didn't know what to do. "But-but, um I don't-" she stuttered.

"Bitch I know you ain't thinking 'bout leaving with that chump cause if you iz, so help me you'll be even sorrier than he's gonna be once I get in there." the pimp threatened.

Havoc grabbed Big Fella's pot of hot chilli and flung it at the door. "Who's sorry?" Havoc asked as the pimp screamed in pain. "Nice guy. Now I can see why you're having such a hard time making this decision," Havoc said, "So what's up, you staying?"

Mercedes pictured her face on the side of a milk carton and nervously climbed out the window. "As soon as you land run for the red Chevy across the street. But do not open the door. Wait for me I'll be right behind." Havoc instructed.

The teenager nodded, hung for a moment, then let go screaming and landed on her plump behind. She was sore and would definitely wake up with bruises tomorrow but just like Havoc assured her, the mattress and trash pile absorbed the blunt of her fall. It was now Havoc's turn and when he climbed out he noticed Diamond Ken was no longer at the door. It was definitely time to leave. When he landed he was staring up at the business end of the pimp's shotgun.

"Leaving so soon?" The pimp asked with a red scorch mark over his greasy face and winded from running down three flights of stairs. "The party's just starting!" He said and kicked Havoc hard in the face. "That's for throwing that hot shit in my face." Havoc tasted his blood and angrily went to stand. "Ah-ah-ah don't even think about it. Not unless you trying to win first prize in a wet t-shirt contest." The pimp warned holding his gun threateningly.

Havoc cut his eyes at Mercedes trembling with fear then eyed his classy cherry red '1957 Chevy Bel Air across the street. Taking hold of the whistle around his neck, he blew into it, but it made no sound.

"Yo homeboy I think your whistle's busted. But if you trying to call the neighborhood watch you're wasting your time. Cause I'm it!" Diamond Ken laughed.

Havoc ignored the pimp and waited for something to happen. Inside of his car a pair of yellow eyes blinked open followed by a deep growl. The Chevy's back door opened and everyone was magnetized as a huge paw stepped into the street making a crunching noise when it's razor sharp nails dug into the ice. Havoc turned back to Diamond Ken with a devilish grin.

"Nah, my dog whistle works just fine." The Trouble Consultant said cockily. The fearless pimp was paralyzed with terror from what had stepped out of the car. Havoc got up and brushed the snow from his legs. "Oh, I see you haven't met my partner. Diamond Ken...meet Mayhem."

The pimp was speechless. As soon as he laid eyes on the tan and reddish canine that stood at an imposing twenty-seven inches high and easily weighed one hundred and thirty pounds with its large wrinkled head, short black muzzle and big drooling jowls sporting a gladiator-pit style spiked red leather collar, he knew he was not dealing with an ordinary dog.

Sixty percent English Mastiff and forty percent Olde English Bull dog. Bullmastiff's were cross bred to be one of the most powerful super dogs on the planet. Prized for their size, speed, intelligence and tenacity, they have had many jobs throughout history. Romans used them as war dogs due to their temperament and aggressive nature. South African's employed them to guard diamond mines. In England they bravely guarded livestock, assisting English gatekeeper's as night watch dogs and were the primary source of defense against poachers during the 19th century. And in the 20th century, the Trouble Consultant's loyal and unflinchingly protective companion against killer psycho pimps and other deviants.

Diamond Ken's face was tight with anticipation of what the freak of nature was thinking about doing to him. Prior to Mayhem the biggest, meanest-looking dog he had ever come across was Terminator, the ferocious rottweiler that guarded the auto body mechanic shop where he had his car phone and Alpine speakers installed. But compared to Mayhem that mutt was a poodle. Mayhem stretched with a yawn displaying sharp teeth that looked like they belonged in a shark's mouth and caused a tidal wave of muscles to ripple from nose to tail. With shaky hands, Diamond Ken swallowed hard and aimed his shotgun at the large beast.

"NO!" Havoc shouted and kicked the gun from the pimp's hands as a shot fired and snow exploded around Mayhem. The Trouble Consultant then landed seven lightning-quick punches to his face and stomach until he folded up like lawn furniture.

Holding his ribs and sucking oxygen, Diamond Ken struggled to his feet. Mayhem jumped into protective mode. Terrified, the pimp took off running. Havoc cut his eyes at his dog anxiously awaiting his next command. "Handle that!" Havoc instructed.

In a flash Mayhem took off after the pimp and using the knock and pin method like its ancestors were trained to do against poachers it pounced on top of him and pinned his shoulders with overwhelming strength. A menacing growl drilled a hole in Diamond Ken's ear but to his surprise it didn't come from Mayhem, it came from Havoc.

"Call off your dog man. Please!" Diamond Ken begged as the snow between his crotch turned bright yellow.

Havoc was so furious with the chicken-shit pimp for almost shooting his best friend that he was tempted to give the command that would prompt the dog to rip out his throat. "Mayhem...come." he called upon second thought, while throwing a kiss in the air and patting his thigh. Mayhem played deaf and leaned in inhaling deeply. With anxious fangs inches from Diamond Ken's face hungry for a bite, the mythical looking beast could smell the fear come out of the pimp's pores and fed off of it. "Mayhem I said, COME!" Havoc called again this time with base in his voice and the dog grunted like it was pissed and trotted over to his side. "Good girl. That's my precious little girl," he said bowing to kiss her on the head and she wagged her tail pleased she made her master happy.

Havoc picked up Diamond Ken's shotgun and placed it to the side of his head like he was about to make a hole in one. The pimp squeezed his eyes shut and screamed out, "Please don't kill me!" More urine ran from his bladder.

Havoc pumped the shotgun spilling blue shells all over the pimp. "You know, I was planning on beating the piss out of you, but I'll fall back. Seeing as how you've already done that for me." He said and dropped the emptied gun then stared at him lying there humiliated and exited without another word. Mercedes trailed behind.

Happy to still be alive, Diamond Ken breathed a sigh of relief that is until he noticed all of the women whose flaws, weaknesses and addictions that he used against them to keep them under his thumb were watching him with Poetic Justice stretched across their lips.

Realizing how weak he must look in his stable's eyes the pimp quickly climbed to his feet worried that if he did not do something right now to regain his power over them, he would lose them as well.

"G'wan! Take her junkie ass! Shit that hoe could use the vacation. But mark my words, she'll be back. I mean shit, where the fuck else is a twenty-four seven, super-duper freaky hoe gonna go?" Diamond Ken called out in a voice as cold as ice chips, adding a sinister laugh for effect. Mercedes stopped dead in her tracks and spun around then marched right back over to Diamond Ken. "What, back so soon? That didn't take long. Come on hoe. Come back to Daddy." the vile pimp smiled with his arms open wide. Mercedes walked towards him and suddenly hauled off and slapped him hard across the face then began sobbing uncontrollably.

Diamond Ken was furious that one of his women had the audacity to hit him and raised his arm to backhand her. Havoc cleared his throat then shook his head letting him know that he was about to make a huge mistake. The pimp's arm wisely swung to his side.

Havoc turned to Mercedes. "Let's go."

With every ounce of water drained from her eyes Mercedes walked past the sad faces of fellow streetwalkers who desperately wished someone loved them enough to send a Brooklyn-Knight in crimson armor to rescue them. As soon as Havoc slid behind the wheel of his ride he removed his heavy four-fingered ring because it felt uncomfortable when driving and impossible to fire a gun while wearing and stuffed it back in his pocket. Then reached under his seat grabbed his Glocks then put them back in their holsters. Now he felt whole again. He glanced over at Mercedes. She was staring straight ahead with a blank look and rocking in her seat. Havoc shook his head with a sigh. Deep down he pitied her. She had borne witness to so many loveless acts of sex and violence yet she wasn't even old enough to sit at a bar and order a drink. He eyed his dog in the rear-view mirror.

"Gimme some," Havoc said reaching an open palm over his shoulder and Mayhem placed her paw inside his hand to shake it. Then with a proud papa smile he twisted the key in the ignition. He was about to pull off when he heard someone screaming and shouting and looked out the window.

As Diamond Ken went from demanding to begging on his hands and knees that his stable not leave him, it was painfully clear that he had collected his last pimp's commission off of them. In the game of Macking and stacking, a Pimp's job is to dress, rest, finesse and let his hoes take care of the rest. And any self-respecting flesh-peddler who can't keep his shit together, much less his bladder might as well turn in his playa' card and fill out an application at some square-ass job somewhere because he was through in this field.

"Damn, I guess it's true what they say. Pimping ain't easy," Havoc said ruefully then disappeared into the night.

He went in, got the goods and came out. Piece of cake.

# Chapter 2

It's the section that put the 'crook' in Crooklyn and the 'Nam' in Brooknam. The New York neighborhood where its occupants convince themselves as they're trying to make it, that they're gonna make it. The area that fills up a huge percent of New York's state prisons. Brownsville, aka Thugs-Ville. Home of the brave where the moto is, 'Brownsville, never ran, never will!'

Barbara Jean Holiday paced her living room floor chain smoking like an expectant father. She was fifty with the blurry features of a woman who must have once been a pretty teenager.

She sat down for a second then got up and paced some more wondering how to prevent what happened from occurring again. After receiving a phone call from Havoc saying that he was bringing her daughter back home safe and sound she could not sit still. In fact, she did not even realize it was a new year until forty-five minutes into it. Riddled with worry and nervous energy she tapped the bottom of a pack of Kool cigarettes then lit one and looked out the window at the drabby, tall brown Tilden housing projects surrounding her, smothering her, caging her. Down below were the kids she watched grow up, some she even baby-sat, tranquilized by malt liquor, squeezing off rounds into the air, laughing and celebrating what they considered was living.

"If I owned Hell and these projects, I believe I'd rent out this place and live in Hell." Barbara sighed.

When she first moved into the projects it was a completely different place to live. She had neighbors of different races and cultures. There were vegetable gardens outside of her window. And weekly tenant association meetings where neighbors brought delicious dishes and discussed things going on in the community and how to better improve it. Now it was a gloomy, depressing place where odd characters came and went at all hours. Daylight drug dealing was common and occasional gunshots were followed by the screech of tires.

Raising two kids on her own was no picnic and doing it in a hard-core high crime zone was even tougher. When neighbors reported that her oldest child Mercedes was spotted hanging out with a rowdy bunch of kids that cut class, drank, smoked and did Lord knows what else, Barbara did not want to believe it. But she had to come face to face with reality when she found a bag full of small plastic capsules filled with tiny white rocks in her daughter's bedroom that she promptly flushed down the toilet. Fed up with her daughter's dances with trouble, Barbara confronted Mercedes about it. Mercedes claimed she was simply holding them for a friend and did not even know what that stuff was.

Barbara may have been born at night, but it wasn't last night, and she refused to believe such a tired ass story. A shouting match ensued which resulted in Mercedes storming out saying that since her privacy was not respected there, she would no longer live there. For weeks Barbara was worried sick and heard nothing. Then on Christmas Eve, her nine-year-old son Elijah came home to report that he overheard the older kids gossiping about how his sister was strung out and prostituting somewhere out in East New York. Barbara did not know what to do. Since her daughter was eighteen she was not a minor, and not considered a runaway. Therefore, New York's finest would not waste their time searching for yet another missing black girl, hooked on the new wave drug, 'crack'. A cheaper form of rock cocaine that caught people like an ambush and turned them into addicts at an alarming rate.

This was too much for Barbara to deal with by herself and she needed help. But where was this help going to come from? Purcell her children's father and a pitiful excuse for a man, left her and the kids with nothing but the pain of abandonment. And her family and friends had their own problems. Then one day while she was at the incinerator dumping the trash and feeling sorry for herself, Maxine, the resident *Wilona,* offered some free advice about her predicament.

"Say gurl, I ain't trying to be all up in your business, but I heard about your trouble with Mercedes. Now word on the street is that there's a man who can help. He'll listen to your story, and he'll make a judgement. If he thinks you're wrong, you're out on your ass. If he thinks you've been wronged, then you'll never have a better friend." Maxine then handed Barbara a black business card with bold red letters that said:

NEED RELIEF FROM THE BEEF?
THEN CALL HAVOC & MAYHEM
TROUBLE CONSULTANTS AT 476-4678
REASONABLE RATES, SATISFACTION GUARANTEED

Barbara studied the card and twisted her face a little skeptical. "Havoc and Mayhem huh, what is this dial a joke?"

"Trust me, he ain't no joke!" Maxine said like she knew from personal experience, "He's a man of honor and when he says he will do something, you can best believe it'll get done."

Left with no other alternatives, Barbara took the card then went inside her apartment and made a phone call...

A sharp knock at the front door awoke Elijah and he sat up on the couch and rubbed the sleep from his eyes. Barbara replaced a picture of the sweet little girl in pigtails, taken at Sears way before she became a junkie prostitute, back on the mantle, gently ran her fingers through her son's curly Afro and walked over to the door. She looked through the peephole, took a drag then exhaled a plume of cigarette smoke through a frustrated sigh before unbolting a series of locks, chains and a long metal bar over the door. Havoc stood beneath a lonely flickering light bulb taking up almost all the space in the narrow graffiti covered hallway with his massive red frame.

"Where is she?" Barbara wistfully asked darting her eye's everywhere. Havoc cleared his throat and held out his hand rubbing his fingers together.

"Oh right, I'm sorry. I'm just real anxious to see my baby." Barbara apologized handing Havoc a thick envelope.

The Trouble Consultant bowed slightly and stepped to the side revealing a worn out looking Mercedes, badly in need of a hot shower, a home cooked meal, a warm bed and most of all, her mother's love.

"My baby," Barbara whispered stepping forward and her eyes filled with water. Mercedes may have only been gone a little over two weeks, but the effects from the fast lifestyle she lived made her look way beyond her eighteen years. Barbara embraced her daughter and they both gave in to their tears. As Barbara led her into their apartment, she looked back to thank Havoc, but he was already gone.

There was no need for thank yous, the Trouble Consultant was simply doing the job he was paid to do.

# Chapter 3

His eyes roving, Havoc nodded to 'You Belong to the City' feeling every bit a man of the street as he streaked past the Galaxy Hotel on Pennsylvania Avenue where hookers tricked and nickel and dime drug dealers stood around pushing weight like it was popcorn at a Saturday matinee. One building dissolved into another, some bustling with life, some empty and boarded over but all the same. Turning off Atlantic Avenue and onto Eastern Parkway, he spilled out behind the Brooklyn Public Library across from Prospect Park and weaved through the entanglement of monuments and green parks where tourists flocked and weekenders played volleyball. This was all that most visitors saw as worthy in Brooklyn, having been fed a steady diet of negative headlines about the rest of his beloved borough, and it pissed him off hearing all the dissenting shit about his beloved hometown from people that didn't know jack-shit.

It was two thirty-seven in the am as Havoc pulled up in front of the Kum-Pow Chinese takeout restaurant on the corner of Myrtle Avenue in the Clinton Hills section of BK. After switching off the ignition he lowered the radio and reflected on yet another job he awaited payment for.

It was a criminal plan hatched from hunger and stupidity, all designed to snare a lousy fifty-dollars' worth of Chinese food, and now, sadly, a man's son may never reach his full potential.

On Christmas Eve of the previous year John Chung, a hardworking immigrant from South China got a call for a huge order at his restaurant. Like always he sent his eighteen-year-old son Timothy to deliver the order. Once young Tim arrived at the nearby Ingersoll Houses he quickly learned that he was set up by a couple of crackheads to be robbed. Outnumbered, he willingly gave up the food but that wasn't enough for the fiends and they proceeded to toss a blanket over his head and pummel him with a brick so that he could not identify them. It was a stupid idea that went bad pretty fast.

The degenerates would have gotten away with it were it not for the fact that they were stupid and bragged about the deed to whoever listened until it eventually got back to the victim's father. With his son in a coma, and those that knew something foolishly honoring the phrase 'snitches get stitches', combined with the police dragging their feet and insisting they needed more proof than hearsay because the call was made anonymously from a pay phone, Mister Chung's grief turned to anger and his anger turned to resolution. It was around that time when he decided to call the phone number on the black card with bold red letters that mysteriously found its way under his windshield wiper. After a week of staking out Timothy's attackers and paying a snitch to get them to admit their guilt on tape, Havoc and Mayhem moved in and did what they do best. Later, in between his last consulting gig of 1987 and his first of 1988, he briefly called Mister Chung to inform him it was taken care of and that he would be stopping by his restaurant at closing time to pick up the other half of his payment.

Havoc observed John Chung pull the gate down over his restaurant then tapped his horn. The balding Asian man was momentarily startled then smiled when he recognized Havoc and went over to him.

"All I hear all day in my restaurant is people talk about how the wicked men who hurt my son got their just deserves. How ironic it is that they hurt my son for food and now they will never be able to eat solid food again without the aid of false teeth." the small man said and handed Havoc an envelope stuffed with money. "Here is payment, for job done well." He bowed.

Havoc bowed his head back never bothering to check if it was all there, because it always was. "So, how's your son doing Mister Chung?"

The Asian man's face dropped and he sighed remorsefully. "Doing much better, thank you. His eyes finally opened. But Doctors say he still has long-long way to go. I am headed over now to see him and give my wife a break."

Havoc's eyes tightened and he reached his hand out the window and gripped Mister Chung's shoulder. "If he's half as strong as his father is then he'll pull through fine." Mister Chung bowed at Havoc's kind words. "If you need me for anything else, you know how to reach me."

"Thank you again Havoc. Oh, and have a happy New Year. And you too Mayhem." Mister Chung said waving until Havoc's car disappeared into the night.

It was too early to call it a night and Havoc knew the hottest nightclub in Brooklyn, 'Smitty's Supper Club,' would be jumping about this time. Not to mention he was starting to get a serious case of the munchies brought on by the weed. Normally after smoking a fat one only his appetite was affected, but for some reason the weed had him feeling paranoid because he could swear that a black Mercedes Benz with tinted windows had been tailing him for three blocks. When the dark German-made car made a left on Belmont and disappeared he felt silly and assumed his paranoia was fueled by the spliff. Shrugging it off he twisted the radio knob to radio personalities Mister Magic and super producer Marley Marl who fill New York's hoods with soundtracks to the streets. When a familiar beat came on he pumped up the volume smiling approvingly, as he sang along with Slick Rick and Doug E. Fresh to their hit song, 'The Show'.

Sitting at a light, Havoc bopped his head to the music as Mayhem began making low angry growling sounds from the back seat. "What is it girl? Timmy's fallen down the well?" her master joked then realized something was up and muted the sounds. Mayhem continued growling, locked on what was past the windshield, baring fangs and snarling. Confused by his dog's erratic behavior, Havoc stared through the windshield to see what had her so spellbound, but only saw dark, barren, windy streets. "Shush! Quiet down Mayhem! Ain't nobody out there." he said. "See?" Suddenly a limp body slammed up against the windshield with a loud thud and rolled down onto the hood. Mayhem went into a barking frenzy. "Oh shit!" Havoc jumped startled, then dipped down and popped back up with both Glock's ready to lick-shots. His heart was tap dancing on his tongue and his fingers stroked the triggers ready to squeeze. He strained at the face mashed against his windshield and paused perplexed when he recognized it. The man stretched out on his car popped open his eyes and he winked with a goofy smile.

"There he is! The man who I wanna be when I grow up." the faker declared.

Havoc shook his head while cursing under his breath and lowered his guns. "Jesus Bug-Out, what the hell's your problem? You trying to catch a bullet?" he yelled then turned to calm his dog down.

Bug-Out was too busy laughing to answer. "I gotcha!"

"No, you almost got **it**!"

"Oh man you should've seen your face. Havoc and Mayhem my ass! Y'all look more like a ghetto Shaggy and Scooby-Doo." he said imitating Havoc fumbling for his guns.

Havoc glared at Bug-Out dividing his attention to Mayhem. "Your ass play too damn much. Easy girl! It's all right, I'm here. It's only Bug-Out's ignorant ass, see."

"I know you are but what am I?" Bug-Out teased impersonating Pee Wee Herman then tapped on the window, "Hav, yo Havoc open up man, it's freezing out here."

"Crap!" Havoc sucked his teeth as he stroked Mayhem's head to calm her down. After a second, he leaned over and unlocked the door.

Bug-Out opened the door and stuck his head in and Mayhem snarled. "Yo what's up with Cujo?"

Havoc glanced back at his dog then smiled sinisterly, "If I bark, she bites." Bug-Out wasn't sure how he should perceive that and paused deciding if he should get in or not. "Man, either get in or shut the damn door!"

"Ok quit illin'," Bug-Out said and swallowed hard then slid his skinny frame in the front while keeping a watchful eye on Mayhem. Five minutes into the ride he turned to Havoc with his hand outstretched. "So happy New Year my nigga!"

Havoc turned his nose up at him like he smelled something foul. "I told you before, address your homeboys with that word not me. I don't play that."

"My bad Homey D. Clown." Bug-Out giggled. Havoc rolled his eyes and shook his head. "Kidding. Geez, where's your sense of humor?"

Havoc sighed. He hated to hear black people mentally oppress one another referring to one other as 'nigger' or it's sub variations, nigga and niggaz. It struck a chord with him that Black kids ignorantly used it as a term of endearment or universal greeting, manipulating it's sound and meaning like it was their own personal word. And it infuriated him that those who said it never once took into consideration the horrific history of that word or that it was the last thing many of their ancestors heard before they died at the end of a rope. Bug-Out, on the other hand, felt Havoc was overreacting and gave the word way too much power when it was only that, a word. Hell, everybody calls each other nigga. From Black people to Puerto Ricans, to the backwards baseball cap wearing white boys that listened to rap and hung out on Kings highway. And if controversial gangsta rappers like N.W.A. said it in their lyrics and respected comedians like Richard Pryor used it in their act how could it possibly be a diss? But since he seldom saw Havoc he did not want to argue.

"I'm sorry, ok? You'll never hear me call you that again." Bug-Out apologize.

Havoc nodded that he accepted his apology and moved on. "Damn dawg, I can't believe it's eighty-eight already. Eighty-seven just flew by."

"Tell me about it. Time in general is flying by. Before you know it, it'll be the year two thousand. I wonder what that'll be like. You think that we'll be like the Jetsons, riding around in flying cars and shit? Cause that'd be dope." Bug-Out said.

Havoc cut his eyes over at Bug-Out and snickered. "Man you always did read to many damn comic books."

"Whatever!" Bug-Out said and took a long sip from his brown paper bag then let out a nasty sounding belch.

"Damn! What're you drinking?" Havoc frowned, fanning the air.

"Peach Cisco. You want some?" Bug-Out offered.

"I'll pass."

Bug-Out peeped the wine coolers on the floor. "Yeah, wine is fine, but Calvin's Coolers, huh?"

"It's better than that liquid crack you're sucking on."

"This here is all good. 'Sides, ain't no other drink on the market's gonna get you fuuugged up like dis here for the low-low price of tree-fiddy."

"I'll let you tell it. Anyway, what are you doing all the way over here this time of night by yourself?"

"Who me?"

"No Mayhem. Of course you, who else would I be talking to?"

Bug-Out sang along with the radio to Prince's, Let's go Crazy, then suddenly laughed out loud, "Yo you think Prince is gay?"

"Huh-what?" Havoc asked confused.

"At first I did, cause homeboy be wearing some crazy looking gear. And what's up with the makeup and high heels? But then I got to thinking, Prince keeps a bad bitch. Apolonia, Shelia E., Vanity. Nah dude ain't no homo. No way."

Havoc cut his eyes at Bug-Out picking up on how he was trying to change the subject but had other things on his mind and let it go. "I'm headed over to Smitty's you wanna roll?"

"And walk up in the club with you looking all Marty McFly? Thanks, but no thanks! My ego is fragile enough."

"Suit yourself. I can drop you home on the way if you want."

"Bet, that'll work." Bug-Out smiled rapping his fingers on the dashboard to the beat. "So, since you're driving this sexy red bitch and you're dressed accordingly, I guess it's safe to assume you just finished consulting somebody's ass. So, who was it this time?"

"Dude, my name ain't Keith so stop sweating me." Havoc said through an exasperated breath.

"Well excuuuuse me."

"You know I never discuss my work. And I hope you aren't going around blabbing we're related."

"Relax, take a chill-pill. It's not like I walk up to fools I don't know and be like, 'Hey you know that dude Havoc that be serving up piping hot beat-downs like IHOP except no syrup? Well he's my little cousin.' Damn near raised him."

Havoc looked at him like he was full of shit, "You told somebody didn't you?"

"Nobody I swear. Word to Big Bird," Bug-Out promised. "Although, according to the ladies I have been known to talk in my sleep." He winked.

"This isn't a joke Bug Out. I have enemies. And I make new ones every day. And if they can't get to me personally then they might try another route. Got it?" Havoc said.

"Chill out cousin. I was just jiving with you. I didn't tell anybody." Bug-Out said with an unconcerned wink. "Look, I know you on some secret squirrel shit but there's one thing I gotta ask regarding your whole Trouble Consulting thing. And then I'll stop sweating you."

"And that is?" Havoc asked eyeing Bug-Out with a dubious glare.

"How is it you don't carry a phone? A beeper? How's a motherfucker supposed to contact you smoke signals?"

"I prefer to use pay phones when I'm moving around in the street. Reason being, what if I'm throwing hands and lose my phone? I'm supposed to trust that little plastic belt clip to hold something big as a VCR on my hip?"

"Maybe one day they'll make phones small enough to fit in your pocket." Bug-Out reasoned.

"Yeah right. Why not have them take pictures and tell you the weather while you're at it."

"Ok but what about beepers?"

"I don't want anybody having twenty-four seven access to me. If we made plans, you know I'm coming."

"You mean them hoes know right?" his cousin grinned.

Havoc shook his head and blew steam through his nostrils. "I swear man the older you get, the younger you act."

"Hey thirty-nine's not old." Bug-Out snapped defensively. He hated being reminded that he was closing in on forty. It was bad enough his knees popped every morning when he got out of bed and his stomach was starting to lap over his belt from too much beer. To make himself appear younger he got his haircut in a Cameo hi-top fade and shaved parts into his right eyebrow. His efforts did very little to subtract years off his appearance.

Havoc looked over at him disappointedly. He wished that his cousin would get his act together. It really bothered him that the man he grew up watching kung-fu movies on Forty second street, riding huffy bicycles and playing skelly with, could not keep a stable job or take care of his own child. Another thing that concerned him was the floating rumor that Bug-Out had lavish habits.

Bug-Out suddenly began coughing violently like he was choking to the point his eyes watered, and his lemon-skinned complexion turned beet red.

"Jesus man, you Okay?" Havoc asked concerned.

Bug-Out leaned back in his seat looking worn out. "Yeah I'm cool. I just can't seem to shake this cold. I've had it for almost two weeks now. Some days it hits me so hard I can't even get out of bed."

"Well no wonder, it's freezing outside and all you have on is that thin ass track suit that's got you looking like you're straight outta Beat Street,"

"That's so funny I forgot to laugh." Bug-Out said then glanced at the blinking dashboard. "I'll give it to you cousin your car is da bomb but it can't compete with my old Brougham." he said.

"Havoc sucked his teeth and cut his eyes over at Bug-Out like he was crazy. "I know you're not talking about that Rickety Rocket looking Cadillac my pops gave you when you turned eighteen?"

"Hey, the Mack mobile was no piece of junk, and it could give any of dem fool ass drag racers behind Starrett City a run for their money."

"Now I dunno what car you're talking about, but the ride I'm talking about was as junky as Sanford and Son's front yard, it leaked oil and you had to roll down the window to unlock the door." Havoc laughed.

"That car was off the hook." Bug-Out said unconvincingly.

"More like, it needed to be hauled off by one. So next Friday my moms and I are throwing Tee-Tee a birthday party. Can you make it? Everybody's going to be there, Nanna and Grandpa Smurf, Sidney, Marie and the twins, Lil Dee, Cameron, Aunt Cookie, Uncle Booze, Aunt Glo-Dee, Faye, Gus, everybody. Aunt Mary didn't tell you?"

"Nah, she and I are taking a break. But how come you're just asking me now?"

"I tried calling but Ma Bell said your phone was disconnected."

"Oh yeah," Bug-Out chuckled embarrassed. "So you said Uncle Booze is gonna be there?"
Havoc nodded. "Yup. Oh you know who else is coming? Olivia. She's driving up from DC with her fiancé some Spanish dude named Hector. I hear Money's a doctor." Havoc said.

"So, homeboy's a P.R.D.R.?" Bug-Out laughed as he thought about his distant family he had not seen in a while. "Sounds like a blast, count me in."

"Cool. Then be at Nicky's next Friday around three."

Bug-Out turned to Havoc looking confused. "Whoa, it's at Nicky's? Your ex-wife Nicky?"

"I was only married to one woman named Nicky."

"But how come you're having it at Nicky's? I thought it was over with you two."

Havoc frowned like he'd been knifed in the arm. "It is over. But our-I mean her place is big enough to house everybody. Besides you know how tight she and my moms still are. And Tee-Tee loves her to death."

Bug-Out frowned like he wasn't buying it. "Aw go-head wit dat Cuzzo. Tee-Tee loves everybody. But I'm saying, why not just rent a spot and have it there?"

36

"Good question. Unfortunately, I don't have a good answer. I figured my moms was just trying to save a few bucks by having it at Nicky's and-son of a bitch!" Havoc hissed when he violently bounced over a pothole. "This is the shit that pisses me off. Why doesn't the city do something about these damn holes? If this were Howard Beach, they would've been fixed this. But since we're in the middle of Bed-Stuy do or die, nobody gives a flying fuck about a brotha's car…What was I saying again?" he asked screw-faced.

"You figured Aunt Carla was trying to save a few bucks by having Tee-Tee's party at Nicky's and-"

"Oh yeah-yeah. I figured she was trying to save a few bucks so I offered to pay to rent out the Empire Roller Skating Rink."

Bug-Out slumped low in his chair smiling. "Damn. I ain't been there since we was kids. Hey 'member how we used to go there on Friday nights and compete to see who'd pull the most girl's phone numbers? Then after it closed, we'd smoke til we was high as muthafuckin Cheech and Chong and go across the street to White Castle's to get our grub on. Oh yo, how about the time Beverly and Tracy was fighting and Tracy's big ol' titties popped out of her tube top? We was hooting and hollering and she was like, 'Grow up! Y'all act like y'all ain't never seen no titties before?'"

Havoc laughed as he reminisced. "And you said, 'We have but, we ain't never seen **your** titties before.'" the two exploded into laughter slapping each other five. "Damn those were the days."

"True dat. When safe sex meant your parents weren't home. I swear I wish we could start off old and grow young." Bug-Out said laughing.

"Now that would truly be dope." Havoc nodded with a slight grin.

"Word you should do that cousin." Bug-Out said jumping back on the subject of Tee-Tee's party. "Skating and reminiscing to Shalamar and Peaches and Herb, Chaka Khan and Rufus. It'd be maaad fun."

"True it would be kinda flyy. But my moms said Tee-Tee's already got her heart set on having it at Nicky's."

37

"So let me get this straight. Tee-Tee would rather have her party at Nicky's instead of at a skating rink?"

"According to Carla Pinkney she would."

Bug-Out twitched his lips skeptically. "If you say so. But won't that be kinda uncomfortable for you?"

"Nah, it's no big deal." Havoc shrugged.

"Really? You're a better man than me cause I'd be like, 'Oh hell no!' Especially when I used to live there and now-"

"Dammit Bug-Out, I said it's no big deal!" Havoc snapped with flared nostrils. His tone made both Bug-Out and Mayhem jump.

"Sooooo-um you want Laquita to make some potato salad or fry some chicken." Bug-Out asked wisely changing the subject.

"Nah don't even sweat that Bee. There'll be plenty of food and liquor there. Just bring Laquita and A.J. around three." Havoc said with an angry face.

"Aight." Bug-Out nodded covering a yawn then leaned back and closed his eyes.

Twenty minutes later Havoc's car slowed into park, a block and a half away from the Marcy housing projects where his cousin lived.

"Bug-Out wake up. Man wake up punk, you're home. Yo Bug-Out!" Havoc said shoving him. Bug-Out mumbled something incoherent, farted, scratched himself and began to snore once more.

While his cousin snored like a buzz saw Havoc noticed his slovenly appearance for the first time. Even though he had a hearty appetite Bug-Out always looked undernourished. As a kid he was a wiz on the basketball court, but he was so skinny he had to put wristbands around his calves to keep his tube socks up. But this time in addition to being rail-thin he also looked sickly. His clothes looked bad too. Instead of a coat he had on more layers than a Duncan Hines cake to battle the cold. His hair needed a comb run through it and he smelled like he could use a shower. Havoc was astonished. Growing up Bug-Out was the shade wearing player type who always rocked a toothpick between his teeth and stayed dip in the illest gear. When Laquita became pregnant, Havoc couldn't remember Bug-Out ever sitting down. He was either returning from one job or headed out to another taking care of his responsibilities. Something was wrong, big time.

"Yo Bug-Out wake up. We're here!" Havoc said so loud that Mayhem sat up curious.

"I'm up-I'm up!" Bug-Out said grumpily stretching with a yawn and another fart. His eyes popped open with a rheumy-eyed look and he stared at his surroundings then sucked his teeth. "Damn! How come you dropped me off here instead'a out front of my building?" he complained about having to trek all the way through Herbert von King Park to get home.

"What are you stuck on stupid? Didn't I just finish telling you to keep us being blood on the down-low?" Havoc said. "Besides you're up in here stinking up my ride with your lethal farts."

"I'd rather fart and be ashamed, than hold it in and bust a vein." Bug-Out laughed as he opened the door to get out.

"Yo Bug." Havoc called. Bug-Out looked back and his sleepy eyes lit up when he saw the one hundred-dollar bill his cousin had in his hand. "First thing tomorrow morning I want you to go down to the Albee Square Mall and buy a coat before you catch pneumonia."

"For real? Aw man, wow. Thanks, Cuzzo. That's really decent of you. Man lately I been so broke, if a mugger robs me, he's just practicing."

Havoc had to laugh at that one. "Don't sweat it we're family. What about A.J. and Laquita? They straight?" Bug-Out's eyes dropped to the ground in shame. Without hesitation, Havoc reached into one of his payment envelopes and withdrew three more hundred-dollar bills and a fifty. A sneaky smile formed in the corner of Bug-Out's mouth that quickly vanished as his cousin handed him the money. "That's enough to get everybody a coat, the phone turned back on plus a toy for little man."

"Thanks, cuzzin. And I promise, as soon as I find a job I'ma pay you back every red cent. With interest. Unless of course you and Mayhem are looking to turn your duo into a trio."

"We aren't." Havoc quickly responded.

"Dang, you could at least front like you gave it some thought before dismissing it. I can be a valuable asset to your team." The skinny man said swinging his fists at invisible enemies.

Havoc shook his head grinning. "Not with them Gumby arms of yours you can't. Look, I told you don't worry about paying me back." he said since he never loaned out money he couldn't afford to get back.

"No, I insist. As hard as you work for yours. Listen, Laquita ain't cook so I'ma run up in Mamma's real quick and order me a center breast and fries. Cool?" Havoc nodded suspiciously. No matter how bad things got he could not remember a time his cousin's girlfriend and mother of his son didn't have a steaming pot on the stove.

"Fine, just make sure you do the right thing with that money." Havoc said adamantly.

"Of course, I am. What else would I do with it?"

"Um, nothing. Never mind." Havoc said regretting he went there.

Bug-Out recognized the accusatory look his cousin gave him. It was the same look he had been getting lately, since the rumors started. "Aw shit! Not you too." He said with a wounded look.

"Not me what?" Havoc asked avoiding eye contact.

"Listening to what them fools on the Ave been going around saying. That I'm basing. That's what!" Bug-Out said getting defensive.

"Relax. I didn't accuse you of anything."

"You ain't gotta. It's written all over your face cuzzin. This is straight up whack! Look man if you're gonna start going by what everyone else says then I don't want your damn money." Bug-Out said, but at the same time made no attempt to give the money back. "You just finished saying that we're family then you turn around and give me looks like I'm a freaking leper or something!"

Havoc sighed heavily and nodded. "You're right man. My bad. It's just that you used to look so well-put together and now...this." He said waving his hand over Bug-Out.

"What can I tell you? Times is hard on the boulevard."

Havoc leaned back in his seat staring up at the ceiling. "Check it out, you keep that-what I gave you, and no more talk about last year's drama. This is a whole new year full of countless possibilities. So, we cool?" Havoc said offering his hand.

Bug-Out glared at his cousin then smiled and shook his hand. "Yeah, we cool. Hey I was thinking. I may know of a way to change my current unemployed situation around and make some loot."

"Doing what?" Havoc asked.

"Writing plays."

"Plays? Cousin what do you know about writing plays?"

"What's there to know? Hell, look at all of them plays they got out now making crazy dough. Momma I wanna sing, The Diary of Black Men, Beauty Shop. If Shelly Garrett can do it why not me?"

"You're serious?" Havoc asked shaking his head.

"As a heart attack. I even came up with a few names for potential plays, check it out." Bug-Out said then cleared his throat. "Coming to the Marcy Project Community Center for a limited engagement. A play by Alonzo T. Strong the man who brought you the off-off-off Broadway runaway hit, Who, drank all the Kool Aid: A Ghetto Mystery, brings to you, Lord Momma done burnt the Chicken, Again." Havoc cracked up at his cousin's foolishness. "Okay that one does sound a little ill but how about, Momma, cause you know all black plays gotta have the word Momma in there somewhere, Momma It's the First of the Month and the Check Ain't Here: A Ghetto Tragedy. And after it blows up you know what's next, right? The sequel, Momma, It's the fifteenth and the Check Still Ain't Here. So what do you think?"

By now Havoc was laughing hysterically at his comedic antics and had to wipe the tears from his eyes. "Hey I can't knock your hustle cousin. If you want to write plays I say go for it. In fact on opening night I'll buy out the first row."

"Thanks flyy guy. So I'll see you next Friday." Bug-Out said as he bumped fists with his cousin and entered a spot on the corner under a big white and red neon sign that read Mama's Fried Chicken. He went up to the bulletproof window and placed his order.

As soon as Bug-Out spotted Havoc drive off in the reflection of the glass plate window behind him he canceled his order deciding he wasn't hungry after all. Instead of heading towards Marcy Projects he jogged in the opposite direction towards a dark block in a rural area lined with run down bodegas, crack houses and one working street lamp, to feed a different type of hunger.

# Chapter 4

As Havoc patiently waited for Mayhem to sniff out the right spots to do her business at, he could hear the muffled sounds of music and celebrating coming from within Smitty's across the street. A group of passerby's approached his car with a gathering awe like desert crash survivors coming upon an oasis. They could not stop staring at the gorgeous amazing piece of machinery with the license plate that read CODE RED and were especially taken by its vintage make and the way everything was bold and beautifully exaggerated, from the eye-bulging headlights to the wide steering wheel and glossy chrome 20-inch rims outlining the tires. As Havoc sat there out classing the Jaguars, Benzes and other expensive automobiles corralled along the block he smiled with pride along with the wide grille on the front of his car. Next to his family and dog, that car was his most prized possession.

The two met when he was out hunting for something that was a joy to drive but mirrored his character when he was working. Basically, a roughneck on wheels with swagger. He searched high and low, hitting up used car lots, police auctions, newspaper ads and car shows but none of the steering wheels he sat behind felt right. Feeling disappointed he decided to cheer himself up with a Shamrock shake and a McDLT. As fate would have it, just as he was about to take a bite out of his sandwich, a car pulled into the drive thru with a FOR SALE sign in the rear window and he felt that same giddy feeling he felt when he laid eyes on his wife for the first time. And just like then he had to have her!

Tommy quickly abandoned his meal and hurried over to inspect the vehicle. Although it needed some work, the vintage blue Chevy was by far the coolest car he had ever seen, multiplied times ten. He made a cash deal on the spot and a handshake later the car was his. After a fresh coat of red paint and some major improvements like tinted windows, red leather interior, push button reclining seats, key remote, a cardiac-arrest-inducing stereo system and a turbo engine that could go from 0 to 60 in seconds courtesy of the talented Borrero brothers, the best auto mechanics in the hood. He had the bomb-ass whip he was longing for!

The back door opened and Mayhem climbed onto the back seat and pulled the door closed behind her. Opening and closing doors with her teeth, paws and tail was one of the many impressive tricks her master had taught her. Outside, Havoc popped open his trunk where he kept an emergency change of clothes. Rummaging through an A&S shopping bag, he removed and slid into a fresh red Chams de Baron shirt that wasn't covered in his enemy's DNA. He then got back in his ride and removed a bottle of Polo cologne from the glove compartment and spritzed his neck. He stared in the mirror, cleaned a speck of random blood off of his Gazelles, approved of his GQ look, then patted his dog affectionately.

"I won't be gone that long girl." Havoc promised as Mayhem licked his hand and gruffed.

Havoc got out and boldly left the doors unlocked. Driving a flashy car in a rough neighborhood might fan the flames of jealousy but he was not the least bit concerned about his car being tampered with since he had a one hundred and thirty-pound Bullmastiff inside waiting for someone dumb enough to come along and open the door. With his coat billowing out behind him in the wind like a red leather cape, he jaywalked across the Avenue and entered Smitty's.

One of the selected few with enough juice to not have to go through the stop, frisk and cover charge procedures like regular folks, Havoc walked up to a surly Puerto Rican bouncer named Gabriel gave him a soul brother handshake and chatted briefly about his wife and kids before heading inside.

The dance floor was packed as tightly as a can of sardines and erupting with energy. Havoc momentarily stood in the archway bopping his head to, Shannon's, 'Let the Music Play', scoping the scene and feeling at ease.

Smitty's Supper Club wasn't like the clubs in moneymaking Manhattan such as The Funhouse, Union Square, The Tunnel, Harlem World or The Red Parrot where if a guy wasn't fresh, dressed like a million bucks, with a pair of Bally shoes and fly green socks, he was nobody. Instead Smitty's had a more laid-back atmosphere where one could unwind and have a good time minus all the flashy B.S. and hype.

The décor was dramatic with white velvet drapes and midnight blue walls that boasted black art. Jazz greats such as Billie Holiday, Nina Simone, Sara Vaughn, Thelonious Monk, Miles Davis and Wynton Marsalis blended in with the likes of Heavy Dee, Karen White and Rob Base to give an eclectic mix. On any given Sunday young urban professionals could stop in for a mimosa and relax while enjoying readings by local talented poets and authors. In addition to its being rich in Black culture, Smitty's also had a dining section where you could order a plate of mouthwatering soul food that gave Harlem's own legendary Sylvia's restaurant a serious run for her money. The house special was the fried catfish, shrimps and grits.

'Groove Me' by the musical trio GUY, was the next jam to spin on the ones and twos. The hit song was a personal favorite of Havoc's and from the crowd's volatile reaction everyone else's too, as expensive outfits soaked up sweat. Bouncing to the beat Havoc weaved past people slurping flutes of champagne and blowing into noise makers while beating up the dance floor with the hottest dances like the Wop, the Smurf, the Cabbage Patch, the Roger Rabbit and the Snake. His stroll apparently had the shiny gold dog whistle and rope chain around his neck swinging enough to hypnotize random folks who stopped dancing and gawked at the bald brotha whose ghetto icon status was arguably untouchable, if not unmatched. The Black man many may imitate but could never quite duplicate. The Flyy Guy who's escaped more pitfalls than that vine-swinging dude from that Atari video game. Havoc the Trouble Consultant. Fellas wanted to be like him with his stoic presence, tough gear and matching attitude. And the ladies wanted to be with him because of his good looks and the way he carried himself with an air of confidence that was so strong it was both intimidating and inviting.

"Careful ladies, you may experience eye straining due to excessive staring." DJ Hurricane jokingly announced as Havoc nodded in his direction while making his way towards a vacant booth.

Across the room a cute honey-brown waitress with a blonde Salt and Pepa a-symmetric haircut and features that put Jessica Rabbit's to shame, closed her Right-On magazine, checked her makeup then cut her 15-minute break short and danced over to Havoc's table. She stood there picturing herself running her fingers through the nest of curly black hair that peeked through the two open buttons of his shirt.

"Hey Ava, Happy Year." Havoc said pulling her from her trance.

"Huh? Oh-happy New Year to you too." She said flustered.

"So what's up? You look a little down." Havoc inquired.

"Oh-nothing, it's just that there's this guy I really-really like who comes in here every so often. He has all the right credentials. Tall, sexy, has his stuff together and is so fine he'd make a nun reconsider her choices in life. But alas he's not interested in me." she sighed.

"Is he here tonight?" Havoc asked looking around. Ava nodded sadly. "Well I don't know who this guy is but why don't you try telling him you like books, music, good movies…"

"Well it's worth a shot," Ava said then leaned forward, batted her eyelashes and whispered, "I like books, music, good movies…"

Havoc grinned. "Cute. I must be slipping cause, I didn't even see that one coming."

"So, what brings you in here handsome?"

"Business."

"Serious or Monkey?" she flirted.

"None of your," Havoc winked.

"Touchy-Touchy. So what'll you have?" Ava smiled removing a pen and pad from her apron pocket.

"Just bring me a large order of hot wings, curly fries, a double-shot of Johnnie Walker RED and a pitcher of bud."

"Scotch and Beer? But honey it's New Years. Check it out. I have a bottle of Moet chilling back at my pad. I get off in a couple of hours. We could have a private celebration. What do you say?"

Havoc smiled. "To be honest, I've had a real stressful day. I only stopped in to see your boss for a quick chit-chat, grab an even quicker bite then I'm out."

"You sure? It's not far."

"Ava to be quite honest, I just wanna go home and go to bed."

Ava licked her lips seductively. "So do I."

"You're kinda young to be coming at me so grown. How old are you if you don't mind my asking?" Havoc inquired.

"Forty-one times five, plus two, minus one hundred and eighty-nine." She sucked her teeth with her hands on her hips and a slight head roll.

"Eighteen huh? I figured as much," Havoc shrugged without even thinking about it.

Being able to add subtract multiply and divide in his head without even giving it a thought only added to the list of reasons why Ava's heart skipped a beat whenever her major crush stopped by. "Yeah that's right. I just graduated from court-case status."

Havoc eyed her from head to toe. Ava was definitely a dime-piece, but eighteen was too young in his book. Like KRS One said, the girl looks so good, but her brain is not ready. Plus, he came into Smitty's way too often to have to deal with a pissed off waitress whose phone calls he knew he wouldn't return after he tapped it.

"Why don't you find yourself a decent guy your age?"

"You mean *boy* my age, no thanks. Look, give it some thought and I'll be right back with your drink." Once she was gone Havoc settled back into his booth on display to all the female admirers clocking him like he was a three-course meal. When some of the men on the dance floor noticed their women paying more attention to the black Adonis than them, they let it be known in no uncertain terms that unless the pretty boy in red was driving them home they had 'Best' remember who they came there with.

Wishing Well by Terrence Trent D'arby played as Ava danced back over with a pitcher of beer, a frosted mug and his double shot of scotch. "Your food'll be up in a minute. So, is there anything *else* I can get you?" the waitress asked putting her curves on display and giving it one more try.

"I'm good. But you could tell your boss I'm here." Havoc said knocking back the shot in one gulp then pouring himself a beer chaser as Ava disappointedly went to relay the message.

A short time later Ava came back and set enough food to feed a small village before Havoc. "Smitty said he'll be with you in a second," she said.

"Thanks," Havoc smacked.

"Oh you missed it, earlier Daddy-O and Wise from Stetsasonic stopped by earlier." Ava said excitedly.

"Word?" Havoc said more impressed with how good his food tasted than the rappers Ava was name-dropping.

"Yup! And they was real cool too. I took a picture with them and everything. See!" she said handing him a Polaroid snapshot of her all hugged up with the famous rappers.

Havoc glanced at it briefly with an, *'Umm-hmm'* and continued chowing down. Celebrities never impressed him. To him they were regular folks who made their coins using their God given talents. Kind'a like what he did. Some celebrities were cool and down to Earth. Like the time he met Big Daddy Kane and Biz Markie, at a charity basketball game at Rucker Park in Harlem but most he encountered seemed to forget that when they stepped into their limos the fans who put them there were getting on the train with a token.

After a minute Ava got tired of watching Havoc strip the meat from the chicken bones and walked off to check on other customers. As Havoc continued to grub the lights suddenly dimmed as the DJ put on the slow jam, 'You Bring Me Joy' by Anita Baker. Every woman on the dance floor laid her head on her man's shoulder as he squeezed her tightly and together they happily anticipated spending a whole new year together. Havoc watched the blissful couples moving fluidly and suddenly lost his appetite and pushed his plate away then rested his chin on his fists.

A well-dressed distinguished looking gentleman with a neatly groomed beard, tight short afro and shock of gray hair on the right side of his temple came over to Havoc's table and sat down across from him. He had the refined look of a 1920's jazz musician and pulled out a cigar case, removed a Havana then turned to Havoc.

"You mind?" The elder gentleman asked and Havoc shook his head. Smitty nodded 'Thanks', clipped the end, lit it, and puffed. "Women, can't live with 'em. Can't kill 'em without going to jail." he winked through a haze of smoke.

"Damn, am I that transparent?" Havoc asked.

"Like a friggin glass house." Smitty said.

Havoc smiled and held out his palm. "Happy New Year, old dog."

Smitty slapped his palm and replied, "Happy New Year, young pup."

The two laughed for a minute then Smitty said, "So what's up with the sad face Youngblood? It's New Year's."

"Actually, I was just thinking about the new year." Havoc sighed staring at the happy couples on the dance floor.

Smitty watched him watching the dancers then asked, "Nicky?"

Havoc sipped his beer and nodded. "It's been over two years since the divorce."

"Yes, Nicky was a gem." Smitty said.

"Man I don't even know why I'm sitting here trippin. I swear love is a maximum of bullshit and a minimum of pleasure!"

Smitty shifted the cigar from one side of his mouth to the other without using his hands. "You don't really mean that."

"Don't I?"

Just then Ava swayed by carrying a tray of colorful drinks and almost bumped into another waitress stealing a peak at Havoc. "Now see, if I was smart I'd accept her invite and go back to her crib and ride that like a Big Wheel til the sun comes up." Havoc said.

Smitty shook his head and bit down hard on his cigar. It hurt him to the core to see the young man looking so sad when he cared about him so much. He had known Havoc all his life and only wanted the best for him. If he had it in his power to get what it was that Havoc was pining over he would have done it instantly, but some things a man has to achieve on his own. The wise older gentleman knew a hell of a lot about achieving things out of one's reach. Dropping out of high school to help take care of his family closed the door on his dreams of going to college. But his fierce desire to succeed made him determined to do more with his life than get drunk and blame the white man for his ill fortune. An ambitious street hustler, Smitty ran both a numbers hole and back door card game until he had enough money stashed to go legit and open his own highly successful nightclub. Many years later after developing a close bond with the streets, he learned that the little boy who used to beg him for ice cream money whenever Mr. Softee drove down the block, had in fact become the infamous Trouble Consultant he was hearing about who beat down punks, pushers, pimps and perverts for a profit. Deeply concerned for the young man's welfare he tried to get him to quit his dangerous profession before it caught up to him and offered to put him through college on his own dime, but the young man didn't accept charity. Plus had other plans. And although Smitty didn't agree with them, he did respect them. After all he was young and full of vigor once himself and back then nobody could tell him anything either.

"But you're smart. That's why you aren't wasting your time on no teenyboppers. But at the same token you can't just give up on finding happiness because things aren't going your way. Every day you put your clothes on and they just get dirty again. So, what're you gonna do? Stop getting dressed? Of course not." Smitty said answering his own question.

Havoc gave him a half nod like he somewhat understood what Smitty was getting at then poured out the last of his beer into his mug. "Let's change the subject. This is depressing the hell out of me. So, my Mom and I are throwing Tee-Tee a birthday party next Friday. Everybody is gonna be there. Think you can make it?"

"Damn, where'd the time go? You betcha. I can't miss your baby sister's big day and have her getting all hinkty with me." Smitty said with a hint of Southern flavor.

"Hinkty?" Havoc cracked up like Smitty just told a joke. "Man, you moved to New York in what? Thirty-seven? And you still sound like you're from Alabama."

Smitty shrugged unfazed by the young man's teasing. "So where's this party gonna be at and what time should I show up?"

Havoc rolled his eyes. He knew once he answered he'd be right back on the subject he just finished dismissing. With a sigh he uttered, "Around three-ish…and it's gonna be at…" Smitty raised his eyebrows and gestured for Havoc to spit it out. "…Nicky's."

"Solid," Smitty nodded and continued puffing. Havoc was dumbfounded. He expected something, anything but funky smoke.

"Didn't you hear me? I said the party's gonna be at Nicky's."

"I heard you the first time Young blood no need to repeat it." Smitty said reaching for a curly fry.

"I expected you to have a comment."

"I ain't get this far in life by stating the obvious."

"And that would be?"

Smitty shook his head at Havoc like he should already know. He was about to explain the writing on the wall when DJ Hurricane began arguing with a man in front of his booth…

"Yo son why is it that you've been taking requests all night from other folks but ain't put my jam on yet?" the angry man demanded.

Dressed in a Malcolm X baseball cap, a 40 Acres and a Mule jersey, and leather Africa shaped medallion, DJ Hurricane shook his head sadly at the drunken man. "Number one I am not your son. Number two N.W.A.'s, A Bitch is a Bitch, is an inappropriate song to play for a room full of black women."

"But it ain't fo dem ho's! It's strictly for da niggas!" The drunk laughed ignorantly showing off his huge gums and baby teeth as women glared in his direction.

"Just what I need, ignorance personified." DJ Hurricane said.

"Yo Money why is you dissing me?"

"Nobody's dissing you. Truth be told, you're doing a damn good job all by yourself."

"What the hell kinda DJ is you supposed to be? Talking out the side of your neck about you don't like gangsta rap music."

"Let me explain something to you. The definition of music is the art of organizing tones to produce a coherent sequence of sounds intended to elicit an esthetic response to the listener, which don't have jack shit to do with being violent, sexist or misogynistic." Hurricane said breaking it down for him.

The blank look on N.W.A.'s number one fan's face said he was utterly and completely dumbfounded. "Fuck you!"

"Great comeback,"

Gabriel noticed the two arguing and came over. "Hurricane is there a problem here?"

The troublemaker looked the swollen bouncer up and down and twitched his lips like he was unimpressed. "Ain't no problem Full Force. Why? -You looking for one?"

Gabriel rolled his eyes, not in the mood. "Okay buddy you've had way too much to drink, so why don't you go home and sleep it off." He suggested following Smitty's code of bouncer etiquette that said, be nice, until you can no longer be nice.

"Back up off me or so help me I'll stick a pin in your buffed ass and let the air out."

"Now see that's why black people don't have anything now because we don't know how to go into a place and act properly." Hurricane said.

"Man ain't nobody trying to hear all that Malcom X-clan preaching shit Farrakhan."

Smitty excused himself from the table and stormed over visibly pissed off. This was exactly why he was seriously considering banning kids 21 and under from coming into his establishment. He did not need the aggravation regardless how much more revenue the younger crowd brought in.

He looked at his DJ for an explanation. "Boss, this guy here wants me to play a song that is degrading to women and I told him no." Hurricane complained.

Smitty nodded then turned to the troublemaker. "Looka' here Slick, here at Smitty's we try to present a certain image where people can come to relax and party in a positive atmosphere without feeling offended. And by playing that junk you call *music*, it would be greatly be tarnished. Now if that's what floats your boat, fine, I could care less, but I don't think my club is the place for you."

"Oh, so now I gotta go cause of my taste in music?"

"No, you gotta go because you're preventing people from having a good time."

The man looked around at all the annoyed faces staring at him. "Fuck you and your tired ass club old man."

"Okay that's it. You're outta here!" Gabriel said and grabbed his arm.

The punk snatched free from his grip and grabbed the neck of a beer bottle from a nearby table and broke it across the bouncer's nose taking him down quick then turned on Smitty holding out the jagged glass in a threating manner. "So what's up old man you want some too?"

Smitty shook his head and re-lit his stogie then took a puff, "Me? Naw, I never get physical. Not my style. I get upset. But the fact of the matter is when I get upset, he-" the older gentleman said pointing over his shoulder at Havoc who rose out of his seat cracking his knuckles with a twisted sneer. "-gets physical!"

The punk swallowed hard as the angry-face man in red with a physique that defied physics, stormed over and melted his heart with an intimidating stare and asked. "Sup?" Unable to look Havoc in the eyes, he dropped his vision to the floor. Havoc glanced at Gabriel then at the bottle the punk was clutching then back at the punk. "You seem to be pretty popular up in here. But have you met my good friend table yet?" he asked the confused punk. "No? Then allow me to introduce you. Table-meet face!" The Trouble Consultant said and palmed the back of the coward's neck then brought his head down fast, smashing his face against table and splitting it half. The pummeled man hit the floor. Afterwards Havoc looked around unfazed and spotted Ava in the shock-faced crowd, "I'll take a coupla' cheeseburgers to go."

# Chapter 5

The scene outside of Smitty's was a people watcher's paradise as the urban scenery bustled with colorful, loud police and ambulance sirens. After Smitty finished giving a full report to the cops about the drama that unfolded inside of his club, they pulled off with the broken nosed troublemaker handcuffed in the backseat. Smitty then went over to the orange and white ambulance bound for Kings County Hospital and spoke with paramedics as Gabriel sat inside holding an ice pack over his own swollen nose. After being reassured that his friend and employee would be fine and that his injuries were not as bad as they looked he patted him on the shoulder, then let him go. Havoc stepped out of the noisy crowd and Smitty smiled proudly.

"Thanks for lending a hand back there Young blood." Smitty said to Havoc as he escorted him to his car.

"Glad I could be of service. I just hope the big guy's gonna be alright."

"Who Gabe? He's one tough son of a gun. That fool just caught him by surprise is all." Smitty said shaking his head.

"So, has anything like this ever happened before?" Havoc asked.

"Not as bad as tonight, but there have been a couple of incidents where Gabe had to roll up his sleeves. Lately, it's been happening all over the city. I swear the youth of today take a lot for granted. They have no idea what brothers like Frank Embree and sisters like Sarah Bartman endured for us. But I sure as hell do! Growing up in Bombmingham Alabama I've seen our people bitten by police dogs and hosed down by fire hoses just because they wanted to sit at a counter and eat a meal or get a decent education. And here these young fools have everything at their fingertips. Opportunities that were unheard of only a few short years ago but instead of taking advantage and advancing, they'd rather walk around in a fog with their pants sagging and having multiple kids by multiple partners...aw forget it!" Smitty said sounding frustrated.

Havoc opened his car door and Mayhem jumped out excited to see her owner. "How's my girl doing?" he asked as he kneeled to receive a hug from her. By the way her tail wagged in greeting, he could tell how badly she wished she could talk back to him. "Hey, I got something for you," he smiled opening up the doggy bag and tossed her the cheeseburgers that she caught in the air and devoured. After licking her chops, the large dog recognized Smitty and came over for more affection.

"Does she even own a leash?" Smitty asked giving the large dog a scratch under her chin.

"Mayhem's not exactly the kind of dog you want to put on a leash," Havoc said.

"So, lemme ask you something. If you're such a bad ass, how come you need her in the first place?" he teased.

"I wouldn't be in this line of work if I was a creampuff. But it's like this. Teaming up with a Bullmastiff is like buying a life insurance policy. You might not need it right away, but it's good to know you got it in reserve just in case you've got to deal with a situation you can't handle on your own."

"I heard that. So what the hell are you feeding her? She's huge."

"She puts away a 15-pound bag and a case of dog food a week." Havoc said proudly.

Smitty whistled astonished. "A week? Damn. I guess kicking ass and taking names must pay well."

"I do alright."

"Alright enough to have stashed away enough revenue so you can retire and get a normal job?" he asked hopeful.

"Normal is a setting on a washing machine. And retire and do what exactly? Paint pictures of happy bushes with Bob Ross?"

Smitty shook his head. "I don't get you. If you feel the need to risk your neck and make a buck then why not become a bounty hunter and catch skip tracers?"

"And split the profits with some lazy ass bails bondsman? No way Jose!"

"Then how's about a cop?"

"Me, a cop? That's funny," Havoc laughed.

"What's so funny? You can still save the world and it's a helluva lot safer. If you took the test, which I know a smart guy like you would score high. You'd be training at the academy in under a few months. Detective in a couple'a years."

Havoc looked at Smitty oddly. "Aside from the fact I wouldn't pass the drug test, I am not trying to save the world. Plus, I can make in two to three jobs what cops bring home in a month."

"Young blood, money is only something you need in case you don't die tomorrow." Smitty said wholeheartedly.

"Well I feel fine. So I'll be needing that chedda' today."

"You will never see a U-Haul behind a hearse. No matter how much chedda' you make, you can't take it with you. The Egyptians tried and all they got was robbed." Smitty shook his head in frustration. "I'm just saying what you do doesn't have much security, but it does have a whole lot of risk. You know it's never too late to become what you might have been. Go back to college. Get your degree-" Havoc's expression said he was not in the mood for a lecture and for the older gentleman to back off. "Okay-Okay. No need to ice grill me like that Young blood. Shit, it's cold enough out here as it is." Smitty rubbed his hands for friction. "Let's warm up inside your car. We need to talk." he said and walked around to the passenger side. "Hell's the matter with you?" he asked when Havoc was still standing there with a bothered look on his face.

"Nothing. It's just that I have this thing about people sitting in my ride."

Smitty looked insulted. "Last I heard I was your father and that should carry more weight than just, 'people'."

"Pop you know I didn't mean it like that." Havoc groaned. Smitty waved at his son like this wasn't up for debate and opened the door then climbed in. It was too cold to argue so Havoc opened the back door so his dog could climb in, closed it shut, then slid behind the wheel. "Okay what's so important? And please don't let it be about me going back to college. Depending on your major, a degree is nothing but a high-priced piece of toilet paper." Havoc said switching on the engine and the heat.

Smitty sat quietly brain wrestling with what was on his mind then turned to his son. "When was the last time you saw your cousin Alonzo?"

"Who Bug-Out? I dropped that knuckle head off at his crib earlier on the way here. What do you want with him?"

"Look, I know you and your cousin are tight and all but-" Havoc held up his hand to respectfully stifle his Dad.

"Pop I already know what you're going to say, so let me stop you right there. I heard the rumors too. And that's all they are, rumors. I'm not about to accuse him of being nobody's addict. And as his uncle you should give him the benefit of the doubt too."

Smitty predicted his son to come to his cousin's defense just like when they were kids. That's why he had proof. "You know a two-time loser named Dead Broke?"

"Yeah I know that piece of shit. He was on the three-train peddling sign language cards fronting like he was deaf." Havoc nodded with a frown. "I have no use for him whatsoever. No one does."

"Word on the street is the owners of just about every bodega and five and dime store in Brooklyn are after him and your cousin."

"What for?"

"Shoplifting and trading in five-dollar rolls of dimes filled with pennies for paper money. They're also selling VCR boxes with bricks or wet newspapers inside."

"If you're dumb enough to do business with or buy anything from those two you deserve to get got," Havoc reasoned.

"You always seem to have the answer for everything, tell me what you would do if somebody hired you to consult your cousin?"

Havoc shot his father a serious look. "Aw man get serious."

"When have you known me not to be?"

"Well obviously I wouldn't take the job. And I'd let Bug-Out know what's up."

"Not very professional are you?"

"Which is another reason why I'm not a cop. Bug-Out's not working and he's got mad responsibilities. You know better than anyone that sometimes you have to bend the rules to provide for your family. Not that I'm justifying what he's done and I'll set him straight. But desperate doesn't always equal basing. It can also mean hungry."

"Sheeeeit you've got to be kidding me! He and his old lady are on every government-funded program that exists. Section eight, welfare, Medicaid, WIC and whatever else there is. Trust me when I say, there ain't nobody starving in that apartment. And everybody knows that piece of trash Dead Broke would pimp out his own mamma for a fix. So you tell me what other reason would Alonzo have for hanging out with a character like him? I heard that he's reduced to selling everything he owns including the coat off his back. Now what does that tell you?"

There was a long silence and Havoc plucked the little red cinnamon smelling tree hanging from the rear-view mirror. He wasn't about to confess that he had just given Bug-Out enough money to get beamed up like Scotty. If memory served him correct, Dead Broke lived in the Atlantic Towers complex which would explain why Bug-Out was so far from home when he found him wandering the streets, and why he didn't have a coat. It also explained why he was so elusive when asked what he was doing there. Havoc turned to Smitty with a hurt look in his eyes. Smitty exhaled and felt his pain.

"This is not easy for me either son." Smitty said.

"Yeah-I know." Havoc said and reached for the pack of Newport's on the dashboard.

"Alonzo's my nephew. My sister's kid for crying out loud. I gave him his first car." Smitty said as Havoc lit a cigarette and shook his head then attempted to massage the growing headache away by rubbing his temples. "Your Aunt Mary and I were talking and she suggested that if I gave him a job at the club, that it might give him a sense of responsibility. But I eighty-sixed that idea for obvious reasons. So, I was thinking maybe if you talked to him, tried to get him to enroll into a detoxification program, he might listen and get his act together."

"I don't know Pop, I mean how the hell am I supposed to convince him to get it together, when deep down I'm not even sure he can?"

"I don't know son. But I do know if anyone can get him to listen it's you."

Havoc felt his head nod but had no idea how he was going to talk his favorite cousin into seeking help for the addiction he claimed didn't exist. "Okay, I'll talk to him. And figure out how to convince him."

A wave of relief came over Smitty. When his sister called him crying about her son's problem he did not know what he was going to do. "Thanks son. I knew I could count on you. So about this party for Tatiana, I see your mother couldn't call me herself to invite me, she had to send you to do it." Havoc shrugged uncomfortably. "And what about food?"

"She's having it catered."

Smitty was slack jawed. "Catered? I own a supper club. I could have done that for free."

"What do you want me to say Pop? She wanted it catered by someone else. I think one of her Church lady friend's has a catering business."

Smitty grumbled but was not about to share what he was thinking with his son about his mother. "I swear sometimes that mother of yours can be so damn difficult. When is she going to let go of the past?"

"I don't know. Maybe when she's good and ready." Havoc snapped cutting his eyes over at his father then blew off some steam and made himself calm down. "Look Pop, let's not do this Okay?"

Smitty shook his head. "Sorry son. I just wish she would talk to me."

"What do you want me to tell you Pop? Write her a letter," he said jokingly.

"You think she'd read it?" Smitty asked desperately. Havoc remained silent and gave him a raised eyebrow look indicating that his father had better not hold his breath waiting for his mother to compromise. "Yeah, it'd be a waste of paper. Well let me go back inside. If I don't talk to you before the party I'll see you there. And one more thing. Try not to get killed out here."

"Everyday." Havoc nodded then pulled off after his father got out. A mile away he remembered that Smitty never told him why it was so obvious that Tee-Tee's party was going to be thrown at Nicky's.

Havoc grew up in two completely different households. During the week he lived a privileged existence with his mother and sister in Canarsie amongst other solid upper-middle class families in what the kids from the nearby projects referred to as the 'The bourgeois ghetto.' And from Friday afternoon to Sunday evening, he stayed with his father in Bedford-Stuyvesant and got his education in street smarts and an edge over his peers by hanging out with his cousin Bug-Out and his crew. As a small boy he thought he had the coolest father in the world. Handsome, charismatic, adored by all and down to earth, Smitty didn't discipline his son. Instead he schooled his son by teaching him how to observe, conduct himself with people and most importantly to work hard for what he wanted. But it wasn't until he was older that he learned his perfect father wasn't so damn perfect.

# Chapter 6

The tranquility that characterized early Saturday mornings in the high-end residential district of the Williamsburg section was felt as Havoc made a left onto Bedford Street and cruised down its quiet cobbled streets. He chose the forlorn neighborhood because as he put it, 'The stress is less and the sun is brighter.'

Passing a hodgepodge of nineteenth-century houses, abandoned factories and an aging Domino Sugar refinery building, the Trouble Consultant pulled up to the only occupied building for miles, a lonely two-story walkup devoid of life he leased and got out along with Mayhem who stretched before trotting over to her favorite hydrant. Havoc removed the massive padlocks from the gate over the garage adjacent to his building, lifted it up and drove inside. After parking beside a midnight black Jeep Cherokee, he locked up his expensive vehicles then unlocked his front door and wearily climbed the seemingly endless staircase leading to his home with stone feet.

"Be it ever so humble," Havoc muttered over a yawn opening the door at the top of the stairs. Mayhem barged past him and made a bee-line for her food and water bowls. His eyes were heavy and all he could think about was the King-sized waterbed across the room as he shuffled inside. The sun was shining brightly through the wide picture framed window that boasted a spectacular view of the Manhattan skyline. Sometimes in the summer he and Mayhem would go up to the roof and have a private barbeque as he marveled at the beautiful sight. He came over and pulled down the shades, closed the curtains, then flicked on the track lights overhead.

Havoc's loft was ridiculous. Huge yet cozy. Brick-face walls. Glossy wooden floors. Just plain gorgeous. The marble mantle over the fireplace was overstocked with constant reminders of his unique and extraordinary profession. There were trophies, shiny medals, plaques, framed certificates and commendations boasting of his skills and accomplishments in boxing and firearms all testifying to his coordination, endurance and aggression. The only awards not on display were for the skills and moves he picked along the way in combat like wrestling and mixed martial arts.

In the corner dangling from a chain was an 'Everlast' punching bag worn from abuse and a workout bench stacked with the weights he used religiously to build his muscles into a protective suit of armor. Walking across the room past a pair of treadmills sitting idly side by side, he pushed back the red door, adorned with a velvet black light poster of a bikini-clad shapely afro sporting sista walking with a black panther to one of his two spacious walk-in closets and flicked on a light switch. Between the walls and garments there was so much red the inside of the closet looked like a crime scene.

In a time where wearing someone else's name splashed across the back of designer jeans was the height of fashion, Havoc made it his business to be up on the freshest styles. Hanging neatly on red wooden hangers were shirts, slacks, jeans and suits all designer label, all red. Gucci, Polo, Benetton, Calvin Klein, Bill Blass, Lee's, Cham's de Baron and Sergio Valente just to name a few. Red leather, shearling and suede coats and jackets hung on separate rods. There was even a special hook just for his red ties, belts and hats. On the bottom of the closet was a shoetree ripe with more kicks than a Bruce Lee flick. Clarks, Ballys, British Walkers, Doc Martins, Adidas, Nikes, Air Jordans, Reeboks, Filas, New Balance, Lottos with the switchable velcro patches, K-Swiss, Gucci and Pumas. If it was in style it was in Havoc's closet. In fact, the only pair of kicks he didn't own was Kangaroos because he thought the pouch on the side was straight up whack. Havoc removed his clothes, hung up his jacket and stuffed the clothes he had on in a bag for the cleaners.

Havoc then went into the kitchenette where he kept cases of Chuck Wagon and Gravy Train dog food stacked high beside a Whirlpool washing machine and dryer. He refilled Mayhem's food and water bowls to the brim, jumped in the shower to wash the funk of the previous night away, then went about the rigorous task of mother and sister proofing his home.

He grabbed the semi-automatic rifle off the mantle, a 38 special from a bowl on the kitchen table, the semi-automatic handguns from the nightstand and tucked them along with his trusty red handled Glocks away in the secret compartment in the ceiling. The Black Tail porno magazines lying on the coffee table were tossed into a box and placed on the top shelf of his closet. The empty beer cans and over used ashtrays were scooped up into a giant Hefty garbage bag, twisty-tied and placed beside his already full garbage can. A half can of Lysol was sprayed to mask the smell of cheeba. Mayhem hid under the kitchen table as her master ran a Hoover over the beautiful and pricey red and gold Asian floor rug he received as a bonus from a furniture store owner whose life he saved after a neighboring furniture store owner tried to kill the competition-literally. He emptied the dishwasher then with a bucket full of Mr. Clean tackled the bathroom. With that done, all that was left for him to do was dust the shelves, the entertainment rack that housed his stereo, CD player, VCR, endless collection of movies on VHS, Nintendo Entertainment system and his TV. Now his home looked presentable for his mother and sister.

Beyond exhausted he had one more thing to do before getting some much needed sleep and that was check his phone messages. There were two separate phones lines. A black one for family, friends and the like. And a red one to coordinate his various appointments, dates and meetings with his clients. He reached for the answering machine box that was hooked up to his personal line first. The light blinked two times. He hit the message button and his voice came on sounding jovial.

*'Hi this is Tommy. I'm probably home. I'm just avoiding someone I don't like. Leave me a message and if I don't call back it's you.'* BEEP! *'Tommy this is your Mom. I wish you'd change that rude message anyway, I wanted to know what happened after you invited your father to Tee-Tee's party. I know he probably said I'm acting foolish cause I didn't call him myself, but I don't care. That's his problem. Besides he's not coming to see me, he's there to see his daughter. Anyway, the reason I'm calling is because I need your help. I'm having a hard time finding this Cabbage Patch doll that Tee-Tee wants for her birthday. Now the white ones are easy to find, no problem. The shelves are packed with them. But the black one's, forget it! I've searched hi and low and had no luck. And don't bother going to Fulton Street because I went to every toy store there and they don't have any. I figured I'd better ask you now because I'll have you know who with me later. Okay honey, expect us at around noonish, love you bye.'*

Havoc scratched his baldhead wondering, where in the hell was he supposed to find the hottest new toy during the holiday season. He hit the button again.

BEEP! *'Hi...it's me Nicky.'* Havoc's head snapped erect when he heard her voice. It sounded so sweet he could almost smell the balmy Egyptian Musk she wore come out the answering machine along with it. *'Listen I know it's last minute but I was wondering if you could stop by tomorrow. I wanted to talk to you about something. Don't trip nothing's wrong. There's just something we need to discuss before Tee-Tee's party. I'll be home all day so drop by if you can. Take care and oh yeah, Happy New Year.'*

After the message was over he contemplated playing it back just to hear her voice but refused to play himself like a Herb. The number light on the business answering machine flashed four times. He hit the button, this time he sounded all business.

*'This is Havoc, at the tone leave your name and message. I'll get back to you.'* BEEP! *'Hello, my name is Gloria Rueben and my situation is a sensitive one.'* The desperate sounding woman's voice explained trying her best to remain dignified. *'I lost two sons to street violence. Just buried my oldest a month ago. And now I fear my youngest is headed down the same path as his brothers. He's been running around with a bunch of hoods and dealing drugs in Marcy Projects for some piece of filth named Johnny Hop. What I was hoping you could do is persuade him to choose a different path. I already tried the Scared Straight program, school guidance counselors even the beat cop that patrols my neighborhood and nothing's worked. I know this sounds bizarre and it's not the kind of call you normally get, but Michael is my only baby I have left. I've heard stories about you. The good things you've done for the community. Helping out people who have nobody to turn to and I think he'd listen if you talked to him. He just needs someone who cares. A role model. I'm desperate please call me at 718-'*

Havoc shook his head then hit the erase button. "Sorry lady but I am nobody's role model."

BEEP! A throaty voice tinged with sobbing came on. In the background was more wailing. *'Um-hello Havoc this is Roxanne Jenkins. We spoke last week about the job you're doing for us. Well I wanted you to know that those stupid ass, no dick having mothafucka's came by my bar and fucked with us again. They beat up my boyfriend Lamar when he tried to stop them. I mean it's fucking New Years, you would think they'd have somewhere to be but obviously not. I know you are supposed to take care of them next Saturday, but I don't think we can wait that long and I'd really appreciate it if you could do it tonight instead. There's an extra something in it for your troubles. If you can do it then please call me back.'*

BEEP! '*Havoc you son of a bitch!*' Havoc raised his eyebrows and twisted his head at the chilling voice that sounded like the caller gargled with ammonia and crushed glass before calling. '*Yo Havoc, you hurt my brother real bad!*'

"I hurt lots of brothers real bad. And each one deserved it! Which one's yours?" Havoc jokingly asked the answering machine.

'*You'd better watch your back cause when you're least expecting it, I'ma sneak up on you like a motherfucking ninja and Bruce Leroy dat ass!*' the twisted voice on the machine threatened.

"Picture that." Havoc said twisting his mouth unfazed by the mysterious caller's attempt at intimidation. Empty threats went along with the territory and he got used to them a long time ago.

BEEP! '*Ello my name es Cynthia Sanchez. I have huge-huge problem and I need your help please. My husband Eduardo. He hit me so I put him out. I got a how ju' say, order of protection from the police. But he no care. Sometimes I see him outside my window standing there staring and I am very much scared. I tell the police, but they do nothing. It's like they are waiting for him to hurt me or worse, before they will do something. If you are interested in taking me on as a client I work the eight to midnight shift at Junior's Restaurant all this week. Just ask for me, Cynthia...bye.*'

After jotting down locations, names and numbers Havoc got down on his knees and thanked God for allowing him to make it home safely then removed his red silk boxers and climbed into bed, clapped his hands twice activating the clapper and it was lights out.

The Trouble Consultant felt like he wasn't asleep for more than a few minutes when the phone rang. He reached out and picked it up with his eyes still shut.

"Who dis?" he mumbled.

"Hey I caught you, good."

"Nicky?" he asked sitting up yawning.

"Yes. I didn't wake you, did I?"

"Huh? Me? Naw-I wasn't sleep." He said grinning as her soft voice tickled his ear like a Q-tip.

"So, did you get my message?"

"Yeah I got it." He said trying to sound nonchalant.

"So, can you stop by? I really need to see you."

Havoc looked over at his clock. "Yeah I guess I can do that." He said stifling a yawn with a balled fist.

"Good. You remember the address?" she teased.

"Oh you've got jokes? I'll see you in a few."

The Trouble Consultant went over to a second walk in closet with the black sliding door where he kept the clothes he wore when he wasn't working and threw on a pair of Guess overalls, hi-top Jordan's and a black Fila V-neck. Even in a hurry he was still fashion conscious.

"No-no girl stay here." he stopped his dog as she went to follow him out.

Anxious to learn what was so important his ex-wife needed to speak with him about, the bald man opened up the garage and climbed behind the wheel of his Jeep Cherokee. Five minutes later while waiting at a light he spotted Bug-Out and Dead Broke on the corner making money hand over fist selling stolen black Cabbage Patch kids. He drove madly up onto the sidewalk and the customers scattered. He jumped out and stormed over. Dead Broke dipped off, leaving Bug-Out who was too petro to move. He got up in his cousin's face so angry he could strangle him.

"I know what this looks like but-"

"Shut-up! If you aren't honest with yourself, how can I trust what you say to me?" Bug-Out's angry cousin reasoned. "I found out about a detox program and you will attend and get off that shit or so help me, I will fly that head. Make a decision!"

Bug-Out's eyes filled with tears and he embraced his cousin. "Thank you man! Thank you! This was all I ever needed. For someone to give a damn."

"Huh?" Confusion was written all over his face. This was not the reaction he was expecting. He thought for certain he'd have to use more than mere words to persuade his cousin. "So that means you're going to the program?"

Bug-Out nodded. "Most definitely! You think I wanna be like this? A lousy husband and pathetic father to my son? You set it up and I am there! In fact, you know what? I don't even want to sell these dolls. Here you want them?"

Shocked at his cousin's willful cooperation, he almost didn't hear his offer. "Sure. Thanks," He said unable to believe his luck as he accepted his sister's impossible to find birthday gift.

"So, you ready?" Bug-Out asked anxious to get a new start on life.

Pressed for time, the bald man checked his watch, "Um no, not right this second. I have somewhere to be, but I promise I will pick you up on the way back."

"Okay then I'll go upstairs and wait for you and thanks again man I really mean it." Bug-Out said then jogged home.

Stunned but very happy that his cousin wanted to get help, he got back in his ride smiling like the Kool-Aid man. Moments later he pulled up to a small red-bricked house in Bedford Stuyvesant. He got out and went up and rang the doorbell. The door opened and a beautiful woman opened the door smiling and allowed him inside.

"I'm so glad you came." Nicky said cheerfully and surprised him with a kiss on the cheek.

"So what's this all about?" her ex-husband asked immediately. He didn't want to get caught up in her big brown eyes.

"Relax. Coffee?" she offered and he nodded a reply. "So how do you want it?"

"Black, just like my woman." He said. Nicky giggled and went into the kitchen and came back out with a big cup of steaming java. "Okay, so what's up?"

She paused for a moment as if to collect her thoughts. "I'm just going to come right out with it. I don't know about you but this past holiday made me realize just how much I miss you. Miss us."

"Whoa, I'm confused. The last time we spoke you made it painfully clear that you were over me."

"I've had time to think things over and I really want to try and work things out." She smiled with love in her eyes.

He could smell something good coming from the kitchen. "You cooked?"

"I was hoping it would be a celebration dinner. So, what do you say? Can we try this again?" She asked taking his hand.

As he stared long and hard into his ex-wife's eyes he couldn't believe how great the year was beginning. First Bug-Out agreeing to go into rehab, Tee-Tee's doll and now Nicky asking him back. Sometimes good things came in three's. "Well I don't know, now that I'm back on the auction block my stock has soared." he said with a sly wink.

Nicky pouted. "Aw you're gonna make a sister beg huh?"

"If anybody should beg it should be me since I messed up." He said and pulled her close then kissed her passionately.

"Hold on we need to set the mood." Nicky said dimming the lights and switched on the stereo. "It feels like ages since we've danced." she said holding out her arms and her ex-husband smiled and they embraced as the stereo volume suddenly jumped. "Isn't the music just a bit too loud?" he shouted covering his ears as it went from a romantic melody to deafening noise.

"Huh? What?" she yelled.

"I said!-"

He sat up in bed abruptly. His stereo was blasting so loudly that his thoughts crashed together. He looked around the room wide-eyed and noticed a confused young woman in her twenties frantically fiddling with the knobs on his stereo. Before he could get the words out, the front door opened and an older woman entered his home lugging grocery bags.

"What in the world!" the older woman carrying the bags exclaimed. She looked at the dumbfounded man sitting up in bed then at the young woman struggling with the stereo. She put her bags down then came over and hit the power button silencing the deafening noise. Mayhem followed behind her wagging her tail.

"Tatiana what did mommy tell you?" she asked sternly.

The young woman poked out her bottom lip then dropped her head like a scolded child and timidly whispered, "Don't move unless it's a fire or a flood."

She then directed her attention at the shocked-faced man in bed and shook her head, "Tommy Strong! It's a brand new-year. Are you planning on sleeping through it?"

"I'm up Ma-I'm up." he said with a stretch and yawn.

"Don't you have something to say to your brother?" his mother asked his sister.

"Sorry I touched your radio Tommy." Tatiana apologized.

Tommy frowned shaking his head. Bug-Out going to rehab, Nicky and him back together, even the stupid Cabbage Patch Doll, it was all a dream, a simple fantasy that he wished was a reality. He rubbed his face and forced a smile. "It's okay Tee-Tee." He said dipping behind the partition to throw something on. His sister giggled pointing at his bare butt.

After sliding into sweatpants and a BVD t-shirt Tommy came over to his mother circling his arms around her waist and planting a kiss on her cheek. "Hey Mommy-O. Happy New Year."

"Hey baby, Happy New Year."

Tee-Tee jumped up and rushed over. "What about me? Kiss me too Tommy!" her mocha-flavored face was decorated with delicate facial features which breathed new life into the phrase 'cute as a button'.

"Happy New Year brat." Tommy said hugging his sister and kissing her atop her head. Tee-Tee squealed then ran back to her cartoons and bowl of cereal with the vivacity of a child less than half her age. "So, how long have you two been here?" He asked his mother.

"Not long. About an hour. You must've been doing some serious partying last night, you didn't even hear us when we came in."

Tommy smelled something delicious and went over and lifted the lid off a huge pot simmering on the stove. "So that's what I smelled."

"And just what are you trying to say about your mama's cooking?"

"Nothing at all. I just smelled it in my dreams." He sighed thinking how right now he was supposed to be eating a celebration meal with Nicky.

"Dreaming 'bout your mama's good-luck collard greens huh? There's no other way to start the year off right. And I put my foot in this batch." she laughed as she removed a bottle of hot sauce from her purse then shook it all over her greens. The green leafed vegetables tasted so delicious everyone called them 'Carla's greens' since that was her name and she cooked them like she created them. "C'mere baby." She called to her son holding a fork full of greens and fed him. "Good huh?" she asked as Tommy licked his lips giving her the thumbs up. "They're almost done. In the meantime make yourself useful and put that away." She said pointing to the bags she brought in.

"What's all this?"

"Groceries. Your cupboards and refrigerator look like you just moved in here yesterday."

"My fridge ain't empty."

Carla opened the refrigerator and looked at him with an arched eyebrow. "My fridge **isn't** empty...and yes, it is." She corrected her son's grammar. "A box of baking soda, a six-pack of beer, a half-eaten spiced ham and cheese hero, Ring-Dings and Cool-Whip is not food. The only thing edible in here is this box of macaroni and the expiration date on it is in Roman numerals." His mother hissed at the garbage can overflowing with empty McDonalds, pizza and Chinese food containers. "I don't know why you eat that junk when it's full of salt. Especially when you know high-blood pressure runs in our family."

"Sure you're right!" Tommy muttered cutting an eye at the simmering pot on his stove filled with collard greens and hefty amount of salty fatback for taste. "C'mon Ma look at me." He flexed showing off his physique that was smooth and hard like polished steel without a trace of body fat anywhere. "Does your son look unhealthy?"

"What's on the outside has nothing to do with what's on the inside Tommy."

"You go gurl! Drop that knowledge," Tommy smiled stealing a kiss on her cheek.

"I'm being serious." Carla said earnestly. Tommy rolled his eyes like he didn't want to be bothered. "You don't like to listen son. Never did, with your hard-headed self." his mother said in a playful but scolding tone and popped him upside his head

"Ow Ma-that hurt!" he frowned rubbing his head.

"It did? But I thought you were soooo tough."

"Hey I'm a grown man now, you can't be abusing me no more. I ain't scared of you." Tommy said from a safe distance.

"Oh boy please, ain't nobody hardly abused your behind." His mother laughed.

"Ma I'm pretty sure beating your kid with an orange Hot Wheels race car track constitutes as abuse." Tommy griped.

"It was only once and you deserved it. As bad as you were Tommy you're lucky that's all I used." Carla said making no apologies.

"I wasn't bad." Tommy said unable to keep a straight face knowing good and well, growing up he definitely tested his mother's patience and love on numerous occasions. "I was merely asserting my independence."

Carla looked at her son like she was two seconds away from grabbing the giant wooden spoon next to the fork hanging on the wall and giving him another whooping. "I'll tell you this much, if I didn't knock some sense into you from time to time you might have turned out like one of those wild boys you used to hang out with. Either in jail or worse." Tommy had to admit, many of the guys that he grew up with were no longer around because their parents did not administer enough love. Mayhem came over to see what happened to her master and was met with Carla's long stare. "Do we have a problem?" Carla asked placing her hands on her hips and staring down the huge dog. Mayhem backed away with her tail between her legs and promptly laid on her mat. Even she knew better than to mess around with Miss Carla 'Take no mess' Pinkney.

Actually no one in their right mind man, woman or beast messed with the dainty elegant looking woman of color who wore fifty-one as if she created the age. Bearing an uncanny resemblance to legendary screen goddess Leena Horne, Carla wore her silver-gray hair in a close-cropped style that perfectly framed her face. But her looks and tiny frame were the only things soft about her. Between raising two kids for the most part on her own, and teaching for the wild-style New York Board of Education, she quickly developed a zero tolerance for nonsense and could give less than a damn about pleasing others. But it was her tough as nails personality that got her offered the position as assistant Principal of Boys and Girls High School, which she graciously accepted.

"What's wrong May Grandma's being mean to her grand dog?" Tommy asked his dog referring to her by the nickname he used around those who didn't know what he really did for a living.

"I wish you'd stop referring her as my grand dog and give me a real grandchild." Carla griped as she turned off the burner under the steaming pot of collard greens.

"And I wish you'd realize that the bond between a man and his dog is just as strong as the bond between him and his wife, or even his child."

"Hmph! I beg to differ. Look, don't get me wrong, I think May's a sweet dog. But she's hardly a substitute for a grandchild." Carla beefed. Tommy pretended not to hear and wrestled with his dog. "So, how's the construction business?" she asked realizing it was pointless to continue.

"I do okay." Tommy lied averting his mother's stare.

"That's good but Tommy do you really want to do just 'Okay' forever? What are your long-term goals? You need some stability in your life." Carla asked earnestly. She was a little disappointed that her thirty-one, year old son was not where she felt he should be in life. More disappointed that he dropped out of college and got divorced with no explanation. As smart and charismatic as he was, she saw her son doing so much more than operating a jackhammer. But if construction was what he wanted, so be it because no matter what she loved her baby-boy dearly and spoiled him as an adult, as she had done when he was a child. But that didn't mean she wasn't going to stop pushing him to do more. It was her God given right as a mother.

Tommy looked to the ceiling for strength. "Stability is overrated. Seriously Ma pace yourself it's January the first. You've got the whole year to pluck your son's nerves." He said opening a Ring-Ding and cramming the entire hockey puck shaped cake into his mouth as he turned to walk off.

"Tommy I don't care how swollen you are from lifting them dumbbells. I'm your mother. I brought you into this world and I'll take you out!"

Tommy leaned against the counter like he was four years old, head down thinking, if his enemies could see him now. "Yes Ma'am."

After getting her due respect, Carla continued. "Now like I was saying, Tommy, you're a grown man but you live like you're still in high school. Honey you cannot live on pizza and beer forever. It is time to grow up. Have a family of your own."

"I wanna Ding Dong! Gimme a Ding Dong!" Tee-Tee suddenly bounced over proclaiming. Tommy looked at his sister then at his mother and busted out laughing.

"Baby they're called Ring Dings alright?" Carla corrected her daughter while glaring at her son's immaturity.

"What?" Tommy shrugged.

"Did you finish your cereal honey?" Carla asked her daughter suspiciously. Tee-Tee nodded with her eyes glued to the box of cupcakes in her brother's hands. Carla was about to give her one when she heard gulping sounds coming from somewhere in the room. She peeked behind the partition Tommy used to divide his place and discovered his dog lapping up the bowl of Smurf Berry Crunch on the floor.

Tommy couldn't help but laugh. Even though his sister had the mind of an adolescent, some of the things she did were very clever and quite 'adult-like' in her scheming.

"You're not helping matters any." Carla said frustrated to her son.

"C'mon Ma you gotta give Tee-Tee her props. She should get the cake just on G.P." He said winking at his sister.

Carla sucked her teeth and opened the foil wrapper over the small cake then handed it to Tee-Tee. "Here, you have your brother to thank for this because your sneaky behind don't deserve nothing." Tee-Tee accepted her award for, 'Most creative way to simultaneously finish her food and obtain a Ring Ding' and excitedly ran back to the television in time to the sing along with the Fraggle Rock theme song. Carla looked at her daughter sadly. Sitting there watching television Tatiana appeared to be a normal twenty-four-year-old woman. But whenever something funny happened on the children's television show she was watching, those same elegant features that she shared with her mother transformed into those of an animated child's. Carla forced a smile then turned to her son. "I'd really like some grandkids."

"Why didn't you tell me? I could've saved a whole lot of money and gotten you one of those instead of the pearl necklace I got you for Christmas." Tommy said sarcastically.

"I'm serious Tommy when are you going to settle down?"

"Whoa! You want me to settle down and start a family. Pop wants me to go back to school and get my degree-"

"I can't believe that I'm saying this but I agree with you father. Partially. With the job market so competitive, you'd be better off with your Masters." Carla added.

"I'm shocked you didn't offer any suggestions on what I should study too."

"Well according to L.A. Law and St. Elsewhere you can't go wrong in either the legal or medical field. And I know I can never go wrong when I'm watching me some Blair Underwood and Denzel Washington. Mmm-mmm-mmm!" She sighed daydreaming.

"Wow Ma, really! You know what you are? An African American yenta." Tommy said letting out a cross between a sigh and a laugh. "Look, I am happy with what I am doing right now and I am certainly in no hurry to have a wrinkled little time clock."

Carla threw her hands up feeling defeated. "Well fine then, but I still don't understand why you and Nicky divorced. She was perfect. Good looks, brains, a sweet personality. And to this day neither of you have ever given me a straight answer."

Tommy shrugged his shoulders like he wasn't about to now and patted his thigh getting his dog's attention. "Get daddy a beer." He commanded to which she happily obliged and let out a bark then galloped over to the fridge and clamped down on the handle and pulled open the door. She stuck her head inside and grabbed a bottle of Guinness Stout by the neck, closed the door with her tail then brought it to her master.

"Nicky called me yesterday." Carla said matter a factly.

"Oh?" Tommy said nonchalantly never mentioning she called earlier or that he dreamt about her. Instead he set the bottle cap on the edge of his counter, held on tight to his beer and brought his hand down hard on the cap to pop it off.

"Tommy can I have a sip of your beer?" Tee-Tee asked.

"No!" Both Tommy and his mother replied.

"Didn't you have enough to dink last night? Carla asked her son.

"So, what'd Nicky want?" Tommy asked deflecting her meddling.

"Just some advice. Her Principal asked her if she'd consider teaching special education next year because of the wonderful work she's done with her class. I told her she should do it. She's a passionate teacher and it's why she got into this profession in the first place, to make a difference. Remember how helpful she was with Tee-Tee?" Tommy nodded. When the special education teachers had a difficult time teaching his sister to relearn the alphabet and tie her shoelaces only Nicky was able to do it. "But that was it. It's not like she's going to say but so much because she knows I live for the day you two will get back together and you can move out of here"

"What's wrong with my place?" he asked gesturing at the Manhattan skyline in his window.

"Who cares about a view, when you're miles from civilization? You might as well be living on a deserted Island looking at a cruise ship."

"I like my privacy." Her son explained leaving out the part about not wanting the scum he consulted knowing where he rested his head.

"Which you didn't care about until you got a divorce."

"**Which** has been almost three years. Leave it alone, please." Tommy pleaded to deaf ears.

"And another thing." Carla began, as she ignored her son face palm his forehead out of frustration.

"You know it's not a coincidence that the word smother has the word mother in it," He pointed out.

"She still cares a great deal for you." Carla mentioned.

"Well of course she still cares about me. The divorce was amicable and we're still friends."

"Well amicable or not, she regrets being so quick to sign those divorce papers."

Tommy did a double-take at his mother. He knew she could be annoyingly intrusive when it came to his life, but did she figure out how to pry in on his dreams too? He gave her un-asked for opinion a brief thought then waved it away like it was mere hearsay dropping his head. "Nah. That train has left the station."

Carla lifted her son's chin. "Tommy I only want what's best for you. Now I'll admit, sometimes I can be a little pushy. But no matter what I or anybody else says, follow your heart. Even though it's on your left, it's always right." Tommy smiled at his mother's lived in but never worn-down words of wisdom. She went over and checked on the collard greens and added another dab of hot sauce. "So, did you get my message?"

"Huh? Oh yeah. I'll try Kings Plaza mall tomorrow but I gotta be honest. We may not find you-know-what until after you-know-when." Tommy muttered while pointing at his sister on the low. "Oh, and I went by the bar like you asked and invited Pop."

"So I heard." Carla's posture tightened at the mention of her children's father.

"When did you see daddy Tommy?" Tee-Tee asked suddenly.

"Last night nosy. I went by his club to tell him about your party next week."

Tee-Tee exploded into laughter. "I spoke to him too! And you know what?"

"No...what?" Tommy asked in a fascinated child-like voice.

"Daddy said he's coming to my party next Fri-yay, and he's gonna get me something real nice for my birthday!" she said excitedly.

"Wow!" Tommy said and turned to his mother with a perplexed look.

"Your father called to speak to her this morning." Carla informed with an eye-roll. Tommy shifted uncomfortably and gave a semi nod of the head. "I'm sorry honey, I know how you hate to be put in the middle of your father's and my squabbles."

Tommy walked over to his mother, kissed her forehead and the three of them enjoyed New Year's collard greens and each other's company without mentioning Smitty, college, careers, marriage or grandkids for the rest of the afternoon. As the afternoon was coming to an end Carla had placed the remaining collard greens in Tupperware bowls and put them in the fridge along with the left-over baked chicken and macaroni salad she brought from home.

"Now if you're not going to eat that food put it in the freezer so it doesn't go bad."

"Got it." Tommy said while tickling his sister.

"Tee-Tee get your jacket Honey. It's time to go."

Tee-Tee's smile turned upside down. "Aww, but I wanna stay here," she whined.

"Young lady we've spent the whole day with your brother. I'm sure he's more than ready to put us out." Carla said nudging Tommy.

"Don't say that Ma, you know I love having the two of you over." Tommy said but quiet as it was kept, he was ready to go back to sleep and hopefully finish his dream.

"Well in any event we still have to go. Nana is supposed to be dropping by so we can watch Golden Girls." Carla said checking her watch.

"Nana does love her Golden Girls. How's she doing anyway?"

"Fine. She told me to tell you that you could pick up a phone sometimes."

"I know, I'm a terrible grandson." Tommy admitted.

After seeing his mother and sister out Tommy turned off the ringers on both phones and went back to dreamland but unsuccessfully picked up where he left off. Two and a half hours later, his eyes opened and he got up. Both answering machines had messages.

BEEP! *'Yeah, my name is um...Bob...Glass. Yeah Bob Glass and I need your help. Today's my baby girl's eighteenth birthday and my last child support payment. I told her, take this check to yo mama and tell her this is the last check she's ever getting from me and tell me the 'spression on your momma's face. An hour later baby girl walked through the door and I said, 'Now what yo momma say about that? And she said to tell you that you ain't my daddy and watch the 'spression on yo face! So I was wondering if you could kill the bitch or at the very least give her a permanent limp? Either will do.'* Tommy shook his head in disbelief then proceeded to the next message.

BEEP! *'Hello Havoc. It's Roxanne Jenkins again. I was wondering if you got my message and if so would you be willing to do it tonight. Like I said I will pay you extra if you do. Call me, bye.'* The female's voice sounded frantic and pleading. And it was obvious she worried that there may be a repeat performance of last night's fiasco.

Tommy felt bad for her, but he did not really feel like busting heads tonight. He moved to the next machine.

BEEP! *'Hey, it's Nicky again. I'm home if you could stop by I'd appreciate it.'*

BEEP! *'Hi Tommy this is Tee-Tee. I'm bored. Mommy and Nana is watching a corny show about old ladies. So, what you getting me for my birthday?*

*'Tatiana who are you on the phone with?'*

*'Uh-oh Mommy's coming I gotta go bye. I love you.'*

Tommy laughed then went over to the window and pulled back the curtains. With the sun setting over the bright lights of the city, New York could easily fool one into believing it was civilized. But Tommy knew better. He left Mayhem at home sharpening her teeth on some rawhide. And forty-five minutes later he was experiencing déjà vu as his Jeep Cherokee pulled up in front of a familiar looking red bricked house on Quincy Street in Bedford Stuyvesant. There was a parking space directly out front and he bo-guarded his way into it before a sleek black Porsche could. After shutting off the engine he got out and walked towards the house.

"Hey, *homeboy* what's your problem? I was about to park there!" the driver of the Porsche angrily shouted in a loud unmistakable-high pitched squeaky voice. As soon as Tommy heard the condescending way he said 'homeboy', like he was lowering himself to speak on his level, he already knew the driver was a pompous ass. He turned around with a sneer. "Well?" the driver said.

Tommy didn't say a word and stared at him with a set of hard dark eyes burrowing through the driver of the Porsche. It was a game he liked to play. Get his point across without having to say one word. When the driver looked away a victorious smile formed at the corner of Tommy's lips. The driver pushed back his glasses with his index finger and sheepishly mumbled something about 'Hoodlums' under his breath before screeching off.

"Punk ass Buppy!" Tommy said shaking his head. As he continued towards the house a bit of nostalgia came over him when he entered the gate and passed the garbage cans he used to drag out to the front every morning. He paused and gritted his teeth at how his old mailbox no longer read Mr. and Mrs. Strong, but now simply said Ms. Nicky Hunter. Annoyed by the changes plus a combination of anxiousness about why he was called over made him mash the doorbell repeatedly.

"Alright already! I'm coming!" A voice close to hoarse, deep and whispery filled with cracks yelled from the opposite side of the door followed by a series of locks and chains being unbolted. "Ring all you want I told you before, you're still not getting a-!" The door snatched open and an annoyed African American chocolate sundae stood in the doorway. "-key! Tommy, it's you!" Nicky said startled immediately changing her mood from sour to sweet.

Tommy stood there gawking at his ex-wife. She had the kind of beauty that when she opened the door and you first met her you felt like you won the lottery. Her head was covered with long braids that slipped across her face and her flawless skin was the color of milk chocolate. Her nose was a sepia button squeezed in between toasted almond shaped eyes. Curves were plentiful, starting at her smooth cheeks, rolling to her sufficient bosom and extending around to her ample bottom. She was barefoot and he stole a peek at her feet. They were perfect, compact and deliciously brown without a corn in sight. The toes he used to pour honey on and suck clean during their lovemaking were mocha morsels topped with a dollop of bubblegum-pink polish.

"Hey." he said.

"Hey yourself," she smiled opening the door further so he could enter. "When I didn't hear from you I was beginning to think you weren't going to show."

"I got in late last night and crashed." Tommy explained. canvasing the place. The house was set up differently from when he used to live there. His feet sank into the plush wall-to-wall carpeting that matched perfectly with the chocolate brown leather sofa and love seat. The walls were adorned with beautiful African paintings and masks. In the corner was a 30-gallon aquarium with a bed of bright blue gravel and beautiful tropical fish. On a coffee table made of glass and iron sat a jewelry chest with a map of Africa etched on its side. Making the picture complete was an oak entertainment center with a large screened TV and stereo beneath. "The place looks, dope." he complimented looking around for a lamp, an ashtray something that he remembered from when he used to call this place home.

"Thanks. So, can I get you something? Beer? A soda?"

Tommy wished that she would offer him coffee like in his dream. Then offer herself to him. "Nah I'm straight." He said and they sat in silence, feeling awkward and uncomfortable.

"My mom stopped by earlier. She told me that you're considering teaching special ed kids." Tommy said breaking the loud silence.

"Yes, actually after talking with her I've decided to become an E.D. teacher."

"What's an E.D. teacher?"

"An emotional disturbances teacher. I have a lot of ideas to make learning more exciting for them and I think it will be a good experience." Nicky said.

"Well I think you're the perfect person for the job. You have the patience it takes. I remember how you had my sister reciting her alphabet when none of her teachers could."

"Thanks, but I do not deserve all the credit. Tee-Tee was a fast learner and I believe that in time she will surprise everyone with her greatness. Speaking of Tee-Tee, I bet she's excited about her party."

"Oh yeah. She's really looking forward to it. Thanks again for letting her have it here."

"No need for thanks, I love Tee-Tee. All the nights she used to stay here. She's the kid sister I never had. That's why when your mom called to ask if I'd mind having her party here I was more than happy to help."

"My mother, asked you?" Tommy asked.

"Yeah she said that she couldn't find a decent place to rent out and that it would mean a lot to Tee-Tee if I could have the party here. What's wrong? You sound like this is all brand new."

Now Tommy knew what his father meant by 'Stating the obvious.' His mother felt that he and Nicky weren't doing anything to rekindle the magic, so she decided to play Cupid and have the party there. Perhaps after a couple of slow dances and sharing some birthday cake they might remember what they once had and get back together.

"No, no I knew that. I'm just trippin' because uh, it's been so long since I've been here." Tommy said which was partly the truth.

"Yeah it has been a while. You look good." Nicky smiled. It had been almost a year since Nicky and Tommy had last seen each other. She almost had forgotten how disarmingly sexy he was but was quickly reminded as her eyes zeroed in on his broad shoulders, wide chest and buffed arms bulging from beneath his mock neck shirt. Then there were his chiseled good looks that completed the package.

"So, do you." He smiled returning the compliment. She too looked madd flyy in a fitting pair of Bubble Gum jeans with zippers at the ankles that showed off her soda bottle curves and an Ocean Pacific pin-striped men's button-down shirt cinched at the waist with a wide designer belt and open enough to tease her lovely cleavage.

"How's Mayhem?"

"She's fine."

"And other things?"

"If you're referring to Trouble Consulting, it pays the rent." Tommy hunched his shoulders.

"Speaking of which, I overheard one of my students bragging to the others about how Havoc and Mayhem took care of a slum lord that was terrorizing his Grandmother and the other elderly tenants in her tenement." Nicky said.

Tommy frowned, grinding his teeth. "That piece of filth knew that roach motel violated tons of safety and health codes. Yet every first of the month he and his fat ass nephew would kick in doors threatening to toss these old people out on the street if they didn't have his rent. But when I got through with them-!" he said slamming his fist into his palm to demonstrate. "-let's just say that not only has the building had vast improvements, the tenants pay even less to live there now."

"The kids speak about you as if you were their favorite comic book superhero come to life. If they only knew, their teacher was once married to their superhero." she giggled.

Tommy winced up like he had just been insulted. "Nicky just because I can throw a punch it doesn't make me a superhero." he said with bitterness.

"What bug crawled up your ass?" Nicky asked.

Tommy blew steam. "Sorry. It's just that lately I've been feeling sorta guilty about taking payment for what I do."

"Not you. Mister, 'I'm strictly in dis here for the loot!'" Nicky said taken back by Tommy's sudden virtuous street-cred ways that drastically contradicted the man who loved being paid in full.

Tommy nodded. "Those old people that hired me were damn near desolate. It's why they lived in that shithole in the first place. And I still took their money. Now you're telling me that their grandkids are discussing me like I give them-I dunno. Hope."

"Sounds like you're struggling under a rather big conscience."

"Perhaps."

"So then why'd you accept the money?"

"If I didn't then everybody would be looking for me to help them out for free."

Nicky rolled her eyes unmoved by his words. "Well you know how I feel about this subject anyway."

"I should, it cost me my marriage."

"No, it cost me mines!" Nicky said raising her voice. "Look let's not take a stroll down memory lane. Let's just discuss why I asked you over."

"No problem. So what's up?"

"There's this guy I've been seeing for a few months. And well, I told him about us being divorced and how close I still am with your mother and sister. And he feels a little jealous. I guess I can understand since most people who get divorced usually break up with the families of their spouses too. I explained that I don't have any family and that you and I are ancient history and he says he understands but I can tell it still bothers him."

"You didn't tell him why we split up?" Tommy asked realizing that's who she was expecting when she answered the door. But it was no longer any of his business. Still he did feel a bit of satisfaction in knowing whoever dude was, he wasn't getting a key to the crib he used to live in.

"Of course not. That's none of his business. If I wouldn't discuss it with your mother, I definitely wouldn't tell him. Anyway, he is feeling a bit insecure about your entire family coming over and wants to come to Tee-Tee's party. I don't really think it's that big of a deal. And I'm more than certain that you're seeing someone. Right?" Tommy half-shrugged an answer that she assumed meant 'yes'. "I'm just a little worried about how your mother might react since she's convinced we're going to get back together someday. I'm curious, how did she react when you started seeing other women?"

"I've never brought anyone home to meet her."

"Chicken huh?" she giggled.

"Remind me, why did you neglect to tell her about your new Schmoopy again?"

"Touché, but we aren't at Schmoopy status yet. I was thinking maybe if you two met he would see there's nothing to worry about and stop feeling so insecure."

Tommy sucked his teeth leaning forward. "So this is what you wanted? For me to meet your new man? Assure him that we are no longer an item?"

"Well yeah, is there problem?"

Tommy calmed down when he heard his tone rising and sat back playing it cool. "Nah, there's no problem."

"So you'll meet him then?"

"I'll even bring a date to Tee-Tee's party." He mumbled.

Nicky was so pleased she leaned over and hugged Tommy. "Thanks, I really appreciate this. You have no idea how this party has put a strain on our relationship."

"Oh really?" Tommy growled. He was even more upset that she did not seem the least bit concerned about who he was bringing. "So when do you want me to meet this guy?"
On cue the doorbell rang. "That should be him now."

As she went to open the door Tommy shook his head. "What if I would've said no?"

"I knew you wouldn't," Nicky smiled and unlocked the door.

A clean-shaven black man with salt and pepper hair slicked back stormed in visibly upset. "I swear this neighborhood is in desperate need of gentrification! You will not believe what just happened! I just had it out with one of your hoodlum neighbors over a parking space!" From where he sat Tommy's back faced the front door, but he immediately recognized the steady and resonant voice. "There I was about to back into a perfect space, right outside your door, when this dimwitted cretin comes zooming up and steals my space! He almost rear-ended me. And you know I was not about to risk my beautiful Porsche getting scratched by his drug mobile, so I being the bigger person allowed him to have the space. Man, he got under my skin! And get this Nicolette, when I reprimanded him about his inconsiderate actions he just stared at me then sashayed off like he owns the block. Probably because he's incapable of complete sentences. I tell you people like that shouldn't be in jail. They should be underneath it!"

"Well never mind that now baby. There's someone here I want you to meet."

"Oh? And whom might that be?"

"My ex-husband Tommy dropped by to discuss the party arrangements for his little sister next Friday."

"Ah splendid, I've been looking forward to meeting the man who foolishly let you go. But as they say, one man's loss is another man's gain." He chuckled with a peck on the cheek then came over smiling and extended his hand. "Corbin Blake Ramsey the third, pleased to make your acquaint-YOUUUU!"

"Hey, how you doin?" Tommy grinned devilishly looking up at Corbin like he was meeting him for the first time, then casually filled his face with Reese's Pieces from the glass dish on the coffee table.

"Thanks for **allowing** me to have the space. Seeing as you're the **bigger** person out of the two of us"

Corbin's slight frame shook with anger. "Nicolette, what is this-this **person** doing here?" he demanded.

"What are you talking about? I just told you. Tommy dropped by to discuss the party."

Corbin shot Tommy a scornful look. "This is your ex-husband? This-this-"

Tommy drew himself up so that he towered over Corbin and fixed a cold stare upon him. "Choose your next words carefully."

Corbin's eyes stretched over Tommy's rock-solid frame and swallowed his pride.

Nicky stepped in, physically interposing herself between them. "Calm down boys! Now what's going on? You two know each other?" she asked confused.

"The hooligan I was just telling you about! The one, who took my parking space, it's him! He's the one!" Corbin blurted out in a frenzy of jumbled words standing safely behind Nicky. Tommy shook his head in disbelief.

Nicky turned to her ex-husband for an explanation, "Tommy?"

As far as Tommy was concerned this had to be a joke. There was no way she could be serious about this old ass Nipsey Russell looking mofo with his corporate suit, tortoise framed glasses and monogrammed sleeves. "Nicky, he's overreacting. Okay so maybe I taxed his space, but so what. This is Brooklyn. If you're slow you blow. Look I feel like this, if I'm willing to let the 'drug mobile' comment go, then he should stop his whining."

"Whining? Who's whining?" Corbin whined.

"Baby, calm down, remember your blood pressure." Nicky said. Tommy flinched like he felt a sharp dagger twist in his back when she called Corbin, 'Baby'.

"I'll have you know sir that whining and stating one's case are two entirely different matters altogether!" Corbin said to Tommy.

"Whatever. Look I'll let it go, if you do the same." Tommy shrugged already bored and looked around the room stopping at Nicky's entertainment center. "So what kind of VCR is that?"

"It's not a VCR, it's a CD player." Corbin snootily explained as Nicky plopped on the couch realizing what a mistake it was bringing her ex-husband and new friend together.

Tommy walked over turning up his nose at the sound system like it smelled funny and picked up a Madonna CD. "What do these things cost? Five-six bucks?"

"Try twenty."

"Twenty? Aw man forget all that, you can't even tape off of the radio. Besides it took me forever to switch my eight-track collection over to cassettes." He winked at Nicky.

"Perhaps, but the sound quality from CDs are much more lucid than those antiquated cassette tapes." Corbin explained like a salesperson at Crazy Eddie's.

"Antiquated? Speak English," Tommy laughed.

"I am speaking English. Perhaps if you spent more time at the library expanding your vocabulary than stealing parking spaces, you might know what it means." Corbin glared. Nicky cut her eyes at Corbin and shook her head. She couldn't believe the level of testosterone in the room.

"Take a chill-pill Old-school. I was just messing with you. I know what a CD player is. Got one myself." Tommy smiled.

"This one's paid for!"

"I also know what antiquated means." Tommy insisted, disregarding being called a thief.

"Yeah sure you do." Corbin smirked in disbelief.

"Antiquated; old, out of date, old fashioned, ancient, a veritable relic, hence the word an-tique!" Tommy smiled enjoying the verbal fencing match, "And just because I like you so much Corky, I'ma use it in a sentence. Wanna hear it? Here it goes! 'Nicky is way too young and fine to be dating your **antiquated** ass!'"

Corbin's top lip curled with detest. He wanted badly to invite his girlfriend's ex-husband outside for an old fashion ass whoopin but he didn't share Tommy's flare for satire nor did he share his burly size seeing as he only used his overpriced gym membership twice in the last year and a half. His frown strained into a tight smile. "So what do you do? -Wait don't tell me, let me guess. I know, you're one of those rapping homeboys who makes noise with their mouth while spitting?" he asked in that same condescending tone Tommy had already come to identify him with. Tommy smiled and shook his head. "No?…Hmmm, well judging from your size my second guess would have to be something that required a lot of heavy lifting, little thinking and paid far below minimum wage."

"I work in the construction field." Tommy replied.

"Typical. I figured you for the type who swings a sledge hammer at their 'ahem' job."

"And what is it you do, mister mouth almighty tongue everlasting?" Tommy asked wondering what kind of game this buster could have possibly kicked to pull a hottie like Nicky.

Corbin grinned widely like this was the moment he had been waiting for. "Me? Oh, nothing really. I'm just a simple investment banker for a little company called Charles Schwab. Maybe you've heard of us, we're one of the leading brokerage firms in the country."

"I have, and I figured you for the type with one of those Wall Street jobs responsible for Black Monday." Tommy said dismissively.

"I may not have been the cause of it, but I sure as hell benefitted from it." He laughed smugly.

Nicky was becoming bored of their dick measuring contest. Especially when figuratively and physically her present couldn't measure up to her past and she wanted to bring this to an end. "Look boys this is obviously not going the way I had intended. So why don't we just call it a night? Tommy I'll see you at the party. If there are any last-minute changes, I'll call your mother." she said.

"Cool," Tommy nodded. He was relieved that she didn't want to call off Tee-Tee's party. His mother would have killed him.

Corbin took off his glasses and cleaned them with the paisley print silk handkerchief in his breast pocket. "No, no honey not yet. My new compadre was just about to enlighten me on what kind of job it is that I have." he said reigniting the beef to which Nicky tossed her hands up in defeat. "So, go on Tommy...tell me, what kind of job do I have? On second thought, let me tell you. I have the kind of job that pays me a lucrative salary so that I can afford my condo on Park Avenue, a summer beach house in Martha's Vineyard and my beloved Porsche. The kind that allows me to travel the world and experience different cultures abroad. The kind that recruited me during my senior year at Harvard and paid for me to go back and get my MBA. And this one you'll love. The kind of job that allows me to shower **my** lady with the finer things in life. Basically, the kind of job you don't have."

"Petty. But finally, something we can agree on," his inner Trouble Consultant remarked.

"Sorry, I can't hear you over my success."

"Calvin, success has nothing to do with being rich or being poor or just being plain average. Everything else is relative. But I wouldn't expect a narrow-minded person like yourself to understand." Tommy said. Nicky lifted her eyebrows half impressed and half perturbed. It wasn't that long ago her ex was singing an entirely different tune. A tune that caused them to break up, and she wondered if the new woman in his life had something to do with his new outlook.

Corbin looked like he wanted to laugh. "Spoken like a true have-not. And for the record, my name is Corbin."

Tommy eyed Corbin from head to toe and had to laugh to keep from hooking off on him. "Kervin, you really shouldn't speak on things you know nothing about, **brotha**." he advised in a facetious tone. High paying Trouble Consulting gigs had his phone ringing off the hook and on the advice of a financial advisor he once protected he put a large amount of money into a high-growth mutual fund and turned an even larger profit. The advisor also helped him create a portfolio and invest in some safe stocks to which he could retire and live quite nicely, if he wanted to.

Corbin shook his head sadly. "Here we go. So I choose an education over hanging on the corner drinking malt liquor with the homeboys and for that I'm considered a sell-out to my race."

"No, you're a sell out for looking down on those homeboys who did not have the same choices you did. I've been A-1 since day one."

Corbin raised his hands in frustration. "Don't speak of choices to me. This country was founded on honesty, truth and the equal rights of all men."

"No, what this country was founded on was the bones of Indians, and the backs of your fellow Africans!" Tommy snapped.

"Oh please! Save the pseudo self-righteous crap you prehistoric throwback. Black people are born knowing that whatever is to be gotten out of life we're always the last to get ours. That the short end of the stick has our name written all over it. But instead of working hard to get ahead, what do most of us do? Bitch and complain about how the white man is keeping us down. So what life's not fair. Boo-hoo! Get over it, and above all else, get yours." Corbin advised pausing to admire his gold Rolex and cufflinks. "Hmph! I know I sure as hell am."

Tommy shook his head. "Boy I tell you, if Martin Luther King had the same outlook as you, we might still be drinking out of colored fountains."

Corbin stood up abruptly. "You know I would continue this battle of wits with you, but from that last comment, you are obviously unprepared, uninformed and unarmed." he said and made an about face for the kitchen.

"A word of advice," Tommy called to him.

Corbin paused smirking, "**You** are giving me advice? This should be good."

"Be careful of the toes you step on today, because they might be connected to the ass you have to kiss tomorrow."

"So insightful. And where pray tell did you pick up that spiritual and enlightening banal cliché? PBS? Masterpiece theater? The unemployment line?"

"Uppercuts Barber shop," Tommy stated as a matter a factly.

"How charmingly ghetto." Corbin laughed and continued into the kitchen.

Tommy shook his head and turned to Nicky. "Seriously Nicky what the fuck? This dude is super whack."

Nicky shrugged. "Hey, I thought it'd be a great idea if you two met before the party to avoid any awkwardness. I saw no reason to think that there'd be any problems."

"And there wouldn't have been, if ya boy Cornball on the Cobb, ain't come in here acting like he's all that."

"His name is Corbin," she corrected.

"You sure about that? Cause the brother doesn't have a stache. And what's up with his hair? Somebody needs to tell Cab Calloway that the conk is dead." Tommy winked causing Nicky to smirk. "Hi-Dee-Hi-Dee-Hi-Dee-Ho."

"Tommy stop." Nicky said unsuccessfully trying not to laugh. Regardless of how upset she was with him he always could get her to smile.

"Aw come on Nick. Don't tell me you're serious about that Oreo-cookie."

"You don't even know him."

"No, but I know his type. Over educated in everything, except what really matters. And how old is money-grip anyway? Strutting around here with Poligrip on his breath."

"Who I date and how old they are is none of your business Tommy. I didn't ask about who you're bringing to Tee-Tee's party now did I?" Nicky asked no longer smiling.

"True dat." Tommy said thinking how obvious it was that she was thinking about it. "Actually, I'm surprised that you are still having it since your 'Ahem' boyfriend and I didn't hit it off."

"Why? This is **my** house. Lord knows I deserve it after all I went through." She said with an all-knowing look that only her ex-husband could decipher. "The party is still on, and Cornba...I mean Corbin...dammit!" She cut her eyes at Tommy who was doing his best not to laugh but said nothing. "Will be attending. My only concern is your mother and Tee-Tee. You two don't have to like each other. I just thought it would have been nice if you could get along since you have to spend time together."

Corbin walked back out of the kitchen with a martini in one hand and a board game in the other. "Finished eavesdropping?" Tommy asked.

"I haven't the foggiest idea what you are talking about." Corbin said and popped the olive from his drink into his mouth with an arrogant smile then opened the box and proceeded to set up the pieces on the coffee table. "Nicky and I are about to play a rousing game of Scrabble. I would ask you to join us, but since purposely misspelled words like def and phat aren't recognized in Webster's Dictionary you might be out of your element."

"Scrabble's a bit too ostentatious for my taste. I'm more of a Dominoes man myself."

Corbin's eyebrows raised at Tommy's use of the word ostentatious. "Big word. I'm impressed."

"Little man. I'm not."

Corbin smiled insulted, "Dominoes huh? You mean that tacky parlor game commonly played by unemployed home-boys sitting on milk crates in the hood?"

"No, I mean that thinking man's competitive game invented by Black Egyptians to simulate war games commonly played by prominent men in the community." Tommy said shaking his head at Corbin like he wasn't worth the effort and headed for the door. He stopped in the doorway and looked back then his eyes lit up. Finally, he recognized something from when he used to live there and the human submarine known as Tommy Strong fired a torpedo, striking the good ship Corbin across the bow.

Savoring every syllable Tommy said, "Nice shirt!" to his ex-wife and walked out grinning. Corbin shot Nicky a confused look and her eyes dropped to the floor. At first, he was baffled by what just transcribed then he zeroed in on Nicky's over-sized baggy Ocean Pacific shirt and knew that there was no way his small frame could fill out a shirt that big. Only a man built like Tommy could.

# Chapter 7

Tommy and Nicky's Brooklyn love story began during homeroom class at James Madison High School when he broke the ice after bashfully sending her a note asking: 'Do You Like Me? Check yes, no or maybe'. She checked yes. That Saturday they rode the number three-train downtown and caught a matinee showing of 'JAWS' at the Duffield movie theatre then laughed over pizza and sodas. It was still early and since the weather was nice they decided to walk over to the Promenade, Brooklyn's version of lover's lane. They found a cozy bench with a fantastic view of the Manhattan skyline and with Tommy's transistor radio serenading them, talked for hours about their hopes and dreams. Then as the moon did the electric slide across the harbor, they took shelter under each other's shadows while Al Green sang, 'Let's Stay Together' and shared their first kiss. Confusion and heat filled them like nothing they had ever felt before. It was simply magic and from that moment on they were connected at the hip. In their yearbook they were voted 'Most likely to get married' and shortly after graduation they moved in together to a railroad apartment in Crown Heights. Less than a year later Tommy asked Nicky to marry him and again she checked 'yes'.

If Tommy had to choose one thing out of the many things he loved about Nicky it would have to be how she carried herself. She wasn't some neck poppin, materialistic, hoochie-mama who would spit on you if you said good morning. Nicky was a rare breed, a female who everyone felt comfortable with. Blessed with girl-next-door beauty she was genuinely sweet and dedicated to her man and he missed her immensely.

As soon as Tommy pulled out his house keys he could hear Mayhem run up to greet him on the opposite side of the door. He walked in still stinging from his altercation with Nicky's new man.

"So what he went to Harvard! I could've gone to college if I wanted. Still could..." Tommy rambled then dismissed the notion of sitting in a classroom surround by pimply-faced freshman at thirty-one. Mayhem, entuned to his body language, realized he was in one of his moods and went back to her food bowl. *"Ooh look at me! My name is Corbitch and I have the kind of job that paid for me to go back to school and get my MBA so I can afford condos on douche street and summer homes in asshole-ville.* " Tommy said mocking Corbin. "Big f-ing deal!" He flipped on his CD player and began blasting Eric B and Rakim's album Follow the Leader. Peeling off his top, he went over to his punching bag and began bouncing spasmodically tossing powerful hooks and combinations into the bag visualizing Corbin's pompous smug grin.

Dissatisfied with pretending he was hitting him instead of hitting the real deal, he wiped the beads of sweats from his face and slid underneath a mountain of steel plates. After several sets of tossing the weight of a Volkswagen into the air and piling callouses on top of blisters, he was still unable to shake his foul mood. With energy to spare, he switched over to his treadmill and began doing angry-faced laps. As he looked to his side his mean mug was replaced by a smile, then a hearty laugh as Mayhem uplifted his spirit by climbing onto her matching treadmill and joined him for a side-by-side workout, tail hanging and saliva flailing.

Feeling better thanks to his best friend, he wearily climbed off and went into the refrigerator and took out an ice cold 40 ounce of Olde English and cracked the top. After slicing up a lemon and stuffing the slices in the bottle he sipped his brew. Mayhem barked like she had a problem.

"What, you want some?" Tommy asked to which his dog replied with a sharp bark that almost sounded like, *'Hell yeah!'* After consideration he shrugged, mumbled, *'Fuck it'* and poured some of his 40 into her water dish, which she immediately began lapping up. He could not help smiling. His business phone rang and he reached for it.

"Talk to me…Hey Roxanne how you doing?… I'm chilling…Nah it's cool. Actually, I was gonna call you cause I've decided to do it…Yeah. Besides, I have some pent-up aggression I need to release so why not get paid doing it…. So how much more we talkin?…Bet that'll work…Aight I'll be there tonight. Peace."

After a therapeutic shower Havoc slid into a pair of baggy red acid-washed Guess jeans, a form fitting red Coca-Cola sweat shirt and a box-fresh pair of red striped shell-toed Adidas. Once dressed, he flicked on the television and sat on the edge of his couch with an old Rudy Ray Moore album cover on his lap as he split open a White Owl cigar with his fingernail.

His second favorite commercial after the 'I don't want to grow up, I'm a Toys R' Us kid' advertisement came on. It was the PSA where a father confronted his son about the stash of drugs his mother found in his room. Havoc mouthed along as the father asks his son, *'Who taught you how to do this stuff?'* and the son yelled back, *'You alright! I learned it by watching you!'* Laughing, Havoc scraped out the tobacco center, licked the outer paper, dumped weed inside, wrapped it tightly, licked it, pulled out a lighter and dried it then put it to his mouth and sparked up. After exhaling a white cloud, he mouthed the end of the commercial. *'Parents who use drugs, have children, who use drugs.'* His personal phone rang and he lowered the volume.

"Who dis?" He answered annoyed.

"Who dis? Is that how you answer your phone?"

"Oh, hey Mommy-O, what's going on?"

"You tell me. Is everything all right? You sound preoccupied." Carla asked sensing something was the matter by her son's tone.

"Not at all." He said changing his tone as he sparked up.

"You might not want to hear this but it still needs to be said."

He sighed already annoyed. "Talk to me Ma. What's on your mind?"

"Well I didn't want to say anything in front of your sister earlier but I noticed your placed smelled like Lysol attempting to camouflage the smell of marijuana. I'm hoping I was wrong."

He looked at his watch. He didn't have time for this. "Ma weed is not a drug. It comes from the earth."

"So, I guess I got my answer." His mother sighed disappointedly.

"Okay yes once in a blue I might indulge a little. No biggie." he fronted downplaying his passion for cannabis.

"No biggie huh? I wonder if your cousin Alonzo started out with that same kind of logic, before moving on to the harder stuff."

Havoc sank into the couch swallowing billows of smoke and cut his eyes at the ceiling. "So that's where this is all coming from."

"Your Aunt Mary told me what's going on. She said your father and you were getting him help."

"Yeah that's right." He exhaled speaking out the side of his mouth as the exhaust clouded his face.

"Well isn't that like the blind leading the deaf?"

"Ma chill out. A little weed is a far reach from shooting up dope and smoking crack." he reasoned and removed a stack of dead presidents as thick as the Sunday Times he kept in a sneaker box and stuffed it into his pocket.

"And silly me here I thought all drugs were against the law." Carla said. "So how often do you, smoke?"

"Hardly ever." He lied through a white cloud.

"When's the last time you, as they put it, indulged?"

"Ma it's been so long I don't even remember...then again weed'll do that to you." he snickered.

"Boy I'm not playing with you!"

"Sorry Ma. But seriously, it's been a long time ago in a galaxy far, far, away since I last smoked." He said, taking a hit and blowing smoke into his dog's face while trying his best not to laugh at her crazy reaction.

"You know I can tell when you're lying."

"Then you'll know I'm telling you the truth. But dang Ma, you're like a travel agent for guilt trips." Her son said glancing at his watch. "Look I don't mean to rush you off the phone but I was on the way out when you called. So how's about I call you tomorrow and we won't discuss this any further Okay?"

"Bye Tommy." His mother said and abruptly hung up.

Havoc sucked his teeth. He loved his mother dearly and wanted to do whatever he could to make her happy, but he just could not stay clear of the things that he knew made her sad, scared and so protective of him.

On the way out the door, he grabbed his red terrycloth bell shaped Kangol and stuffed a plastic bag from the cleaners into it to give it that perfect smooth round look. He then pulled it down over his shaved dome, covered his eyes with a red pair of Gazelle frames, slid on a red leather bubble goose down then paused, "Wait a minute. How in the hell does she even know what marijuana smells like?" and he wondered if his favorite PSA pertained to him.

▄▄▄▄▄▄▄▄▄▄▄▄▄▄▄▄▄▄▄▄▄▄▄

Bath Beach, Bay Ridge, Bedford-Stuyvesant, Bensonhurst, Bergen Beach, Borough Park, Brooklyn Heights, Brownsville, Bushwick, Canarsie, Clinton Hill, Cobble Hill, Coney Island, Crown Heights, Cypress Hills, Dyker Heights, East New York, Flatbush, Flatlands, Fort Greene, Gerritsen Beach, Gowanus, Gravesend, Greenpoint, Howard Beach, Midwood, Park slope, Prospect Heights, Red Hook, Sheepshead Bay, South Brooklyn, Sunset Park, Wingate and Williamsburg are all the districts Brooklyn is comprised of. Each one has its own unique and distinct flavor setting it apart from the rest. But none is quite as inclusive and diverse as Park Slope. Largely populated by the gay community, it is a small but tight-knit village of carefree people who just want to live their lives in peace and be left the hell alone. Unfortunately, certain outside individuals who do not approve of their lifestyle sometimes make that extremely difficult.

For the past month and a half, a rowdy pack of no life having thugs from the Gowanus Housing Projects, a neighboring tall group of brick buildings that sit isolated from the rest of the community, would get drunk and invade Park Slope like a venereal disease. The 'Gay Bashers' as the Village Voice labeled them would drive around in their funkdafied jeeps fueled by ignorance, hate and a male sense of inferiority searching for homosexual men to taunt and savagely beat-down then sink into the shadows under the cloak of nightfall. When the bashers could not find any victims, they would take it over to 'Rhythm & Dudes', a popular coffeehouse by day, extravagant dance club by night, where openly gay men would go and hang out.

Rhythm & Dudes was packed and a good time was had by all as Sylvester had the dance floor bouncing with energetic young men under the shimmering mirrored disco ball to the tune of 'Do You

Wanna Funk.' Roxanne Jenkins strolled through his establishment meeting and greeting his clientele. He was a tall self-made and self-named, wafer-thin handsome man; 50 percent Cuban, 50 percent Black and 100 percent gay. His combination of model good looks and exquisite taste in fashion had him constantly turning down advances from both sexes. And if he had a nickel for every time a starry-eyed admirer used the line 'Roxanne-Roxanne, I wanna be your man,' he could retire and live on a private beach in the Maldives.

Every so often Roxanne would nervously eye the Keith Harrington clock over the bar. He knew they were coming. And when they did, he knew the police were not. The 'boys in blue' had already made it painfully clear what they thought about 'his kind' the last time they came out to remove the bashers from his establishment. Roxanne eyed the big man under the red bell Kangol at the bar tossing back shots of Johnnie Walker Red Label and prayed this would work.

"Yo, leave the bottle!" Havoc growled at the dainty little bartender.

"Sor-ree! I ain't know the two of y'all was on a date." the slim bartender with perfectly arched eyebrows and ready for the world jheri curls said, then promptly placed the bottle of scotch back in front of him. Havoc huffed at his remark and continued sinking shots. "That is so not a healthy attitude to start off the new year with." the bartender said as a matter of factly in a feminine manner.

Havoc rolled his eyes like he did not want to be bothered. He wasn't homophobic or anything like that, just not in the mood to be cordial to anyone. Gay or straight. The Trouble Consultant turned up his shot glass then poured himself another.

"Slow down Hot Sauce, my goodness! Girlfriend must be some special kinda woman to have you drinking like a fish."

Havoc looked up glassy-eyed. "Huh-what'd you call me?"

"Hot Sauce. Cause you look like a bottle of hot sauce with all that red on. I could just shake you all over a fried fish sandwich." The bartender said forcing Havoc to snicker and drop his tough-guy demeanor. "And for heaven's sake pick up a fashion magazine. Red is out, cranberry is in." the bartender said modeling his dark wine-colored designer threads.

Havoc pursed his lips. He was not about to drop his trademark red because Madison Avenue said so. "You got jokes."

"Oh my goodness! What's up with your voice? There's so much boom I feel like I'm hearing you in surround sound. Is it live or is it Memorex?"

"I got it as a kid from yelling up to my mother to throw down money for the ice cream man."

"Who has jokes now?"

Havoc smiled. The bartender was amusing in his own unique way and reminded him of Blane, Damon Wayans's flamboyant gay character on the television show, In Living Color. "Sorry I didn't mean to be such a big jerk."

"I wouldn't say big...huge...massive...Paul Bunyan comes to mind." The bartender winked. "But don't sweat it Hot Sauce, all men are. Shantae Dupri, part-time bartender, but full-time diva honey." he grinned holding out his hand to shake and eyed the huge four-fingered ring on his customer's hand.

"Nice to meet you Shantae. And I'm Havoc, full-time Trouble Consultant."

"Oh, so you're Miss Roxy's secret weapon against the ignorant forces of closed-mindedness? But I thought you traveled with a big ol' scary dog."

"I gave her the night off." Havoc said.

"Well good cause I'm too much bitch to get along with other bitches. Now, back to Miss Thang that's got you one sip away from AA?"

Perhaps it was the Red Label or the realness that Shantae exuded but the next thing Havoc knew, he was admitting his cousin's addiction, his parents feud, still having for his ex-wife and his ex-wife's pain in the ass new man.

"Boy I declare, you've got more drama than Miss Erica Kane. And honey she's the Queen of drama!"

"Tell me about it." Havoc sighed.

"Well my advice, for what it's worth, is to be gentle when you approach your cousin about seeking help for his demons. Especially since you seem to be the only person he trusts and he doesn't even recognize he even has a problem. When it comes to your parents, stay as neutral as possible. Don't get in the middle of that mess by taking sides and let them work on their drama themselves. As for your ex, well it sounds to me like she's looking for a completely different type of relationship. She's already been there, done that, with the young wild and spontaneous type, that being you, and it didn't work. So now she's going for the older more stable type. I don't know why you two broke up but evidentially she must still feel something or she would have burned your shirt instead of worn it. I should know cause I still wear my ex-boyfriend Glen's shirt to bed, and sometimes when I'm feeling weak, him."

Havoc sipped his drink darting his eyes around. That was more information than he really needed to hear. But even still, Shantae's advice and wisdom made a whole lot of sense. "It's funny you should say that because I feel-" his thoughts were ambushed by the appearance of seven tough looking men that walked in. 'I feel Love' by Donna Summer was the next song to play but nobody was in the mood to dance. The way everyone reacted from their presence plus Roxanne's frightened nod told him they were whom he was there to see. Havoc punched his internal clock. Break time was over, it was time to make the donuts. "Shantae what do you say we pick this conversation up later. I just spotted some friends."

"Yeah I see them, right on schedule. The closet cases."

"Closet cases?" Havoc repeated.

Shantae nodded narrowing his contact covered hazel eyes. "Umm-hmm. It's a term some of us use in my community for guys who have eyes for other guys but can't come to grips with it. So they cover their feelings with aggression and hostility."

"They're gay? Wait. You sure?" Havoc asked. He didn't consider himself an expert on the topic but from where he was standing, nothing about these jokers said gay. Instead they were the opposite and fit the typical thugged-out stereotype, which was tough looking, leather jackets, gold teeth, humongous gold chains and diamond medallions the size of dinner plates.

"What's wrong Hot sauce? You find it hard to believe those B-boys are on the down low because they don't perpetuate your archaic notion of gay, which is snapping and switching, swishing and swaying? We gay men come in all shapes, sizes and varieties. But I'll cut you some slack since you weren't born with the luxury of having gaydar like me. So, think of it like this, why on God's green earth would anyone come here to party every other night if our way of living disgusts them?"

"You make an interesting point."

"Sometimes, not everything is so obvious. And sometimes that's exactly what it is."

Havoc nodded in agreement and realized he had to change his way of thinking. He studied his soon to be opponents. None were strangers to the gym. The smallest weighed about fifty pounds more than he did but that didn't bother him. In the past he'd taken out chumps so big he needed a ladder to reach them. The group headed over to the nearby pool table and handed out menacing looks forcing the men who were already playing to abandon their game. With a grill that could make babies cry and enough gold in his mouth to shake up Fort Knox, Lights-Out, the tallest and biggest in the group, headed over to the bar as his crew racked the balls for a new game.

"What can I get you?" Shantae asked with detest written all over his smooth baby face.

"Well, for starters you can get me a bartender that looks like a man and not a wo-man!" Lights-Out wise cracked.

"Oh please! I am more man than you and more wo-man than you will ever get." Shantae hissed with a Z-snap and two fingers in the air.

Lights-Out screwed his face up. "Gaylord!"

"Okay, I'm sure that's a devastating comeback in the break room at The Wiz. Now unless you want something, poof-pow-be gone." Shantae said gesturing Lights-Out towards the door.

"Just get me a Goddamn beer on tap fruity-pebbles." Lights-Out growled.

Havoc was impressed and snickered out loud. For a little guy, Shantae had more courage than a lot of so-called hard rocks he knew. As Shantae filled a mug with beer, Lights-Out cut his eyes over at Havoc and made a mental note to check him later for laughing. Shantae returned with his beer. Lights-Out took a sip, frowned and spit it out on the floor.

"Ugh! This beer tastes like piss! Here you drink it!" Lights-Out said and doused Shantae with it.

"No you didn't!" Shantae screamed. "I may be small but so is dynamite!" he growled as a second bartender prevented him from diving over the bar. On the sly, Havoc turned and nodded at Roxanne who nodded back then unbeknownst to anyone, locked the front door. And everyone inside.

"Closet case." Havoc snickered loud enough for Lights-Out to hear then turned up his glass.

"What the hell did you just call me? Huh, faggot? What did you say? Say it again!" Lights-Out growled in the Trouble Consultant's direction daring him to repeat it.

Havoc looked up from his drink unmoved. "I called you a closet case. You come here and terrorize a group of marginalized people who already have enough problems in their life so that you can seem like you're the hero. When in actuality, you're secretly trying to hide your own homosexual desires by talking negatively and causing physical violence to decent folks who are comfortable enough to actually be honest about their sexual preference." he said logically tapping his temple.

"Whatchoo talkin' 'bout Willis? I'm so straight I keep my eyes closed in the shower cause I don't want to see my own dick." Lights-Out hissed trying to sound extra manly.

"And I think thou protest a bit too damn much." Havoc smirked between sips of his drink.

Lights-Out stomped over and his boys rushed to his side. "You're new. I've never seen you in here before."

"That's your idea of a pick-up line?" Havoc asked.

"Hardly. Just an observation. So, who the fuck you are supposed to be anyway, LL Cool Gay?" he asked pointing at Havoc's Kangol receiving laughs from his crew.

Havoc cut his eyes at Lights-Out and sucked his teeth. "You're so gay, it could be raining titties and you'd manage to get hit in the face by a dick." he said, receiving louder laughs from patrons.

"Oh so we have a comedian in our midst? A funny fairy? Well I'll tell you what Tinkerbell. You're gonna sit right here like a good little bitch while I light up this joint. And after I'm nice and lifted, I'm going to beat your sissy ass just enough to keep you out of the hospital. We'll see how funny you are then....nigga!" Lights-Out snickered then brought a flickering Bic to his mouth.

From across the room Roxanne looked horrified.

The Trouble Consultant's eye tightened at the disrespect. Then in a flash his hand darted out like a cobra and clamped onto Lights-Out's wrist that held the lighter. "What'd you call me?" Lights-Out was taken by surprise by both Havoc's speed and strength as he unsuccessfully tried to pull his wrist back.

"Motherfucker lemme go!" Lights-Out protested borderline begging. Havoc disobeyed his request and twisted Lights-Out's wrist upright. "Hey man what the hell are you doing?" Lights-Out demanded.

Havoc ignored him and filled his cheeks till they were bulging with whisky and slammed the shot glass down on the bar.

"Oh no!" Lights-Out whispered when he realized what was about to go down.

Havoc wiggled his eyebrows at Lights-Out then spit the liquor in the troublemaker's face. When the alcohol came into contact with the burning Bic it ignited, creating a blow torch that scorched his face. Lights-Out screamed frantically beating himself about the neck and face. After putting himself out, he twisted just in time to read the word 'HAVOC' on the four-fingered ring as he was brutally knocked to the floor. Havoc then stepped over him as his homeboys surrounded him with evil looks.

The Trouble Consultant grinned like this was his most favorite thing in the whole wide world and quickly incapacitated the closest thug by splitting his lip down to the gum with the back of his fist taking him out of the fight. The man on Havoc's right advanced and Havoc deflected his attack then grabbed him by the shoulders and head butted him to sleep. Three others decided to jump him while one stood frozen with fear. Havoc struck the solar plexus of two of their necks temporarily dazing them then push-kicked the third attacker away. Returning to the two simpletons holding their throats, he unleashed punches and strikes to their faces and guts then smashed them together scattering their teeth. The third inexperienced fighter recovered and threw his entire arm forward with a misguided punch. Havoc shifted out of the way brutally side elbowing him in the head, gained control of his arm then lifted him in the air culminating in an epic body slam to the ground.

With those foes taken care of Havoc tuned to the remaining punk still frozen in place. Glancing over his friends laid out, he cowardly spun on his heels and bolted for the door but it was locked. He frantically looked around for an alternate escape route and spotted Roxanne standing there. "Open the door!" the punk demanded. "Did you hear what I said, faggot?"

Something inside Roxanne snapped and he clenched his fist. Suddenly every bully who ever teased and tormented him from adolescent to adulthood for being who he was, stood before him. He squeezed his eyes shut and swung. When he opened his eyes, the punk was lying at his feet stretched out cold and he took a bow as Shantae and the others cheered, 'You go gurl!'

As Havoc nodded his acclaim, Lights-Out stood up behind him with smoke coming off of him and the word 'HAVOC' imprinted on his face. Havoc turned around, took one look at the human billboard, snickered and snatched a cue stick off a nearby pool table then tossed it to him. Lights-Out caught it confused.

"I'm curious to see if I'm as bad as I think I am." Havoc explained cracking his knuckles.

Lights-Out snarled and swung the cue stick missing Havoc by a mile and the Trouble Consultant immediately went to work. He didn't crack his skull, he didn't crush his larynx and he didn't break his ribs or punch his hand through his chest. He did just enough, to keep him out of the hospital.

Once Lights-Out was down for the count, Havoc put the heel of his right Adidas on his chest and looked deep into his raccoon eyes. "The way I see it you've got one of two options. We can tango again and I assure you this time I won't go as *easy* on you. Or you and your confused crew can agitate the gravel and never darken the door with your ugly faces again. The choice is yours."

Without saying a word, Lights-Out staggered to his feet then he and his crew left with bruised bodies and shattered egos as the club's patrons tossed them goodbye kisses. Gloria Gaynor's 'I Will Survive' fittingly played and the party was back in full swing.

After Roxanne paid Havoc for a job well done Shantae offered him a drink on the house but the ever-busy Trouble Consultant graciously declined because he had somewhere else to be.

# Chapter 8

It was a whirlwind romance straight out of a Hollywood screenplay. A college night watchman named Eduardo Salvador routinely stops in the Junior's Restaurant across the street from his place of work at the Long Island University campus every night for a slice of strawberry cheesecake and cup of Café Bustelo just so he can be waited on by Cynthia Sanchez, an elegant Dominican waitress that he has a secret crush on. One night, Eduardo works up the nerve and tells Cynthia that he thinks she's the most beautiful woman he's ever seen and that he would like to take her out on a date. Cynthia is flattered but turns him down. She does however take his phone number. A week later she calls him, only after praying to St. Ann, the Dominican patron of single women. The two began dating and two months later Eduardo proposes with a glittering diamond.

Within a year a beautiful baby girl named Jennifer was born, that's when things started to change. Eduardo began to feel tied down. Stifled. He started seeing other women, but he also wanted to keep Cynthia around selfishly. When she attempted to leave he turned violent even threatening her at gunpoint while their daughter looked on. The police were called and they removed Eduardo but he still lingered around, standing outside her window for hours attempting to woo her back by serenading her with their wedding song, Consuelo Velasquez' "Besame mucho." When she called the police, he disappeared. With her child suffering from nightmares and her nerves on edge from threatening phone calls, Cynthia finally called the number on the black card her best girlfriend gave her when she was experiencing a similar situation.

Sporting a well put together red ensemble, Havoc blended into the red leather booth in the back of Junior's Restaurant like a chameleon. Once the hunk of cherry cheesecake vanished from his plate. he chased it down with coffee then dabbed the corners of his mouth with a napkin.

"That hit the spot," Havoc said pushing the plate away.

"Bendito," Cynthia smiled, "Would ju' like another slice?" she asked in a lilting Spanish accent. She loved to watch a man eat.

"Nah, I'm straight." Havoc said patting his stomach. "So go on, continue your story."

107

Cynthia paused, unsure if she should continue. Up until now she had been uncomfortable with sharing her story of pain and heartbreak. "There's really no more to tell. Like I said my husband he beat me and I had him put out, then he began showing up outside my building. Peeking through my window. I reported it to the precinct and they said there was nothing else they could do. He called me today, said he wanted to get back together for our daughter. 'Put it behind us, he says'. But how am I supposed to pretend he wasn't with other women? That he never beat me and threatened to kill me with his gun? No, not even for my daughter would I take him back!"

Havoc sat forward in his seat and folded his hands under his chin watching her with pity in his eyes. He got more spousal abuse calls than any others. Sadly enough, they were his bread and butter. He looked Cynthia over. She was gorgeous with an olive complexion, full red lips, long flowing strawberry blonde hair and shimmering jade eyes. What kind of man would hit a beautiful Boricua like her, or any woman for that matter?

"You mentioned he carries a weapon?" Havoc asked.

"Si," Cynthia nodded and blew a cloud of smoke then flicked the ashes from her Virginia Slim into a glass of water. "It's for his job but he always keeps it on him. Even when he sleeps."

Havoc leaned back and thoughtfully took a sip from his coffee. "I've heard enough. I'll take you on as a client. My fee is…" he paused just short of saying one thousand flat and that he expected half up front then he realized there was no way a single mother working as a waitress could come up with that type of cash. Plus, the fat bonus Roxanne just paid him more than covered her half. "Five hundred. And I expect half up front. Also I need at least a week to check out your husband and make sure your story is legit. We can start with the police report you filed against him."

"But why when I just es'plain to ju' what kind of a man he is." Cynthia said annoyed by his request.

"Sorry Mamacita, but it's how I do things. Take it or leave it." Havoc said fixing a hard stare on her, his expression betrayed nothing.

Cynthia pulled out a large wad of bills which made the Trouble Consultant wonder where a waitress would get so much money from. She counted out two hundred and fifty dollars smacking each one down hard on the table while mumbling something in Spanish under her breath. Havoc was not fluent in her language but recognized a couple unflattering words he knew were aimed at him. He was unfazed by the sudden change in her behavior since it was this very type of human detail he looked out for when deciding to take on a client.

Cynthia paused and looked up with a suck of the teeth, "Can't ju' just trust me and do dis on my word?" she said trying to hypnotize him with her long lashes.

Havoc scrunched up his face, "Trust you? Miss, I don't know you from a hole in the wall."

Cynthia was about to hand over the money then stopped just short of putting it into his hands. Her sweet demur evaporated into thin air. She sucked her teeth then dropped her cigarette into the glass and leaned forward. The gleam faded from her eyes and revealed the person whom she really was, "Okay here's the real deal. I've been trying everything I could think of to get out of my marriage but he wouldn't leave." She said clearly and unapologetically.

Havoc sighed at the transformation. "Proceed." he said through a glare detecting bullshit.

"Yo Mera don't be judging me when you don't even know how it was. Look I tried to be a good wife honest to God, but he is so freaking boring!" she said then gave her situation some thought, "But I will take part of the blame."

"How generous of you." Havoc said.

"I should'a known better than to marry a man almost three times my age. But he was nice you know? Respectable. Not like them stupid guys from the projects who only want to sell drugs and shoot each other. But all he does is work his loser job and come home and go to bed and that's it. We hardly even had sex because he's forever bitching about being tired. And when we did try it…God, I don't even wanna go there. So, I got tired of all his nonsense and got me a tender-roni that knows how to make me happy. Three times in a row! Ed couldn't take the hint so I told him, 'Look Poppi this marriage thing, it ain't working out. So the best thing for us is to do is get it annulled.' But he told me, 'No Cynthia please I don't want to break up! I love you!' and started crying. God I hate to see a man cry. It's-"

"Pathetic," Havoc rolled his eyes thinking that's exactly what she was.

"Exactly. I even told him about my new man Carlos and he said that he didn't care and that he still loved me. Stupid Cabron! So I was like fuck it I'ma just bounce, but then he threatened to sue for custody of my daughter. He said he'd tell the courts that I'm an unfit mother who associates with criminals and that I drink too much if I left. That's when I got to thinking-"

"That I could persuade him to back off so you and Carlos can be free to do whatever and still keep your daughter?" Havoc said shaking his head. "Lemme' guess. Carlos is from the projects, sells drugs and shoots people and makes lots of cash. But he's not like those other stupid guys because he loves you. So much that he said he'll take care of you and your daughter?" he said purposely repeating the traits of the kind of man she not even two minutes ago said she'd sworn off of.

As his point sailed over her empty head, Cynthia was dumbfounded by his astute ability to predict what she was about to say before saying it. "Wow, are you related to Dionne Warwick or something?"

"Or something." He said staring at her in disbelief. Mind blown.

"Well since we have an understanding, don't beat him up too bad. After all he's still my baby's daddy-I think." she snickered.

"Wow," Havoc shook his head.

"And he still gotta work, you know?" she winked.

Havoc stood up abruptly and slid into his coat. "Nah, I don't know!"

"Wait, where you going? I thought that's what you did. Bust sucka's asses for money."

"Oh I do,"

"Then what does it take to hire you?"

110

Havoc met her cold glare with his own. "Money and a just cause."

"And this ain't one?"

"Your old man doesn't deserve to get his ass kicked. But he does need a good swift kick **up** the ass so he'll wake up and recognize how trifling you are. And speaking of trifling, what the hell happened to your thick ass accent?"

"I figured you'd have sympathy for a poor abused single mother who don't speak good English." Cynthia shrugged with a sly grin. "So, let's get down to business. I could pay more. You say you wanted five hundred? What if I pay you double?" Cynthia asked digging into her purse.

Havoc laughed at himself when he heard her offer his going rate which he cut in half because he pitied her. He frowned at Carlos' money like it was crawling with maggots. "Sweetheart you don't have enough money in your little bag of tricks to buy me." he said putting on his red Kangol then headed for the door and looked back at her. "Just be glad I don't take cases against Putas!" and with that said he was gone.

The Trouble Consultant entered his crib and undressed thinking were it not for his thorough approach to examining characters and context, a decent man whose only crime was being a sucker for love would have been wrongly punished. He switched on the stereo and 'I need Love' by LL Cool J was playing. His personal answering machine informed him someone called while he was out and he checked it.

BEEP! *'Heyyy bay-bee!'* As soon as Tommy recognized the sultry voice he grinned licking his full lips. *'I just got back in town and you're the first person I called soon as I touched ground. I haven't even called my momma yet. Aren't you flattered? You'd better be! Just playing, listen honey, I'm going to the crib to drop off my suitcase, take a shower and then I'm hitting Bentley's for a much-deserved night of fun with my girls! If you're not busy then meet me on the second floor by the bar at twelve-thirty. I was thinking, maybe we could go back to your place and ring in the New Year right. Well, there's my cab. Fuck you later-I mean see you later.'*

Tommy stroked his chin smiling devilishly. After his divorce there was a brief period where he moved through women faster than a flea changing dogs. Then he met Donnie Campbell and all that went out the window.

Donnie had it all, brains, beauty, social grace and class to spare not to mention a high paying job as an accounts receivable analyst for one of the top entertainment law firms in the country. With all these attainments her homegirls found it hard to believe how badly her love life sucked.

Everyone and anyone who had known Donnie's college sweetheart turned fiancée Sam for more than a minute formed a bad opinion of him. He was rude, obnoxious and uncouth and those were his good qualities. Donnie didn't even know why she was still with him since she had outgrown him during her senior year. But it was something about those bad boys that she couldn't resist.

When she made up her mind to end the relationship Sam laughed and said, "Bitch it's over when I say it's over, and not before!"

When Donnie put her foot down so did he, literally. "Oh hell fucking no!" Her best friend Pumpkin said when she found out Sam's loser ass was acting hands happy with her best friend. "Lemme ask you something and be honest. Do you still love him?" she asked.

"Hell no! But what am I going to do? He won't leave me alone." Donnie cried.

Pumpkin reached into her purse and handed her a black card with bold red letters, "Here. Call this number and explain your situation to the deep voiced brother that answers and trust me, Sam's bitch ass will leave you alone with the quickness!"

Donnie wasn't the one for violence and wanted to handle things more civilized. But, as soon as she told Sam that he could not show up at her home drunk whenever he felt like it, his insecurities kicked in and he took it as if she were implying she may have another man coming over. He became so enraged at the thought of her seeing someone else that he smacked her and then ignored her pleas to stop as he forced himself upon her.

Unable to tolerate his shit any longer plus weighed down with the humiliation and fear it might get back to her job if she called the police, Donnie called upon the Trouble Consultant instead. A few days later Havoc met her at a trendy outdoor restaurant in Carroll Gardens to discuss the possibility of him taking her on as a potential client. Just as he was explaining his strict policy about needing proof that her boyfriend was the despicable person she claimed him to be, Sam entered the restaurant storming over causing a scene.

After that Havoc needed no proof as Sam aggressively grabbed Donnie's arm ordering her to leave with him. When Havoc advised him to let the lady go, Sam told him where he could go instead and swung a clumsy fist. Havoc blocked the lousy attempt and planted a punch on Sam's chin instantly taking the fight out of him. After being mortifyingly helped outside by the Trouble Consultant, Sam sat on the pavement and over pitiful sobs begged Donnie to forgive him to which she replied with a stern "Hell no!" But just to make sure he understood her, Havoc made Sam repeat after him word for word as he calmly explained that if he ever darkened her door again he'd be sorry. Really-really-REALLY sorry! And just like Pumpkin promised, Sam's bitch ass left her alone!

Havoc never bothered to bill Donnie since he completed the job before accepting it. A week later Tommy received an unexpected invitation to dinner from Donnie. He was flattered but declined explaining his strict rule about never dating clients, regardless of how fine the client was. Donnie worked around his rule by reminding him that she was never technically his client. Tommy pondered over the offer then decided what the hell and accepted. When he arrived ten minutes early at The Lennox Lounge, a popular Harlem night club he suggested that offered dinner and a show, he was surprised to see her at the bar waiting on him and came up behind her smelling like Johnson's baby powder and Polo cologne.

"And here I thought women were supposed to be fashionably late." he said.

Donnie turned to him and flashed a perfect smile then in a flirtatious voice said, "I'm always fashionable, but never late."

Once seated, they were serenaded by a talented singer who performed a spot-on rendition of Roberta Flack's, 'Just When I Needed You.' Tommy was glad he accepted Donnie's invitation. She was more than just a pretty face. She was also, comical, intelligent and she had a real centered kind of energy. In layman's terms, she had her shit together. He was also surprised to learn Ms. Corporate America had a passion for hip-hop music and considered herself Mike Tyson's number one fan. Just like him. And not since Tyson and Givens had a man been so outmatched in the ring.

Donnie was also pleasantly pleased with Tommy who arrived armed with charm and came across as a nice guy who somehow stumbled into a provincial line of work for which he was uniquely suited. And like him, she too wasn't mad at the fact that he had lady-killer good looks, a physique like a linebacker, and the soft eyes of an R&B heartthrob who could offer stimulating and intelligent conversation.

Half way through the date Donnie knew things were going well when the singer complimented them and asked how long they had been dating. The attractive couple chuckled letting her and everyone in attendance in on the fact that it was their very first date. At the end of the night when the waitress brought Tommy the bill and he went to pay Donnie took it from his hand and insisted on paying because she invited him out. Tommy resisted explaining that wasn't how his Momma raised him but eventually gave in when they agreed he'd take care of the bill next time.

Standing outside of her Bay Ridge condominium she admitted to Tommy that she had not had this much fun since the Girl Scouts and didn't want the night to end. "Then why does it have to?" he asked her. She stared into his dreamy bedroom eyes and they shared a long kiss good night. This led to groping and her inviting him upstairs for a nightcap. That night, although they arrived in separate cars, they had an orgasm in the same bed.

Six months later they were still hooking up whenever their demanding schedules didn't collide and having the most incredible, mind blowing, forget-about-all-your-past-lovers, Prince doesn't even do it like this sex. Afterwards they would chill in bed sharing a spliff together as Tommy told her Havoc and Mayhem's latest exciting battles on the mean streets of Brooklyn. It was so ghetto, but at the same time so real, and she loved it. Eventually Donnie realized that she could not go back to the typical nine-to-five guys she used to date. At work she found herself laughing on the inside when her female coworkers talked about their lame boyfriends who couldn't fill Tommy's jockstrap. But truth be told, there was one thing the girls at work had over her. Their men came home to them every night.

Meanwhile she was lucky if she saw Tommy twice in the same week. After careful consideration she felt it was time to rectify that.

One morning beneath the sheets after a blissful love making session the two were sharing their usual spliff. Maybe it was the combination of Bartles and Jaymes wine coolers plus the weed. Or the fact she felt like she was in limbo and unable to keep it in any longer. Donnie confessed that she was falling in love. She told Tommy that she knew his heart still belonged to his ex-wife and did not expect him to reciprocate her feelings. Tommy didn't say a word choosing to seal himself away from emotional melee that he felt would impede his productivity and possibly any chance at getting back together with his ex-wife. Common sense and a crew of close girlfriends told Donnie to move on and get her own man but she didn't listen and settled for seeing him whenever she could…

Tommy agreed with Ladies Love Cool J. He too needed some love. So he showered, changed clothes, vehicles and found himself caravanning over the Brooklyn Bridge. Destination, Manny-Hanny.

During the day Manhattan is an overcrowded, cramped metropolis where millions of people pass by with no connection to each other whatsoever. But at night the city is swarming with tinted-out SUVs, BMWs and Mercedes Benzes pushing the speed limit, switching lanes headed to the clubs to get their party on!

Tommy sat parked across the street from the Bentley's nightclub on 54th Street smoking a blunt and mashing buttons on his electronic head to head football game. Half-way through his marijuana filled cigar, the club's doors opened and a crew of incredible looking women four deep bounced out. The song 'Flyy Girl' by the Boogie Boys exited with them and they marched in cadence to the synthesized beat just as bad as they wanted to be.

All of them had runway looks. They were the type that every dealer, hustler and wannabe playboy wanted to get with, had to have and wanted to sport-to show they had it going on! They ran thick each one as flyy as the other but even amongst the crew Donnie Campbell was without a doubt, the flyyest out of the bunch. Tall and statuesque, she had the kind of crippling beauty that made weak men fidget uncomfortably and avoid eye contact when speaking to her. Whipping each leg ahead with a bold snap from her little waist in an 'I'm not conceded, I'm convinced!' stride, she had a light complexion with a sprinkling of cracked-pepper freckles over her cherub nose, sparkling green eyes, perfect teeth, cheekbones that could cut glass and a small sexy mole over her plump lips. Her body was curvaceous and her dark curly hair reached the center of her back. A dab of gel kept her baby hair greased down in the front. Her gold cursive 'Donnie' nameplate nestled between her collar bones, two pairs of bamboo earrings, silk-wrapped nails, full-length sable mink coat and Gucci thigh-high boots was a warning to all men thinking about approaching her that they had best come correct, or don't come at all.

Four men tried to stop their groove; four men were dissed and dismissed. But number five feeling bold perhaps from the bowl of Wheaties he had for breakfast, blocked Donnie's path with a wide cheesy grin.

"Dang why you all in my grill and ain't even been invited to the bar-b-que?" Donnie asked slightly creeped out.

Ignoring her obvious repulsiveness, he moved in close and asked, "Yo baby yo don't I know you from somewhere?"

"Yeah and that's why I stopped going there." Donnie replied and kept it moving as her girls cracked up while Romeo picked his face off the floor.

As they continued up the block a horn blew. Donnie looked across the street then smiled that million-watt smile when she saw Tommy sitting in his urban assault vehicle looking like all that and a bag of chips. While singing along to Slick Rick and Doug E Fresh's club banger, 'La Di Da Di', he took a deep pull on his spliff leaning further back in his seat lazily licking his lips and slowly exhaling a wispy cloud of smoke. Never once did he glance at her. He didn't have to. He knew she was clocking him.

Caught up in Tommy's flyy-ness Donnie tossed her car keys to one of her girls then jetted over. Tommy spotted Donnie approaching in his rearview with pot-soaked peepers and smiled turning the music down, "Welcome home Honey-dip."

"Hey bay-bee," Donnie said with a flirtatious smile and leaned in for a brief tongue wrestle, afterwards she opened her mouth to say something but felt a light yawn coming on and covered it.

"Tired?" Tommy asked.

"A little. I guess I'm still feeling that three-hour time difference." Donnie said then eyed what he was holding. "You know, you can pass that Dutchie pon' the left-hand side." she said and received Tommy's blunt then brought it to her lips.

"So how was Cali? Did you like meet any totally cool surfer-dudes?" Tommy asked in a Valley accent cracking himself up.

Donnie frowned exhaling a cloud of smoke then passed it back. "Well let's see. In the space of sixteen days I toured the California office. Sat through endless boring ass meetings. Got ptomaine poisoning from crabmeat and wanted to die very badly for a day and a half."

"Bummer." Tommy said tapping the ashes on the ground before taking another hit.

"So why are you asking about California anyway? If you really wanted to know you would have called me while I was there to find out. Or you could join the rest of the world and just get a pager or at the very least a celly." Donnie pried with a confronting stare.

"Either you know where I am. Or you don't. It's that simple." he said as Donnie lip synched along indicating she was well aware of his deal about cellular phones and beepers already. He shrugged defiantly. "Besides, like they say absence makes the heart grow fonder." Tommy said pointing like the words were hanging in the air.

Donnie raised her right eyebrow. "More like the nose grow longer."

"Sugar, looking at you, that ain't all that's growing, know what um sayin?" Tommy snickered.

"Nasty ass," Donnie smiled and slobbed him down some more.


A souped-up pearl colored BMW full of giddy women pulled up alongside of Donnie blasting 'Paper Thin' by Mc Lyte. The girl behind the wheel sucked her teeth then looked at her Swatch like she was timing their kiss. "Alright enough with the tongue-fu already! C'mon Dee get in, we're headed uptown to the Rooftop. Oh, hey Tommy, I didn't know that was you. That chain you're rocking is stupid fresh."

"Yeah whateva." he replied skeptically since she never had good things to say to him any other time.

"No for real." she said with a mischievous grin. "Now all you need to do is get that cubic zirconia pinky ring offa lay away and your slum jewelry collection'll be complete." She said making the entire car shake with laughter. Tommy had a snake and mongoose type of relationship with Donnie's crew but his main sparring partner was her best girlfriend Pumpkin the woman who ironically introduced them.

"And what you need to do is to keep your head straight when you laugh cause that cock-eye of yours starts to rolling around and looks real crazy. Question, when E.T. phoned home, did you pick up the phone?" Tommy replied coyly.

Pumpkin stopped popping her Juicy Fruit and gasped insulted. "Forget you Tommy Morehead!" She was a one-woman party with sleepy eyes that always made her seem like she was high, a vivacious mouth, java colored complexion and sharp tongue more lethal than a vampire's fangs.

"My last name is Strong. Get it right." Tommy retorted.

"Well you could'a fooled me, cause you got **more-head** than hair."

Tommy twisted. "Oh, now I know you ain't talking when your head is so big it's a freeway sign. Exit left for Largeheadass boulevard. And on top of that you're rocking a New Year's weave!" he said causing Pumpkin's homegirls to snicker then unsuccessfully try to cover their mouths when she glared back at them.

"I swear why is it you two always have to diss one another every time y'all see each other?" Donnie scolded. She wanted the two to be civil to each other, but it was as difficult as trying to align the mismatched sides of a Rubik's Cube.

"Talk to your girl. She's the one acting like she's got a patent on being obnoxious," Tommy growled in Pumpkin's direction.

"Anyways I don't see nothing wrong with having a weave. Shit-if you can't grow it, sew it. Can't achieve it, weave it. Your hair's not able, then break out the staples!" Pumpkin said shamelessly defending her sew-in as she dug a fingernail in her scalp and scratched.

"I swear the two of you must have been siblings in a past life. So anyway, what can I do for you?" Donnie asked Tommy.

"I thought you wanted to hook up tonight." He asked twirling her hair around his fingers.

"Oh, so that's all I'm good for is hooking up?" Donnie pulled back.

Tommy sighed and looked to the sky for strength. He hated it when women put on a show for their girlfriends. "Maybe this was a bad idea." he said and revved his engine.

"Hold-up! Why are you tripping? You know I was just playing." Donnie said switching up her attitude then turned to her homegirls.

*"Yeah I thought so."* Tommy muttered under his breath.

"So what's up Dee, you ready to bounce or what?" Pumpkin asked with major attitude.

"Um-actually why don't y'all go on without me." Donnie said in a mousy voice.

"Whoa-rewind. Same question."

"I'm gonna roll with Tommy." Donnie said. The girls traded disgusted looks as Tommy immaturely grinned at Pumpkin.

"Damn Dee why you got to be a flat-leaver? I swear, we're chilling all night, having fun, and then **he** steps on the scene and you're ready to abandon your girls. That is so foul." Pumpkin said pissed off.

"C'mon now gurl you know it ain't even like that. Ah sista is just trying to get her freak on that's all." Donnie winked at her best friend hoping she'd understand.

"Well maybe if you stopped wasting your time on Headdie Murphy and came with us, you might meet someone to get your freak on with." Pumpkin said pissed.

"Donnie if you're rolling with Witchy-Poo, cool. If not then let's bounce cause I feel a hate crime coming on!" Tommy said and Pumpkin rolled her eyes back at him.

"C'mon P, why are you acting like this?" Donnie asked her best friend.

"Because it's supposed to be girls night out." Pumpkin whined.

"But, you know how I feel about Tommy," Donnie said out the side of her mouth hoping Tommy didn't hear her. But he did.

"Yeah but when he ain't show up to meet you inside the club, you was like, 'Fuck Tommy with his ol' big-headed-self!' Now you're acting brand new. I mean damn Dee, is the dick that good?"

Tommy ran his hand over his baldhead smiling boastfully, "Well not for nothing-"

"Tommy!" Donnie cut him off. She realized her friend was only looking out for her best interest but she didn't understand. After being with a steak and potatoes man like Tommy Strong she couldn't go back to a burgers and fries type of guy. Tommy was a complete package. Good looks, self-confidence and the most incredible lover she had ever had. Real men like that were not waiting for her at the Rooftop. That was for damn sure.

"Look, take my car and y'all go on. I'll pick it up tomorrow and we can do lunch. My treat." Donnie said cheerily to her girlfriends.

Pumpkin sucked her teeth and shot Tommy a look he wanted to frame and hang on his wall, "Carmine's. And I'm ordering the most expensive thing I can't pronounce on the menu." she hissed at Donnie

"Yo Donnie what's up, your girl can't pronounce pork and beans?" Tommy asked and cracked himself up.

Pumpkin gave him the finger then peeled off. Donnie shook her head. Pumpkin was just going to have to be mad. She needed some D-I-C-K in the worst way. She climbed into Tommy's ride beside him and before pulling off he turned to her and asked, "So you said I got a big head huh?"

Donnie leaned over and stole a kiss then palmed his crotch and smiled. "Umm-hmm, real big!"

As they headed for Brooklyn a black Mercedes emerged from the shadows and tailed them making sure to blend in with the background so as not to be seen.

Tommy and Donnie entered his loft kissing and biting each other wasting no time. Extremely turned on from the smell of Tommy's cologne and masculine hands groping her everywhere she pulled off her mink and his eyes bulged. In the soft light of his loft, Donnie was something this side of spectacular. She was rocking a purple velvet skintight cat suit with a plunging neckline that showed off her ample cleavage, small waist, plump ass, round hips and long legs.

"Di-zamn! Check you out, looking like page fifty-five in Jet magazine!" Tommy said salivating and grabbed his crotch.

"You're so silly. So what is it with you men grabbing on your penises?" Donnie giggled.

"Hey if you had a pocket full of gold, you'd touch it once in a while too." Tommy winked boastfully.

"Whatever, I'm just glad you appreciate this outfit since I went through hell wearing it just to make you happy."

"What's that supposed to mean?"

"You know I don't even dress like this. I wore it especially for you since we haven't chilled in a minute. But you never showed up. And I was left fighting off a hundred stupid ass guys that wouldn't take no for an answer." Donnie hissed annoyed as she recalled the drunken guys pawing at her.

"Aw sorry to hear that baby. But forget those lames. Captain Caveman is here now." Tommy came over smiling then leaned in and sucked her lips while curling his tongue around hers. He pulled away and took a step back eyeing Donnie from head to toe while smiling like a kid on Christmas morning. "Shit!"

"What?" Donnie asked.

"Nothing. It's just that you look so damn good." Tommy admitted.

"No need for flattery. I'm a sure thing." She giggled.

He could smell the perfume wafting from her and was becoming more anxious by the second to get her undressed and if she didn't start stripping soon he was prepared to rip off her clothes and chase her around the room like a Benny Hill sketch. Donnie saw the desperation in her lover's eyes and batted her long eyelashes then cleared her throat while pointing at the zipper. Tommy came over and pulled the zipper down with his teeth then pulled off his shirt and undershirt into one big ball tossing it to the side. When Donnie turned around and eyed his muscles that were so tight and well-proportioned they appeared to be the efforts of an erotic sculptor, she felt her insides get moist. Tommy peeled her cat suit and boots from her body like a banana then unhooked her bra from the center and a pair of large, gracefully curved breasts spilled out. He licked in between and all over them until her nipples were erect then ran his tongue down her flat stomach. Pausing at her Victoria's Secret panties he inhaled the sweet smell of Calvin Klein Obsession perfume she sprayed down there. He licked his lips as he tried to part her legs but she resisted and he glanced up like, 'What's the problem?'

"Umm, I haven't showered." She said shyly.

Tommy squeezed her thigh and looked up into her eyes. "I'm tryna' taste how your day was."

"Dammnnn baby!" Donnie whispered then parted her legs and sucked off all of her lip-gloss.

Tommy chewed the tiny flower on Donnie's panties like a cartoon Billy-goat pulling them down to her ankles. Balancing herself on his shoulders she stepped out of her underwear completely naked and uninhibited. He sat her down, parted her thighs and buried his face in her crotch. Starting with long licks and a nose bump on her joy button, he smiled and held on tight as she squirmed then he brought in a finger to massage a bit and licked like crazy. He paused to look up and his entire face and head were dripping with her juices. Donnie met his gaze with a relaxed smile. Wiggling his eyebrows he reached over to hit the power button on his stereo and they were serenaded with a steady rotation of slow jams spun by WBLS' Vaughn Harper on his Quiet Storm radio show, beginning with Luther Vandross and Gregory Hines' 'There's Nothing Better Than Love.'

"C'mere baby." Donnie whispered pulling Tommy up by his shoulders and they sucked each other's tongues. "Umm, damn you can kiss."

"You've got some delicious, luscious lips yourself," Tommy moaned coming up for air.

Donnie smiled then kissed and ran her tongue over the battle scars on his chest and shoulder blade, perks from his profession, then dropped to her knees and unbuckled his pants to return the favor. The head of his penis was poking out of his silk boxers.

"I just love your ass. It's so perfect." she giggled cupping his tight cheeks in each hand.

"Ahem-if you'll notice, that's not the only thing down there perfect." Tommy said out the side of his mouth.

Donnie grinned then preceded to perform fellatio on him like it was the biggest, sweetest, juiciest Popsicle she ever tasted and she wanted it to last forever.

After a few minutes Tommy couldn't take it and backed away. "Keep that up and I won't be any good to you." he said trembling.

Donnie giggled and climbed back up his torso then paused when she noticed something that was not there the last time she inspected his body.

"So those are new." Donnie said eyeing the dark stylized geometric shapes that emblazoned his meaty arms.

"They're called Adinkra symbols. And they're from an ancient cloth in Africa called Ashanti Adinkra."

"Oh really?" Donnie asked fascinated in a dreamy voice, a sponge for his conversation

Tommy nodded and held out his limbs. "Yeah I read about them in this book about Africa. See there are all these different symbols that represent different things on the cloth and it's used in ceremonies when honoring rites of passage. The one on my left arm is called Okodee Mmowere. It symbolizes strength, bravery and power.

This one on my right is called Ohene Aniwa, it represents vigilance, protection, security, and excellence." he said.

"Wow, you really know your stuff." Donnie smiled impressed with his sense of style and sophistication that was built on everything that came before, and pointed the way to a lot that was up and coming.

"Yeah well according to the book they're supposed to protect you and I can use all the help I can get out there on the streets. Know-what-I'm-saying? Besides I can't see getting something as permanent as a tattoo and it not having any serious meaning."

"Like a cartoon character, or someone's name?" Donnie said.

"Precisely," Tommy nodded, "I remember there was a sign on the wall in the tattoo parlor that says, 'Ninety-eight percent of all tattoos outlast relationships, so think before you ink.'"

"Makes sense." Donnie lied. Truth be told, she would have loved to see 'PROPERTY OF DONNIE' tattooed across his washboard abs with an arrow pointing down South.

"So, you likes?" Tommy asked flexing.

"Oh, I likes. And you chose the right symbols. They definitely describe your character."

Tommy blushed. Donnie kissed both tattoos then wrapped her arms around him grinding and kissing him as she inched him towards the bed. Tommy stopped short. "Hold on I wanna try something a little freaky." He said with a gentle kiss.

"Baby I don't think there's anything freaky you and I haven't attempted at least once." Donnie said while nibbling on his ear. She was so hot she was dripping like an ice cube in a steam room.

"There's one thing," Tommy pried her from his waist. "Be right back." He promised and went into the bathroom then stuck his head back out, "Hey do me a favor."

"If I get one in return."

"Take the pillows and the sheets off the bed."

"The sheets? Baby now is not the time to be changing sheets. If anything, it's time to mess them up!"

"Donnie just do it."

"Okay, Okay!" Donnie said and pulled the blanket and sheets from his waterbed.

Tommy came back out carrying a shower curtain and a large bottle of baby oil. He flung the shower curtain out over his bed.

"Here help me, smooth out the ends on your side." He said. Donnie did what he said and watched as Tommy poured out half the bottle of baby oil onto the curtain.

"Now, get in bed." Tommy ordered.

Donnie's eyes stretched wide and she knew this man was going to rock her world. She willingly climbed into bed. "Oh my! You're right this is new." She said rolling around. "Umm, it feels slippery, sexy. I like it! Come here baby."

"No not yet. There's just one more ingredient. Turn around." Tommy said motioning her with a twirling finger. Donnie did as he requested and got on all fours with her ass pointed out at him. Licking his lips, he grabbed a Pokka-dot tie lying over the partition and blindfolded her with it.

"I don't believe you've got me acting out some nine and a half weeks type mess!" Donnie smiled.

Tommy climbed into bed with her and emptied the rest of the bottle over her shoulders making her quiver with delight as the oil crept down her body slowly and seductively. Suddenly he pulled her by her ponytail as he massaged her from head to toe then laid her down and played with her body touching her in all the right places her last lover forgot to. Not knowing where his big hands were coming from drove Donnie insane. All the outercourse was making her fiend for intercourse. Her body temperature was rising and she felt as if she was going to explode if she did not have him inside of her right this instant.

She could no longer take it. In a fit of wild of passion, she yanked off the blindfold, climbed on top of Tommy, pinned down his shoulders, bit the wrapper off of a condom, rolled it down his thick throbbing penis and took what she wanted. As soon as Tommy hit her G-spot she began twisting and writhing wildly.

"Oh God! Oh shit! I'm coming! Oh-Oh-Oh-YES! Oh right there! TOMMM-MEEEEE!" she shrieked Tommy's name like she was in hard labor with 12-pound twins while riding him like a cowgirl. "Oh shit! Fuck!" Donnie said between gasps of air. "Damn-shit! Baby you just boned away all a sista's hopes and dreams!" Tommy laid there covered with oil, sweat and accomplishment. Across his thick lips was a pretentious smile with his hands behind his back like he was the man. Donnie looked down and shot him a wry look. "Oh, so you think you're all that?"

"I don't wanna toot my own horn but, Toot-Toot." Tommy teased and Donnie rolled her eyes, "Hey you're the one who said I've got the power to bone away hopes and dreams," he reminded her.

"You know you're not the only one with skills. In fact, I think it's high time you learned about P.O.P." Donnie said then bit on her bottom lip with a devilish smile. Tommy rolled his eyes like whatever then suddenly his shoulders jerked forward like he was having a seizure combined with an exorcism and lifted halfway off the bed moaning and bobbing his head wildly as Donnie contracted the muscles in her pelvis. His eyes closed tight and his mouth was open with a slight smile like he was in another place. A beautiful place. That place was her.

He began to moan, as he came he reached up and grabbed Donnie's shoulders pulling her to him and thrusted himself deeply inside of her while kissing her passionately. After his orgasm he opened his eyes with an exhausted look. "Wha-what the hell is P.O.P.?" he asked slightly convulsing.

"Power of the Punany! Beep-Beep." Donnie said with her own arrogant smirk and licked the sweat from his forehead.

The two laughed then for the rest of the night went on a non-stop two-man orgy like a couple of nymphos on death row.

Three hours and five orgasms later, the clouds parted like the legs of a ready lover, as the sun burned brightly through informing Tommy and Donnie how long they had been going at it. Their bodies were exhausted but they felt elated. They wanted to sleep but first

126

they had to clean up the bed so they removed the shower curtain and put it back up in the bathroom then took a shower together. A peck goodnight and Tommy's eyes dropped like twin guillotines. Donnie watched him and smiled at how sexy he looked sleeping then giggled.

"What's so funny?" Tommy asked yawning.

"Why is it men always fall asleep immediately after sex?" she asked.

"Well...I can't speak for all men but I'm sleepy...YAWN...because you wore my...YAWN black...ass...YAWN...the fuck out..." he said and drifted off.

Donnie leaned in and kissed Tommy on his head thinking to herself that, real men, correction **Strong** men like Tommy were definitely not in the clubs. Afterwards she spooned him and drifted off as well.

# Chapter 9

Donnie sat up stretching and looked over at Tommy across the room sitting at the kitchen table sipping on a steaming mug of Taster's Choice while using a pencil to rewind a Public Enemy cassette after his stereo chewed it up. She smiled thinking longingly of last night. Seeing him sitting there gave her a warm tingly feeling that began at her head and rushed down to her toes. And her eyes said what she would not. That she loved watching him, spending time with him and making love to him.

"Morning sleepyhead," Tommy smiled devilishly at her nude body.

"What time is it?" Donnie asked covering a yawn.

"Almost noon." he said twisting the pencil in the cassette to manually wind the tape slack.

"Dang, why is it so hot in here? I know it's cold out but you got the heat turned up like we're up in the PJ's and what-not." Donnie laughed wiping the sweat beneath her breasts.

"And what does your Ivy League background know about the projects Miss Corporate America?" Tommy teased as he inserted his repaired cassette into his cassette player on the table and smiled when it played.

Donnie wrinkled her brow at Tommy. "Don't sleep. I can go from the boardroom to the block and keep it real in both places." she said snapping her fingers.

"Shit, scared of you, Hood Bougie." Tommy winked shutting off Chuck D' then went over to the kitchen and grabbed a can of dog food.

Mayhem snapped to attention at the sound of the electric can opener then scrambled over to her bowl as Tommy emptied a can into her bowl. She sniffed the brown chunks of meat in her bowl then grunted disapprovingly and walked away without touching it.

"Hey where are you going? According to the TV commercials it's a mouth-watering home-cooked meal in a can." he said to his dog.

Mayhem twisted at her master with an expression that said, *'Then you eat it!'* and jumped half onto the bed with Donnie to receive a scratch behind the ears. When they first met Donnie was taken back by her intimidating size and appearance, but she eventually warmed up to the gentle giant when she discovered that Mayhem was nothing more than a big ol' sweet puppy dog.

"Hey pretty girl," Donnie said as Mayhem licked her fingers and wagged her tail excitedly. "So what other tricks can she do?"

"Everything but beg. Not her style." Tommy winked.

"So, how'd you train your dog to do all the things she can do?"

"It's easy when you have a willing participant."

"Oh really?"

"That's right. You see Mayhem's not your average pooch. In fact, I'm positive she was human in a past life,"

"How come you never mated her? I'll bet she'd make some beautiful pups,"

"I tried once. A buddy of mines had a Rottweiler. But it was a catastrophe. As soon as the other dog tried to climb on she went off. Almost killed him. So since then I never tried."

Donnie smiled at Mayhem, "Tell him a girl likes to be romanced before she's climbed on top off. Ain't that right?" Mayhem panted a jovial response.

"Whatever." Tommy said as he washed his hands before coming out of the kitchenette with his arms behind his back. "Okay ladies break it up you two. Hey baby close your eyes and open your mouth and I'm gonna give you a big surprise."

Donnie closed her eyes smiling. "It'd better not be that stuff Mayhem wouldn't eat." She said and Tommy laughed as he fed her a fork full of Salmon cakes and grits. "Umm this is good. You made this?" she asked smacking her lips.

"No doubt!" Tommy nodded proudly. "I seldom cook but depending on the company, I've been known to chef it up a little somethin'-somethin'."

Donnie shook her head in awe. "I swear, every time I think I have you figured out and labeled under completely predictable, you show some new wonderful side of yourself that messes up my whole system."

Tommy blushed, "Well thank my Nana. She's the one who taught me how to cook. She would always tell me if I wanted to catch a woman I should know how to cook because it's not fair to expect her to do it all the time."

"Well my Grandmother had a different philosophy about landing the opposite sex. She'd say to me, chile, if you want to catch a man then you have to be a cook in the kitchen, a maid in the living room and a whore in the bedroom.'"

"Well I can't vouch for the cooking and cleaning but Grandma damn sure got that last part right Miss P.O.P.!" Tommy laughed as he brought her over a tray filled with food.

Donnie took one look at the smorgasbord and held out her hand like a traffic cop. "You know what? Let's do this at the table, I can't eat on your bed." she said bobbing around like a beach ball.

"Fine by me." Tommy said and placed the food back on the table then went into the refrigerator for some orange juice. When he turned back his face scrunched up at Donnie. "Hold up. Is that sugar you're sprinkling on your grits?"

"Yeah, that's how I like them,"

"Look, it could be some salt and pepper, butter, even some hot sauce…but sugar? Nah, you gots to go." He smirked.

As they laughed over her odd choice for seasoning her grits, he noticed she had slipped into one of his oversized shirts and it made him think about how Nicky had on his shirt the other night. He looked up and was snatched from his trance as Donnie waved in his face

"Did you hear one word I said?" she asked.

"Oh, sorry I had something on my mind."

"Sure it wasn't **someone?**"

"So anyway, what were you saying?" Tommy asked not wanting to go there.

"Actually, it was a question. I was asking what are you doing today?"

"I have to find this doll my sister wants for her birthday. And speaking of which, what are you doing this Friday?"

"Working beside that no plans, why?"

"Well I was wondering if you'd like to come to her party."

"Whoa, I-um." Donnie was speechless.

"Bad idea, me asking right?"

"No, no it's not that. I'm just a little surprised that you invited me to a family function."

"It's no big deal." Tommy said feeling guilty about his ulterior motives since if Corbin was not coming there would not have been any need to invite her.

"It is a big deal and of course I'll come. I'd be honored to. So, I'll finally get to meet your mother."

"Yeah, but if she asks don't tell her how we met."

"Why not? Doesn't she know what you do?"

"Oh hell no! Not Carla Pinkney. Our relationship is crazy enough as it is. If she knew, she'd go ballistic. Probably break out the belt and whoop my ass. So if she asks, make something up."

"I think you'd better handle that. I'm not trying to lie to your mother."

Tommy rolled his eyes. "Fine."

"So who's going to be there?"

"Well it's just some of my crazy family, my parents, and oh yeah, *my ex and her boyfriend*. Nobody really!"

Donnie looked up from a fork of grits. "Your ex-wife's gonna be there?"

"Um-uh yeah." Tommy said darting his eyes around and quickly sipped his coffee.

"I see. And out of curiosity, why is she and her new boyfriend going to be there?"

"Well it's um, gonna be at our-her. Her place." He said covering his mouth and tripping over his words.

Donnie glared with her arms folded over her chest. "I see. So basically, you're only inviting me to show your ex that you have somebody too?"

Tommy wrinkled up his face. "You got it all wrong. I just figured it would be nice to meet some of my family since they're all going to be under the same roof."

Donnie twitched her lips. "A minute ago it was no big deal. Now you figured it would be nice if I met your family." she said thinking how if Pumpkin knew this she would never let her hear the end of it. "So why is Tee-Tee having her party at your ex-wife's house?"

Tommy was not in the mood to talk. Quiet as it was kept he wanted to get back in bed and bump bellies but if he didn't answer her it wasn't going to happen. "Okay it's like this. Remember when I told you how my sister's mentally disabled?" Donnie nodded. "Well back when I was married Tee-Tee was always over, and she and Nicky became real close. Ever since our divorce they don't see each other as much. Actually, at all and Tee-Tee wanted to have her party there. Kinda' like for old times' sake."

Donnie nodded. "Okay I guess I can accept that. I mean it does seem a bit suspicious how out of the clear blue you want me to meet your family when we've been...I don't know. Whatever it is we call ourselves doing, at a time when your ex-wife is flaunting her new man in your face. But if you say that it's not like that, and you really want me there, then I believe you and yes I will come."

"Then it's settled. I'll pick you up from work on Friday." Tommy said then came over and kissed her on top of her head as he massaged her shoulders while slipping his hands into her shirt and fondling her breasts.

"Tommy?"

"Yeah baby?"

"What are we doing?"

"Well, if you gotta ask, then I must be doing something wrong," He smiled.

Donnie pushed his hands away. "No that's not what I meant! What are we doing, with each other?"

Tommy slumped back into his chair. "Aw geez, I don't know Donnie, having fun,"

"But all we do is have **fun**. I mean yeah we have great sex and all but something's missing."

"And what might that be?"

"Romance. Tommy you never plan any activities for us. Whenever we have gone out it was always my suggestion. I wonder if I should cut my losses and move on. Sometimes I feel like all I do is take the good with the bad-"

"You take em' both and there you have, the facts of life," Tommy sang jokingly as he tried to put light on the matter then sighed. Going from ambivalent, to elated to crushed in one minute was too much to deal with and he wanted to go back to bed. "Donnie you know what I do for a living." He said.

"What's your point?"

"My point? C'mon baby, the world I live in is insane, complex and gritty. And although you seem okay with it now eventually you're going to ask me to change my life and everything just like-" Tommy realized he was talking too much and paused.

"Go on and say it. Just like Nicky. That is what you were going to say right?" Donnie accused. Tommy shrugged contemplating on having a shot of Bacardi with his breakfast. "So Tommy, do you still love her?" she asked.

"Aw dammit Donnie! I never ask you about your past relationships now do I? So why the hell are you sweating me about mines?" There was a loud silence and as soon as Tommy saw the hurt in Donnie's eyes he wished he had put what he said in a thought balloon.

Donnie was not as concerned with him getting loud as she was with what was said. "Tommy you can ask me anything you want, I don't have anything to hide."

"And neither do I baby." Mayhem jumped up and came over. She placed her head in her master's lap. Tommy patted her then sent her away. "I'm just a private person is all."

"Okay fine I can respect that but this is not just about you."

"Where's all this coming from any way? Pumpkin put you up to this didn't she?"

"Pumpkin doesn't have anything to do with this. I feel I have a right to know if you are still in love with Nicky and make a decision to continue seeing you or not. So again I am asking you, are you still in love with your ex-wife?"

Tommy walked over to the window and looked across the water at the illuminated skyline lost in his own private thoughts. The little voice in his head said, *'Whatever you say do not tell her the truth! She may say she wants to know, but she really doesn't!'* But that wasn't his style. He may have been a lot of things, but he was no liar. Not a malicious one anyway.

Tommy shook his head. "I dunno. Maybe." he turned around and admitted.

"Oh-I see." Donnie said. She calmly got up and gathered her clothes and went into the bathroom. Not even five minutes later she came back out dressed with red eyes. "Call me a cab."

"Aw c'mon Donnie let's talk about this." He pressed but she said nothing. "Ok then let me drive you back to-"

"No. We've said enough."

"You know most men would have lied, minced words, but not me! I told you the truth and for that I am being punished. Damn Donnie, what else do you want?"

Donnie didn't even have to think about an answer. This was something she thought about a lot. "Someone to brush my teeth with in the morning. Someone to ask me how my day was when I walk through the door. Someone to hold me in the middle of the night. Someone that when the phone rings I already know it's him. Tommy I'm tired of casual relationships and casual sex. I'm ready to move past the condom stage!" Tommy shot Donnie a baffled stare and she knew what that look was about. "Yeah I know when we began this we agreed this would only be a sex thing and nothing more. But forget all that! I'm allowed to change my mind when it comes to my feelings! I'm getting older and to the point where I want something that has a little meaning to it. Although we never really discussed it, you know about the shit I endured with my ex. It's time I had something that will withstand the test of time. Yes, you're right, I asked you for the truth. And I thank you for your honesty, because you're right, most men would have lied. But face the facts, you're not like most men. And that's why I feel the way I do about you. But just because I admire you for telling the truth doesn't mean I have to accept it. And I am not punishing you, but if I stayed, I would be punishing myself." Donnie said and wiped a tear.

Tommy felt bad. He knew this discussion was a long time coming and did everything in his power to avoid it. He dialed a cab, spoke for a second and hung up. "They said to come downstairs in five,"

"I'll go down and wait." Donnie said then came over and kissed Tommy on the cheek. "Love you…Hate you." she said then left.

The door shut behind her and Tommy could hear sobbing. He went over to the window and watched Donnie for five minutes until the cab pulled up and pulled off. She never even looked back. What bugged him out was until this very moment he never really gave their arrangement that much thought. But now that it was over he felt like part of him had walked out the door and drove off with her. His Nana once told him that you only get one chance at love, twice if you're lucky. But that's it. Tommy plopped down on the edge of his waterbed worried that he might have just thrown away his only other chance.

"This is exactly why I didn't want to get serious-dammit! I ain't got time for this shit!" He based at the four walls. He reached over and checked his messages on both machines. One was about a consulting job scheduled for later on that night. There was another one from his mother anxious to continue their conversation from last night but he was not in the mood for that. And an incoherent message from Laquita asking him to call her back once he received this message. He dialed Bug-Out's crib.

"Wa'sup little man this is cousin Tommy. Lemme speak to your moms...Hey Laquita, calm down and tell me what he did now... WHAT!?...Where's he at?...Aight I'm on the way over now. Keep him there!"

Tommy slammed his phone down livid. He couldn't believe that Bug-Out could stoop as low as to take his five-year-old son to the park and get high. If it wasn't for a neighbor from the building that spotted AJ walking around by himself crying that, 'His daddy was on the ground shaking with spit-up in his mouth,' who knows what could have happened. Tommy's Jeep Cherokee dug skid marks into the street outside of the Marcy Projects. He jumped out and glared at each and every face he passed daring them to mess with his ride. Mashing Bug-Out's doorbell like he was running from the cops, he stormed inside when Laquita opened the door. She was petite with a mushroom hairstyle that accentuated her light skinned gaunt face.

Tommy looked around his cousin's crib and shook his head. The place was practically barren except for a tattered couch and shaky looking card table surrounded with scratched up folding chairs that was used as a dinette set. There wasn't a television set or stereo because Bug-Out had sold them for drugs.

"Excuse the apartment." Laquita said embarrassed.

"How's AJ doing." Tommy asked staring at the traumatized looking little boy sitting on the couch.

Laquita shook her head sadly. "He's Okay, thank God. But Tommy what if someone reports this to BCW? They could take my baby away from me." She began crying and collapsed in his arms. Tommy consoled her and felt a tug at his Eight Ball jacket. He looked down at his little cousin and patted his head affectionately.

AJ was a handsome little boy. The spitting image of his father. Although he sported a golden grin Tommy could see the faint marks of ghetto pain tattooed on his five-year-old face. When Tommy looked back up Bug-Out was standing in the hallway looking pitiful. Tommy glared at his cousin then stuffed his hands into his jacket pockets for fear that if he didn't, he would shake hands with his voice box. "Get your coat. We're going for a ride!"

## Chapter 10

Tommy smacked loaded magazines into his weapons then fingered through a stack of newsprint targets deciding on one that detailed a thug in a ski mask holding an Uzi in one hand and a female hostage in the other. He then clipped the 20 by 24-inch paper target onto its hanger and sent it out about 30 yards into range, twisted his head all the way to the left then all the way to the right until he heard his neck crack, closed his left eye and then, **BLAM, BLAM, BLAM!** he fired in short bursts of three. Off to the side with his hands pressed firmly over his ears, Bug-Out flinched from each loud shot.

Ambidextrous when it came to shooting, Tommy switched from right to left until the magazine ran out then reeled in his target. Back in the day he used to drag Nicky here. At first she hated coming because it was noisy and the gunpowder smelled, but eventually she allowed Tommy to show her how to shoot and got pretty good at it to the point she was hitting the bullseye with almost every shot.

"Yo Tee?" Bug-Out said.

Tommy ignored his cousin and studied his handiwork. From the right side of the ski-masked terrorist's chin all the way to the top of the head was perfectly perforated by bullet holes while the woman wasn't touched. Were it an actual man the wad would enter his spine and he'd feel his legs go dead even as his heart exploded. He smiled with an elated chuckle. It felt great to master shooting from a sportsman perspective but he hoped he would never have to use his shooting skills to settle differences.

He turned to Bug-Out with a disgusted look and said, "We're out."

Tommy scratched the stocking cap covering his dome as he careened his Jeep Cherokee through his old stomping ground with Bug-Out sitting uncomfortably beside him. Tommy had not said a word to him since he picked him up three hours ago and all this silence was starting to get to the slim man. Bug-Out turned to his cousin who was still wearing an ice-grill.

"Yo man I know I fucked up royally! I had no business taking A.J. with me. He didn't need to see me doing that."

Tommy cut his eyes over at him while at a yellow light. "You looked me dead in the eye and told me that you were not on that shit!"

"I know."

"Put me on a guilt trip for thinking what I knew in my heart was the truth!"

Bug-Out looked down at his sneakers and shook his head pitifully. "I know man. Sorry I lied. But you were the only one who still believed in me. Well you and my son. Now even he's calling me a nasty junkie."

"Well isn't that what you are?" Tommy asked coldly and his cousin drop his head ashamed. "But you're not entirely to blame. This is partly my fault as well,"

"How, is that possible?" Bug-Out meckly asked.

Tommy faced his cousin with no emotion. "I should've known you were lying. Cause your lips were moving!" he said unsympathetically. Or at least he did but pretended to be. "I don't understand what the hell made you get hooked on that garbage in the first place!"

"Man, a whole bunch of shit."

"Like?"

"No job. No money. Laquita cheating on me. It just happened."

"Laquita cheated on you? With who?"

"This one-eyed fool from my projects named Johnny."

"Johnny Hop, the one who heads up the Black Top crew?"

"So you know him?"

"Yeah I know his crippled drug dealing ass. That punk's as soft as Church music."

"Yeah well Church Music boned my wife!" Bug-Out hissed bitterly.

Tommy searched his face for the truth and came up short. He slammed on the brakes so hard that Bug-Out's head hit the dashboard. Tommy spun to him pissed off. "Don't play me, play Lotto, you'll win quicker! Now that don't hardly sound like Laquita. She's put up with way too much of your shit in the past to start messing around now! What aren't you telling me?"

Bug-Out clamed up and looked over at his cousin waiting for an answer. "Okay, I owed Johnny Hop some money. Serious money. And I couldn't pay him back. He said maybe we could work something out that benefited all of us. Then he said he always liked Quita and that...the only way I could settle my debt was if-if...he slept with her."

"So, you pimped out your wife? Why in the hell didn't you come to me for help?" Tommy demanded. "You never had a problem taking money from me in the past."

"Like I said this was serious loot. I'm talking gee's. I couldn't ask you for that kind'a money. And besides, I didn't want you to know."

"And just how did you come to be in his debt in the first place?"

There was more silence then Bug-Out whispered, "He was letting me cop drugs on credit. Before I knew it, I was in way over my head." Tommy closed his eyes and shook his head. "But you don't understand cousin. That bastard knew I was weak. He took advantage. I was the victim."

"When I hear the word victim it makes me think about the innocent people who hire me to protect them-from people like you. How can you call yourself a victim when you are running around with these drug dealers, getting high and involving your family? You're no victim, you're a volunteer. The only victim is Laquita for having to degrade herself." Tommy said then turned to his cousin. "Now get out before I do something we both regret!"

Bug-Out checked out his surroundings and noticed the large red and white sign that read, 'Brooklyn Hospital'. "Yo Tee man why are we here?" He asked confused. Tommy angrily blew through swelled cheeks and cracked his knuckles. Bug-Out jumped out with the swiftness.

The two entered the Hospital's automatic doors and Tommy went over and briefly spoke with the woman seated behind the information booth. She nodded and made a phone call. Minutes later a tall, thin Hippy looking white man with wire-rimmed glasses and salt and pepper hair tied in a short ponytail came over to the booth and the woman pointed him in the direction of Tommy and Bug-Out.

"Tommy Strong?" He asked them both in an uncertain voice.

Tommy stood up with his hand extended. "Hey man, how you doing?"

"Fine, fine and this must be your cousin Alonzo? Pleased to meet you." He said offering his hand.

Bug-Out looked at the stranger's hand like it was infected then turned to his cousin. "Tee, who is this Doctor Snuggles looking cat?"

"Chill-out," Tommy warned his cousin.

The white man smiled unbothered by Bug-Out's defensiveness like he was used to discourtesy. "Sorry. I'm Andrew Carmichael and I run the detoxification and outpatient programs here at the hospital where our moto is, 'There's no hope in dope."

Bug-Out frowned and looked at Tommy peculiar. "What is this some kind of joke?"

"Nah this ain't no joke! You heard the man. He runs a detox program. The same detox program that you are about to admit yourself in."

"Yo man I don't know about this." Bug-Out said nervously.

Tommy looked at Bug-Out like his head was spinning. "You're acting like you have options, when you don't!"

Andrew cleared his throat. "Um Mister Strong we do not want to make your cousin feel uncomfortable about all of this. Keep in mind he needs our help not anger."

"I got this," Tommy grunted at Andrew then spun back to Bug-Out. "Now Bug-Out don't get me wrong, I love you like a brother…Hell, we are brothers. So I'm asking you, begging you, please admit yourself into detox and get some help."

Bug-Out looked deep into his cousin's eyes and could see the pain his addiction was causing him. It was the same look of anguish he saw in his mother's eyes, his uncle's eyes, his son's and everyone else who loved him. He had to do something, if not for himself then for them. He twitched his lips and sized Andrew up and down then nodded his consent.

"Right this way Alonzo," Andrew said.

"Yo call me Bug-Out."

"Whatever makes you comfortable, Mister Bug-Out." Andrew smiled.

"No just Bug-forget it man." Bug-Out said agitated. "Aight man I'll do it, but what about Laquita and A.J.?"

"Don't sweat it. I'll tell them." Tommy said.

Bug-Out blew out his frustration and hugged his cousin then spun on his heels and walked away confident he would defeat his demons.

"Represent kid!" Tommy called out as his cousin and Andrew disappeared through the swinging doors at the end of the hall.

*"It's ten o'clock, do you know where your children are?*

The poster boy for pedophile pedagogues, thirty-six-year old Melvin Smiley fit the criteria of a monster. He had a smile that would make a dentist cringe. He was short, pear-shaped and hairy everywhere except for his balding head. He wore shirts with dingy collars and yellow sweat stains under the armpits to work at the Brooklyn Public School where he taught fourth grade. Students described the educator with poor hygiene as moody, lurching from nice to nasty and parents complained to school officials but nothing was ever done. Nothing that is until a student came home and informed his parents that Mr. Smiley told him to stay after class so that he could help him with an assignment he was having problems with. What happened next was the worst cases of teacher student betrayal to ever occur in the school's history.

Charged with sexual misconduct and endangering the welfare of a child, Melvin's stay in prison was alarmingly brief thanks to his cunning lawyer who was a pro at manipulating the truth and the system in his clients' favor. Parents were boiling with anger and railed bitterly at education officials for allowing a suspected child molester to continue teaching.

So, to ease tensions the principal transferred Melvin to an administrative job at another school. Melvin knew he was under watchful eyes and had to be on his best behavior, but his hunger for little boys would not go away. So, he began lurking around places at risk adolescents frequented. Once he picked up a homeless Dominican boy named 'Angel' near the Times Square Covenant House with long eyelashes and a curly Afro. He couldn't believe his luck. The immoral encounter only cost him the price of a pack of smokes and a two-piece dinner at Popeye's fried chicken.

Tonight, Melvin was at Eddie's Arcade on Flatbush Avenue, with his beady eyes set on a tan-skinned boy playing Dragon's Lair and sipping on a quarter water. The black child looked no older than thirteen. He was small, around five feet tall, weighed roughly about ninety pounds, with big romantic eyes and close-cropped hair. After Melvin witnessed the way the boy's Devil jeans hugged his lower torso, he was in lust, picturing in his sick and twisted mind how soft the child's skin would feel against his bloated body.

It was close to midnight and something evil was lurking in the dark. 'Mickey' by Toni Basil played on the sound system. Most kids were clearing out but the young Dragon's Lair fan was still there committed to rescuing the damsel in distress Princess Daphne. It was a sure sign to the pervert the child did not have a family somewhere overly concerned about his whereabouts. Perfect. When the boy's game ended and he angrily announced he was out of quarters Melvin saw his opportunity and slithered over.

"Howdy," Melvin said smiling creepily.

The angry-faced child looked up at Melvin with his bottom lip poked out. "Sup."

"I see you like video games. Pity they cost so much huh?" Melvin inquired.

"And this one's fifty cents." The boy complained.

"Wow that's a lot. But you're in luck because I happen to have every video game at my place and you can play for free."

"You do?"

"I do. So, what do you say?...Wanna come home and play with me?"

"Hey kid." A deep voice called out.

Both Melvin and the boy looked over to see an imposingly large man leaning against a Ms. Pac-Man game console dressed in red from head to toe biting down on a peppermint chew stick ice-grilling him with a slow-burning simmer in his eyes. Never breaking eye contact with the child molester as the boy skipped over, he gave the kid a crisp C-Note and told the ecstatic boy, "As promised. Now go home!" then shook his head disappointedly at Melvin.

Melvin's heartbeat accelerated. Whomever this guy was Melvin was certain he wasn't a cop. After he was found not guilty, the arresting officers that were present to support the victim's family were visibly upset and voiced their dissatisfaction with the verdict. The Judge presiding reminded them that Melvin was judged by a jury of his peers and found not guilty, then warned them not to harass him or they'd face harsh disciplinary actions which could result in suspension and or losing their badges.

The man in red had Melvin so petro that he lost his appetite for adolescents and decided maybe it was in his best interest to go home and masturbate to some child pornography. He quickly left the arcade and headed for the subway. After a minute a graffiti covered D train noisily snaked around the platform and Melvin quickly boarded it. *'Stand clear of the closing doors please'*, Once Melvin heard the most recognizable voice in New York followed by the accompanied bing-bong chime, he began to breathe a little easier. Then his heart dropped in his Pro-Keds as a pair of arms thick as tree stumps pried the doors apart, reached inside and snatched him back out slamming him onto the platform. When he looked up he was staring into the angry headlights of the fire truck from the arcade.

"Take my wallet just don't hurt me!" Melvin begged.

"Get up!"

"My heart. I can't. Please help me." the obese man pleaded clutching his chest.

Not in the mood to deal with paramedics, Havoc growled then blew exasperated and kneeled in. "Here, take my hand."

Melvin nodded 'thanks' then he took Havoc's hand and suddenly pulled him forward and sprayed a blast of Binaca in his face. As Havoc cursed up a storm rubbing his burning eyes Melvin scrambled to his feet and took off running down the staircase at the end of the platform. The fat man ran frantically through the train station until he found himself sucking oxygen and clutching his chest on another platform. An iron horse pulled in and he was about to make his getaway when suddenly without warning he was knocked to the ground.

"You should've used Mace!" Havoc advised with irritated eyes. At that very moment the child molester felt the helplessness his young victims felt. He climbed to his feet running for all he was worth, pumping his arms and legs as he focused on the staircase at the far end of the platform. "I am not about to chase your fat ass!" Havoc said shaking his head, then calmly planted his foot on the outer lip of the departing train and held onto the grooves sticking out of the door as it pulled off. Melvin's lungs were slamming against his chest plate as he neared the stairs. When he looked over his shoulder he shrieked spotting Havoc gain momentum. As the Trouble Consultant train surfed his way a group of graffiti artists across the platform tagging trains cheered him on.

When Havoc was right upon Melvin he let go of the train and tackled him from behind and they tumbled and bounced down the stairs crashing at the bottom. Havoc stood up and brushed himself clean then came over to Melvin who was clutching his sides rolling around in agony.

"My ribs, I think I broke them!" Melvin cried dramatically.

"Don't flatter yourself! If anyone broke your ribs, I did!" Havoc said then dragged Melvin out the station and through the street over to where his Chevy was parked.

"Who are you? What do you want?" Melvin asked.

"Since we live in a society where our judicial system allows monsters like yourself to walk away scott-free after molesting children, the only way to make sure you get what's coming is if you admit your guilt on your own recognizance to the police."

Melvin cleared his throat, "I have nothing to feel guilty about because I didn't touch that kid."

"Just like you weren't going to touch the kid at the arcade?"

Melvin avoided Havoc's pensive stare. "My attorney advised me not to discuss-" BAM! Midsentence Havoc slammed him hard in the nose with sharp scarred knuckles, sending the pedophile down, landing on his fat ass.

"I'm not interested in what your scumbag lawyer advised you Melvin!" Havoc barked.

Melvin sat on the ground holding his face, "Beat me all you want. You'll get nothing outta me! I'm not smart but I'm far from stupid! Being dubbed a child molester would be like a bulls-eye to the other inmates and prison guards."

"Tell me something Melvin. How do you fit so much evil and sin in that stubby little body of yours? You know what, forget it!" Havoc growled frustrated then shoved him on his back.

"What are you doing? Hic…Oh-hic great now-hic-I have the Hic-hiccups….Hic!" Melvin said over spasmodic breaths.

"The way to cure them is to relax and breathe slowly. Hiccups are due to a lack of oxygen entering your lungs and this is their way of getting it back in. I've also read scaring someone can cure hiccups. But I'm not sure bout that one. Unless I'm not doing a good job." Havoc explained to a surprised-face Melvin. "What, you think all I do is kick sloppy punks like you up the ass all day long? I read! Matter a fact just the other day I was reading this book all about methods of torture."

"Oh-hic, really?" Melvin asked wiping more blood from his nose.

"Oh yeah. Fascinating shit," Havoc explained taking out a box of Newport's and tapping the bottom. He offered Melvin one and the pervert shook his head left and right frantically. "See, you are smart.

These things'll kill ya." Havoc said and lit up. "So basically, for more than 500 hundred years, torturing accused criminals was the standard operating procedure in Europe. It was also the primary means of determining guilt. And there were countless types." Melvin swallowed hard. He did not like where this was heading one bit. "Let's see, there was the water torture where a handkerchief was shoved down the throat. The nose was pinched and gallons of water was poured into the mouth via a funnel. Once the victim was beyond bloated, his or her head was tilted down to increase pressure on the heart and lungs. Another method was where a man's wrists and ankles were bound to four chains attached to the ceiling. He was then lowered onto a pointed iron rod, which was inserted, in his ass. By sheer muscle effort, he had to support himself for hours to avoid sitting on the pointed iron, which pierced him with insufferable pain only prolonging the inevitable. But I'd have to say out of all the sick and twisted things man has concocted to get a confession, the worse in my opinion was during the Korean War. See when the Korean's were looking for answers from uncooperative captured GI's they'd take a big fat diseased rat and put it in a jar then place the jar over the GI's stomach. Then they'd heat the jar up with the rat still inside. Once the jar got hot the rat would start going crazy, spinning around like a damn tornado in a bottle, trying to escape and since it couldn't chew through glass it would gnaw through the G.I.'s guts. Fucking nasty! Sometimes those rats would dig into the poor bastard's belly and halfway into his heart before he broke down. And by then, it was too late." Havoc explained with a twisted smile then flicked his ashes onto Melvin's chest. "Now I don't make it a habit of carrying around rats, but I do always carry this." He said and produced a small can of dog food with a pull-top lid. Melvin sat there confused as he continued. "Melvin I'm gonna give you one option, non-negotiable. If you don't accept, we take this to the next level."

"Hic-The-hic-next level?...Hic," Melvin asked confused.

Havoc shook his head frustratedly, then removed the lid from the dog food and proceeded to dump its contents all over the crotch of Melvin's Lee jeans.

"What the hic-hell are you doing? Hic," the pedophile demanded.

Havoc pulled his gold whistle out of his shirt then blew into it. "Now for the last time are you going to do the right thing," he implored as the car's back door opened. "Or, am I gonna give her the command to-EAT?" All it took was one look at Mayhem's ferocious grin and Melvin nodded his head like a woodpecker. "Look on the bright side Melly Mel. At least you don't have the hiccups anymore."

Luckily for Melvin central booking was only six blocks away from the subway, since there was no way Havoc was letting him inside his fancy ride with Alpo covered jeans to muck up his rich Corinthian leather. When they got to the precinct Havoc waved him over.

"Okay pervert, go inside and ask for Detectives Angus Fisk and Jay Rockford."

"Huh, Fuh-Fuh-Fisk?" Melvin stuttered nervously.

"Did I stu-stu-stutter fat-boy? Fisk and Rockford."

"And what do I tell them?"

"The truth. That you molested a student you were entrusted to protect and that you were planning on picking up another minor tonight. Oh and feel free to admit any other sick and twisted things you've done. If someone asks why the sudden confession and are you being forced to do so, tell them that you couldn't carry around the shame any longer and you need to be off the streets before another child is victimized. Capiche? That's Italian for nod your fucking head!" Melvin nodded while darting his eyes down the street. "I wouldn't if I were you. My dog'll be all over you like white on rice before you reach the end of the block. And once she's done I'm gonna stomp whatever's left into the cracks in the sidewalk. Ball's in your court." Havoc said. Melvin dropped his head somberly then inhaled his last bit of air as a free man and walked inside to answer for his sins.

A couple of hours later, Havoc was sitting in a vacant Sunnydale grocery store parking lot cracking up as Arsenio Hall interviewed Eddie Murphy while puffing on a blunt. A blue Ford Crown Victoria pulled up and flashed its headlights three times. Havoc switched off his Watchman, stored his blunt in his mouth and switched on his ignition then tailed the car to an abandoned building inside the Brooklyn Navy Yard. A snow-topped white man with a permanent scowl and a broad shouldered black man with salt and pepper facial hair got out and came over. Havoc rolled down his window releasing the aroma of marijuana into the night air and returned the blank look they shot him with a raised eyebrow.

The Black detective leaned forward and sniffed the air then looked over at his partner funny. "See Fisk, I told you hiring 'A Man called Hawk' was a bad idea." He said then looked back to Havoc with a sly grin.

"Well-well-well, if it ain't Brooklyn's own Murtaugh and Riggs. You two fossils ok? You look like you're getting to old for this shit!" The Trouble Consultant wisecracked then reached out his hand and shook theirs.

"Havoc, after the day I've had I could use a hit of that." The White detective said hinting at his marijuana filled cigar.

"Anything for New York's finest. So, did he confess?" Havoc asked already knowing the answer as he honored Fisk's request and passed him the blunt.

Fisk nodded exhaling a cloud before passing it to his partner Detective Jay Rockford. "Yeah, that sick son of a bitch admitted to everything and then some. He even said earlier tonight he was at an arcade in Flatbush looking to pick up a minor. That shit bag's done."

"Brother I dunno what your methods are and frankly I don't wanna know. But you must've put the fear of God in him because he smelled like shit! We had to hose him off before we could even take his statement." Rockford chuckled with mellow eyes after a deep pull from the shrinking blunt and returned it back to its owner.

Havoc smiled satisfactorily. "Yeah Mayhem has that effect on some folks. Don't cha' girl?" he said reaching his arm back and patting his dog. "It's funny, my old man's been on me to get me to quit my day job. Take the road less traveled. Even suggested I become a cop. Picture that. Me? I told him it's highly unlikely I'd pass the drug test. But the way you two are hitting this blunt I'm not so sure."

"Shit it's impossible to be in this line of work without having some sorta' vice." Fisk said removing a flask from his coat.

"Amen to that." Rockford co-signed.

"Not saying you wouldn't make one hell of an Officer, Havoc. Hell, it even has a nice ring to it. But I can name at least several serious as fuck situations when you were able to get shit accomplished that my brothers in blue couldn't. Including my own personal damn dilemma.

No, you're needed right where you are, Trouble Consulting! Doing what we can't, that needs to be done! And, that's coming from a seasoned vet of over twenty years." The white detective said handing Havoc a thick envelope he placed in his glove compartment.

"Respect. So, how's the kid?" Havoc asked concerned.

"He'll probably be in therapy until he's thirty." Fisk sighed as his partner placed a consoling hand on his shoulder.

"Sorry to hear that." Havoc frowned.

"But at least that piece of shit is finally where he belongs. I know people on Rikers Island who owe me favors. On both sides of the bars. Trust me, Melvin Smiley is about to learn the true meaning of pain and suffering!" Detective Rockford said bitterly.

"I love a story with a happy ending. So, you boys headed back to the Office?" The Trouble Consultant inquired.

"Nah. I'm gonna take my Caucasian brother over to Smitty's to knock back a few brew skis. They have a live Jazz band performing tonight. You wanna' roll?" Rockford offered.

"Can't. I got one of those serious as fuck situations, that needs my attention." Havoc said then took one last hit and offered the remainder of his weed to the Detectives. "But here. For the road."

"Much obliged. And Havoc if I can ever return the favor. Let me know." Fisk said.

"Careful. I might just take you up on that one of these days." Havoc remarked as he bumped fists with the Detectives before they headed back to their car.

Occasionally the unflappable Detective Angus Fisk enlisted the services of Havoc and Mayhem when the straight and narrow approach didn't work because he knew the Trouble Consultant stepped over lines and could get things accomplished that he couldn't. Like a confession from the perverted substitute teacher who molested his 9-year-old nephew.

## Chapter 11

Tommy's very first job as a Trouble Consultant was the kind of story best sellers are made from. It was the middle of the summer during a record heatwave. A scorching ninety-five degrees. Bodies were glistening in the heat as men walked around bare-chested and women wore tube tops and halters. Crime was at its highest form and the stick-up kids were robbing any and every one. Every fire hydrant on every block in Brooklyn was on full blast as kids and adults alike tried to beat the heat and have fun at the same time. Tommy Strong entered the neighborhood bodega to buy a pint of orange sherbet for his wife and unknowingly walked in on a robbery in progress. He tried to do an about face and keep it moving but the pantyhose-masked gunman stuck a gun in his back and promised if he tried to make it out of the door, that he wouldn't! Reluctantly Tommy stepped back inside and was motioned into a corner with a group of terrified people. The gunman then proceeded to rob every one of their valuables. When it was Tommy's turn to ante' up he stood there unresponsive and uncooperative.

The others were scared but Tommy wasn't. Instead he was pissed and refused to give up his hard-earned bread. The robber became impatient. He wanted to get paid and be out in a hurry. He warned Tommy that this was not the time to pull a Charles Bronson and threatened that he would pull the trigger by the time he counted to three, if he did not cooperate. The gunman began, 'One!' and Tommy quickly said, 'Two-three!' then disarmed him by grabbing and bending his wrist and forcing it down then violently twisting until it popped. The gunman let go of the weapon screaming in pain.

The gun dropped to the floor and made a sound like light weight plastic instead of heavy metal. Immediately Tommy lifted the punk into the air then furiously sent him crashing through a glass freezer in the blink of an eye. Sometime later after the police took away the wannabe stick up kid and statements were taken, a cop with sergeant stripes had to ask Tommy, "Hey kid, how'd you know?"

"How'd I know what?" Tommy asked confused.

"That the gun wasn't real? It was a cap gun."

Tommy shrugged and shook his head with no reply. Because he didn't. Impressed and eternally grateful, the storeowner offered

Tommy whatever wanted from the shelves as gratitude for his heroics. Tommy nodded thanks playing down what he did then grabbed a pint of orange sherbet for his wife and filled a couple shopping bags with ice cream bars to hand out to the neighborhood kids. That evening after his wife finished ranting about the insane risk he took she joked about him beating down small-time crooks on a full-time basis since he hated his construction job so much. She even created a name for it. Trouble Consulting.

Later that night he found himself dozing in front of the television when an animated voice said, *'Hello, my name is Tom Vu and I quit my dead-end job as a bus boy and followed my dreams. Now I'm happy and successful and you can be too!'* Tommy's eyes opened to a hyper Vietnamese man on a yacht dancing in a conga line with beautiful blonde women in bikinis rambling about his rags to riches idea that turned his life around. As the shyster on the infomercial continued hawking his ridiculously priced bogus seminars on how to sell distressed properties at a hefty profit so, *'You too can be a millionaire like me!'* Tommy's mind drifted to how he could turn his life around with his own legitimate idea. But he kept coming up blank. Then he glanced over at the melted bowl of sherbet and a lightbulb went off in his head.

His wife might have been joking about him becoming a Trouble Consultant but the more he thought about it, the more he thought it was a good idea. And why not? In America, a crime is committed every two minutes. But in Brooklyn, it was more like every two seconds. And as rough and tumble as his beloved borough was, his services were definitely needed. The time it took for the police to finally arrive, after the store robbery he prevented, was proof of that. True it would be dangerous but it wasn't like he was a stranger to fighting. Besides when he thought about it he'd never lost a fight in his entire life. And he'd been in quite a few serious brawls in his heyday. From his first three o'clock high slug match against the so-called school yard bully, to the countless barfights and constantly having his cousin Bug-Out's back when his mouth wrote a check his ass couldn't cash. The couple of times he got out his aggression while making some extra cash in illegal underground matches, right on up to the clown he handled at the bodega earlier. He was undefeated thanks to the brutal skills he honed on the streets of Brooklyn and perfected at Gleason's Boxing Gym. In fact, he was often told by trainers he was a natural and had what it took to go pro if he was interested. Which he wasn't when he saw how many didn't make it compared to the chosen few that did.

There's only one Mike Tyson and plenty of Mitch Greens. But the more he thought about it, what he was considering wasn't any more dangerous than his current gig where he handled hazardous cancer-causing toxins as well as corrosive, flammable and explosive gasses. In fact, it was less dangerous.

But the truth of the matter was, Tommy was at his lowest point. He was tired. Tired of stretching his meager paycheck around his neck three times and still being broke. Tired of robbing Peter to pay Paul and dipping in their cookie savings jar that had nothing left but pennies and prayers. Tired of the groove his life had fallen into that ran so deep, it would take an eight-pointer on the Richter Scale to knock him off that track. And above all tired of the misery and paralyzing stress he felt when the alarm woke him up every morning to get up for a job he despised. A job he was supposed to be grateful for having because if nothing else it was safe and reliable. So, against his wife's wishes he made a U-turn in life and replaced a period with a question mark. He quit his safe and reliable job. Trusted his gut and began a new and exciting career cruising Brooklyn's shadowy districts as the Trouble Consultant.

In the beginning while following his intuition and figuring out this whole Trouble Consulting thing, jobs were few and far between which meant no money was coming in. It was then Tommy started worrying he might have played himself when he told his boss to take his job and shove it! But instead of turning down the doubt, he turned up the faith, in himself. He had a well thought out plan and followed it. Referring to himself as Mister Fix it, he spent his days in the gym to prepare for his nights in the streets. When the sun set he was out on the blocks, in the projects, strip clubs and seedy joints to make connections, pass out business cards and build his reputation. After a couple of successful consulting gigs word began to spread like butter on toast throughout the hood about the brother, half man half amazing, who was 'settling beef for a fee'. That's when the calls started pouring in, followed by the cash!

Now that the Trouble Consultant was confident that he found his calling, he needed a better street name than what he was presently going by. He didn't feel Mister Fix-it sounded rugged enough nor defined him. In fact, some people called mistaking him for a plumber. He wanted a name that made his enemies as uncomfortable as a circumcision. Then ironically got it from the unlikeliest of places. The low-life he was hired to step to that was preying on senior-citizens cashing their Social-Security checks. After molly-whopping the piece of garbage until he saw quadruple, the punk dubbed his two-fisted Karma with the name 'Havoc' as he recounted his story while being packed into an ambulance, *"All I remember was this big guy with a shaved head and a voice like Arizona sand appeared dressed in red, then HAVOC followed!"*

After receiving the rest of his payment plus the new name folks were already referring to him by, the Trouble Consultant strolled into a random bar to celebrate another victory and his new and appropriately given moniker. Mainly a Guinness Stout connoisseur, he jokingly referred to the bartender as Isaac from the Love Boat asking what he'd recommend for a momentous occasion. Taking the ribbing in stride, Isaac suggested a two-finger shot of his personal favorite top shelf scotch Johnnie Walker, leaving him to decide if he wanted black or red label. While pondering Havoc, dressed in all red from head to toe stared back at his reflection in the mirror and took notice of how superbly the color hid blood stains from his recent consulting gig.

"...Gimme a shot of both," he finally answered unable to decide. After tossing back both shots and experiencing the sweet and spicy flavor and robust smoke with a warm finish from each, he vowed he'd always wear red when he was working, he'd only drink red label when he was and black label when he wasn't.

A few hours later Havoc stumbled out of the bar and into 'Irie' the local Caribbean spot for a bite to eat. On the way out, he heard a whimper coming from behind a dumpster in the neighboring alley. He went over to investigate and behind the dumpster discovered a filthy, frightened, malnourished puppy living on the street. She was cold, shivering and had difficulty standing on its injured front paw. The sizeable puppy didn't seem like the typical stray and instantly reminded him of the Italian Stallion's companion Butkus from his favorite movie Rocky. When he held out his hand, the puppy backed away growling defensively. After promising he wouldn't hurt it, he proved it by offering the rest of his ox tails and rice. Starving, the pup took a gamble and limped forward, sniffed and licked his hand affectionately, wagged its tail then feasted. Once he gained her trust he brought her home.

That night she hid under the table afraid of everything and Tommy could see how tough life for her had been. Finally, he said, "I'm just going to take her to bed." He carried her upstairs and placed her in a crate beside him. And in the morning, it was like a different dog. She was connected to Tommy and a mystical bond between them was formed.

It wasn't long before she was healthy and running around like she owned the house causing 'Mayhem', snapping at pants legs and gnawing on anything. Mayhem wasn't like any dog either Tommy or Nicky had ever encountered. She had her own unique personality and attitude. She was also very smart, and with patience her master was able to train her to do simple commands like sit and get him a beer out of the refrigerator. Eventually she graduated to more serious ones like tackling an enemy and tossing a weapon. Never purposely far from her the man who saved her life, Mayhem began accompanying Havoc on trouble consulting gigs, proved her value and became his loyal companion.

Time had passed and Nicky still could not believe all this began as a result of a stupid joke she made. In fact, after Tommy became a Trouble Consultant whenever she made a joke depending on its severity, she made it a point to let him know that she was only playing and for him not to take her seriously! She hated him taking on one death-defying mission after another. She hated how many candle lit dinners went uneaten. She hated lying to everyone about what her husband did and she especially hated how jaded her husband was becoming from all the violence.

Tommy on the other hand saw things differently. He loved his new job and assumed he had everything under control. But he learned the hard way that assumption was the motherfucker of all mistakes!

It was their anniversary and Tommy and Nicky celebrated with dinner and a movie. Later that evening they decided to take a romantic stroll to the Promenade. As they held each other under the moon reflecting on the time between their first date and the present, a man who Havoc recently consulted happened upon them looking for payback. With revenge in his bitter eyes he cowardly snuck up and attacked Tommy from behind. Nicky was terrified and screamed as the two men tussled. But she was even more frightened and shocked by how violent her husband could be. Unable to watch anymore she begged Tommy to stop beating his attacker before he killed him. Furious, Tommy obeyed his beloved but not before ordering the half-conscious man to apologize to his wife for ruining their evening.

155

That night after Nicky finished cleaning and dressing Tommy's wounds with trembling hands, she told him she always thought she could cope with what he did if she ever had to experience it firsthand, but she was wrong. She said she wanted kids in the future and worried what would happen if the father of her children went out one night and did not return. The only logical thing for him to do was quit being a Trouble Consultant, immediately! Tommy disagreed, arguing that there was no way he could go out and find a job that would pay him the kind of money he was making as a Trouble Consultant. And since his pride wouldn't allow him to borrow money from their parents or a bank to pay the mortgage and college tuition, he saw no other alternative. Nicky argued that she didn't care if they rented a room and lived off of boxed macaroni and cheese, as long as they were together. But he did.

Tommy felt like he was on Let's Make A Deal. Behind curtain one was a backbreaking job with shitty pay and shittier benefits. Behind curtain two, long cash, thrills, chills and adventure! The way he saw it, money may not be everything, but it was way ahead of what was ever in second place. And he could not go back to his old life.

Nicky looked at him as if to say, *'So what was it going to be? Curtain one, or Curtain two?'*

So, after some serious fussing, fighting, crying and arguing, Tommy chose curtain two. Nicky was so angry with Tommy that it was a year before she could even say his name without cursing. Whenever Carla called to see what she could do about getting her and her son back together Nicky remained respectful but let her ex-mother in-law know that she did not want to talk about it. Eventually she began going out with her girlfriends after work and that's when she met Corbin Ramsey at a Grant's Tomb jazz concert.

There were plenty of men fronting like they were there to hear jazz but were actually there to pick up women. What made Corbin stand out was that he actually came to enjoy the music. Nicky surprised herself and made the first move and before she knew it, they were sipping wine and conversing like old friends in the back of a cozy little jazz club in the East Village.

Corbin Ramsey the Third was definitely not the type of man Nicky was used to dealing with. For starters he was nine years her senior. He very rarely wore anything but a tailor-made suit and when he did dress casually the furthest he would take it was a pair of penny loafers, khakis and an open collared shirt. Sometimes if he was feeling a little daring he would put pennies in his loafers but that was the extent. Nicky admitted to her girls that sometimes he could be a bit dull but she also felt that maybe an older mature gentleman, who appreciated Miles Davis more than Big Daddy Kane, was just what she needed. A few months passed and although she was not in love, she believed she was over Tommy.

"Come on Latrell. You're smarter than this! You just aren't applying yourself!" Nicky vented aloud to herself as she went down her student's math test marking bold red X's.

Corbin looked up from his newspaper at Latrell's test and sighed shaking his head, "Thirty-two? My goodness! Is that his test score or the age the little car-jacker will be when he graduates? This is why I will never again use brain surgery as the bar against which intelligence is measured."

"Corbin, I asked you before not to talk about my kids like that." Nicky said defensively.

"You said yourself the boy sits in the back off your class goofing off and covers his hands with Elmer's glue just to peel it off. Look, all I'm saying is if these little imps want to be nothing, that's just what they are going to be."

Nicky sighed. "You don't understand Corbin-"

Corbin chuckled inwardly. "Honey I don't mean to come off condescending but, 'Don't understand?' I have an IQ in the triple digits. Graduated magna cum laude from Harvard University. I can even speak Latin fluently. So what don't you think I understand?" he asked in the same pompous manor Tommy disliked him for.

Nicky rolled her eyes. "What you don't understand is that we are in a state of emergency, with the AIDS and crack epidemic, we simply cannot afford to raise a generation on ignorance under Nixon's benign and neglect policies. Unfortunately, our young culture frowns on people who think too much. They have this perverted sense of authenticity and fear of being seen as rejecting their roots in favor of trying to be what they believe is selling out or white."

"So basically, who cares about where the universe came from or how the Greeks hammered Troy, when rappers like Iced Tea have a new album out in the stores?"

Nicky nodded not even bothering to give him the correct pronunciation of Ice-T's name. "Yeah, basically. But don't put the entire blame on my kids. There are a lot of things wrong with the way the educational system is set up. Like for Instance, our schools are overcrowded and dilapidated and we public school teachers do not get the support and the conditions we need to help children meet higher standards not to mention our salaries lag far behind teachers in the suburbs and private institutions. As for the children, the majority of them are misunderstood. They know their calling is greater than poverty. That the ghetto they live in is a third world country within America. They want a decent future and they understand that the only way they'll get it is if they study hard. But unfortunately, the textbooks they're issued are outdated and it's kinda hard to concentrate on fractions when drug dealing, threats of violence and gang fights are a part of everyday life."

Corbin held up his hand and rubbed his thumb and pointing finger together with an unsympathetic look. "Shh, I'm playing the world's smallest violin." Corbin said in a compassionless voice.

That's not even funny." Nicky griped.

"I apologize if I sound disparaging but I have a real hard time buying the homeboy from the streets with a chip on their shoulder and a quip in their heart act. Look Nicolette, you know as well as I do if not better, that you could give those heathens an entire university's worth of up to date mint condition text books and within a week the pages would be defaced with misspelled graffiti. Face it the only D, C, B or A coming their way is if they're standing on a subway platform." Corbin said making himself laugh.

"I can't believe you just said that." Nicky said.

"Why because I'm as your ex-*Tommy* would say, 'Keeping it real?'"

"You know something Corbin, when it comes to the corporate world I'll give it to you, you are on the top of your game. But when it comes to life, you're so lost that you're wandering around in the daytime with a flashlight. It's obvious their plan is to keep brothers on lock down because if you've been to jail then you cannot vote. And that means fewer minority votes. And fewer minority votes means no Blacks and no Latinos are voted into office. So ultimately what happens is that only whites will be elected because you know they aren't voting for a Black or Spanish person so he or she can be given all that power and responsibility." Nicky said breaking it down for him.

Corbin chuckled and shook his head like something was funny. "Christ Nicolette not you too!"

"Not me too, what?"

"You sound like one of those angry militants who see everything through race tinted glasses. They stand around downtown with their paranoia and silly conspiracies trying to think of an alternative way to spread their revolutionary ideology to the masses and keep McCarthyism alive. They're so incredibly laughable because they fail to realize that they're only a threat to themselves. When it comes down to it, no matter how passionate they are about their beliefs they lack intelligence, direction and focus and are basically just saying a whole lot of nothing."

"Whoa, back up! I know you did not just call me a joke in my own damn house!" Nicky asked pointing a long finger his way.

Corbin's bottom jaw swung open. He had momentarily forgotten that he was dealing with a strong independent black woman who was educated and owned her own home with no qualms about throwing him out on his ass. "No-no my dear you've misconstrued what I was saying. I would never disrespect you. In your home, or anywhere for that matter. All I was saying was that perhaps you should consider abandoning such inconsequential concerns. We both know that the people we are speaking about should be doing something much more constructive with their lives. It's a documented fact that at least seventy percent of men between the ages eighteen through thirty-five of Black and Hispanic descent are either in jail, on probation, or on parole."

Nicky shook her head sadly. "You really shouldn't believe everything the media tells you."

"I don't and I also don't throw the race card down at the drop of a hat every chance I get to blame the white man for the dilemma black people are in either. Maybe a few years back, they had a leg to

159

stand on. But now it's only a crutch. These are the eighties, things are different now."

"And you truly believe that?"

Corbin brushed some imaginary lint off the sleeve of his expensive sports jacket, "Indeed I do."

"Even though every four years the President still has to sign the Lynden Johnson 1966 civil rights act so that black men like yourself can be treated what is considered equally?"

"Well of course we still have a ways to go, but there has been some progress. At least we aren't forced to sit on the back of the bus any longer. And what gets me is what about the Black and Hispanic men that aren't in jail? They don't vote! They don't even care about such matters. All they care about is buying gaudy jewelry whose value depreciates as soon as they put it on and expensive cars that cost more than the homes they live in. It sickens me to no end!"

Nicky could not argue with Corbin there. She had quite a few students who always forgot to hand in their homework assignments but heard them in the cafeteria banging on tables while reciting all the words to latest hit rap song. And it disgusted her that throughout New York there were schools that bore the names of great Black leaders like Paul Robeson and Martin Luther King but failed to live up to the legacy of the person for whom they're named, but regardless of the fact she was not about to count out her race. Unlike certain people she knew.

"It's obvious we do not see eye to eye on this subject, so let's not even continue discussing it Okay?" Nicky said trying to avoid arguing.

"I couldn't agree with you more. Hey I've got a joke for you." Corbin said attempting to switch the mood.

Nicky sighed. She had a lot of papers to grade and a lesson plan to write but a joke could lift the tension between them. "Okay is it funny?"

"I'll let you be the judge. Wayne told it to me and the guys the other day and it was uproariously funny."

"You're saying Wayne like I'm supposed to know who he is."

"Darling I've mentioned Wayne from work before. Wayne Braithwaite head of marketing? He's the one I told you who suggested I get a Porsche like his because it makes a bold statement."

"I guess, let's just hear the joke." Nicky said unimpressed.

"Alright, what happens when you stick your hand in a jar of jellybeans?"

"I don't know, what?" Nicky smiled.

"The black one's steal your watch!" Corbin said then exploded into laughter. "Don't you get it? The black one's steal-"

"Oh yeah, yeah I get it." Nicky said unable to find the humor in his play on racial stereotypes.

"Oh that's a riot. It gets funnier every time I hear it." Corbin laughed rubbing tears from his eyes. He was so amused he failed to realize how unamused Nicky was. "Hold on Wayne told me another one, what do you call a Black-"

Nicky sucked her teeth thinking about what Tommy had said about Corbin standing by the water cooler telling racist jokes about his own kind. "Corbin let me ask you something? Aren't you the only Black man on your floor? In fact, the only Black Man with a Managerial position?"

"Um-I suppose, unless you count Jackson our Mailroom Manager, but what am I saying, he runs errands and delivers my mail. He doesn't count. So, I guess it's safe to say yes. Why do you ask?"

Nicky gathered her things, ticked off. "You have an I.Q. in the triple digits-figure it out." She said and went into the living room to continue working. Tommy would never hear her admit it, but she was beginning to think he was right about Corbin and his less than real ways.

Tommy sat on the couch with a drink in his hand and an ear cocked towards the stereo as Teddy Pendergrass vocalized his thoughts in the background.

♫ If you don't know me by now, you will never, never, never know me. ♫

It was Thursday evening. One day before Tee-Tee's party. He had not heard from Donnie since Sunday after he admitted he still had feelings for Nicky, and she left with tears in her eyes. Since then he couldn't get Donnie off his mind and he missed her terribly.

♫ All the things that we've been through. You should understand me. Like I understand you. Now baby I know the difference between right and wrong. I ain't gonna do nothing, to break up our happy home. ♫

In the past depending on their schedules, sometimes as much as a week or two would pass without them seeing each other. And it was no big deal because eventually they would connect, in more ways than one. But this was different because the calls had ceased all together. It wasn't just the sex he missed. It was the 1am phone calls just to say she was thinking about him. The things she did like pick up a shirt at the mall she thought he would look nice in. Basically, the little things that meant a lot. He sat there all alone reflecting and let out a heartfelt sigh as the smooth crooner depicted his current status.

♫ Oh don't get so excited when I come home a little late at night. Cause we only act like children when we argue fuss and fight. ♫

As he listened he realized how he had taken her for granted. He knew he was not an easy person to deal with and not many women would tolerate half the things he put her through.

♫ If you don't know me by now. You will never, never, never know me. ♫

He picked up the phone and placed it back on the receiver. He picked it up again and placed it down then shook his head. For a guy who made a living being fearless, sometimes he could be a punk. He sipped some whisky for courage and dialed Donnie's number. Oran Juice Jones' song, 'The Rain' came on after the third ring followed by her saying,

*'Hey this is Donnie. You called the right number, but at the wrong time. So, if you'll kindly leave your name, number and a brief*

*message after the beep, I will gladly return your call at my earliest convenience. Have a blessed day. '-*BEEP!

Tommy emptied his glass in one huge gulp then spoke. "Hey-um Donnie it's me, Tommy. Um-listen, I was just calling to see how you were doing and to um-uh, that is to say, I miss hearing from you. Man I hate leaving messages! In any event, I was hoping that you would give me a call sometimes and that we could still be friends. I mean Okay yeah-I said I still had feelings for my ex, but that doesn't mean that I don't have feelings for you too. Okay maybe that didn't come out right-see this is why I hate leaving messages! What I mean to say is that I have feelings for you but sometimes a brother doesn't show them. Look, I'm just rambling on and on." On the opposite end of the phone line, Donnie felt Tommy had suffered enough and reached for the phone but Pumpkin stopped her as he continued, "Maybe it's the Johnnie Walker talking. I dunno, but regardless, I do miss hearing from you, so call me sometimes...If you feel like it."

Pumpkin rolled her eyes, "You know he's only begging cause his ex-wife's gonna be at his sister's party and he don't want to show up without nobody on his arm looking like Buster."

"Maybe." Donnie said.

"Maybe? C'mon Dee don't tell me you're falling for his ghetto Jedi Mind tricks!" Pumpkin said in the middle of Donnie's home using a lot of hand gestures.

Donnie's place was decorated to match her personality, regal yet real. Nothing over the top it was simple but very elegant and modern. Pumpkin followed her into her bedroom and sat on the edge of her canopy bed. Everything was lavender, from the satin sheets, pillowcases and comforter to the curtains, carpet and floral wallpaper. Sitting on Donnie's antique mahogany dresser was framed picture of her standing in between her beaming parents in her cap and gown on her college graduation day, a picture of her and her crew posing in front of a felt sheet that said 'Paid in Full' on Forty-deuce and a big heart framed picture of her and Tommy.

"Aren't you the one who always says that drunk tongues speak sober minds?" Donnie asked.

"Oh so now you choose to listen to a sista? Look, all I'm saying is I don't trust him and neither should you." Pumpkin said then

163

turned to the wall mirror and frowned. "These hair barrettes are so My Little Pony," she said and pulled the colorful hair barrettes out of her hair then spotted a pair of Donnie's doorknocker earrings and held them to her ears smiling. "Donnie could I-"

"No,"

"Why not?"

"Remember when you borrowed my gold bangles?" Donnie asked.

"What gold bangles?"

"Exactly. Now let me ask you this, if Tommy's lying and just wants me to accompany him to his sister's party then how come he never mentioned the party in his message?" Donnie asked.

Pumpkin sighed and shook her head at her sister from another Mister's naivete. The two met in middle school and due to their mutual crush on Willis from Different Strokes, became best friends. Through the years the older they got, the closer they became, even though they were as different as night and day. Pumpkin avoided higher learning like the plague, had a jacked-up attitude and used sex as a tool to get what she wanted from men. While Donnie was studious, sweet natured and as Pumpkin put it, 'A Bum-magnet,' who always seemed to attract guys who were broke and did the same to her heart. As a result, Pumpkin took it upon herself to prevent her friend from becoming another notch on Tommy's belt.

"He wants you to believe that he misses you. If he said he only needed you to go to this party, then it would show him for the dog he really is. I told you, dating Tommy was a heartache ready to happen. So, c'mon Dee help a sista out. One of my doorknockers got smashed when my daughter sat on it." Pumpkin begged staring at her friend's large gaudy earrings.

"Boil them in Crisco oil to unpucker them. That's what Nelda said she did when the same thing happened to her earrings."

"Now how you expect me to take the advice of somebody who irons dirty jeans and believes grease and water makes your hair curly?" Pumpkin said then spritzed her neck, chest and shoulders with some of Donnie's expensive designer French perfume.

"Ease up gurl! That ain't Jean Nate'." Donnie reminded her.

"I know. You used my discount to get it," Pumpkin reminded her back.

"Any-who getting back to Tommy. I don't know Pumpkin. I mean think about it, all this started because he was being honest. So why would he turn around and be dishonest now?"

"Who knows how his twisted mind works? Tommy is a manipulator. He'll say anything to get you back. But right now, as we speak, two of Brooklyn's most eligible bachelors are waiting downstairs to take us out and spend crazy loot. So forget about Tommy and his small potatoes ass!" She said.

"Pumpkin I make my own money. A man can't buy me anything that I can't buy for myself. Oh, and for the record, Tommy is hardly small potatoes." Donnie said as a matter-a-factly.

"You know I've been meaning to ask you, exactly how much does Tommy make? And how much of it does he spend on you? Pumpkin asked applying a fresh coat of lipstick. "I'm only saying if he don't make dollars, then it don't make sense. Cause like the song goes, you gots to have a J-O-B, if you wanna be with me." Pumpkin laughed.

"A word of advice. If you want a man, get a man. If you want money, get a job Patrice."

"Un-uh! No, you didn't just diss me with my government name!" Pumpkin flinched. "I have a job! O-K?"

"Gurl please. How're you gonna diss somebody when you got two kids, are still living at home with your mama and work as a cashier at Macy's?" Donnie asked causing Pumpkin's chin to hit her trachea. "Now I'm not saying there's anything wrong with that, but you're looking down on Tommy like your name is Shelia E. and you're living the glamorous life, when we both know it's more like the scandalous life." Donnie said bringing her back down to earth while fighting for mirror space to apply some eyeliner.

"Excuse you? A cashier is someone who dropped out of high school to support their baby and rings up groceries at Pathmark. That ain't me. I am in charge of my own fragrance counter and in addition to my salary Calvin Klein pays me a hefty commission. As for my daughters, they're very well taken care of thank you very much!"

Donnie was two seconds from asking Pumpkin if it was like that, then how come she hadn't paid her back the three hundred and fifty dollars she borrowed last month for the girls' tuition yet? And it was no secret that she was swiping cash from her register at Macy's.

"We ain't got time for this. We are supposed to meet Lenny and Ray-Ray." Pumpkin said.

Donnie's expression said she could care less. "I hope this guy is not expecting to get lucky at the end of the night, because if so then I will not hesitate to whip out my American Express card and pay for my own meal." She huffed.

"Whateva'." Pumpkin said with a wave of the hand then went back to fawning over herself in the mirror, "So many men, so few who can afford me.

"I swear you ain't changed since the eighth grade," Donnie shook her head exasperated. It bothered her that her best friend's priorities were so screwed up. Publicly, Pumpkin did mad impetuous things and flirted with everyone she met, but there was so much more to her. If only she would have taken her best friend's advice and learned some type of skill instead of messing around with guys that hustled dope and ran 3-card monte games. Then she would be a more independent woman, able to care for her kids on her own instead of having to depend on not so dependable men. Another thing that bothered Donnie about Pumpkin was the provocative way she dressed. Her breasts were practically spilling out of the porn star in training T-shirt she sported. Donnie wasn't a prude but she did have moral misgivings about letting her stuff hang out and felt a little cleavage, maybe some stomach in the summer, was enough. But Donnie was not about to waste her breath. If the way guys disrespected Pumpkin and verbally demeaned her did not tell her she should rethink what she wore before coming out the house, then nothing she said would.

"Stop bugging-out, Ray-Ray ain't like that. He's a perfect gentleman." Pumpkin said.

"I can tell by his name."

Pumpkin screwed her face up like something smelled bad, "Why you acting all Tom Petty? I swear, try and do a sista a favor and hook her up with a brother with some flava' and she start trippin'!"

"Girlfriend don't eeeven try it. You asked me to do *you* a favor and double date with you and your boyfriend's cousin, let's not forget. I was perfectly content with sitting at home reading a book."

"Okay true dat, true dat. But I only asked because I was tired of seeing Tommy play you."

"Oh so now I'm a charity case? I need you to find me a man?"

"Donnie you know it ain't even like that. Trust me the way guys be clocking you when we go out, I know you do not need me hooking you up. But you're my gurl and I want to see you happy. Is that a crime? So is we still gurls or what?"

Donnie smiled and hugged her friend. "Yeah we're still tight."

"Well let's have our Kodak moment later. Cause I want some sex on the beach until I can't walk straight and I ain't talking about the kind where I wake up with sand on my booty either!" Pumpkin said dancing towards the door.

"Hold up." Donnie said and handed Pumpkin her doorknockers.

Pumpkin smiled and put them on. "So how do I look?"

"Very cute." Donnie said.

Pumpkin sucked her teeth. "Cute? Shoot, I was cute when I was three. I'm fresh to def!"

As Donnie followed Pumpkin out she glanced back at her answering machine smiling. She couldn't wait until her date with 'what's his name' was over so she could come back home and replay Tommy's message.

After working out it occurred to Tommy that he hadn't spoken to his mother in a few days or heard anything about his cousin's progress since dropping him off for that matter. He called Laquita first

167

because he knew once he spoke to his mother he'd be mentally drained and not up for another conversation. His cousin's wife told him that she had gone to see Bug-Out and that he seemed in good spirits. Although he was a bit concerned about his blood tests being late, he had jokes, saying he never was good at taking tests because instead of going to high school, he went to school high. He sent word to Tommy not to worry about him and that the program was letting him out for the party because of his positive attitude. Laquita was proud and bragged, 'They don't let just anybody come home, cause they might slip up and start basing again. So, my baby must be doing good!' Tommy blushed at the best news he heard all day. Next, he dialed his mom.

"Hello?" Carla picked up on the third ring, laughing.

"Hey Mommy-O."

"So my prodigal son remembered to call his mother."

"Aw stop it, I just spoke to you a few days ago."

"I spoke to Nicky."

"Do, tell." he sighed already drained.

"When where you going to tell me about Nicky and you seeing other people?"

"She mentioned that huh?"

"Yes she did."

"Well it's what people do after getting divorced. They move on."

"Don't remind me. To this day I still don't know what really happened between you two that you couldn't work it out, and every time I ask, you both skirt around the topic. In my day you took your vows seriously."

"So, is that why you and Pop never divorced even though you've been apart for all these years? Til death do us part, or whoever kills the other one first?" he joked.

"I'm not laughing."

"Sorry. So, did Nicky also tell you I met her boyfriend? And that he'll be there?"

"She did."

"Yeah well I bet she left out that he's old enough to be her father."

"Actually, she did mention he was a little older."

"A little older? Ha! Dude could be the spokesman for Ben Gay."

"So what about your friend? Is she of a certain age too?"

"Who Donnie? No way. She's just the opposite. Young, vibrant, fine, successful, down to earth. Young. Did I mention she's young? Cause she is."

"Then why haven't I met this perfect young lady yet?"

"I dunno Ma. I just wasn't sure if she was the one, so I figured, why bring her home until I am?" Tommy said wondering who was that Tee-Tee was talking to in the background.

"So how long have you two been seeing each other?"

Tommy could have sworn he heard his father's voice in the background but he wasn't sure if it was the television. But if it was why did it also sound like his mother was trying to unsuccessfully stifle someone? "Huh? Oh, almost a year."

"That's a long time not to be sure of someone. Are you bringing her to Tee-Tee's party?"

"No. Something came up." Tommy said disappointedly.

"Oh. That's a shame. What happened?"

"Mom," he said in a tone he wasn't up for explaining himself.

"Okay. I'll let it go." Carla said. From the tone in her son's voice she could tell whomever Donnie was, she was special to her son and he was hurting.

"You still need me to get that Cabbage Patch doll for Tee-Tee?" Tommy asked.

"No, your father already did."

"Pop?"

"Can you believe it? And on the day before her birthday no less. We-I mean he had to drive all the way to New Jersey to get it." She chuckled nervously.

"Oh really?" Tommy said suspiciously. "It sounds like you have company. Anybody there with you?"

"No, just me and your sister."

"So where is Tee-Tee?"

"Watching television."

"Let me talk to her."

"Why do you want to talk to her?"

"Why do I need a reason to talk to my sister?"

"When she's watching Annie."

"Again? Oh, never mind." Tommy nodded once he realized his sister was watching her most favorite movie in the whole wide world. "So, Ma. I know you were trying to get Nicky and me back together. She told me that you asked if you could have Tee-Tee's party there. Please stop."

Carla sighed. She was hoping Nicky would keep her asking to have the party at her place to herself. But it's not like she asked her to. "You two were meant for each other. I just wanted to remind you, but then I find out that she is seeing someone and you're seeing someone. I should have stayed out of it. Sorry, I just wanted you to be happy. And I believed Nicky was the woman to do it."

"You're a Mom. It's your job." Tommy said forgiving her.

"Are you going to be alright with this new guy there? It sounds like you two didn't get off to a good start."

"We didn't, but if I allowed everyone I didn't get along with to hold me back I wouldn't get very far. Besides, it's Tee-Tee's day and I can put my feelings aside for her."

"You're such a good big brother."

"I try."

"Well let me go. I have to fix dinner. Love you son, bye."

"Love you too Ma." Tommy hung up unsure what just happened. As long as he could remember there had never been one time his mother spoke about his father without having something bad to say.

# Chapter 12

It was Friday. The day of Tee-Tee's birthday party. After calling to wish his sister happy birthday and refusing to tell her what her present was, Tommy threw on some clothes and headed to the neighborhood barbershop Upper Cuts. Coming in out of the cold, Tommy was instantly greeted with a warm reception.

"Yo Tee lemme holla at you," A man in a cipher of young men waved Tommy over and he slapped palms with each of the local cats he knew from 'round the way patiently waiting for a haircut.

"Money Making Mitch. What the deal playa'?" Tommy greeted the tall man in an 8-Ball jacket.

"Maxing and relaxing. Yo Tee do me a solid and help a brother out. I need you to settle a debate between me and this cat Vaughn regarding boxing." he pleaded.

"Ok," Tommy nodded.

"And what makes him an expert on the subject? I mean no disrespect." Vaughn cut in to which Tommy replied with an unbothered 'none taken' shrug.

"Cause fool not only is boxing in his DNA. I've personally seen him put in serious work over at Gleason's gym." Mitch said then turned back to Tommy. "Now Tee, I say Mike Tyson is the toughest and hardest fighter to ever enter the ring. He intimidates his opponents in a way no other fighter does. True he has the height and reach disadvantage but uses it as an advantage and functions like a machine, KO'ing fools in seconds. No other fighter in the history of boxing can go more than five rounds with him. But Vaughn here says he's overrated." the animated overzealous fight fan explained then directed the conversation towards his friend seated across from him.

"Look I agree, Mike Tyson is a very talented and skilled boxer. I just think that there are a lot of other boxers in the heavyweight division who can be considered better than him in the history of the sport. Like Ali. The greatest of all time." Vaughn explained rationally.

"Man, you straight tripping." Mitch argued then spun on Tommy. "Settle this Tee. Who's the greatest heavyweight ever?"

"I mean if we're debating who's the best at the glove game then I'm rolling with Brooklyn's son. Without a doubt Mike's untouchable and unbeatable. His defense is impregnable and his power is unmatched by any boxer past and present. A lot of people think Mike's slow and dances around his opponents with that peek-a-boo style that's the same speed as a middleweight. But in my opinion, there's no point in comparing him to any boxer because he'd win." Tommy rationalized like a fight commentator.

"Even Ali in his prime?" Vaughn countered and Mitch rolled his eyes sighing.

"Hell, Ali said it himself. You can't hit what you can't see. Power punchers like Jack Dempsey were much slower than Mike and almost every heavyweight lacks his explosive power, his iron chin and his unbreakable will… In the ring. Not his personal life mind you, cause if he marries that actress Robin Givens, her new name will be Robbing Tyson." Tommy said getting chuckles. "But if for no other reason the fact alone he holds the record as the youngest boxer to win the heavyweight title at only twenty years old plus he's the first heavyweight boxer to hold and successfully unify the WBC, WBA and IBF makes him the undisputed world heavyweight champion ever."

"I guess when you put it like that." Vaughn said back peddling.

"See told ya! Tommy knows what he's talking about." Mitch said rubbing it in his doubting friend's face. "Yo Tee we gotta hangout sometime man."

"Sounds like a plan." Tommy nodded and kept it moving.

Upper Cuts was long and narrow with eight barber's chairs lined up and in use. In the back the older men hung out playing chess and passing around bottles of Thunderbird and Malt Duck as they reminisced about the good ol' days when they were, young, dumb and full of cum. The ghettotastic wall of fame was covered with posters of the latest and popular hair styles like the Gumby, Caesar and Hi-top fade. In addition, there were Polaroid flicks of local heroes and two handwritten signs. The first read, **'No hair too kinky. No tip too Big!'** and the second reminded people to, **'Be careful of the toes you step on today, because they might be connected to the ass you have to kiss tomorrow.'**

"Have a seat Tee." the shop's owner Mister Randy said to Tommy as he brushed lose hair from his chair then snapped his cape clean. He was thin and tan with a beard and head full of scraggly gray hair that had him looking like Grady from Sanford and Son. "So what'll you have?"

"The usual. An Isaac Hayes and tighten up my goatee." Tommy said removing and hanging his coat, scarf and hat then settling into the barber's chair. He reclined back and closed his eyes as Mister Randy covered him with his cape then went to work.

After lathering Tommy's face and dome then pruning his facial hair to topiary standards, Mister Randy's straight edge razor stopped just short of scalping him and he shook his head. "I don't get you man. Here you got some of the best hair I've ever seen on a black man's head and you go and shave it all off. Meanwhile these boys be putting all types of chemicals and what-not in their hair so it can look half-way good as yours does without even trying."

"You know me Mister Randy. I ain't hardly trying to be no pretty-boy Floyd." Before Tommy became a Trouble Consultant, he used to wear his hair in a curly fade, like Al B. Sure but he lopped it off because he doubted anyone would take an R&B looking brother seriously in the streets.

"Well I will say this in your defense. At least you have the right kind of head for a baldy. Perfectly round and smooth. Not like some of these brothers who shave it off knowing good and well they got dents, lumps, bumps and craters. And then there are the ones with necks that look like a pack of franks,"

"I guess you aren't a fan of the sudden dreadlocks craze either?"

"Man please. Them ain't nothing but naps that grew up." Mister Randy sucked his teeth.

Tommy's father and Mister Randy went way back like car seats, the two sometimes hustled together as kids. One dreamed of owning his own bar, the other a barbershop. Both proved that what the mind conceives, the body can achieve.

When it was time for his very first haircut, Smitty took his son to his oldest and closest friend and he was the only one who's cut it ever since. Over the years Mister Randy watched Tommy grow from a spoiled little momma's boy who had his first sip of beer in the back of his shop, into a strong black man literally and figuratively whose name rang bells on the streets of Brooklyn. And like his father, Mister Randy wished he would choose a safer profession.

"But funny you should say that. Your dad and I were just laughing at all the Jafakins suddenly popping up everywhere." He said shaving Tommy's head.

"Word, my father came by?" Tommy asked.

"He was my first customer today. You should've seen him, he was all excited about your sister's party."

Tommy grinned. "Yeah it's later on today. Will you be there?"

"With bells on."

"Good cause my father made a big ol' jug of pot liquor for you guys." Tommy reported causing Mister Randy to smack his lips practically tasting the strong concoction of collard green juice and other down south secret ingredients that went into the homemade alcohol. "Hey how is Cleveland doing?"

"You know my son. I told that boy, don't go and marry the first woman to give you a piece of tail. Experience life before settling down. You're only twenty-one. Travel, see the world! But nooo, he's gonna tell me he's in love, and I don't know what I'm talking about. Now two kids later, my son wants to go out and chase poo-tang all over Brooklyn like he don't have any responsibilities. And just last night his wife caught him coming out of the short-stay over on Macon Street with another woman. The boy don't think! I mean how in the hell is you gonna cheat on your wife and park your car directly outside of the Goddamn hotel a few blocks from where you live?" Mister Randy asked the room.

"Maybe he wanted to get caught." A barber two seats over reasoned.

"Bullshit! I love my son but he ain't the brightest color in the crayon box. But I gotta give props where props is due. Maggie wasn't having it. She rolled up on my boy like an angry God on judgment day that caught him raping an angel and whooped both they asses! Had that fool running like he was Lionel Richie getting chased by Brenda!" Mister Randy said causing the entire barbershop to erupt with laughter. "So he begged her not to leave him and now they're gonna spend the weekend in the Poconos and try and rekindle what they had that brought them together in the first place. For his sake I hope it works cause he can't move back home with his momma and me. We like walking 'round the house buck ass naked." he said receiving more laughs.

"It'll work Mister Randy. That's why Mister Smitty's doing it." A barber named Gabby said grinning.

"What's that my father's doing?" Tommy asked opening his eyes.

Mister Randy glared at Gabby. "Dammit boy, I swear you got the perfect name, Gabby! Cause you always flapping them big ass soup-coolers! Didn't the man say if his son came by the shop to keep this on the humble?" He asked. Gabby hunched his shoulders and stared at the floor.

"Keep what on the humble? What's going on with my father?" Tommy asked them both. Gabby returned to cutting his customer's hair and began whistling. "Oh, so now you're gonna clam up huh?"

Mister Randy turned to Tommy. "Simmer down, it ain't nothing to get your dander up over. Your Dad came in earlier all worked up cause he's planning on surprising your mom with a trip to New Orleans next week. Obviously, he wanted to tell you himself." He said and cut his eyes over at Gabby.

"Yeah. Obviously." Tommy said looking dazed.

Gabby came over looking pitiful with his big chapped lips all poked out. "Yo Tommy man my bad. It slipped out. Do me a favor and don't let tell Mister Smitty that I told you."

"Don't sweat it Gabby." Tommy said smiling to himself. 'Well I'll be damned. It was him in the background.'

*"Hey Tommy it seems we are playing phone tag, so tag you're it. I'm at work so give me a call-"* As Tommy entered his home he could hear Donnie's voice on his answering machine.

"Move Mayhem! MOVE!" Tommy shouted running like OJ Simpson through the airport in the Hertz commercial, leaping over barbells and piles of clothes spread out like obstacles. His foot tripped over his dog who lazily refused to budge and he banged his knee as he fell against the coffee table and landed on his face. "Man's best friend my ass!" he hissed as she wagged her tail. He grabbed the phone before Donnie could hang up. "Hello? Hello? Donnie you still there?"

"Oh, you are home." Donnie said.

"Yeah, I just walked in from getting a haircut. So, how are you feeling?" He asked getting up and limping over to the bed then collapsing. As he massaged his aching knee it dawned on him that he just flew through his home like a bat out of hell to get the phone like his life depended on it, when he could have easily called her back.

"Like Donna Summer cause they got a sista working hard for the money. So anyway, I got your message and I was thinking about what you said about us still being friends and all."

"And you're just getting back at me?" Tommy asked.

"I was busy." Donnie said reflecting on her lousy double date with Pumpkin. Just like she thought Ray-Ray was a, 'Waste of time Wlllle.' He didn't have a job, money, or ambition and then had the nerve to ask her for her number. And his cousin Lenny was just as bad, with his ghetto jailbird ensemble and uncouth ways. The high point of the night was when she got back in and replayed Tommy's message.

"Oh, Okay." Tommy said.

"So you got your haircut huh?" Donnie asked. She loved how Tommy smelled and how soft his skin felt after he got a shave. She pictured his baldhead rubbing all over her neck and in between her thighs and felt her temperature rise.

"Yeah I needed it. I was starting to look a little shabby." Tommy chuckled as he laid back getting comfortable like he was back in high school mackin' his crush.

"Oh please. **You** look shabby? Impossible." Donnie smiled twirling the phone cord in her fingers while flirting with the man she just called friend. The portable radio on her desk played Earth Angel by New Edition.

Tommy noticed the time and sat up. "Well as much as I'd like to sit here and kick it, I've got to shower, get dressed then run Uptown and grab my sister's gift." He said.

"Oh that's right, today's her party."

"Uh-huh." Tommy said downplaying it.

Donnie smiled from ear to ear thinking, Pumpkin was wrong. Tommy never once mentioned the party. If he wanted to use her to make his ex jealous he would have mentioned it by now. "So, am I still invited?" She asked after a long pause.

Tommy stretched his eyes stunned. He did not expect that. Then again, he did not expect her phone call either. "Huh? I mean, do you still want to go?"

"I would not have asked if I didn't. So am I still invited? …Tommy?" Donnie said after a long silence.

"…I'm nodding my head." He laughed nervously as he gave her the address. "So what time can you get there?"

"Well I get off at three and I want to get a mani-pedi before I go home and change. So expect me around five. That's not too late is it?"

"No-no five's perfect." Tommy said.

"Yeah I'll bet it is." Donnie said slyly.

"Don't start. I really do want to see you." Tommy could hear himself talking but he couldn't believe what he was saying.

"Really? That's sweet. Well let me finish up a few things here and I'll see you then."

"Bet. Oh, Donnie one more thing."

"I know-I know, don't mention your day job."

"Also, around my family Mayhem is May."

"You're weird. But what does that make me?" Donnie giggled and hung up the phone.

Tommy hung up pondering the situation. Was Donnie the yin to his yang? He remembered feeling like this once before and having someone feel that same way about him. It was when he was in love with Nicky. But he couldn't be in love with Donnie, could he?

As he sat on the edge of the bed rubbing his knee pondering, Tommy looked over at his dog. Mayhem was looking out the window with her huge paws rested on the sill. Her long head extended through the gap looking down on the Manhattan skyline.

"What's the matter with me girl? Am I losing it or what?" He asked his best friend. Mayhem came over and wagged her tail receiving a pat. She loved him so much that he sometimes felt unworthy of her worship. He reached over and picked up a box of Milk Bone dog biscuits off the floor and she became excited. He gave her one of the treats and she quickly devoured it. "Damn! Are they that good?" he asked then took another one out the box, sniffed it, and took a tiny nibble. "You know it is kinda good." Tommy said and Mayhem started barking in protest. "Stop being stingy I share my beer with you don't I?" He laughed and decided he would sort out this thing with Donnie later then dialed Nicky's number.

"Hunter residence." Corbin answered.

Tommy laughed. "Yo man why Nicky got you answering the phone on some Mister Belvedere shit?"

"It's a little something I like to call phone etiquette-Nicolette, telephone!" Corbin hissed.

Tommy could hear a lot of people in the background as Nicky asked who was on the phone. Corbin made a snooty sound like he was clearing his throat and handed it over. From Corbin's response she knew immediately who it was.

"Hello Tommy."

"Hey wa'sup, the caterers there?"

"Yes. They're setting up now and the DJ just arrived. Your mother wants to know what time you're going to get here."

"Lemme talk to her."

"You just missed her. She and Tee-Tee went to pick up Nanna and Papa Smurf."

"Oh Okay. So she met Cornball huh?"

Nicky sighed. "Corbin. And yes."

"And?" Tommy asked.

Nicky went into the kitchen dragging the long telephone cord behind her. "And what? You know she wouldn't approve no matter who he is. She wants us back together."

"Yeah well."

"Well nothing. I love your mother don't get me wrong. But it really doesn't matter what she thinks. I'm seeing Corbin and it's as simple as that. And while we're on the subject, you aren't planning on bringing your dog are you?"

"Why?"

"Corbin isn't fond of dogs."

"Hilarious."

"What's so funny? Plenty of people are scared of dogs."

"And their shadows. Anything else I should be informed of?"

"No but why didn't you inform me that your friend isn't coming?"

"Carla?" he said obviously.

"Who else?"

"Hey did somebody pick up the other phone?" Tommy asked suddenly.

Nicky became silent for a moment listening out. "No."

"Oh, because you know how your boyfriend likes to eavesdrop."

"Tommy nobody's eavesdropping. Now tell me about your friend!" Nicky asked slightly agitated.

"You sure he didn't pick up?"

"Tommy!"

"Okay, Okay! Donnie will be coming after all."

"Oh…Is that right?…That's nice." Nicky's voice said but her tone said different.

Tommy didn't expect her to do handstands but he also didn't expect her to be so blasé. It was as if she was happy when she heard Donnie wasn't coming and now she was disappointed that she was. While he pondered over his realization, the phone clicked very lightly as if someone were doing their best to hang up the other line without making a sound.

"Now tell me you ain't hear that." Tommy said.

"I didn't hear anything Tommy." Nicky said.

Corbin suddenly walked into the room dressed in a sharp looking suit. "Are you still on the phone with Tommy?"

"Yeah why?" Nicky asked.

"Please tell him to forgive me if I am a bit too over dressed for his sister's soiree, but I came here straight from a meeting at work. I'll feel just awful if everyone were to compare us based on my tailor-made Brooks Brothers suit versus what he pulls from his closet." He laughed and walked back out the room. After that Nicky was convinced Corbin was not permanent. In fact, she wanted to tell him he could leave but she needed someone on her arm when Tommy's new *friend* showed up.

Tommy sucked his teeth. After the last time Nicky put him in his place about Corbin and his ego he decided to keep his comments to himself, besides she'd see it for herself eventually. "Well anyway, when my mom gets back tell her that I will be there in an hour, aight. Later!" Tommy said and hung up. As he passed the punching bag he tagged it with a solid right hook sending vibrations through the floor and sprinkling sand on the floor. He went over to his closet mumbling under his breath and pulled out two garment bags and a shoebox then placed them on his bed. Mayhem came over wagging her tail to see what he was up to. "So Cornball wants to battle who's got the freshest vines? Somebody should'a warned him!" Tommy said with a devilish grin.

## Chapter 13

Less than one minute old, Tatiana Strong was wonderful, precious and made from love. Her first word was 'Remarkable'. Her mother read somewhere that babies should be taught to say words that have at least three or four syllables. So at night Carla would stand over her daughter's bassinet and say, 're-mar-ka-ble', 'be-au-ti-ful' and 'mag-ni-fi-cent'. It was the portent of things to come.

Carla loved both her children tremendously and was equally proud of them both, but it was frustrating to have to fight with her son tooth and nail to get him to turn off the TV and pick up a book. Fortunately, she didn't have that problem with her daughter Tatiana, 'Tee-Tee' for short. Tee-Tee loved school and was always winning some type of academic award or certificate for her achievements. As she and Tommy got older their conflicting attitudes towards higher learning resulted in matches of sibling rivalry but no matter how many dictionary sized words Tee-Tee threw at her brother, when it was all said and done he had the option of going to see his girlfriend Nicky or hanging out with his friends. Alas she did not have that luxury because her intense study habits made her a social leper.

At school Tee-Tee was the one who annoyed her fellow students when she asked for extra-credit homework assignments, aced all her tests, won science fairs and spent all her free time in the library. Guys never approached her because regardless of how beautiful she was all she ever talked about were topics school related. Girls were either jealous of her beauty or thought she was too nerdy to hang with. Even though the other kids avoided her like the plague Tee-Tee didn't care what they thought about her. Her idea of fun was reading about far and distant lands or figuring out complicated mathematical equations, not jumping up and down in miniskirts and shaking pom-poms while acting dizzy whenever pimply faced-boys with a mouth full of train-tracks walked by. In fact, none of the boys at Canarsie High School interested her. Then her attitude changed that fateful day her teacher introduced the new kid, Lance Cooley to her class and her books before boys theory, went out the window.

Lance moved from Philadelphia to Brooklyn in the middle of the semester and within his first week made more friends than Tatiana had during her entire academic career. Cooler than Shaft and dreamier than Billy Dee Williams, he was tall, muscular and handsome with smooth ebony skin and a perfect ivory smile. A sharp dresser and natural born comedian, Lance could sing and dance like he was signed to Motown and was a threat on the basketball court. Everyone liked him even the teachers and Principal. All the girls were fighting for his attention and the hip guys welcomed him into the fold right off the back. But what made Lance stand out from all the other popular kids was that he was smart. Real smart. And the fact he could be accepted in their exclusive world and still get straight 'A's' gave the nerds hope.

Tee-Tee had a major crush on Lance but did not think she had a snowballs chance in hell with all the fashionistas mimicking Pam Grier's provocative style in hopes he would notice. Then one day while she was walking home someone called her name. She turned around and it was Lance, looking as dapper as ever. At first she thought there must be someone standing behind her with the same name until he came over and began speaking. He asked if he could carry her books and walk her home. When she noticed all the jealous-faces looking appalled, she held her head high and graciously accepted. By the time they reached her front step they had a date planned for that Friday evening. It turned out that although Lance liked hanging out with the popular kids when it came to dating he preferred his girlfriend to have brains as well as beauty. Tatiana had both.

All weeklong all Tee-Tee could think about was her date on Friday with Lance. During the week he had come by the house for dinner and met with her parents. After standing strong against the intimidating glares and intense grilling from her overprotective father and brother and holding an intelligent conversation with her mother, her parents agreed, Lance was the perfect gentleman to take their daughter out on her first date. Even Tommy had to admit he was cool.

Friday or as she excitedly referred to it Fri-yay, finally came and Carla, assisted by Tommy's girlfriend Nicky, helped Tee-Tee out with her hair and make-up. The past week had been extra stressful for Carla who in addition to having to accept her baby girl was growing up also had put her differences aside with her children's father so he could come by and meet with Lance and give his daughter a proper sending off into the wonderful world of teen dating. Downstairs the Strong men informed Lance that they were entrusting him with the most important sixteen-year old on the planet and if he stepped out of line there was no place he could hide from them. Lance respectively assured them that they had nothing to worry about because he was and would remain a perfect gentleman.

Tee-Tee cleared her throat and asked her father and brother to stop interrogating her date. All three men stood and Smitty instantly whipped out his Polaroid OneStep camera and began flashing away. It was the first time Tommy did not have any wise cracks to say about his little sister. She was a vision of beauty. Adorned in her Mother's heart shaped locket and a dress Cinderella would be envious of, Tatiana was a vision of beauty. Lance felt like the luckiest guy in the world. He promised his date's family that he would have their precious cargo home by eleven sharp and they left arm in arm.

As they approached the bus stop Lance led Tee-Tee past it and towards a sleek royal-blue Thunderbird parked across the street. He told her that since this was such a special night he snuck his father's car keys out of his coat while he was on the couch counting sheep. Tee-Tee was not sure this was such a good idea, but Lance assured her that he had been swiping his father's car since he was a kid and was an excellent driver. She still was not convinced then Lance flashed his sexy convincing smile. After that Tee-Tee was adjusting the passenger seat to accommodate her petite frame. But still unable to shake that bad feeling.

The night was what every first date should be. Fun, exciting and memorable. They went bowling, shared a personal pizza, then drove out to Jones beach and walked along the shore holding hands. It was definitely worthy of a few pages in her diary. The night was going so well and they seemed so compatible that Lance suddenly turned to Tee-Tee and asked if she would be his steady. Without hesitation she said yes and they sealed it with a long passionate kiss. It was Tee-Tee's first kiss and when she squeezed her eyes shut she could see fireworks just like on the tv show Love American Style.

Lance glanced down at his watch and his jaw dropped. He only had fifteen minutes to get Tee-Tee home. They rushed to his car and he sped off trying to beat the clock. He was not about to start things off on the wrong foot with the parents of his brand new girlfriend! Then in the blink of an eye promise turned to tragedy. The light up ahead was turning red, there was no way he'd make it, if he was in any other car besides a Thunderbird that is. Lance winked at his girlfriend then shifted gears slammed his foot on the gas and darted ahead. By the time they realized they were in the path of an oncoming sixteen-wheeler there wasn't anything either driver could do about it. The truck rammed into the driver's side with a magnificent force that sent Lance and Tee-Tee flipping out of control. By the time the paramedics arrived the Thunderbird was demolished, Lance was dead and Tee-Tee was in a coma. The news hit her family like the impact of two trucks colliding head-on.

Weeks turned to months and Tatiana Strong still lay dormant in her hospital bed hooked up to all types of machinery. Her family visited her round the clock and prayed constantly for her to awake from her deep sleep. Then one day her eyes miraculously opened and she sat up. At first everyone was excited their prayers were finally answered until she spoke and then they realized the bright gifted young woman with her whole life ahead of her was gone forever.

As a result of the crash Tatiana obtained irreparable and permanent brain damage and for a long time she was unable to present her thoughts coherently or even clothed in words that aptly conveyed their meaning. It wasn't easy but everyone pulled together and adjusted to the new, younger-behaving, tantrum-throwing Tee-Tee. Some days were easier than others were, but all were tough. Home attendants came by every day to work with Tee-Tee and she had to relearn basic skills like using utensils and tying her shoelaces on her own. Some times when Carla watched her daughter struggling to use a knife and fork she thought about the surgeon she could have been and would burst into tears. Smitty dealt with his pain by showering his daughter with all the toys and anything else she wanted. Losing his baby sister had a profound effect on Tommy. But he refused to give grief the satisfaction of ripping him apart and instead went with the flow. Sometimes he would read her 'Flat Stanley, Curious George and the Man with the Yellow Hat' or 'Snowy Day' by Ezra Jack Keats doing all the different voices. She loved when he did that and no matter what, he loved her...

Sister Sledge appropriately sang 'We are family' as countless friends and family members celebrated Tee-Tee's twenty-fifth birthday. Nana and Grandpa Smurf cuddled in the love seat feeling no pain as they sipped rum and coke. Cousin Marie and her latest boyfriend Dennis chased behind her twins Desiree and Destiny. Olivia used any and every opportunity to show off her engagement ring and her Doctor fiancé Hector. Guy, recently released from juvey felt like a kid in a candy store as he gorged himself on food and drinks. Lil' Dee pushed the furniture out of the way and entertained everyone with his break dancing and pop-locking skills. Cameron walked around with his petite redheaded white fiancé who looked like the girl from Small Wonder on his arm grinning like he struck gold. Aunt Mary, Aunt

Cookie and Carla were joking and laughing and Smitty stood in a huddle with some of his old buddies drinking pot liquor. Every now and then he and Carla would steal doting glances at each other from across the room giving family members something to whisper about. Nicky had forgotten how much she missed Tee-Tee and was catching up on lost time. Off to the side Corbin stood with his nose turned up like everyone had some life threatening disease and he was worried he might catch it.

Carla came over to where Nicky and Tee-Tee were playing Connect Four and kissed her ex-daughter in law on the cheek. "I can't thank you enough for allowing my baby to have her party here.

"Oh Mommy. I'm not a little baby no more." Tee-Tee fussed and crammed a fistful of Pop-rocks into her mouth.

"Whatever you say baby." Carla smiled then turned to Nicky. "Everything's wonderful! I tell you, it feels so good to get this many black folk together under one roof without it being a funeral."

"Amen to that Miss Pinkney." Nicky said. She envied how big and close Tommy's family was and since her own family was spread out over the states and spoke only on holidays she enjoyed having a house full of down-home warm black folks.

"Connect four!" Tee-Tee yelled and began clapping and pointing at the row of red checkers.

Carla shot Nicky an odd look. "Nicky as long as I've known you, you've called me Ma. Now just cause you two lost your minds and split up don't mean you have to stop. So you keep on calling me Ma okay?" She said sternly.

Nicky nodded and smiled. Carla had been there so many times for her in the past when her own mother hadn't that she loved her like she was a second mother. "Yes Ma'am. I mean Ma."

Carla smiled, "That's more like it. Now what's taking Tommy so long to get here?"

"He should've been here by now." Nicky said wondering the same thing herself.

"Y'all looking for Tommy?" Guy asked down on one knee cleaning his sneaker with a toothbrush. He was big, brown and built like the Chicago Bears running back William 'The Refrigerator' Perry. "Yes. You spoke to him?" Carla asked.

"Yeah, my bad Auntie Cee, I forgot to tell you. I was coming out the bathroom when the phone rang and answered it. He said to tell y'all that he's running late cause he had to make a stop and pick up Tee-Tee's gift."

"Cousin Guy, what'd my brother get me?" Tee-Tee asked excitedly.

"Dunno Half-Pint, he ain't say." Guy shrugged his shoulders.

"Now why did Tommy wait to the last minute to get her gift? I swear that son of mines." Carla sighed then noticed Corbin standing in the back being antisocial. "Nicky, I know I said I'd mind my business about you and Tommy's personal lives, but this new guy you're dating. I don't know. He takes himself way too seriously. Look at him standing there, like he's too good for us common black folks. He's so full of himself he needs to hang a cup outside of his ass just to catch the excess."

Nicky had to chuckle at that one. Corbin was being an extra jerk today and she was embarrassed. She felt like going over and telling him to go but she decided she would wait until the party was over and everyone had left.

"So who's this girl that Tommy's seeing?" Nicky asked.

"Her name is Donnie." Carla said.

"Donnie and Marie!" Tee-Tee giggled and began singing, 'I'm a little bit Country, I'm a little bit Rock and Roll.'

"Have you met her?" Nicky asked.

"No I just found out about her. But she can't be all that If Tommy never mentioned her before." Carla said encouragingly.

Nicky nodded staring off into space. "You still like Tommy?" Tee-Tee asked.

Nicky was caught off guard while thinking about him. She turned to Tee-Tee. "Of course I still like your brother honey."

"No! I mean do you still like-like him?" Tee-Tee pressed.

"Oh Tee-Tee go ask your father to dance." Carla said as The Stylistics 'You're A Big Girl Now,' played. Tee-Tee jumped up and excitedly ran over to her father. Carla watched smiling proudly as Tee-Tee snuck up behind her father and put her hands over his eyes then laughed out loud as he pretended not to know who it was.

Nicky watched Carla watching Smitty and Tee-Tee dance proudly. "You still love Smitty don't you?" She asked.

Carla turned to Nicky and grinned slyly. "I could ask you the same question about my son."

"This was a nice turn out." Nicky said quickly changing the subject.

"Umm-hmm", Carla replied twitched her lips but let it go. Nicky did not have to answer. She could see with her own eyes that Nicky was still interested in her son. Carla was confident things would work themselves out. Besides, if Donnie was half as much of a dud as Corbin was then perhaps he and Donnie would hit it off and Tommy and Nicky would get back together.

On the other side of the spacious living room, Corbin went over to make a plate of food. Guy was working on his third plate of lemon chicken and Swedish meatballs. He wiped his hand on his sweater then offered it to Corbin.

"Guy Forde." He said graciously.

Corbin placed a napkin in his hands before shaking Guy's hand. "Corbin Ramses the third."

"Nice little get together huh?" Guy asked dancing in place while piling more food sky-high onto his plate.

"I suppose." Corbin answered rolling his eyes like it pained him to answer.

"And great job with the food my brother. These fancy little meatballs are the bomb. But why am I telling you for? You already know." he said popping one in his mouth.

"Actually, I wouldn't know because I'm vegan."

"I tried that but they told me I can't eat pussy so I said fuck that shit!" Gus said laughing and held his palm up for Corbin to slap it. "Up-top."

Corbin left him hanging with a vile expression and was confused as to why the raunchy guest was complimenting him for something he had absolutely nothing to do with. Nicky walked up smiling and gave Guy a kiss on the cheek. After she made him promise that he was not going back to juvenile detention she continued to the kitchen never once acknowledging Corbin. He caught the cold shoulder treatment and wondered what that was all about then assumed she was also upset about all of these intruding freeloaders roaming her home. That was enough to piss anyone off.

"Man, I hope Tommy and Nicky get back together."

"Pardon me?" Corbin said.

"Oh sorry, just wishing out loud about my cousin Tommy and Nicky, the fine sister that I was just talking to. They used to be a couple back in the day. Jesse and Angie ain't got jack on them. And I was hoping they get back together."

"Well I do not see that happening ever. Especially since Nicolette and I are involved!" Corbin snapped.

"Hold up. Wait a minute. You? And Nicky? Git the fuck outta here! Dude, I thought you were like the head caterer or something." Guy burst into laughter. Corbin found nothing amusing. "I mean no disrespect buddy, but there's more chemistry in the dirt on the bottom of my Adidas than there is between you two." he said unable to contain himself, to which Corbin replied by angrily slamming his plate down and stormed off into the kitchen.

Nicky was admiring Tee-Tee's birthday cake with some of the actual caterers. It was a delicious work of art. Three fluffy layers of delicious mouth-watering strawberry cake with a crème filling, covered with creamy vanilla frosting. 'Happy Birthday Tee-Tee' was spelled out across the top in candy letters and a smiling miniature Strawberry-Shortcake cake doll topper made the image complete. And then Corbin entered.

"Nicolette why wasn't I informed that criminals would be attending this party?" Corbin asked sucking the life out of the room. The caterers traded looks and took it as their cue to leave.

Nicky calmly counted backwards from five before speaking. "Lower your voice! And calm down. I'm trying to enjoy myself. I haven't seen a lot of these people in a while."

"And I can think of several reasons why. In fact, I was just talking to one of your charming guests who had the audacity to mistake me for a caterer. Me a caterer? Perish the thought."

Nicky shook her head and walked back into the living room. Corbin followed her out like a stray cat and was about to ask what was wrong when the doorbell rang.

"That'd better be my son." Carla said eyeing her watch.

"I'll get it." Nicky said rolling her eyes at Corbin then headed for the door. He observed her briefly checking herself in the hanging mirror before unlocking the door and made a mental note then stormed upstairs. Nicky opened the door and her big bright smile dropped at the appearance of a beautiful freckled faced woman smiling and holding a gift-wrapped package. "Yes?" Nicky asked.

"Hello, I hope I'm at the right place. You're Nicky right?" The woman asked.

"Yes I am." Nicky nodded.

"Hi my name is Donnie. I'm a friend of Tommy's. He invited me."

"Oh...sure come on in." Nicky said. She was a bit taken back at how beautiful Donnie was.

"Di-zamn!" Guy said loudly as Donnie removed her jacket. She was wearing a beautiful silk dress that accentuated her curvy svelte figure in a classy not trashy way.

"Put your eyes back in your head Guy. This is Tommy's friend." Nicky said taking Donnie's jacket.

"And why am I not surprised?"

"Hi, Donnie Campbell, pleased to meet you." She said to Guy.

"The pleasure is all mines." Guy said kissing the back of her hand. "Real talk, when I grow up, I wanna be like Tommy!" he said drooling.

"You mean you're still growing?" Carla teased stepping forward and patting her nephew's stomach. "Hello, I'm Carla Tommy's mother."

"Oh, I'm Donnie pleased to meet you." Donnie said leaning in for a hug.

"Oh, you're a hugger. Ok." Smiling uncomfortably, Carla pulled back from the brief embrace and hated to admit she was impressed with Donnie's appearance. She was pretty, smelled nice and from her style of dress accustomed to the best.

"So, where's Tommy?" Donnie asked.

"He had to make a stop and pick up his sister's gift." Nicky informed her.

Tee-Tee suddenly came flying around the corner with her cousins chasing behind her. "I heard the bell! Is that Tommy? Is my big brother here yet?" She asked hopeful.

"No not yet honey." Carla said.

"So this must be the birthday girl. Hello Tee-Tee. My name is Donnie. I'm a friend of your brother's." Donnie said smiling.

"Oh hello." Tee-Tec said bashfully. "You're pretty." she said.

"Why thank you. You're pretty too. And I just love your hair." Donnie said causing Tee-Tee to blush.

"My Mommy and me went to the beauty salon this morning. And then we got our nails painted see?" Tee-Tee said showing off her bright pink nail polish.

"Wow they look nice." Donnie said then turned to Nicky. "Nicky your home is beautifully decorated."

"Thank you." Nicky smiled. Donnie was so nice and pleasant she was making it extremely hard to dislike her.

The DJ put on Eric B. and Rakim's 'I Ain't No Joke!' just as the door rang.

"Now that's Tommy!" Both Nicky and Donnie said simultaneously then stared at each other awkwardly and quickly laughed it off.

Carla raised an eyebrow and reminded herself she promised her son she would not meddle in his personal affairs. No matter how hard it was.

"I got it, I got it!" Tee-Tec yelled excitedly running to the door. She snatched it open and squealed with delight as her brother's dog barged in and showered her with sloppy kisses.

"What about me baby sis? Don't I get a kiss too?"

With Rakim singing his theme song, Tommy's entrance was too cool for words. He was sharp as a tack. Dressed to perfection in a cream leather trench coat, double-breasted black Armani suit and cream turtleneck that fit his strut like it was painted on. His dark alligator shoes shined like they were still breathing and the gold and Onyx pinky ring plus matching Rolex glistened tastefully. The diamond stud in his left ear rounded off the ensemble nicely. There was no denying it, Tommy Strong was, 'No Joke!' With one arm he lifted his sister into the air and the other held a garment bag and a six-pack of Guinness Stout. Both Nicky and Donnie sighed secretly wishing it was them being squeezed by Tommy's strong arms.

"Tommy-Tommy-Tommy!" Tee-Tee shouted repeatedly and hugged him back. She was ecstatic to see her big brother and it was evident how close the siblings' bond was.

"Happy birthday day baby sis." Tommy said then noticed both Donnie and his ex-wife hungrily staring him down like a Big Mac on the Fat Boys' tour bus. He bowed his head in their direction then respectively walked over to his mother and kissed her first. "Hey Mommy-O."

"Don't hey Mommy me. Weren't you supposed to be here earlier?" Carla started in on him.

"Sorry about that but it was out of my control. For real. The guy I commissioned to make Brat's gift wasn't done until today. But wait til' you see it. Trust me it was worth the wait." Tommy explained holding up the garment bag while conveniently leaving out the part about making a quick stop at the bogus candy store on the corner of Fulton and St. James for some Bud before picking up her gift. He hugged Donnie and whispered "I'm happy you're here" in her ear causing her to blush and Nicky to wince.

Nicky cleared her throat. "Hello Tommy."

"Hey Nicky," Tommy said leaning in for a brief awkward hug from his ex-wife.

"So, I see you brought your dog." she said kneeling down to receive a sloppy kiss from her.

"Yeah about that I didn't think you'd mind. You remember how she hates to be left alone."

"Didn't mind?" Nicky cut her eyes at him, "What I do remember is us discussing that-"

"So, have you guys met Donnie?" Tommy spoke up. Nicky cut her eyes at Tommy for rudely cutting her off in mid-sentence.

"Well we have, but your father hasn't because she just got here a few minutes before you." Carla said.

"Oh word? Yo Pop! C'mere a sec." Tommy shouted across the crowded room.

Smitty excused himself from playing Spades with his buddies and came over and hugged his son. "Young pup."

"Old dog." Tommy grinned.

So who do we have here?" Smitty asked eyeing Donnie's long shapely legs, but feeling the heat from Carla's glare, he quickly averted his eyes and cleared his throat.

"Pop this is Donnie. Donnie this is my dear old Dad, Smitty."
Tommy introduced.

"Tommy, you didn't tell me how handsome your father is."
Donnie complimented, causing Nicky to roll her eyes. "Nice to meet
you Mister Strong,"

"Why thank you young lady and you can call me Smitty."

"Okay, Smitty." Donnie smiled.

"Hey where's Bug-Out at?" Tommy asked looking around.

"He hasn't shown up yet." Nicky said pretending not to be
irked by her ex.

"Yeah but he is still coming right?" Tommy asked anxious to
see how his cousin was doing since being in rehab.

"As far as I know he is." Nicky said feeling the need to remove
herself. "Why don't you give me your things so you can introduce your
date to your family." She said taking his sister's birthday present and
placing it amongst the huge pile of gifts, then headed into the kitchen
with his beer.

"Oh, okay thanks. Well Donnie let me introduce you to the rest
of my family." Tommy said and took Donnie around to meet his
grandparents, extended family and everyone else in attendance. As he
was making the rounds Corbin was coming down the stairs and spotted
him then came over.

"Armani huh? Decent quality, for off of the rack." Corbin said
blatantly.

Tommy glared then turned to Donnie who was wondering why
the old guy with major attitude was trying to diss him as fine as he
looked in his suit. "Donnie this is-"

"Corbin Ramses. I'm Nicolette's suitor, pleased to meet you."
Corbin addressed Donnie speaking up before Tommy could get off a
cheap shot at his name. He then eyed Tommy. "Your friend is quite
stunning. You're a lucky man...As am I," and with a scowl he stormed
off into the kitchen.

"Did I hear correct, that's your ex-wife's new man?" Donnie asked.

"Boggles the mind don't it?" Tommy asked.

"No comment. But I will say this much, he sure doesn't like you. Or your suit. While I'm extremely fond of both." She flirted.

"And that's all that matters." Tommy winked then spotted his dog playing with his sister and some of his younger cousins across the room. "C'mere girl." He said patting his thighs and throwing a kiss in the air to get her attention as she obediently trotted over. "Go get daddy a beer."

Faithfully she went off to answer her master's bidding as he watched grinning devilishly.

"What are you up to?" Donnie asked.

"Who me?"

"Yes you. You've got this look in your eyes,"

"What kind of look?" Tommy smiled like the Grinch.

"Like you're plotting something diabolical. I'm curious, has Corbin ever met Mayhe-" Tommy cleared his throat as a reminder. "Oh right, May. Has he met May before?"

"You mean before today? Nope!"

"Tommy!"

"What? I just want a cold brew." Tommy said innocently as his dog pushed the kitchen door open and went inside. "Baby count along with me. Five-four-three-two-"

Suddenly on cue a loud scream came from the kitchen then Corbin came flying out in a frightened panic shouting. "OH MY GOD!" Nicolette! In your kitchen! A-dog. A HUGE-dog!" Corbin said over spasmodic breaths holding his arms apart to over exaggerate May's size. At the same time, she came out the kitchen carrying Tommy's beer in her sharp teeth beer clueless. When he saw the gentle giant, he screamed again and ran behind Nicky like a frightened child.

"What's wrong Cupcake? Don't tell me you're scared of my little ol' puppy dog?" Tommy asked cracking open his Guinness and patting her for a job well done.

The room became deafly quiet then a man dressed in a loud plaid suit spoke up, "Maybe he's a cat person. Meow." and burst into laughter along with everyone in the room.

"You have the maturity of a zygote!" Corbin said to Tommy and stormed off.

Tommy shrugged like whatever as Nicky stormed over. "Seriously?" she said.

"Hey he started, all I did was finish." Tommy said.

"And you told me you weren't going to bring her." Nicky complained pointing at his dog but Tommy could swear she was pointing at Donnie.

"I never said that." he smiled and took a sip of beer.

"No but you implied it. All these years and you still haven't grown up." Nicky snapped then briefly cut her eyes at Donnie before going after Corbin.

Tommy smiled and continued drinking when Guy popped up from out of nowhere and shouted, "Tee-ski in the place to be!" with outstretched arms.

"Look who it is. So how was license plate camp?" Tommy asked embracing him.

"Oh you got jokes huh?"

Tommy laughed and turned to make the introductions. "Guy, I'd like for you to meet-"

"Oh I already know who **this** is. What I wanna know is do she got a sister?" Guy asked eyeing Donnie.

"Yes, but she also has taste." Tommy wise-cracked.

"Hardy-har-har," Guy said then leaned in close and threw an arm around his cousin. "Yo I heard what you did for cousin Bug-Out. I think that was really top choice."

"That's what family does for each other." Tommy said bumping fists with his cousin.

Tommy cut his eyes across the room at an almond complexioned woman in her early fifties conversing with a group of people. "Aunt Cookie's still mad at you."

Guy sucked his teeth, "Yeah man, I don't know why she be tripping."

"Maybe it's because she's embarrassed when people ask where her son is and tells them that you're away at Penn State, when in actuality your ass is really in the State Penn." Tommy scolded.

"Whatever. It was only Spofford. Not Sing-Sing." Guy said watching his mother across the room. By the sad look on his face it was evident he missed their relationship.

"Go on over there and talk to her." Tommy said.

"I don't know. She's still pissed about me getting caught with the Lo-Lives." Guy shrugged.

"I must really be out of the loop. What are the Lo-Lives?" Donnie asked.

"They're this gang of juvenile delinquents that run into department stores, snatch entire racks of Polo clothing, then bolt." Tommy explained. "Everybody gets away but this one here, who claims he stopped all that mess."

"Word is bond Tee, I did stop boosting Tee. But I needed to cop this dope ass Polo sweater for a Def-jam concert I was going to later that night and I ain't trying to spend money on the white man's clothes like no Herb." Guy explained trying to sound tough but came off sounding like a fool.

"So, you steal them instead and wind up in the white man's jail? And you wonder why your mother is fed up? Boy if you don't take your Bookman having buffalo-butt ass on over there and beg for your mother's forgiveness I swear I'll-" Tommy threatened raising his hand like he was going to backhand his younger cousin.

"Okay-okay! No need to get physical. I'm going." Guy said then nervously dragged his feet over to his mother. She looked at him upset then gave in and held her son. Tommy smiled at the scene.

"Well cut my legs off and call me shorty! If it ain't my favorite nu-nu-nephew!" said the man who called Corbin a cat person, as he walked up cradling a tall can of Schaefer, grinning like he hadn't a care in the world.

"Hey Uncle Booze." Tommy said embracing him then quickly turned his head after catching a whiff of his intoxicating breath.

"Now I gots'ta give it to you nephew, when it comes to stylin' you don't play. That is a baaad out-fit! Ron O'Neal ain't got nothing on you. But your uncle don't play either. Dig my new threads." Uncle Booze said holding out his arms and turning to model a loud colorful outfit that was an LSD trip on material. "Now is your Uncle also a bad dresser or what?"

"Oh yeah Uncle Booze, it looks…pretty bad." Tommy fronted with a plastic smile.

"See that's why you was always my favorite nephew. You got taste. Now your cousin Guy wouldn't know taste if it bit him on his ass. He's gonna tell me I look like a low-budget Huggy Bear but I told him, don't hate the playa, hate the game." Booze said cracking himself up then emptied his beer in one sip.

Tommy laughed at his Uncle's antics. "So I see you didn't waste no time getting your drink on."

"You know me youngster. I gots'ta have my nerve medicine." Uncle Booze said then raised his brow when he turned to Donnie. "Man O' Manishevitz! Who is this vision of beauty sent from the heavens up above?"

"Simmer down Uncle Booze, this is my friend Donnie. Donnie this is my Uncle Sheldon. My mother's brother." He leaned in to Donnie and whispered on the sly, "But for obvious reasons we call him Uncle Booze."

Before Donnie could ask what obvious reasons? The strong smell of alcohol coming off of Booze's breath punched her in the nose and she stepped back holding out her hand. "Nice to meet you."

"The pleasure's all mines. Man Tommy, I needs to hang out with you boy. Yes siree! Cause this one here is as fine as a square of butter on a warm corn muffin. Hot and yellow!"

"Um thanks...I think." Donnie said.

"You're welcome Sugar."

"So how're the ladies treating you Uncle Booze?" Tommy asked.

Uncle Booze shook his head pitifully, "I never did do good in relationships. My ol' lady gonna tell me she's thinking about leaving her husband. I told her if you leave your husband, then we're through!"

"You're too much," Tommy said as he and Donnie cracked up at his uncle's foolishness.

"Now if you'll excuse me, I see a sweet young thang that look like she could use a sip of Booze." Uncle Booze said eyeing an attractive woman across the room.

"Careful you're not as young as you used to be." Tommy teased.

"And you know what I got to say to that? A man is a young as the women he feels." Uncle Booze said and danced off.

Soon after, Tommy was approached by countless other relatives to pose for photos with and listen to old stories of when he was yay-high. Ever the gentleman, Tommy listened quietly, thoughtfully scratching his head in an effort to remember his family lineage. In the mix of things, he turned to Donnie who was gazing at him through wide infatuated eyes.

"My family. The Huxtable's we ain't," Tommy joked.

"I think your family is great." Donnie said. Watching him interact with his family made him more attractive than all the times she had seen him flexing without his shirt on.

The door rang and no one seemed to hear it so Tommy got up from his Nana and Grampa Smurf's side to answer it. On the way he noticed his father whisper something in his mother's ear that was so funny she almost spilled her drink. It was sort of weird to see them behaving like a young couple in love and he was not sure why it was happening but he was grateful it was. He unlocked the door and Laquita came in carrying AJ. She looked a bit haggard leaning in for a kiss then stepped aside for Bug-Out to come through. Tommy had been anxiously waiting all night to see his cousin so he could tell him how proud he was of his progress, but when Bug-Out walked in he was taken back by his emaciated appearance.

"Hey man how you doing?" Bug-Out asked smiling.

Tommy was speechless. Bug-Out was thinner than he had ever seen him before. "I'm chilling man." He said moving and speaking like the effort may do him in.

"What, no love?" Bug-Out asked with wide arms.

Tommy leaned in and hugged him. The depth of their bond was evident from the water that they both fought back in their eyes.

"Damn this party is all the way live!" Bug-Out said waving to family and friends as he removed his coat.

Tee-Tee came running up and threw her arms around Bug-Out so forcefully she almost tackled him to the floor and he looked embarrassed at his lack of strength.

"Tee-Tee let the man take his coat off and get settled in before being a brat." Tommy said.

"How rude!" Tee-Tee said then stuck out her tongue. "Guess what? Tommy's got a new girlfriend and she's real pretty!"

Tommy shook his head at his sister for having a bigmouth but was glad the spotlight was removed from his cousin.

"And she's here? That's kinda weird ain't it?" Laquita asked.

"Nah, besides Nicky's new boyfriend is here too." Tommy said.

"Where?" Bug-Out asked.

"There," Tommy said pointing at Corbin out looking sour across the room.

"Where?" Bug-Out asked again.

"Right there."

"Quit playing. Not the grumpy looking old dude? You can't be serious," Bug-Out asked surprised.

"As a heart attack!" Tommy said just as stunned.

"Talk about things that make you go hmmm." Laquita commented.

"Damn all that. I wanna meet your girl cause knowing you playboy, I'll bet she's bad and not bad meaning bad, but bad meaning good." Bug-Out sad nudging his cousin in the ribs.

"I am standing right here." Laquita reminded him.

"Just messing wit you sugar pie." Bug-Out said and kissed her.

Tommy introduced Donnie to Bug-Out and Laquita and Bug-Out admitted on the down low that his cousin's new lady was just about as fine as you can get without crossing over into cosmic regions.

James Brown's, 'Sex Machine' made people put their drinks down, grab the closest arm and hit the dance floor. It was a sight to see Smitty and Carla doing the bump as they hammed it up for the crowd and cameras flashed like paparazzi to get proof of the monumental moment in case it was denied later. Uncle Booze pulled Donnie on the dance floor and made up names for bogus dance moves like 'Reeling in the fish' and 'The frog in heat' as he shouted, "Watch out there now! Girl you don't know nuthin 'bout dis here!"

Guy started a Soul Train line when New Edition's 'Candy Girl' came on and began pop locking like Rerun down the center. The DJ kept the flow going with an eclectic mix of old and new hits by artists; The Sugar Hill Gang, Eric B. and Rakim, DJ Jazzy Fresh and The Fresh Prince, Marvin Gaye, Run DMC, Big Daddy Kane, Salt N' Pepa, Whitney Houston, Kool and the Gang, Earth Wind and Fire, Kurtis Blow, The Commodores, Public Enemy and many others. Tommy and Tee-Tee boogied to Cyndi Lauper's, 'Girls Just Want to

Have Fun' as the family chanted, 'Go Tee-Tee! It's your birthday!' and she jumped about thoroughly enjoying her party.

After the song ended Tommy came over to where Donnie and Nicky were standing.

"This party is da bomb!" Tommy said wiping sweat from his forehead.

"Yes, it is going rather well. Tee-Tee's enjoying herself." Nicky agreed watching the birthday girl across the room.

The infectious beat of Levert's, 'Casanova', came on as Corbin walked up.

"Come on Corbin let's dance." Nicky asked.

Corbin darted his eyes around at people dancing and looked nervous. "Um I'd like to but I have this really bad cramp." He said stooping over.

"That time of the month?" Tommy laughed then turned to Donnie and led her to the middle of the room and danced close enough to be Siamese twins.

Corbin asked Nicky a question but she was angry with him for making her look bad by not dancing that she ignored him. This pissed him off and he stormed off into the kitchen. A few minutes later Guy was rubbing his belly, starving like Marvin for some more of those delicious little meatballs. The hot trays were empty so he poked his head in the kitchen. What he saw made his mouth drop and eyes bulge. He slapped his hand over his mouth so he wouldn't burst into laughter and felt somebody had to see this and waved everybody over.

People came over to see what had Guy about to pee on himself and peeked inside. There standing in the middle of the kitchen with his back to the door was Corbin trying to mimic Tommy's smooth soulful dance moves. But instead of mimicking Tommy he looked like he was having a seizure as he flailed his arms about minus any rhythm. Nicky came over to see what was going on as Corbin attempted to perform the Snake and banged his head against a cabinet.

"Looking good Mister Kotter." Guy said unable to contain himself any longer and burst out laughing. Corbin spun around shock-faced.

When the rhythmless black man saw that he had an audience he felt like Fred Flintstone shrinking from embarrassment. Tommy made eye contact with him and shook his head then headed back into the living room.

"What was going on in there?" Donnie asked.

"Nothing important. Trust me." Tommy smiled and led her back to the dance floor in time to slow dance to 'Lady In Red' by Chris De Berg

"I'm really glad I came." Donnie admitted.

"Just now? While we were dancing? I know I'm good, but damn!" Tommy smiled as Donnie shook her head at his foolishness. "Look Dee I know you think that I only wanted you to come today so that I could have a date. And I admit in the beginning it kinda was the reason I asked. But, I don't know, after you left upset the other day it made me realize that you were right. True this may have started out as a method of connivance for two people with hectic lives who like to have sex without any strings, but it has become so much more than that. I also realized something else."

"And that is?" Donnie asked hanging on to every word.

"That I have strong feelings for you." Tommy said then twirled and dipped her.

Donnie looked up at Tommy and felt butterflies in her stomach. "Don't say it if you don't mean it."

With the back of his hand Tommy gently brushed Donnie's cheek. "That's why I won't just yet. It's like I have these feelings inside but I want to express them to you in the right way."

Donnie nodded but she was a little disappointed. It wasn't like she expected him to drop to one knee in front of everyone and propose. She was not even ready for that. But it would have been nice for him to say those three words she longed to hear. Still she was grateful he was not attempting to toy with her emotions. "Well you know how I feel Tommy. But don't expect me to wait forever." Donnie said. She had convinced herself while getting dressed to come to Tee-Tee's party that no matter what she was not going to allow herself to be hurt by Tommy again and if it meant that today was the last time she would ever see him, then so be it.

"I know." Tommy whispered staring deep into her eyes at her soul. He could actually see the love this woman had for him and he felt honored yet undeserving at the same time.

Carla came over. "Hi, can I borrow my son for a minute?"

"Of course." Donnie smiled feeling uneasy around her.

As mother and son walked off Donnie sighed inwardly, "God, either I'm really naïve, or really self-destructive." She glanced across the room taking in the party and caught Nicky staring at her. The awkward moment ended when Nicky immediately went into the kitchen. "Great."

"So, what do you think Ma?" Tommy asked anxiously. "Isn't she great?"

"She seems very nice Tommy." Carla replied nonchalantly.

"Ma. Nice ain't a word. It's an insult. Donnie is a dime piece. In fact, she's a Susan B. Anthony!" Tommy insisted trying to persuade his mom to see what he saw in the beautiful woman.

"Tommy what do you want me to say? I only met the young lady an hour ago. And if memory serves, didn't you say she wasn't even coming and that you were no longer seeing her?"

"Well yeah, true. But we're good now."

"Exactly why I don't go by first impressions. Shoot I didn't even warm up to Nicky when I first met her and now look at us." Carla replied.

Tommy rolled his eyes and sighed. "Why don't you say what's really on your mind Ma. She's not Nicky right?"

"Well truth be told, I've known Nicky for a long time. I've come to love her like a daughter." Carla reasoned.

Tommy shook his head a little disappointedly. Regardless of how old he was, it was still nice to get his parents approval. "Well Pop likes her."

"Yeah well all your father sees is a pretty face. Plus she stroked his ego. You men eat that stuff up."

"What's up with you two anyway? You seem awfully chummy." Tommy asked changing the topic.

"Later. Right now it's time for your sister's cake."

"Yeah. But you're not off the hook that easy young lady. We'll discuss this later." Tommy teased kissing his mother on the cheek then went into the kitchen.

Corbin and Nicky were trading angry words and when Tommy entered they stopped. Corbin highly upset, brushed by Tommy and stormed out. As the door closed behind him Tommy heard Uncle Booze announce, "That's five y'all, drink up!"

"Yo Nicky, Uncle Booze started a drinking game on how many times your man storms out of a room," Tommy laughed.

"Great. At this rate we'll have to drive everybody home." Nicky rolled her eyes and pulled out a book of matches and a pack of Virginia Slims.

"You're smoking now?" Tommy asked surprised. She was such a health nut when they were married that he could not believe she smoked. Nicky shrugged and took a drag. "Since when? How long?"

"Only a few months?" Nicky said then blew a cloud like an old pro. "What's the big deal? You smoke cigarettes and weed."

"Yeah but you called it a nasty habit and said you would never smoke cancer sticks."

"That was then, this is now!" Nicky snapped.

"O-K." Tommy could see she was tense and dropped the subject. He began to light the candles.

Nicky shook her head with a grin. "Sorry I should not have blown up at you."

"It's cool." Tommy waved, already over it. "You and he alright?" he asked gesturing at the door Corbin walked out of.

"All things considered…relatively speaking…from an objective point of view…in the context of the moment…" Nicky stopped beating around the bush when Tommy shot her a look that he was not buying it. "Aw who am I fooling? Stevie Wonder can see Corbin and I aren't exactly happy." She finally admitted.

"So I take it he's not the one?" Tommy asked.

"Hmph! He's not the one, two, three, four, or five!"

Tommy quietly stroked his goatee. This was obviously one of those situations where he was supposed to listen but not comment. Nicky stared at the flickering candles for a long moment before speaking. Outside in the living room she could hear Whitney Houston singing 'Where do broken hearts Go?' and it made her feel even worse.

"I remember it like it was yesterday when all those people out there were my in-laws."

It sounded to Tommy like Nicky regretted getting a divorce but he was not about to assume anything.

"You know why I took up smoking?" she asked. Tommy shook his head clueless. "Because I needed something to take my mind off of being lonely. Not to mention lack of sex."

"Hold up, wait a minute, you mean you and he aren't? You two've never? You're saying that you and Joe College don't-" Tommy asked uncomfortably finally using X-rated hand gestures to say what his mouth wouldn't.

Nicky rested against the refrigerator. "Let's just say it ain't happening. So now I smoke or do extra work with the after school workshops to keep busy."

"Sorry to hear that." Tommy lied.

"Don't be. The kids are benefiting and the extra money allowed me to remodel my kitchen."

"That's nice and all but it's not what I meant." Tommy said.

"Yeah-I know." Nicky said looking riddled with self-doubt as all her youthful features started to sag like air being let out of a balloon. "Corbin's nice but I never was really into him. I was lonely after we divorced and well, he seemed like a change-"

"From me?" Tommy asked.

Nicky shrugged. "So Donnie seems nice." she said tired of hearing about her life.

"Yeah she's cool." Tommy smiled the way he used to smile when he thought about her and it bothered her.

"But I had no idea you were into 'Not-Quites.'"

"Huh?"

"As in Not-Quite-Black."

"Oh cut it out, Donnie's black."

"Please that girl is light bright and damn near white."

"I know you're not trying to say that I'm dating Donnie because she's light skinned." Tommy asked. Nicky did not answer, but her actions all pointed to yes. "That's ludicrous! You and I were high school sweethearts. Married for years. For that matter I can argue that the reason you are dating your man is because he is educated and has seen the world, unlike myself."

Nicky sighed. "So does Donnie know about what you do?"

"It's how I met her."

Nicky looked surprised. "Oh really? And she's Okay with that?" Tommy nodded giggling like a little boy being asked about his girlfriend. "So, I take it she's the one?" she asked pointedly.

Tommy thought about her question. *Was Donnie the one?* His behavior as of lately pointed to yes. But when he looked at Nicky standing there in the kitchen looking as delicious as the icing she was licking off of her fingers while informing him how sexually deprived she was, old feelings resurfaced and he smiled.

"What's so funny?" Nicky asked.

"Nothing. It's just that you're accusing me of having a thing for redbones, and…here I am in the mood for some chocolate love." Tommy said licking his full lips. LL Cool J style.

Nicky came over and hugged him while grinding her pelvis against his crotch causing his nature to rise. Tommy wondered what the hell he was doing when he felt his arms circle her waist and squeeze her tightly. Her shoulders slumped and she let out a sigh as his large hands traveled down to her firm ass and squeezed. Nicky pulled away and gently caressed his face then planted a wet kiss on his lips and looked at him with a hungry look in her big brown eyes. Both were close to the point of knocking everything off the table and doing it right there.

Bug-Out suddenly stuck his head in the door. "Yo Aunt Carla wanna know how long it takes to light the…candles-Oh snap!" Both Tommy and Nicky jumped back, busted. Bug-Out's thin face outlined a sly grin. "I'll-um tell 'em you need a couple minutes more." He winked and closed the door behind him.

Tommy and Nicky stood before each other feeling as awkward as their first date.

"Um, you know what?-I'ma uh, finish lighting these candles!" Tommy stuttered.

"Yes, you do that." Nicky said smiling uncomfortably and put some distance between them.

Tommy felt stupid. What was he thinking? He wanted to know. And what if his mother or worse Donnie had walked into the kitchen? What then? Only moments ago, he assured his girlfriend that she had nothing to fear and here he was standing beside his ex-wife with a huge boner.

"We'd um better take the cake out now." Nicky said.

"Give me a minute." Tommy said as he thought about baseball and anything else to lower his boner.

Out in the living room Carla rounded up everyone as Smitty got his oversized video camera ready. Tommy walked out of the kitchen with Nicky carrying Tee-Tee's cake and placed it before her as the family sang along with Stevie Wonder's 'Happy Birthday to You'.

Tee-Tee shut her eyes and mouthed her wish then blew out her candles. Everyone applauded then presented her with her gifts.

Tee-tee made out like a bandit. She received a pair of Kerbangers, a large Black Barbie styling head, an E-Z bake oven, a talking Teddy Ruxpin, a Monchhichi, Lite Brite, an Etch-A-Sketch, a big bag filled with her favorite candy and birthday cards stuffed with money. Her father gave her an engraved charm bracelet. She squealed with joy, when she tore open the African American Cabbage Patch doll her mother eventually found at the last minute. Nicky gave her a collection of picture books to help strengthen her reading skills and Donnie gave her a beautiful handmade African Princess doll with long braids dressed in a dashiki she found in a quaint little store in Harlem and Tee-Tee loved both. With all the attention heaped upon her the birthday girl was very gracious.

Tommy knew that no one was going to give his sister the kind of gift that a young lady her age should receive and took it upon himself. He proudly presented her with a flyy denim jacket with leather sleeves that had her name and portrait beautifully spray painted on the back. He had it made by Dapper Dan, the legendary Harlem clothier who created one-of-a-kind gangster chic garments. His client list included everyone from the young capitalists rich from the crack trade to famous entertainers and sports figures. It was also where Tommy got a lot of his custom made stylish outfits as well. Out of all her gifts Tee-Tee loved it the most. When she slipped into it and modeled it for everyone Tommy knew he made the right decision and he felt good when he saw her almost behaving like a normal young lady with a clothes fetish.

As it started to get late people began to head out and Tommy's parents asked him to walk them outside. He told Donnie he would be right back and left her chatting with Laquita and playing with AJ. Thanks to Gabby's inability to keep a secret he already knew that they were planning a trip to New Orleans, and keeping his word, he planned to act surprised. He figured they'd invite him along since the four of them had never did anything together as a family when he was a kid.

The winter air was sharp and Tommy wished he had have worn a hat. They got to his mother's minivan and he and his father loaded Tee-Tee's gifts inside. Tee-Tee thanked her brother again for her jacket then got inside and rummaged through her stash until she found her Cabbage Patch doll. Tommy sighed. For a brief moment he hoped she would remain an adult.

"So you've noticed by now that your father and I are working on getting back together." Carla said suddenly.

"Yeah, I thought something was going on." Tommy said.

"Well we did not want to say anything to you until we were sure it would work. But for the past week that I've been staying with your mother and sister it has been pure bliss." Smitty said.

"A week?" Tommy said shocked. He knew they were speaking but he had no idea about this. "So that's why you kept Tee-Tee from me. Afraid she would blab."

Smitty and Carla looked at each other with love in their eyes. "Like your father said. We just wanted to make sure it would work." Carla said.

"And we are." Smitty added.

Tommy nodded. "Yeah, well I guess better late than never."

"Speaking of which. So, your mother and I were thinking. Back when we got married we never really had an official honeymoon, because we were officially broke. So, we decided to do something spontaneous and go to New Orleans to renew our vows." Smitty said. When his son didn't respond he and Carla traded worried looks. "Everything OK son?"

"Yeah," Tommy nodded. "But I'm not gonna lie, it's a lot to take in. I mean for as long as I can remember, the two of you have been at each other's throats with my sister and me stuck in the middle. And now you're all lovey-dovey. It's weird."

"We figured you'd be happy to finally see us getting along." Carla said.

"And I am. It's just gonna take some getting used to. Lemme ask you something, you happy Ma?"

Carla looked at the father of her children like a smitten teenager and nodded. "I am."

"That's all I need to know. So, this trip. When and for how long?"

"Only for a week and we'd leave this Sunday."

"That is spontaneous. And it doesn't give me much time but I guess I can move some things around. Donnie can stop by to check on my dog. So yeah, cool. I can meet you down there by the middle of the week." Tommy reasoned.

"Son you're not invited," Smitty said flatly.

Tommy felt like a needle scratching a record. "Ouch. Don't want a third wheel huh? Got it. Although with Tee-Tee you kinda' will have one." He joked.

Smitty and Carla looked at each other nervously then at their son. "Tatiana's not invited either." Carla replied.

"Huh?" Tommy looked confused at his parents. "Sooo, who's going to watch her?"

"Son we really need your help in order for this to work out. And you know nobody can handle or tend to her needs like us...Or you." Smitty explained.

Tommy was slack-jawed and slowly turned to Tee-Tee as she poured a pack of Pop-rocks onto her tongue and giggled as they snap, crackled and popped in her mouth. He felt light headed and turned to his parents with a worried look.

"But..." Tommy said.

"Now I know it is a huge responsibility but I don't trust anyone else. Besides I figured you'd want to spend some time with your sister. You hardly see her as it is." Carla said.

"But..." Tommy said.

Smitty put his hand on his son's shoulder. "Son I know it is a big inconvenience on your life but it's only a week and it would give your mother and me an opportunity to make up for a lot of time we weren't together. So what do you say?"

"But..."

Carla turned to Smitty with a sad look. "Maybe we are rushing things. I mean you're closing up your bar and I'm taking off from work, when I think about it we may be going a bit too fast."

"Yeah, I suppose." Smitty said sounding disappointed.

Tommy watched his parents put on a brave front. It was obvious that they were really looking forward to spending some time alone together. What was he thinking about? There was no way they could have brought Tee-Tee along if they were going to recapture what they once had before she was born. Before he was born. Even though they were not together they gave him a far better childhood than a lot of kids that grew up in two parent households. Alonzo Junior was proof of that! If they were just now beginning to get along, who was he to prevent that? Watching Tee-Tee for a week would not be so bad. He looked over at her as she picked her nose and wiped it on her new jacket then swallowed hard and uttered the words he couldn't take back. "Okay, I'll do it."

"Are you sure?" Carla asked excitedly.

"Yeah sure why not? It'll be fun, in fact let me tell her," He said and rapped on Tee-Tee's window and she rolled it down. "Hey brat, Mommy-O and Pop are going away on a trip next week so how's about you come stay with me while they're gone?"

Tee-Tee lit up like the Rockefeller Christmas tree. "Yaaaaay!"

Tommy turned back to his parents. "It's official. Now you have to go."

Carla hugged her son. "Thank you honey. Wait a minute. What about your job?"

Smitty cleared his throat. "No fret my pet. When he came to see me the other night at the club our son informed me how he's so tight with his boss he makes his own hours. Ain't that right son?"

"Sure Pop. I make my own hours." Tommy smiled shaking his head.

Carla detected there was something behind those coded looks but was too happy about her trip to ask. "Great, then I have to go home and pack. I have a million things to do between now and Sunday. Honey are you coming with me?" she asked Smitty.

"No, you go on back to the house Sweetness. I want to hang out with my son a little more. I'll get a ride." Smitty said.

"Okay Tommy. I'll see you on Sunday and thank you again."

"My pleasure Ma." Tommy said.

Carla kissed her son and husband then got in her minivan and pulled off leaving Tommy and his father standing on the sidewalk. After she was gone Tommy cut an eye at his father with a chuckle, "Sweetness?"

"She's my weakness." He smiled unapologetically.

"Damn Pop, Mom's got you smiling like a blind singer." Tommy teased swaying like Stevie Wonder.

"Where are you parked wise guy?" Smitty asked. Tommy motioned to his Jeep Cherokee up the block and they walked to it. Inside Tommy put on the heat and found an oldies station his father would like.

"So where we headed." Tommy asked.

"I'll get one of the fellas to drop me off. I wanted to talk to you right quick."

"Okay what's on your mind?"

Smitty pulled a silver flask out of his coat pocket and two plastic cups then poured some brandy out and handed one to Tommy. "Here's to the Strong men, may we live each day like our last and live each night like our first." he said and brought his cup to his son's.

"I'll drink to that," Tommy said then took a sip, smacked his lips and enjoyed the moment. This was what it was all about. Building with his father over drinks and bridging the gap between them. "So Pop, what's the deal? You've got to tell me, how in the hell did you pull this off with Ma. Cause it's tripping me out." He admitted.

Smitty chuckled and rubbed his chin. "I know you're expecting some wild story but to be honest, I just got to thinking about how upset your mom has been with me for all these years. Only speaking to me when necessary and when possible sending messages through you. I felt it was time to make amends. So I took your advice."

"What advice?"

"When you said if she won't listen to me then I should write her a letter."

"You didn't?"

"Look I know you weren't serious when you said it. But I figured, what have I got to lose? So that night after I closed up the club, I poured myself a drink and wrote her a long letter apologizing for all the shit I put her through. You know; taking her for granted, not being there for her, everything and mailed it to her. I guess she was ready to put the past, in the past and move on too because after she read it she called me and said, that's all I ever wanted to hear. Then in a bold move I asked her out to dinner. I took her to City Island and sitting across from her I took a deep breath and started off by saying, 'I don't know if the word sorry means anything coming from me but it's something I feel every day for what I did. I was young and stupid and I am sorry. She agreed it had been a long time and she accepted my apology and afterwards we went back to her apartment and had a long talk. We realized that we never stopped loving each other. Then one thing lead to another. Feelings were rekindled. A bottle of wine. Some Marvin Gaye, and the next thing you know we were-"

"I get the idea Pop. And for the record, no matter how old a guy gets, he never wants to picture the image of his parents doing-the vertical limbo." Tommy said with a frown.

"Point taken." Smitty smiled.

"So that was your secret weapon? Saying sorry?" Tommy asked stunned. The way his mother seemed to despise his father he figured it would take at least a diamond tennis bracelet to get her to even meet with him. Then on second thought his mother could not be bought. "So you mean to tell me that if you had just admitted you messed up, the two of you could have been chilling a long time ago."

"No I doubt that. I think some time needed to pass."

"To this day I still don't know the full story of what went down with you two. All I remember is you and Ma yelling and that's when you..." he paused and continued. "Then me and Tee-Tee moving in with Nana and eventually our own place. I remember Ma crying a lot too." Tommy's voice cracked and he looked his father directly in the eyes. "I was a little kid. I ain't need to see that"

"I know. Back then I was a different person. A selfish person. The way I saw it, as long as I gave your mother money and my kids had a roof over their heads and food on the table then I was living up to my part of the bargain. I didn't understand what family life and nurturing was all about. I was young with my own successful nightclub. All I wanted to do was have a good time. I loved you kids and your mother, I just wasn't ready for being a committed husband and parent. I felt like I was trapped. So I did anything but be a man." Smitty paused for a minute as the old memories he had pushed to the back of his mind resurfaced. He hoped after he explained to his son what happened that he would not hate him. "The first time your mother caught me messing around you were pretty young and your sister was a baby. I had hired this girl Brenda, to bartend and started sleeping with her. Your mother busted us and made me fire her and promise I would never do it again. Call it women's intuition, but a month later your mother sensed something wasn't right so one day she followed me."

"And were you still cheating?" Tommy asked.

Smitty couldn't answer and looked away, "We argued. I lost my cool...and hit her. I looked down and there you were standing there, shocked." Tommy winced and emptied his cup recalling the memory he'd put out of his mind like it was happening all over again. "Most women would've had my ass locked up. And I would have deserved it. But not your mother. She had too much integrity and class for all that and instead said to hell with me took her kids and went on with her life. Enrolled in college. Got her Masters. Started teaching. Got a life. Even started dating. In fact, whatever happened to that guy your mother was seeing for a while? I think he was an electrician."

"Who Lonnie?" Tommy chuckled at the mention of his name. "Homeboy made a big mistake and tried to put Ma in her place, boss her around. It was the first time I ever saw a grown man cry."

Smitty chuckled to himself. "I tell ya' son, I pray this trip works."

Tommy nodded in agreement, "Yeah, about that. I need to say something. Now Pop you know I love and respect you even if you've made mistakes when I was growing up."

"Uh oh, I feel a but coming on." Smitty said and poured himself another drink.

"That's because there is one." Tommy informed his dad, "But that's my mother. The woman who gave birth to me. Raised me and my sister practically on her own. Was there for us when you weren't. I guess what I'm trying to say is, if you hurt her again-it's you and me." He turned his head so as not to see his father's expression but meant it none the less.

Smitty faced his son. A small part of him felt insulted but a greater part felt proud. He nodded understanding fully. "I respect that son and from the bottom of my heart all I have is love for you mother. I really want this to work between us."

"Well okay then." Tommy said and shook his father's hand.

"You know I apologized to your mother, but I never apologized to you."

"It's all good." Tommy dismissed it.

"No, it's not. I'm sorry son. I'm sorry for hurting your mother. I'm sorry for hurting you and your sister. I'm sorry for everything. Can you forgive me?"

Tommy sighed and stared at his father's outstretched hand. Then after a moment he shook his hand and embraced him. Smitty caught a tear with his thumb and smiled proudly at the man his boy had become. "That's my boy. So tell me, what's the story with you and this new girl?"

"I don't know. Everything was going great. Then she had to go and complicate things by throwing feelings into the game. I mean shit, the only feelings we were supposed to share was when we busted a nut together."

Smitty chuckled. "So that's what you kids are calling it now-a-days? Busting a nut? Listen son you can't expect a woman to remain a

217

roll in the hay forever. Eventually she's going to want to know where it's heading."

"Love," Tommy muttered shaking his head and sipped his drink. "She doesn't even know what my favorite color is, but yet she's in love."

"Son I think she knows what your favorite color is. I think everybody knows."

"That's funny. But the weird thing is that after I told her I may still have feelings for Nicky and she stormed out, I automatically started missing her. And I got to be honest, it wasn't just the sex. I honestly missed **her**." Tommy said, like even though it was happening to him, he couldn't believe it. "After my divorce I won't lie, there was a stretch where I did my share of hoeing around. Then I met Donnie and things changed. I changed. I actually enjoyed waking up next to her and having breakfast. Chilling. Prior to her I'd flip through my little black book and pick a random name. And when what's her name complained that I didn't take her out to dinner after we got it on, I tossed her a candy bar and would tell her it was nice knowing her."

"Damn son. That's some cold shit." Smitty raised his eyebrows.

"I dunno Pop. They say confession's good for the soul, but if you ask me, it's lousy for relationships." Tommy said sounding frustrated.

Smitty poured out some more liquor into their cups. "Sounds to me like it's more than just sex with you and Donnie. Besides I thought that Nicky was happy with this older uppity cat."

"Yeah I thought so too but then tonight Nicky sends me these mixed messages and tells me how they aren't happy and suddenly I'm thinking with my second brain, back to wanting her."

"I saw you and Donnie out there dancing and personally I don't think you want Nicky back." Smitty said as a matter of factly.

"So, I should stick with Donnie?"

"No-I didn't say that."

"So, Nicky's the one?"

"I didn't say that either son. But your mother probably would. She's loves Nicky. Even I've grown fond of her after all these years. She's a good woman."

"Then what are you saying Pop?" Tommy asked confused.

"What do I know?" Smitty cleared his throat and shrugged like he owed no one an explanation. "Shit-I'm a lucky son-of-a-bitch who's fortunate enough to get a second chance to do things right with my soulmate. But since you feel the need to hear some of your old man's worldly advice I will say this, son do whatever it takes to ensure that you don't wind up gray and alone because as much as we all fantasize about living the bachelor life it pales in comparison to a full-time relationship."

Tommy turned to his father with an understanding nod and a simple smile. "This is more stressful than being a Trouble Consultant!"

"I'm glad you brought that up. Now son, I hope I don't have to tell you that what you do for a living is on hiatus until your mother and I return from our trip and pick up your sister. I'm saying this because earlier you mentioned that you pick and choose your own hours and I was wondering if that meant you planned on going out after she was asleep. You are aware that Tee-Tee needs a lot of supervision?"

"Come on Pop, I would never work while Tee-Tee was staying with me."

"Good. Maybe the time off will give you the opportunity to think about changing career paths."

Tommy twitched his lips. "I did, when I walked away from construction."

"You didn't have to do that. Or this. You had options. Still do. You just refuse to accept them."

"No, I just refuse to accept a handout from my folks and instead stand on my own two feet."

Smitty sighed. He couldn't even get mad seeing as how his son inherited his stubborn and prideful genes. "Bottom line. You can't run the streets forever. And I know if you gave it a chance, you'd enjoy running a night club solely."

Tommy looked at his father awkwardly. "Running the club solely? Pop, you thinking about retiring?"

"Hell to the no! Smitty's is as much a part of me as-as-"

"As your name?" Tommy asked coyly.

"Exactly, but what I was thinking is maybe opening up a second spot. We'd go half on the cost, but you could run it."

"Me run a nightclub?" Tommy said with a doubtful look. Just listening to the words come out of his own mouth sounded like bad idea.

"Why not? You said it yourself, you aren't the college type and where else could you make the kind of money you're making now busting heads on the streets? Smitty's caters to people who are too old for hip-hop and too young to sit around watching TV. A second nightclub would be ideal. I looked into it. There's a huge audience not being served and not a single place in all of Brooklyn for them to go. So every weekend these kids pile into their daddy's car and go to the lower east side to party. Now think about all that cash that you could be getting with your own place."

"A second club huh? Brooklyn's own black version of Studio 54?"

"Minus the drugs and weird shit. But yes."

"What would you call it? Smitty Junior?"

"It'd be your place son so you would name it whatever you want. But, I'd put a little more effort into it." Smitty said.

Tommy shook his head indecisively. This was not something he could just say yes to without giving it considerable consideration. "I'm not saying it's a bad idea but why me? You've been doing this since forever. You know the business inside out."

"Why? Because you're my kid. Besides, I don't know today's youth. You do. And trust me anyone can learn the club business. Hell, I did it without a high school diploma and I know more than my own

220

accountants do about facts and figures, or Joe College when it comes to running a business. That's why I understand what you meant when you said depending on what type of degree you have, all it is a high-priced piece of toilet paper. When you and your sister were kids all I wanted was for the two of you to have the opportunities and experiences that I did not, which is why I stressed going to college. But then she had the accident and..." Smitty took a swig of liquor and pushed his daughter's catastrophe out of his mind. He looked over at his son and grinned proudly. "I remember the day when your mother told me she was pregnant with you. I was working at the pool hall on Kingston Avenue and she called and told me she had just come from the doctor's office. And that the rabbit died. I was like, 'Okay, I'm gonna call you right back.' It took me about fifteen minutes to get back to her cause I had to let it sink in that I was going to be a father. Man I was shitting bricks. I remember being in the room and watching your birth. It was amazing. You could feel it in the room that a new life was being born. When the nurse placed you in my arms, I was like, 'Wow! This is my seed. My boy. I guess the reason I'm saying all this stuff is because I worry about you out there on the streets getting into all kinds of danger and what could happen. I know your name rings bells but to me, you're just an older version of the same little boy who couldn't sleep without a nightlight."

"Hey don't tell people that." Tommy said.

Smitty chuckled. "Son you may find this strange coming from me because of the hell I give you about what you do for a living, but I admire anybody who refuses charity, stands on their own two feet like a man and won't take anybody's crap. Problem is these fools coming up today are plum crazy! Don't you get scared?" Smitty asked his son wholeheartedly.

Tommy made a smug faced and shook his head. "Not at all, since I'm the one doing the scaring."

"Just because I admire something doesn't necessarily mean I agree with it either. Hell, I think Felix Mitchell and Nicky Barnes are some bad motherfuckers, as was Bumpy Johnson but on the same token I don't agree with their lifestyles either. Son I constantly worry about you. You're my only boy. The one who has to carry on my name when I am gone. What's the point of having a legacy if I can't leave it to my kid?" Smitty said. Word about his son's battles often reached his club before his son did and he felt physically ill and helpless when he heard them. He loved his son more than life itself and if something ever happened to him he did not know what he would do.

"C'mon Pop. You know I hate it when you talk about dying. And please don't start reminding me about life insurance policies and burial plots again."

"Oh, so you can put your life on the line every day and I am supposed to be okay with that but the mere mention of me passing upsets you?" Tommy rolled his eyes and sighed. The discussion was ruining his buzz. "I've heard stories about you getting shot at and almost killed and played it cool. I don't know how you do it. You've been lucky, but son luck doesn't last forever."

"Pop, I'm good at what I do. You can't make it in my line of work on luck." Tommy winked cockily.

Smitty shook his head at his son's audacious attitude. "You're a grown man Tommy. You got all the answers. I can't force you to follow my advice. But I hope you at least listen to it."

"Aight Pop. But I will say this, it's nice to have choices."

Smitty unlocked his door. "Well when it comes to choices, you can either go left, or do what's right. Dig what I'm saying?"

Tommy nodded scratching his head. His Pop was always fond of trite maxims. "Yeah I dig what you're saying."

"Good because regardless of how good you are, you can't do this forever. And if your luck did run out, I don't have to mention what it would do to your mother do I? Especially when she doesn't' even know." Smitty asked. Tommy shook his head and sighed. "Son learn from the mistakes of others because you can't live long enough to make them all yourself." Tommy half-smiled and shook his head like he got what his father was trying to say. "I'll see you Sunday." Smitty said and went across the street to catch a ride with one of his buddies

When Tommy walked back into the house more guests were preparing to leave. Guy was putting on his coat and Nicky was wrapping up plates of food. The caterers and DJ were finishing cleaning and packing up. After paying them plus giving them huge tips for a job well done he spotted Corbin angrily staring at his dog across the room then storm into the kitchen.

"Uh-oh there he go! Wait, I lost count. How many times is that?" Uncle Booze asked tipsy then emptied his shot glass with a shrug.

Tommy shook his head at his Uncle's foolishness when his Nana came up behind him and took his hand. "Baby, this was a nice get-together you and your mama threw." She had a cherub face with shimmering gray hair and the more his mother matured, Tommy could see how she would look when and if he ever made her a grandmother.

"Thanks Nana." Tommy smiled. "Say, you and Papa Smurf need me to drive you home?"

"No that's alright baby like we told your mother, we're gonna stop by and visit some friends of ours who live nearby. But what you can do is look after your cousin Alonzo. That boy's so thin. I declare it look like he got the sugar."

"Okay Nana I'll look out for him,"

"Good, now you go and sit with your beautiful lady friend. We had the nicest talk while you was helping your parents take Tatiana's things to the car."

"Boy if I was you I'd pitch a tent with that one." Tommy's grandfather said nudging him in the ribs. His full white beard and lop-sided blue applejack hat earned him the nickname 'Papa Smurf'.

"Oh yeah Papa Smurf, and why's that?" Tommy smiled.

"Elementary my boy. The way she looks at you. Reminds me how your grandmother used to look at me when we was kids."

"What do you mean used to?" Nana demanded and pinched her husband of fifty-three years on the behind.

Tommy laughed as a cab pulled up outside the window and honked. He saw his grandparents to the door, kissed his Nana and promised he would call more often. He hoped when he reached their age that not only would he be as energetic but have someone to be energetic with as well.

Uncle Booze stumbled over and zipped up his loud outdated jacket then handed his nephew an empty beer can. "Smashing shindig nephew. We must do this again sometime." he said then let out a cross between a burp and hic-up.

"You're not driving are you Unc? Cause I can call you a cab or take you somewhere myself." Tommy asked concerned.

"Don't worry yourself nephew I'm in good hands. Now you get back to that buttered muffin of yours…" he said as an older attractive woman Tommy recognized as the owner of the catering service for his sister's party walked up putting on her coat. "And I'll get back to mines."

"You ready Sheldon? I'm parked around the corner." she asked. Uncle Booze rattled a pack of Tic-Tacs then brought it to his mouth and tossed it back like it was a shot of liquor. He winked at his favorite nephew and the pair left.

Tommy shook his head impressed as a pair of hands covered his eyes followed by the sweet smell of perfume. "Guess who?" Donnie asked.

"Janet Jackson? Vanity?"

"You wish." Donnie laughed. AJ was standing beside her looking up at her with an infatuated sugary smile as he snacked on Fun-Dip candy. "I think someone has a crush on me." she gestured down.

Tommy kneeled before his pint-sized cousin. "Hey little man, you trying to take my date?"

AJ laughed and nodded his head. "Yup. She's pretty ain't she?"

Tommy looked up at Donnie and frowned, "Eh, she's aight."

Donnie cut her eyes at him slyly. "Oh really? And I was going to follow you back to your place tonight. But since I'm just aight maybe I should just go-"

"Sike! I was just playing." Tommy said quickly as Laquita laughed at him clean it up. "So Quita where's Bug-Out at?"

Laquita wrinkled up her face like it had just occurred to her that her husband was missing. "He was here a minute ago."

224

"Cousin Tommy, Daddy went outside." AJ said and went back to gazing at Donnie.

"Thanks shorty. Now I'm going outside to see your daddy and while I'm gone don't steal my date got it?"

"Got it." AJ blushed.

Tommy rose to his feet smiling and faced Donnie. "Oh so suddenly I'm your date?" she asked with an arched eyebrow.

"Oh yeah, that and more." Tommy said leaning in and gently pecked her on the lips before strolling outside. As he walked out Donnie and Laquita both exhaled.

"Girl you is so lucky! Now don't get me wrong I love my man to death, but Tommy got it going on wit his fine self. Nicky must've been smoking some brand new shit to have traded in his sexy fine ass for that whack guy she's with now. I don't know what she was thinking 'bout anyway, cause you know old men give you worms." Laquita laughed.

"You are wrong gurl, you know you are." Donnie said unable to stop giggling and when they turned around Nicky was standing there holding wrapped up slices of cake.

Laquita and Donnie looked at each other with 'Oh shit' written across their faces unsure of what to say. Nicky feeling equally awkward said, "Cake anyone?"

"Oh um, thanks." Donnie said.

# Chapter 14

Tommy spotted Bug-Out standing in between two parked cars and walked up on him. "Yo cuz, what you saw in the kitchen is not what -" he paused and his heart sunk. "I don't fucking believe this shit!"

Bug-Out turned around high as a satellite smiling goofily then took another snort of the white powder. With pupils wide as frying pans, he grinned as the drug took effect. "Damn I ain't never been this high in my life! And I been to the top of the motherfucking Empire State Building."

"What the hell are you doing?" Tommy demanded.

"Oh this? Check it out, I know it looks fucked up. But it ain't what you think cuz."

"Is that right?"

"Nah, I don't even like coke...just the way it smells." Bug-Out said and burst into laughter. "Fun fact. Coke was basically Tylenol about a hundred years ago. It was prescribed for practically everything from toothaches to headaches. Your man Sigmund Freud, was a major cokehead."

Tommy's top lip curled. "I came out here to tell you how proud I am that you're making so much progress in rehab. And instead I get a history lesson on drugs."

"Man please. Rehab's for quitters." Bug-Out said then opened a folded dollar rubbed his finger roughly on the rear of the bill and sucked the coke residue from his finger.

"Why don't you just pray for the earth to open up and swallow your ass cause that's where you're headed!" Tommy snapped. Bug-Out shrugged like he could give a damn about what his cousin was saying and began swaying in time to a tune playing in his skull. "Why Bug-Out? You were doing so well" he growled and snatching Bug-Out by the collar.

Bug-Out turned to his cousin with pain written all over his face. "You're right I was doing well! Then I got my blood test back...I got the monster yo."

"The monster?" Tommy's jaw dropped and his grip loosened. "AIDS?" He whispered. Bug-Out nodded sadly. Tommy instinctively looked at his hands like they were contaminated then felt embarrassed under his cousin's hurt glare. "Are they sure?"

"Positive. That's what took them so long to get back my results. They checked and re-checked. But each time the results said the same thing…'Sorry Mister Strong, that's the breaks!' I don't get it! They got you believing this shit is a gay disease or something started by perverts fucking monkeys in the jungle! But they don't tell you there are other ways to catch it? Hell no!"

Tommy was not about to tell his cousin that information on AIDS prevention was as close as the nearest clinic or bus stop advertisement, and that it was common knowledge that unprotected sex and sharing needles was a surefire way to obtain the deadly virus, so instead he consoled him. He had read enough on the disease to know that he could not catch the virus from bodily contact but was concerned how others would react. AIDS was a new alien specter, and public fear and ignorance turned people unfortunate enough to catch it into outcasts. Even he freaked for a second when Bug-Out said he had it.

"So, what're you gonna do?" Tommy asked.

"I don't know. Go home I guess. Get Superman high and temporarily forget." Bug-Out shrugged rubbing his face. "Tonight was the first time I've seen my mother in weeks since our last argument. And you know what she just told me? That she's proud of me for getting my life together. Then she hugged me with tears in her eyes. That's why I came out here and took a hit."

"Look man, I read that there's this medicine that-"

"Save it. You sound like them jokers at the hospital. Medicine for what? They don't know shit about this disease."

"Maybe you should give it a try."

"What for? C'mon Tommy, there ain't even a cure for the muthafuckin common cold or cancer! Now you tell me how in the hell is they supposed to fix this shit?" Bug-Out demanded.

"But the medicine will suppress the ailments. You know, make you feel better. When you get sick. And you will get sick."

Bug-Out shook his head sadly. "Nah screw that. I go back to that hospital and all that's gonna happen is they gonna run experiments on me like a lab rat until I expire. I can't see it. I'd rather be out here on the streets making every second count."

"Daddy?" AJ called. The child came outside looking for his father.

Bug-Out turned to Tommy. "Nobody can know man. Promise me you won't say anything."

"Jesus Bug-Out, what about Laquita, she should be tested too."

"I'll talk to my wife. But please let me do it my own way. Now promise me." Bug-Out begged holding out his hand.

AJ was coming closer and Tommy sighed and palmed his cousin's hand. "Okay, but you have to tell Laquita. You owe it to her, and your son."

Bug-Out nodded as his son ran up cheerily. "You got a hug for your old man?" AJ squeezed his father's neck and was lifted into the air.

"What's wrong with Tommy, Daddy?" the child asked his father as he observed his cousin stare back at him with a combination of pain and sorrow.

"Um, your cousin's feeling sad cause he remembers the time he dropped you when you was a baby."

"He dropped me?"

"Oh yeah," Bug-Out grinned. "One time he was over at the house, when you was about one, and a roach got on his arm and freaked him out! Man he jumped up and started screaming running all around shouting, 'Get it off me! Get it off me! And that's when he dropped you."

"Did I cry daddy?" AJ asked giggling.

"My son cry? No way! But you did bounce around like a basketball. Dribbled all around the room. And then you landed in your crib." Bug-Out teased. AJ was laughing so hard he had tears in his eyes when his father turned to Tommy, "Oh by the way cousin, I'm way

ahead of you. What happens in the kitchen, stays in the kitchen."
Tommy nodded. "It's cold out here. I'm heading back inside, you coming?"

"In a minute." Tommy said sadly.

Bug-Out and his son went back inside leaving Tommy standing there feeling like he swallowed a razor blade.

Donnie was the first to notice the change in Tommy's mannerism. When he walked back inside she asked him what was wrong. He shook his head like he didn't want to discuss it. After Bug-Out and the rest of his family left the only guests still there were Tommy and Donnie. Corbin stuck his head out the kitchen then frowned and pulled it back in when he saw that there were still some people left.

"Nicky, I had a wonderful time. And thank you for making a potentially awkward situation a very comfortable one." Donnie said. Although she couldn't picture the four of them double dating she did find Nicky sweet beautiful and hoped that she would get rid of her moody older man and find someone much nicer and more deserving.

"You're very welcome Donnie. And yes, it was a tad bit awkward, but it was nice having you over. You too Tommy." Nicky said playfully poking his arm then kneeled down to pat his dog goodbye.

Tommy snapped out of his daze. "Huh? Oh yeah thanks again. Take care." He said and left.

"Jesus I can't believe those heathens finally left. It's pretty obvious why you divorced Tommy. Who'd want to be related to those uncouth tyrants? And was it really necessary to bring that large smelly mongrel?" Corbin said finally coming out the kitchen spraying Lysol. "You realize you'll have to have your couch and rugs cleaned? And I hope you took an inventory of your valuables because I'm certain things are missing."

Nicky glared at him. "We need to talk."

# Chapter 15

Donnie followed Tommy back to his place and parked out front. There were snow flurries blowing around but not quite sticking to the ground. A light layer of snow coated the trees and streets turning his dreary block into a picture postcard. Tommy told Donnie to go upstairs and make herself comfortable then went to walk Mayhem. Donnie was not sure why Tommy was acting so strange and hoped that it had nothing to do with him seeing Nicky with her new man. She could see why Tommy married a woman like Nicky. She was pretty, smart, sweet and unless she was acting, a decent person. Under the circumstances she wasn't sure she could have been such a gracious host. In fact, she knew she couldn't. She could also see if and why he would want her back and that worried her. It also made her question his sudden mood swing.

Tommy came back in with his dog and the lights were dim, candles were lit and Larry Graham was singing 'One in a Million'. Donnie was standing in the middle of the room in her sheer bra and panties holding the drink she made for him. She was a vision of beauty but sex was the last thing on his mind after learning about his cousin's dilemma.

"That's for me? Thanks." Tommy said and gave her a peck on the cheek, then took the glass to the kitchen table.

"You're welcome." Donnie said suddenly feeling awkward after he walked right past her in her sexiest and most revealing underwear. Realizing if this was going to happen she would have to take matters into her own hands she hopped into Tommy's bed. "Well would you looka' here. A bed. And not just any bed." She said bobbing up and down. "A waterbed! Hmmm. Now what could we do in this big ol' bed?" She asked provocatively.

"Donnie I'm not really in the mood." Tommy sighed working on his second drink.

She could not believe it. The Bastard played her, again! Evidently her name was Boo-Boo the fool! Donnie went over and angrily shut off the music. "I wonder if Nicky and her boyfriend have anything to do with your pissy mood." Tommy shook his head like she was annoying him and emptied his glass. "So here's the part when you tell me where you were wrong-again. And that you really do have feelings for your ex. Well save your breath cause I've had it! I told you earlier that I wasn't waiting around for you to get your act together!"

"Donnie." Tommy said in a low voice.

"Save the drama for your mama! See I finally figured it out. You don't have a commitment phobia. You just have a phobia of committing to me." She said and angrily got dressed. When she turned to Tommy he was staring at the bottom of his glass with a sad face. "What's the matter? Racked with guilt? Well you should be! You blew a good thing! And another thing-Aw just forget it! I'm outta here!"

Donnie stormed towards the door then paused. She was giving him ample enough time to stop her from walking out the door but he never said one word. That was it! His last opportunity to make this work. She looked over her shoulder one last time and was at a loss for words. Tommy was sitting there silently crying. This was totally unexpected. She came over and Tommy looked up at her with pitiful red eyes. In this numbed state he possessed a vulnerability that Donnie had never seen. She cupped his chin and he looked up at her. The hardness that usually enveloped his rough face was gone and she wiped away his tears.

"C'mere baby." She whispered and Tommy stood up and climbed inside her embrace.

After getting himself together Tommy explained how a perfect evening was ruined when he found out Bug-Out was infected with the AIDS virus. Donnie felt terrible about jumping to conclusions and he assured her it was okay. Under the circumstances he would have reacted the same way.

"Is there anything I can do?" Donnie asked him.

Tommy nodded drying his eyes then said, "Stay."
Donnie took him by the hand and led him to bed where they laid holding each other fully clothed until they drifted off.

"What are you trying to say Nicolette?" Corbin asked not believing what he just heard.

"I don't think you and I are right for each other Corbin." Nicky repeated lighting a cigarette.

"You're joking right?" Corbin asked. Nicky shook her head. "But-but why? What'd I do?"

Nicky could not believe he was that full of himself that he actually believed that the way he acted all night was appropriate. "There are a lot of reasons, but let's start with today. You alienated yourself from everyone and treated people coldly whenever someone tried to include you in a conversation. I was embarrassed for you and me."

"How did you expect for me to act? These people are your ex in-laws. This woman Carla, Tommy's mother, she made it obvious how much she would just love for you and her son to get back together."

"Don't even try it Corbin. That was exactly why I introduced you to Tommy before the party to reassure you that you had nothing to worry about. So try again."

"Nicolette I-"

"And another thing, I prefer Nicky. I do not like Nicolette, especially the way you say it."

"And what's wrong with the way I say your name?" he asked incredulously.

"Nobody calls me by my full name. Not even my mother and she gave it to me. Everyone calls me Nicky. Everyone, except for you. And when you say it you sound pretentious." Corbin rolled his eyes. "Bottom line is your arrogance and self-important bourgeois ways are too much for me." she said then inhaled.

"But Nicolette-Nicky! I don't understand. I'm in love with you and I thought you felt the same way too."

"Corbin you can fall in love just as easy as you can fall out of love. The word 'fall' means you have no control over it." Nicky sighed.

"Oh spare me the BS, you're just using tonight as an excuse to break up because you still have feelings for your ex-husband."

"Oh really?" The conversation was so dull that she found herself noticing that she needed to change the water in her aquarium.

"The way you were so disappointed when he told you he was bringing his friend to the party. And how he insulted my name like a juvenile. You didn't even come to my defense! And let's not forget about my phobia of dogs and you allowing him to bring that hound of his here."

At that moment Nicky realized that Tommy was right about everything he said about Corbin. Down to the last detail. "You were eavesdropping!"

This was not the reaction Corbin hoped for. He thought with the evidence thrown at her Nicky would back down. Maybe even apologize. "I wouldn't call it eavesdropping."

"Oh? What then? Hanging up in slow-motion?"

"Put yourself in my shoes. I give you the phone and it's your ex-lover. You talk for a minute then go into the kitchen for privacy. Any man would have done the same thing."

"No, not any man." Nicky blurted.

Corbin shook his head with a sad smile and went over to mini-bar and poured himself a scotch and soda. "You're right, not any man would have as you said, eavesdropped. Just a man sick with jealousy."

"God, Corbin. You're not sick with jealousy. You're just sick. Look, we can still be friends, but that's it. It's a new year and we should make a clean break. As successful as you are I'm positive you'll find somebody else in no time."

"Nicky, I don't want someone else." Corbin said and got down on one knee.

Nicky watched hoping he was not about to do what she thought he was about to do. Corbin dug into his pocket and took out a small jewelry box, opened it and presented her with a diamond ring so big that if it came from anyone else it had to be fake.

"Nicky, I know I can be a bit flighty perhaps eccentric at times. But I love you. What we have is real. It is pure. It is forever. Will you be my wife?"

Nicky's eyes stretched at the glistening rock and for a minute pictured it on her hand. But there was no way she could accept it and shook her head.

"I'm sorry but no. Look Corbin, you are not a bad catch. But you are just not for me. I'm not perfect either-"

"Yes you are!" Corbin said.

"No I'm not. When I met you I had just come out of a long marriage. I was lonely and should not have let it get this far. It was not fair to you. And for that I am sorry. But I cannot marry you. I am nowhere near ready to be married again."

"So you're saying it's over?" Corbin asked with a shaky voice and tears in his eyes.

"Yes Corbin it's over."

"Oh God, c'mon Nicky don't do this. Please reconsider."

"I'm sorry but my mind's made up."

Corbin rose to his feet with a vile look on his face. "It's your ex isn't it? You want him back."

"No Tommy has nothing to do with this." Nicky promised.

"Yeah right! Then I guess there's nothing else left to say. It's over!" Corbin said and shoved the ring back into his pocket, angrily put on his coat and grabbed the bottle of scotch. "For the road." He said holding up the bottle. Nicky shrugged. At this point he could have left with the whole damn liquor cabinet as long as he left. Corbin got to the door and leaned for a good-bye kiss and Nicky took a step back and held out her hand.

"Take care of yourself Corbin." She said.

"Yeah right. So I guess you're rushing me out so you can call your ex and celebrate with a fuck?"

Nicky snapped her head at him. "See I was trying to be nice to your snooty ass. Let you down easy. But to hell with that! Get out!"

"Gladly! I need my head examined for even dating you in the first place. You're not even in my class. You're just as ghetto as that thug ex-husband of yours and his ghetto dysfunctional family."

"You know what Corbin? With all your money and expensive things, you can come back two life times and never accomplish what those so called 'ghetto people' have."

"And that would be?"

"Well for starters happiness, but I'm not even going to go there with you Corbin. You're too much of a clown and I'm too much of a lady. But answer me this, if I am beneath you then why were you just begging me to marry you?"

"Well we'll see who's begging who when you call Tommy and ask him to get back together and he tells you that he and his new girlfriend are happy."

Nicky looked at him with disgust, "Tommy was right. You're just a sad old man."

Corbin felt his ego drop to his shoes and he had no comeback. He looked at himself in the mirror by the door and saw exactly that, a sad old man. He looked at Nicky and realized the huge mistake he made. If only he had have given her time and been more thoughtful and considerate to her and her feelings, who knows? Maybe she would have said yes and he wouldn't be standing there kicking himself in the head, scared to death he was losing her, and probably his last opportunity with someone other than the cold fish he met in the work field. He turned to her sadly.

"Nicky, please. I did not mean what I said."

"Well I sure as hell did. Now if you'll excuse me my ghetto ass would like to be alone."

"Please hear me out." Corbin begged and dropped to his knees, grabbing onto her legs and held on for dear life. "I can change! Please give me another chance."

Nicky cringed. "Corbin please leave."

Corbin let go and stood trying to retain some dignity. "I'm sorry. I don't know what came over me. I'll go now. But after you've given it some time if you change your mind, know that I'm simply a phone call away."

"Good-bye Corbin." Nicky said.

"Hereafter, in a better world than this, I shall desire more love and knowledge of you." Corbin said making one last attempt to win her back with some Shakespeare. Unimpressed Nicky rolled her eyes and opened the door. Corbin nodded and walked out into the freezing air. Once he was inside his car he held his face in his hands and sobbed pitifully.

Tommy lay awake in bed listening to Donnie lightly snore as the wind did a tap dance across his window. He was in no mood to work but somehow managed to climb out of bed, shower and get dressed. When Tommy's alter ego tickled Donnie's face with his goatee, her eyes opened and she looked up at him smiling.

"What time is it?" she asked propping herself up on her pillow.

"Late." Havoc said with a second gentle kiss.

"You're going out?"

"Yeah, I have to."

"Are you sure? I mean earlier you were so upset."

He smiled at her concern. "I still am. But I can't neglect my responsibilities."

Donnie pulled him on top of her lightly flicking her tongue between his lips as she kissed him full on the mouth. "Now remember, play nice with the other kids." she winked.

Havoc grinned then threw a kiss at Mayhem prompting her to follow him out the door. Once he was gone Donnie's smile turned to a frown and she wondered how in the hell Nicky was able to do it.

# Chapter 16

For the past hour and a half Misa Scott sat in her booth with her head in her hand, nursing her drink. She liked to go to the local bar in her Crown Heights neighborhood for two reasons. The drinks were cheap and the bartender would serve them minus the annoying questions about why such a pretty girl wanted to drink alone.

Seated amongst the handful of drunken patrons scattered throughout the place, she removed her journal from her backpack, flipped past old entries until she found a blank page then the sad faced young woman began writing:

*Date: Saturday January 9, 1988 Time: 1:30 am*

*It's hard to believe how much can happen in such a short period of time.*

*In three months I turned eighteen, got dumped by my boyfriend, was raped by my mother's piece of shit boyfriend, and found out I'm about to be a teenage mother.*

*But out of all the tragedies going on in my life the thing that hurts the most is that my mother called me a lying tramp when I first told her how I caught her boyfriend Frankie spying on me when I came out of the shower. How could she take that creep's side over her own daughter? Then again, she hasn't been the same since Daddy died from cancer.*

*Drinking, smoking, out to all hours of the night. God, I wish my father was here. What's she even doing with this asshole? He's the type of person she would have crossed the street to avoid when Daddy was still alive.*

I wanted to tell Grandma but I was afraid to. Frankie said if I told anyone he'd deny it and tell my mother to put me out on my ass. And if 'Mommy Dearest' did not believe me when I told her that her man was coming on to her only daughter before, she most definitely would not believe me especially now that I am pregnant.

I felt so depressed and alone, like nobody loved me. Like all was lost. Then one day I was leaving a GYN appointment when I heard all this commotion coming from behind an abandoned building and nosily went to investigate. What I saw changed my life. It was this one guy single-handedly taking on five guys!

Now growing up in Brooklyn, I've seen some pretty tough characters before, but there's no other like this guy. Dressed in all red and unbelievably skillful, he had two large-barreled guns strapped to his sides but never even bothered to use them instead letting his fists do the talking as he cut through the gang like nobody's business!

After it was over and all the punks were lying on the ground crying for their mommas, the guy in red (which might I add is drop-dead gorgeous) was about to head to his car when he noticed me. It was like he could see into my soul and recognized my pain. I was paralyzed as he came over to me. I had no idea what he was going to do. That's when he handed me his business card with all his information.

Grandma always said angels come in different forms and in this case, mines was a six-

*foot plus, bald black man dressed in red. His name is Havoc and for a fee he guarantees to make any problem disappear. Since he doesn't wear a badge he can do things cops couldn't, wouldn't or shouldn't! But I wasn't sure if this was how I wanted to handle my problems, that is until Frankie made me give him a blowjob while Mommy was in the next room. The sick Bastard said the risk of getting caught turned him on. Once we were finished and he went to get a beer, I had a brief cry then called Havoc and arranged a meeting with the Trouble Consultant.*

*Havoc said he would help me but first he needed proof that Frankie was the piece of shit I said he was so I arranged for Frankie to meet me here at the bar in a little while and inform him I'm pregnant...amongst other things!*

A tall man with the features of a rat stormed in and surveyed the area with his beady eyes. He spotted Misa then stomped over. "Okay I'm here. So, what the hell is so damn urgent you had to meet me here at this hour?"

Misa glanced at Rat-face and continued writing in her journal.

*Frankie just walked in. Everything is going according to plan.*

"What's that you're writing?" Frankie asked.

*He's looking over my shoulder reading what I am writing and from his reaction he just discovered that I am pregnant.*

"Plan? What's this shit Misa?" Frankie demanded. "You're pregnant? Answer me bitch!"

*He's cursing me and disrespecting me. Nothing new. But soon he will know what it feels like to be treated like crap!*

"You little skeezer!" Frankie hissed. "I'll tell your mother that it was you who came onto me when I was drunk and took advantage of the situation and she'll believe me and throw your worthless ass out in the gutter where you belong! Hey what's this?" he asked snatching her journal away and began reading it. "Oh, so you got some punk to kick my ass? Don't tell me he's one of these drunks!" he laughed.

Misa stared at Frankie long and hard then shook her head sadly. Almost as if she pitied him. She finished her Shirley Temple, cleared her throat then asked aloud, "So, is this enough proof?"

The drunk a table over seated before a half empty glass of Johnnie Walker RED label with his head buried in the fold of his arms rose out of his seat. He was dressed in a red hooded sweatshirt, red jeans, a pair of red boots and a pair of red tinted shades. Straight business! He pulled back the hood covering his baldhead.

"More than enough. I'll take it from here!" Havoc growled.

The laughter died in Frankie's throat and he dropped Misa's journal, along with his jaw on the floor. Misa bent down to retrieve her journal as Frankie bolted for the door then froze. She continued writing:

*Now I've seen some big dogs before but never one as big as Havoc's dog Mayhem. And from the look of pure terror on Frankie's face, neither has he. Oh this is rich! Now Frankie wants to talk. He's begging me to explain to Havoc that this was all just one big simple misunderstanding, so he can bitch his way out of getting his ass kicked! Well the only misunderstanding is that he actually believes that the baby I am carrying is his when in actuality it belongs to Kendu, my loser ex-boyfriend who broke up with me when I told him he was going to be a daddy. Luckily for Kendu*

*Havoc doesn't beat up guys for running from their responsibilities.*

*For all that tough talk, Frankie's such a pussy! He's not even attempting to defend himself. Dang, the fight's over before it even began. Havoc is on some Iron Mike Tyson shit! I would have liked for Frankie to suffer some more. But, I guess I'll just have to settle for him only losing three teeth. Oh well. Havoc 's cool though. A man's man. Like Daddy. He just strongly advised Frankie to do the right thing and admit everything he's done to me to Mom. He also said if he finds out that he didn't, he'll knock out the rest of his teeth. Frankie's looking at me promising he'll tell her. And I believe him. Unfortunately, I won't be around to see the look on Mommy's face when he does.*

*Instead of taking the pay for kicking Frankie's ass, Havoc told me to use it to buy a one-way bus ticket to Chicago where Grandma lives and that's just what I'm going to do. In fact, looking at my Gucci, it's about that time.*

*So, in closing, I don't know what I'm going to do about my situation but when I spoke to Grandma she said just be on that Greyhound and when I get there we'd figure it out, together.*

*Even though you will never read this Havoc, I want to say thank you. You saved my life.*

━━━━━━━━━━━━━━

Marcy projects like any other inner-city enclave was a last holdout of affordability for the lower middle class. And like most large apartment complexes, it had its fair share of decent law-abiding residents who got up every day and went out into the world to make an honest day's wages. But there were also the undesirables whose only goal in life was to get over. Undesirables like Johnathon Stokes who grew up fatherless and chose thugs and criminals as role models to rear his Bed-Stuy bred delinquent ass. As a result, young John spent his entire adolescence doing bids upstate in Sing Sing, Attica and Fishkill correctional facilities to name a few. His Parole Officer often lectured him about the direction his life was heading if he didn't change. Johnathon listened in silence seeming to agree, but the violent trappings of gangdom would stay on, mobilizing his circumstances against such advice. And since money, drugs and hoes were his primary interests, he became well connected in the get-rich-quick business. A few drug deals and shootouts later, Johnathon Stokes became Johnny Hop after losing his right eye and gaining a permanent limp. But in the process, he became one of the most feared and deadliest street pharmacists in Bedford Stuyvesant where the mantra, Bed-Stuy Do or Die was a way of life.

The scene within the sprawling Marcy Housing project was typical. The basketball rims were bent and net less, and the only sounds were the birds chirping, and shots going BLANG instead of SWOOSH as a couple of kids determined to make it out of the hood on basketball scholarships dribbled up and down the cracked asphalt court. Dressed in a cocaine-colored fur jacket with a matching brim, Johnny Hop sat perched on a parked motorcycle pimped out in the finest gear blood money could buy. Around his neck, wrists and fingers he sported the average man's salary in gold. Covering the eye he proudly lost to the street life was a specially made Louis Vuitton eye patch that would make Slick Rick envious. A few feet away his chariot, a gold rimmed, dark tinted Audi 5000, with license plates that read, '**EZLIFE**' was packed with a team of flyy girls. Nearby his cipher of drug clockers that shared the same 'united we're unfuckwitable' mentality, stood in a huddle engrossed in a friendly game of cee-lo.

"A-yo what do drug dealers and prostitutes have in common?" Johnny Hop asked the members of his notorious Black Top Crew. Hunched shoulders indicated that nobody knew. "A prostitute could wash her crack and resell it." everyone cracked up out of fear not humor and their boss dug further into his bag of jokes, "There was a Black man. A White man. And a Chinese man. So they-" the Pusher man paused mid-crass joke, as he spotted a modish cherry red '57 Chevy bright as a comet tear across the field throwing up dust and clumps of grass. The car swerved to a stop before them, the door opened and Havoc stepped out sporting his trademark red Kangol, straight-legged red leather pants, Air Jordan's with red trim and a red Polo goose down jacket with an image of a man skiing on the back. But he didn't so much emerge from the car as grow from it, as if he were an extension of the power and prestige such a vehicle afforded.

Johnny Hop turned to a muscle-bound dark-skinned man with a grill that read 'Not to be fucked with who looked as if he could dent a brick wall with his fist and catch a bullet with his teeth. Only using hostile facial expressions, he ordered him to attack. Havoc jumped into action and slid across the hood of his ride kicking the would-be assailant off his feet and sending him crashing to the floor. Livid, the drug dealer further humiliated his useless bodyguard as he climbed to shaky feet and ordered him to take a seat on the bench because he was on a time-out.

Havoc shook his head then went inside his jacket. Hands automatically reached inside jackets for weapons as the Trouble Consultant pulled out a tube of cherry red Chapstick and coated his thick lips smugly.

Johnny Hop found The Trouble Consultant's grandiose entrance both entertaining and amusing, and his mouth of gold-plated enamel clenched into a nasty unconcerned grin. "What do you want?"

"To quote, Roddy Rowdy Piper, I'm here to kick ass and chew bubblegum…And I'm all the fuck out of bubble gum!" Havoc said opening his arms with an invitation. While driving home from his last job he couldn't get Bug-Out off his mind and decided to confront the scumbag drug dealer who added to his cousin's list of problems.

Johnny Hop grinned then noisily revved his bike before shutting it off. "Some people call motorcycles death on two wheels. But I disagree. When I'm riding one, it's the only time I feel alive." He sighed eyeing the walking cane his flunky held. Havoc's poker face said he wasn't here for small talk. "So that's what this is all about. Somebody hired you to step to me? You know they warned me you'd be coming."

"Who's they?"

"Oh, a little birdy whose business offer I'm seriously considering. But regarding your offer. Afraid I'm going have to decline. Because as much as I would love to dance with you, eye can't." he said lifting his designer eye patch to reveal a white cloudy eyeball then rose off his bike and reached for his cane from his flunky to lean on. "Plus, I'm crippled so it wouldn't be very fair."

"Fair? Why you little one-eyed poison pedaling mother fucker! You have the audacity to speak to me about fair?" Havoc shouted seconds from losing it. "Is it fair that decent people have to look out their window and see a crack dealer slinging rocks to his own people? Is it fair that kids can't come outside and play because their parents are scared they'll either get shot or recruited by you?"

"Is it fair I gotta be interrupted from having a good time with my crew to listen to you lecture me on some ABC afterschool special shit?" Johnny Hop wisecracked.

"Okay I'm through talking to your morally bankrupt genocidal ass! Since you don't have the heart to take me on yourself, I'll settle for your best man. Right here, right now!" he snarled.

Johnny Hop patted a yawn. "Just so you know Havoc, the only reason I'm even entertaining this corny shit is because of that little favor you did for me the other day."

"Favor? What the hell are you talking about?"

"When you snatched that hoe from Diamond Ken you pulled home boy's skirt in the process. Okay true it may not have been done for me personally but I damn sure benefited from it. Now that Diamond Ken's out of business the majority of his customers now cop from me. Shit, fuck around, I may just start pimping his hoes too." The drug dealer laughed and held out his palm for one of his men to slap.

Havoc was becoming seriously irked, "Man all you're doing is talking shit and swallowing spit! While I'm ready to put somebody's head to bed. So, who's it gonna be?" he said cracking his knuckles.

The half blind crippled drug dealer eyed his army who were anxious to prove their loyalty and paused at a Frankenstein tall steroidal soldier under a Fisherman's hat who was sipping on a 40 ounce of Private Stock. "Yo Dun."

"What up boss?" the enforcer barked a reply.

"Remind me why you're on my payroll! And Dun, don't embarrass me!" he warned.

"Ain't no thing, but a chicken wing." The large man smirked assertively and sent the bottle crashing over his shoulder as he diddy-bopped towards Havoc.

"Havoc, say hello to Dun-Deal. He'll be kicking your ass this evening!" Johnny Hop remarked confidently as his posse snickered in the background.

The Trouble Consultant looked the taller man up and down like he was short and smiled, "Hey there little guy. So, what do you wanna be when you grow up?"

"You got jokes. But you won't be laughing in about two minutes...Nigga!"

"What did you just call me?" Havoc glared at Dun-Deal for calling him by the toxic word he despised and balled his left hand he wore his four-fingered '**HAVOC**' ring on, into a fist!

The big man scowled back and said, "I called you nig-"

**BOOM!** With hands hard as steel and fast as lightning, Havoc killed the N-word by hitting him with a shot so loud it sounded like a 22. caliber rifle. His fisherman's hat spun one way and the big man spun the other landing at his boss' feet, KO'd. The other goons were so stunned by Havoc's awesome power they grabbed their jaws in disbelief muttering, *'Oh shit! Yo did you see that?'*

"Impressive." Johnny Hop said, staring repulsed at the unconscious man on the ground he hired on the spot after watching him mercilessly win a match in an underground fight-club bout.

"Ain't no thing, but a chicken wing," Havoc shrugged mimicking the defeated man's boastful taunt then turned to the remaining men. "Which one of you clowns is Michael Rueben?"

Everyone turned to the smallest out of the bunch who was nervously shaking more than the ass on a hoochie mama in a Two Live Crew video. Under all the stares he tried to look tough and stepped forward. "I'm me...I mean, that's me." He whispered.

Havoc grilled the man-child, "Your mother's name is Gloria right?"

"Uh-huh." Michael gulped wondering how he knew.

Havoc looked down at the frightened little boy no more than twelve, who could have easily been him if he'd gone down a different path in life. And he felt compelled to put the boy on the right one. "Yo lil man peep this. Don't nobody belong in the game, who ain't built for the game. And **you**, ain't built for the game. You feel me?" Michael nodded nervously and darted his eyes at the Black Top Crew. "Look at me." he instructed and had the child's undivided attention. "Don't worry about them. You have my word there won't be any repercussions. Will there?" The Trouble Consultant glared up at Johnny Hop.

"Nobody's forcing him to stay!" the drug dealer shrugged.

"See? You got your walking papers. Now run don't walk home to your Momma!" and with that said Michael jetted, grateful to Havoc for helping him do what he had been wanting to do for the longest. Havoc turned to the rest of Johnny Hop's crew and sucked his teeth. "Aight, who's next?"

Another Herman Monster sized man with his head half-corn rowed, half-wild and a buck 50 outlining his jaw, stepped forward. "That'd be me!"

Johnny Hop halted him with his cane, "That won't be necessary Baby Pa." he said realizing he was running out of enforcers and if his last scarecrow went over there he'd either wind up on the bench with Tank or the ground with Dun-Deal. He limped over to Havoc. "Let's talk."

"Lead the way." Havoc replied.

Johnny Hop stopped before his ride and an attractive young woman leaning against it sucking on a blow-pop. "Kitten, pat our guest down for weapons." After thoroughly enjoying herself fondling more than frisking, she turned to her boss. "He's clean." she said licking her lips then added. "And fine."

The dealer glared with a nod then motioned the other ladies to get out of his ride. "Step into my office," he instructed then climbed in after Havoc and closed the door behind them. Once inside the loathsome dealer whipped out a nine-millimeter Glock and pointed it at Havoc. "Maybe you haven't heard Havoc but I run shit over here." Johnny Hop arrogantly boasted causing Havoc to snicker. "That's funny to you?"

"Actually, it is. In the hood, the Jews own the real estate. The Chinese own the laundromats, the Chinese restaurants **and** the soul food restaurants. The Pakistanis own the fried chicken joints. And the Arabs own the corner stores. So, I find it amusing when I hear a Black man loudly boast, that he runs the block." Havoc coolly stated.

"You won't find shit amusing if you don't tell me what I want to know. Like who sent you? Was it my competition? Or did the losers from the neighborhood pool their money together and hire you to clean up the community?" he demanded holding his weapon in a threatening manner.

Havoc looked more annoyed than concerned, "I'll take that," he calmly said motioning at the gun aimed at him.

Johnny Hop laughed, "Yeah right. So, what I'm just supposed to just give you my biscuit?"

"Or I could take it." Havoc coyly said.

"Well, I'd like to see you try it!"

In a flash the Trouble Consultant, using urban tactics, quickly grabbed his gun and took it up and out of his face, brought the weapon down and with his enemy's finger trapped in the finger well of the pistol, laid two stinging punches to Johnny Hop's face, snatched the gun away then pointed his own gun at him.

"Ow my nose! How the fuck? Yo man you gotta teach me that!" the disarmed drug dealer said impressed holding his throbbing nose.

"Shut-up! Now we're gonna have a little Q and A, and at the risk of sounding redundant, please make your answers genuine. Now normally I'd never betray my client's confidentiality but this is a unique situation that's personal to me. And since I'm more than confident there won't be any backlashes from you, I don't have a problem asking if you're familiar with a gentleman who goes by the name of Bug-Out?"

"Bug-Out? That walking punch line? You gotta be shitting me. **He's** the one who hired you?" Johnny asked dumbfounded. "What the hell for?"

"Oh, lots of things, but let's start with you using his old lady as your personal plaything because he couldn't pay you back for the drugs he owed you."

"You're joking right?" Johnny asked bursting into laughter.

"Do you see me laughing?" Havoc asked with a scrunched-brow glare.

"No but I sure the hell am." Johnny Hop could barely get the words out he was laughing so hard.

"Hop, I'ma give you to the count of three to wipe that raggedy ass smile off your ugly face or I will!" Havoc warned. "One!"

Johnny held up his hand doing his best to drop his smirk but could not stop giggling. Havoc's eyes went dark. "Two!"

"Ok-ok. I'm trying. But me and that skee-zoid?" Johnny Hop grinned disrespectfully.

"Three!" Havoc lunged out grabbing him by his throat ceasing all laughter immediately and rammed the back of his skull hard against the window. No longer finding anything to grin about, the drug dealer gagged as Havoc calmly squeezed his esophagus. "Open your mouth!" Havoc ordered, forcing the barrel of Johnny Hop's Glock down Johnny Hop's throat. "Tell me something motherfucker, you ever see an old drug dealer before?" Unable to answer the drug dealer nervously shook his head. "That's cause they don't exist! Am I making myself clear?" he asked. Turning red from choking, Johnny Hop frantically nodded and Havoc released his grip. The street dealer gasped sucking up air then turned to Havoc coughing and frantic.

"Man iz you crazy? You could'a killed me!" Johnny Hop complained not use to being treated by anyone like this before.

Outside the dealer's goons became concerned and tried the doors then banged on the tinted window calling out to him. The window came down to eye level. "I'm Okay! Get back to your posts!" their boss ordered then pushed his window back up and went back to Havoc who looked like he was ready to inflict more punishment. "Now before you tried to twist my head off I was about to tell you I ain't screw that hoe!"

"That's not what he told me." Havoc growled.

"And you believe a lousy dope head? I thought you were sharper than that Havoc! Man look out that window. Go ahead-look!" Havoc cut his eyes at the sickeningly attractive wasp-waisted women standing outside unsure if they should run for help or continue standing there shivering in their barely there dresses. "I push more powder than Johnson and Johnson and live the Montana life style minus the motherfucking scar! And I only bang model-looking-bitches! So why in the fuck would I screw a nasty crackhead hooker?"

"Fuck you! Laquita's not a hooker."

"Fuck me? No fuck you!" Johnny snapped back then immediately regretted it as the cartoon speed knot on the back of his head reminded him of the repercussions. "Look, I'm just saying you need to open up your eyes wide and realize! Now I don't know what kind of lies them two been feeding you, but I did Bug-Out a favor! Dude came to me begging for work, so me being the softhearted chump that I am, I hit him off with a brick of hash to push and he played me!"

"And how'd he do that?" Havoc asked.

"The son of a bitch took egg whites, thyme, oregano and crushed bay leaves, mixed it up molded into blocks and sold it as Purple Haze."

"And why would he do that?"

"Oh, I don't know. Maybe so he and his girl could get high off of my shit!" Johnny Hop said.

"C'mon Hop, you didn't get where you are by falling for the okey-doke. If you knew all this then why'd you trust him with your product?"

249

"Cause my girl's equally loser brother vouched for him."

"Let me guess? Was it Dead-Broke?"

"Yup, birds of a feather. But it was only a bullshit seven-gram so I ain't care. And I didn't know he was a fiend until he pulled this shit. I will say this much, Bug-Out may be a lot of things but stupid's not one of 'em. He knew that since you got to smoke haze with other shit to get lifted most niggas would never know the difference."

Havoc stroked his goatee mulling things over. He didn't want to believe it but Laquita's appearance at the party was shabby. And Bug-Out had been lying about everything thus far. The gun lowered, and the one-eyed dealer noticed a change in his composure.

"Hopefully this clears up the how-full-of-shit-I-am opinion you've formed of me. Followed by, 'My fault Hop, this won't happen again'." Johnny Hop said while massaging his throat.

"Are you a hundred percent certain what you told me is the truth?" Havoc asked not even entertaining the ridiculous request.

With his one good eye, Johnny Hop looked Havoc straight in his two, "I swear on everything I love, them two is madd fiends! Bug-Out be chasing that Snow White like she's a real live bitch! And Laquita sucks the pipe and the occasional dude in the project's staircase for money."

Havoc knew Johnny wasn't lying about the coke since that's what his cousin was doing when he busted him. He inhaled and exhaled deeply then yelled, "Fuck!"

For a guy who was supposedly hard-core Havoc seemed a little too emotional and concerned about a couple of three-time losers and it suddenly occurred to Johnny what this was all about. "Son of a bitch! Why didn't I figure it out before? You're related to him in some way ain't you? That's why it's personal," he asked. Havoc did not answer but his face and body language did. "You gotta be or why else would you give a shit? Cause it ain't like they could afford to hire you." The Trouble Consultant cut his eyes at him and opened the door. "Hey Havoc tell your brother, cousin or whoever the hell Bug-Out is to you that he better pay me what he owes, or he ain't gotta worry about me fucking his wife, cause I'll be fucking him...Ok that sounded gay. But you know what I mean!"

Havoc turned back and tore Johnny Hop's eye patch off his face. Then looking into his mismatched eyes said, "I'm warning you stay the fuck away from Bug-Out and Laquita! Or I'll give you a matching set One eyed Willie!" after getting his point across he tossed his patch and weapon back at him, then stepped out into the cold rudely bumping shoulders with Johnny Hop's goons and hopped into his car then peeled off.

The men looked to their boss for answers as he shrugged unconcerned. "Don't even sweat that fool y'all, his time is coming!" Johnny Hop said focusing his good eye on the black Benz in the distance and nodded accepting his little birdy's offer. "Trust me…And would somebody help Dun-Deal's ass off the fucking ground? Shit's embarrassing!"

# Chapter 17

Havoc stood outside of the tall building where Disney printed sheets doubled as curtains in the windows of several apartments and sighed. Hating what he was about to do but given no other choice, he and his best friend entered the building where his cousin resided.

A couple of young men were hanging out in the lobby drinking beer, free-style rapping and beat boxing. As Havoc waited for the elevator he wrinkled up his nose at the sickly sweet medicinal odor of burning cocaine mixed with weed, tobacco and a little bit of angel dust in the 'Ruler' the sherm heads passed back and forth.

"Yo Big man, the elevator ain't working." One of the men informed Havoc while keeping his beady eyes locked on Mayhem.

Havoc nodded 'thanks' and the Trouble Consultants began the hike up to the fourth floor mindfully stepping over puddles of urine, tobacco and empty crack vials. When he reached apartment 4C he heard loud music and a lot of activity coming from inside. With a headshake of disapproval, he covered the keyhole with his hand then rang the doorbell.

"Who Is it?" A voice fought to be heard over the music and what sounded like barking. Havoc did not answer and rang the bell again. "A-yo Bug-Out, somebody's at your door man!" the voice reported.

"Well did you ask who the fuck it is?" Havoc's blood pumped when he heard Bug-Out's voice.

"Yeah, but they ain't answer. And they covering the peephole."

"What? Oh, so niggas wanna play games?" Bug-Out angrily demanded.

*"Easy girl. Simmer down,"* Havoc said to Mayhem who let out an agitated growl, anxious to mix it up. He mashed the bell three times in a row.

"God dammit! Who the fuck is it?" Bug-Out asked again. After getting no response he unbolted the locks leaving the chain on the door and nervously reached into his pocket. "Whoever's on the opposite side of this door is about to get they ass whooped like Kunta Kinte!" Suddenly, the door kicked open breaking the chain! "OH SHIT!" he screamed when he saw Havoc and Mayhem standing in his doorway.

Havoc grabbed Bug-Out as he tried to run and flung him like a rag doll across the room. The Trouble Consultant stepped inside and looked around. Disgust was written all over his face. His cousin's apartment had become a crash pad for base heads who walked around like zombies in some bugged-out urban horror flick. Out of nowhere Dead Broke came running up clutching a baseball bat and frothing at the mouth like he had rabies. Shouting expletives, he swung it horizontally at Havoc. The Trouble Consultant moved forward instead of retreating and closed the distance to avoid the business end of the bat. Timing it perfectly after a missed swing, his hands exploded forward and trapped Dead Broke's wrists, forcing him to drop the weapon on the floor.

The frail black man with a pack of Newports tied to his doo-rag looked down at the bat then cringed meekly at Havoc. "Just not in the face," he begged.

Havoc grunted then bitch smacked him and he collapsed. Junkies scattered like roaches with the lights on as Havoc stepped inside their circle welcoming any and all challenges. A couple of simpletons high enough to believe they could actually take the large man on attacked and were toppled like bowling pins. Someone came up from behind Havoc and threw their arms around his neck putting him in a full nelson. With his free arm Havoc reached back and yanked them off and was about to knock their lights out then quickly stopped in total shock. It was Laquita. Their eyes locked and she dropped her head in shame. Havoc couldn't believe it. Johnny Hop was right. His cousin and his wife were a couple of fiends!

"Where's AJ?" Havoc demanded. Laquita rolled her eyes and shrugged. "Don't make me ask again?"

"Damn man, leave her be! The kid's in the john," A crack fiend spoke up then quickly dropped his head, afraid to look Havoc in the eyes.

"Pathetic," Havoc hissed with a glare then went over to the bathroom. He could see movement inside from the space between the door and the floor. "AJ? Hey little guy, it's your cousin. Don't be afraid." he said and twisted the door knob then opened it slowly as the crack fiend looked up smiling sinisterly. "AJ?..." Instantly a ferocious barking pit-bull leaped out attacking him.

"Yeah, tear his ass up Roscoe!" the owner shouted to his dog.

Havoc stumbled backwards bringing his knee up and crossing his arms in front of his face to protect himself as the fierce mongrel sprang forward. With its lethal jaws snapping wildly, the dog chomped down on his coat and pulled. Then a deep growl was heard over all the commotion and suddenly it occurred to Roscoe and his owner that another dog was on the scene too. And this dog was bigger, meaner and deadlier!

In a flash Roscoe was removed from Havoc by Mayhem as she clamped down on the pit-bull's hind leg and flung the dog like a frisbee. Letting out a painful yelp, Roscoe slid across the room then spun around to face the angry, sharp teeth baring Bull Mastiff. Everyone stepped back as a whimper that could be interpreted as *'oh shit!'* in dog speech was made by Roscoe. Mayhem moved forward snarling to attack. After being bitten and handled like a rubber chew toy, Roscoe didn't want any more of what Mayhem had to offer and scampered out the front door while he still could with his master running behind. Mayhem victoriously trotted beside Havoc ready for anything else.

After rewarding his dog with a pat on the head for a job well done, he told her, "Anybody moves... 'Suppertime!'" then stormed past Laquita with his sights locked on the door at the far end of the hall covered with 'Garbage Pail' stickers and a child's arts and crafts. He twisted the doorknob, cracked it partially and peeked in with his gun drawn to make sure the coast was clear. After deciding it was safe he holstered his weapon and entered.

"Who the fuck does he think he's talking to? I'm a grown ass man! My own momma don't tell me what to do!" Dead Broke complained to Bug Out then started for the door. Mayhem growled and he promptly sat back down.

Dressed in Spiderman Underoos little AJ sat wedged in between the space of his bed and the wall with his hands clamped tightly over his ears trying to block out the loud ruckus from yet another one of his parents' wild drug parties. He lifted his head when he saw his cousin standing in the middle of his room and jumped up and ran over crying uncontrollably.

"Get your coat and favorite toy little man. I'm taking you up out of here." Havoc said lifting the child into the air.

"I ain't got a coat or toys no more. My daddy stoled it for crack." The child whimpered and gave into a flood of tears. A look of dismay came over Havoc.

Havoc walked back into the living room cradling little AJ wrapped up in his own leather bomber. Everyone was still planted on the floor. Bug-Out and Laquita were huddled on the couch scared to move. But as soon as Laquita saw Havoc exiting with her child she became frantic.

"Oh hell no! Where do you think you're taking him? That's my child!" She demanded.

"Like you really care!" Havoc snapped. "I'm not surprised at Bug-Out. But you Laquita, you really had me fooled."

"I could give less than a fuck what you think about me. Just put my son down and take your dog and get the hell outta' my house!" Laquita jumped up demanding then backed down when Mayhem let out a warning growl. As Havoc leaned in to settle down Mayhem, he could feel the boy's grip tighten around his neck and shoulders. AJ definitely did not want to stay in this rat hole.

"Oh I'm leaving, but the kid's coming with me!" Havoc said.

"Sorry cousin but I can't let you do that." Bug-Out said rising up.

"Bug-Out as far I'm concerned we're no longer family. You've used up all your sympathy with me. Regardless of what we spoke about." Havoc said looking through his cousin and headed for the door.

Laquita turned to Bug-Out. "Don't just stand there! Do something!"

"Yo man I ain't playing around! Don't make me do something we'll both regret!" Bug-Out said and with shaky hands reached into his pocket and pulled out a tired looking revolver. Mayhem growled awaiting her orders. Havoc slowly put AJ down and looked into his eyes with a hard stare.

"No daddy! Don't!" AJ cried.

"So what's up, you gonna shoot me?" Havoc asked then held out his arms to give him a better target. "Well here I am. Go ahead, do what you gotta do."

Bug-Out clenched his teeth and curled his finger around the trigger. The crack he smoked was coursing through his veins making him sweat like he was in a sauna. He glanced down at his son and knew that he could not do this.

"Dammit! Just leave my son and go!" He tried to sound demanding but it came out more like pleading.

"If you want to fuck up your life fine by me. But I'm not going to stand by and watch you wreck shorty's. So you do what you have to do. And I'll do the same! In fact, I'll make this easier on everyone involved." Havoc said and pulled out his wallet. "So how much? One, two, three hundred?" He said pulling out crisp big-faced bills.

"What are you talking about?" Bug-Out asked confused.

"How much will it cost to buy your son from you? Come on give me a price. Seven, seven-fifty, eight. Talk to me."

Bug-Out's eyes bulged at all the money. So did Laquita's. Havoc counted out eight hundred and eighty-three dollars.

"This is all I got on me. Talk to me. Is it enough, cause I can easily get more?" he asked openly.

Bug-Out and Laquita traded wide-eyed stares then Bug-Out dropped to a level he never thought he'd go and nodded his head.

"See just like you said, everyone has a price. Well, come get your money." Havoc said.

The walk across the room was the longest distance Bug-Out had ever traveled in his entire life as he went over to claim the money for his son. Laquita never said a word. As far as she was concerned the money was already spent on her next high. Bug-Out held out his hands to receive his money but was unable to look his cousin in the eye. Havoc went to hand it over and dropped the money on the floor.

The Trouble Consultant shot him a slick smile and shrug. "Oops."

Bug-Out bent over to pick up the money and Havoc gave him a swift kick in the ass that shot him down the hall like a hockey puck where he banged his head against the wall. He then got up, bent over, heaved, spit out something chunky then cleaned his mouth with the bottom of his shirt.

"Daddy!" Little AJ screamed and ran to his father.

"I can't believe you were really going to sell me your son. Your own flesh and blood." Havoc said shaking his head ashamed of his cousin.

"What can I say? Life tossed me a curve ball." Bug-Out explained full of sorrow.

"And what, you're using your son to get a hit?" Havoc yelled then forced himself to calm down because he was scaring AJ. "That bullshit you're kicking may sound like poetry to you, but to me it sounds like bullshit! C'mon shorty let's go," when he went to take the child's hand, the boy angrily snatched it back. After seeing his father on the floor stirring in pain and his mother crying, AJ changed his mind about leaving and wanted to stay. They may not have been much, but they where his parents and he still loved them regardless.

"I hate you!" the child screamed and began to cry.

"No…don't say that son. Your cousin is only trying to help you. Do what he tells you and go on ahead with him." Bug-Out said sadly realizing his cousin was right. He couldn't do 'Jack' for his son let alone himself.

With tears rolling down his cheeks AJ obeyed his daddy and took his cousin's hand. Havoc stopped in the doorway then turned to his cousin very disappointed.

"How could you let this happen?" Havoc demanded.

"I dunno," Bug-Out sighed heavily, "One day I was headed to where my God given talents would take me, then I made a turn, and another, and another until…there was no turning back."

"He'll be at your mother's," Havoc said referring to AJ then signaled for his dog and walked out.

After they were gone Bug-Out sat there feeling like shit….

"Damn nigga I ain't know Havoc was Yo cousin." Dead Broke said to a stone-faced Bug-Out breaking the loud silence.

# Chapter 18

Sitting in drunken darkness, Corbin refilled his glass with the cognac he received as a Christmas gift from his secretary Kate. His original plan was to drive home but somehow he wound up behind his desk at work drowning his sorrows in a glass of alcohol. Since he was not a big drinker he was stone drunk after his second drink.

"Sad old man! How dare you cu-call me a sssad old man!" He vented with slurred speech and picked up Nicky's picture off his desk. "I hope you realize that you blew it young lady! You were the best thing that ever happened to you. No! To me. No, I mean I'm the best thing that ever happened to me! No-I mean, oh to hell with it! The bottom line is that you could have had it all Nicolette! Carte blanche! I'm an important man who's going places! Unlike that loser ex-husband of yours! What could he do for you huh?" He demanded then laughed at himself for yelling at a portrait. "Oh God Nicolette, you gotta take me back. I love you so." He traced the outline of her lips then kissed her picture and picked up the phone and dialed. After the fourth ring Nicky picked up. "Nicolette, I mean Nicky? It's me. Please don't hang...up. Fuck!" He swore as she slammed the phone in his ear. He dialed her again. "Nicky If you'll just hear me out, I know we can...DAMN!" he tried her again but this time it was off the hook. He angrily cleared his desk with one swipe then poured another glass of cognac and turned it up to his lips.

Soon the room was doing back flips and he felt the contents in his stomach trying to escape. He quickly grabbed the waste paper basket just in time to barf into it. After throwing up until his stomach was in painful knots, he opened the window inhaled some cold air then sat back down and removed an old picture of Nicky and Tommy that he had stolen from her photo album. He stared at them embraced and smiling. Laughing at him. Mocking him. How come she never held him like that? Or even took a picture with him for that matter? The heartache was too much. He felt like that little ugly thing from that Alien movie had burst out of his chest and ripped his heart to shreds. The pain was too much and he threw up again. He wiped the sweat, drool, and water from his face with a downward swipe then ripped the picture down the center. He gently kissed Nicky's picture and placed it into his breast pocket then set fire to Tommy's. As Tommy's smiling face bubbled, curled and melted in the flames Corbin felt some satisfaction but it wasn't enough. He would have preferred Tommy's face actually burning in flames. A sudden knock on his office door snatched him from his thoughts and the door pushed open before he could respond.

"Mister Ramses I presume?" A raspy voice said in the doorway.

"Who's there?" Corbin looked up.

"Please forgive my intrusion," the dark figure apologized concealed in the shadows.

"Show yourself!" From where the intruder stood Corbin could not make out their face clearly in the darkness. He switched on his desk lamp and he gasped. "Dear God!"

"I realize that my appearance is a tad bit disturbing, but I assure you that there is no need for alarm. I am not here to harm you. In fact, it is your help that I desperately need."

"H-how do you know my name? Who sent you?" Corbin asked unable to hide his fear.

"Before I answer any of your questions there's something I need to know. Do you want retribution for the personal injustice you have endured from the man who I am assuming is in the picture burning before you?" Corbin looked down just in time to see the remainder of Tommy's mocking smile vanish into a pile of ashes and found himself nodding 'yes'. "Excellent." The mysterious figure said and tossed something at Corbin. He caught the key and held it up by the Mercedes Benz emblem. "Let's talk business." The twisted voice said as Corbin's office door closed.

# Chapter 19

"Damn, with all that plastic surgery, hair and makeup, I can't tell if that's Latoya or Michael." Tommy laughed commenting on the gloved one's Bad video.

"See this is why Tito was always my favorite Jackson, cause he keeps it real, big nose, nappy fro and all." Donnie joked.

"The only Jackson who kept it real was Joe-Dammit Mayhem! Hold still!" Tommy said frustrated with his dog as she moved her head about while he tried to brush her teeth. "You know what? Just forget it. When your teeth fall out it's your fault!"

Mayhem happily retreated to her water and food bowls licking Colgate from her jaws. Donnie sat regally crossed-legged on the edge of the bed silently dunking Oreo cookies into a glass of milk before stuffing them into her mouth. Ever since Tommy had returned from dropping AJ off at his grandmothers earlier, he was moody and irritable. When he walked in he was so livid after learning the truth about Bug-Out and Laquita that he stomped over to his punching bag and assaulted it for a solid fifteen minutes before he could even speak. After finally recharging his battery with some much-needed rest, she was glad he awoke in a better frame of mind.

Video Music Box ended so Tommy picked up the remote and began absent mindedly channel surfing. "Aids, crack, and Reganomics are devastating Urban America and all Nancy Reagan has the audacity to say is 'Just Say No' knowing goddamn well her husband is the reason crack is even in the hood!' Tommy hissed at the First Lady's commercial.

"And how'd you come to that conclusion Archie Bunker?" Donnie asked.

"Hell, it ain't no secret Ronnie and Castro are in bed together. How else could coke come into this country." Tommy reasoned as he laced up his shell-toed Adidas with fat red and white checkerboard shoelaces then turned to Donnie with his mouth open like a baby bird and she placed a cookie into his mouth. Crunching, he thanked her with a wink and continued flipping then stopped at the Thunder Cats cartoon. "My dude Lion-O! Now we're talking! Yo babe, you mind if we watch this?"

"Fine by me." Donnie said and snuggled up beside her man as he excitedly rooted like an eight-year-old for the ThunderCats to defeat their nemesis the evil Mumm-Ra.

"That's right bust his ass Lion-O, handle your business!" the big kid shouted. After a moment passed Donnie looked up at Tommy and inadvertently let out a sigh. "S'matter baby?" Tommy asked.

"Um…" Donnie said then shook her head like she didn't really have anything to say.

"I hear that 'um' is the best way to start a conversation." Tommy said and kissed her lovingly on the tip off her nose.

The last thing Donnie wanted to do was kill the mood with annoying bothersome questions. But there was something that she had to know. "How long have you been a Trouble Consultant?" she asked.

"Long enough."

"What's long enough?"

Tommy stroked his chin, "Long enough that I can distinguish one crew's secret whistle from another and differentiate the colors of crack capsules sold by rival drug lords. Why?"

"I know you make a lot of money and all but I don't see how you do it. It's so dangerous."

"I think H. Rap Brown said it best, violence is as American as cherry pie," Tommy smirked but Donnie found nothing to smile about. Tommy muted the volume and turned to his girlfriend, "Okay I admit, Trouble Consulting definitely has its moneymaking highs and violence prone lows. But there are bright sides to being the handyman of the hood. Like that fact that I help a lot of people. And let's not forget it's how I met you. Look, crime's a big business. It's what makes the world go 'round. Think about it, if the world were suddenly one big happy place with everybody living harmoniously then more than half the jobs in America would be done away with. All of these idiot Senators sitting in Congress would have nothing to do and everybody from the police to correction officers would be out on their asses. Why do you think building jails takes precedence over building schools? It's because the powers that be need crime to make money. They need crime to survive. Circle of life baby." Tommy explained like he taught a course on the subject.

"And what about you? Do you need crime to survive too?" Donnie asked openly.

Tommy thought about it, "Yeah, I guess in a way I do."

Donnie glanced over at his guns on the nightstand. "Have you ever killed someone?"

"And if I have?" Tommy inquired and got a frustrated sigh and head shake from her as a reply. "Thoughts?"

"I just wonder how it can be right to kill people who kill people, knowing that killing people is wrong?" Tommy, returned her gaze unflinchingly. She was beginning to get too intrusive and personal about stuff that he himself hadn't fully figured out yet. He scooted toward the edge of the bed and reached for his jacket. Too lazy to roll himself a spliff, he opted for a slightly bent Newport. "I'm sorry. I'm asking way too many questions aren't I?" she asked regretting the question.

Tommy waved a hand in the air indicating it was alright. "I've put countless cats in ICU but never the morgue. I did come close once and lost a lot in the process."

"What happened?" Donnie asked.

Tommy paused replaying a harsh memory then snapped out of it with a somber look. "Not worth going into. But at the end of the day if it comes down to them or me, I'll send flowers,"

"Don't you worry that someone might one day send **you** flowers?"

"Try not to. But I do sometimes." He said and looked off in a daze.

"What is it?"

"Your question, it got me to thinking about this consulting gig I did a few years back. On the day this guy proposed to his girlfriend. His side mistress showed up at the restaurant and threw a monkey wrench in his plans. He swore he had no clue who the other woman was but evidently, she knew things only a mistress would. His lady wouldn't listen and tossed his ring back in his face. But dude wasn't trying to hear all that jazz. At first he was on some kiddy shit. Crank phone calls in the middle of the night, showing up to her place. Her job. Then he turned up the heat and things got physical. That's when she called me. I tried talking to him first. Man to man. And call me crazy but I actually believed the guy when he said he was set up and had absolutely no idea who the woman that accused him of having an affair with her was. But by then it really didn't matter because his girlfriend was back with an ex-boyfriend and he was too far-gone to listen to reason. So, we had to do things the hard way. I'll give it to him for a chubby guy his knuckle game was fairly decent. But after he got one look at Mayhem he took off running, to the roof. We chased after him, jumping from one ledge to the next. Damn he was fast. Then just when I thought he was going to be the one that got away, he jumped down to an adjacent roof. Or at least what he thought was a roof." Tommy paused and shook his head at the memory. "I remember it was winter, around this time of the year. But a helluva lot more snow. It covered everything. Cars, mailboxes, fire hydrants and glass skylight ceilings. The poor slob took a nosedive straight through falling at least fifteen feet. Like a safe dropping through a frozen pond. It all went down so fast there was nothing I could do. Blood was everywhere and I'm thinking this poor sap's lying here half-dead and all he was guilty of was wanting to be with the woman he loved. The threats and intimidation was just a by-product of that love. I called for an ambulance and hung around until they arrived and whisked him away."

His life sounded unbelievable, so his words at first seemed unbelievable, but Donnie knew Tommy's statements to be true and it wasn't because they were tailed by, 'ask so and so' or a kiss to his right palm before raising it to swear on everything he loved, but because of the similar situation in her life that he alleviated when no one else could. "So, whatever happened to him?" she asked enthralled by the tale.

"I went my way and they went theirs." Tommy shrugged and put out his cigarette. "There are a lot of reasons that I chose to become a Trouble Consultant but the main reason is I was afraid of becoming one of those people with predictable lives. Pushing papers all day. Catching the vapors when a rival got that phat promotion I had been kissing ass for. I just couldn't see it."

"Well Congratulations. You've certainly succeeded there." Donnie remarked. "But I can identify with not wanting to be predictable. My cousin Kerima in Texas, she's got two kids, a dog, nice picket fenced home and a practical family car to get around in. To most she is living the 'American Dream.' That were me, I'd go crazy in a week!"

"Well I'm with her regarding the dog. But you understand why I do what it is I do."

"I didn't say all that. What gets me is this is all you see yourself doing when there's so much more to you than that." Donnie said. Tommy glanced over his shoulder at her like he did not have the same confidence that she did. "Don't look at me like that, it's true."

"Oh really? Like?" Tommy asked spinning at her.

"Well you front like you're this mean, surly, nasty, rude person but in actuality you're strong, sweet and sensitive."

"Am not." Tommy grumbled.

"Oh really? And who was it that cried during E.T.?"

"Hey, you swore you'd take that to the grave!"

"You're also smart, intelligent, intellectual-but still thuggish in an alluring sort of way. You have this reserved, dignified demeanor that I find sexy as hell. And you can charm the pants off of anyone; I can vouch for that."

Tommy grinned like the face on a pitcher of Kool-Aid. "You sound like you could go on for days."

Donnie leaned forward and kissed him softly on the nose. "I could. But that's because you are more than just, 'Havoc, the Trouble Consultant.'"

"You sound like my Pops. Whenever an opportunity presents itself he tries to convince me to quit and go back to college or anything else."

"And that's a bad thing?"

"I'm not saying achieving higher learning isn't important. I'm just saying there's different kinds of learning. What you learn from books is one kind of knowledge, but what you learn in the streets is another. And the knowledge it takes to put them together is probably the most valuable lesson you're ever going to learn. The problem is, they don't teach a class in that. At least not in any class I ever attended."

"I think your father's just worried about his son. So am I."

"No need. I weight train five to six days a week, plus boxing and firearms and I get paid lovely to defend those who can't defend themselves. Now back in the day when I was working construction, broke and miserable there was a need to worry. But he's so determined to get me to quit, he recently offered me my own club to run."

"Wow that's great. Are you going to do it?"

Tommy shrugged. "My Pops makes it look easy but trust me it's not."

"And what you do is?"

"It makes me mad loot."

"To paraphrase James Baldwin, 'Man cannot live by profit alone."

Tommy sighed. "See, there you go! I told you that you'd be looking to change me."

"Relax Tommy, I'm not trying to change you. But like your father, I just wanted you to be aware that you have other options."

"Check you out. Sounding all concerned about my welfare like you we're in a relationship or something." Tommy teased.

"Well aren't we in a relationship?" Donnie asked daring him to say no.

Tommy stared at her taking in her tight posture and glare. "…Yeah, you're my girl." He smiled after a pause. If there were any doubts Donnie put them to rest last night when she was there for him. No question she was his lady. "Now I guess it's my turn to reciprocate some of the qualities that I find attractive about you?"

266

"It would be nice to hear. But if it's going to be a big deal then don't bother." Donnie said already anticipating he wouldn't.

"I never said it was a big deal." Tommy said. He had not done the romantic thing in a long while and he had to become reacquainted with whispering sweet nothings.

Donnie flashed a vanilla smile and gave him her undivided attention. Tommy eyed her over in her black silk nightgown and ran his hand over her thigh. He pondered on what she meant to him and his face brightened up like something just came to him.

"I can sum it all up, you, me, us, everything, with one word…Honeybee."

"Honeybee?" Donnie repeated ticked off. "Now here ah sister go and break down all the things I love about you, and the best you can come up with is that I remind you of a bug?"

"Chill-out. Dang. Before you go off, don't you at least wanna know why I chose a Honeybee?" Tommy asked.

Donnie sat up with pursed lips hoping he had a good come back. "I'm listening."

Tommy cleared his throat. "It's because your race is black, but your complexion is a golden saffron. Bright like the sunshine. You have this engaging and bubbly personality that keeps you in natural flight. But when you get mad, gurl-you have one hell of a stinger! Now when we make love-aw shit! You make this sexy erotic buzzing sound just when you are about to cum, and it drives me insane." Tommy said turning Donnie's frown upside down as he spoke from the heart. "And not to mention when you rub your legs together, you make some sweet tasting honey." He said and began sucking on her neck while reaching under her gown and rubbing between her legs.

"Talk about reinventing the compliment." Donnie whispered and bit down on her bottom lip. "That sounds nice and all but truth be told, it only pertains to sex. What do you think about me, the person?"

Tommy looked around the room thinking. "I'll be straight up with you. When I try to put words together to describe you all I come up with, are words that don't really go together." Donnie's face said, 'try anyway'. "Aight, you're smart, sweet-innocent, well not *too* innocent." he rethought after thinking about their sex-capades. "You are kind and giving but not to the point you allow yourself to be played for a sucker. That's important because if you're going to be my lady, you cannot be weak. You're patient, independent, loyal, an incredible lover and the best friend I could ask for."

Donnie felt a buzz coming on and got out of bed.

"Hey where are you going?" Tommy asked as she headed into the bathroom and shut the door behind.

"Well after the baby oil episode I got to thinking, why is it that you always get to be creative in bed? So I decided this time we'd try something that I came up with."

"Don't tell me you got another girl in there with you." Tommy asked energetically.

"Sorry Mister Strong but when it comes to my man, I do not share." Donnie said and came out the bathroom donning only post-it notes on her most intimate areas.

"Oh word?" Tommy said eyes wide, wearing the mischievous grin of a child about to act a fool as soon as his parents turned their back. "So what do I do?"

Donnie came over to the edge of the bed. "Well if you look closely, you'll notice that each note has an instruction for what you are to do, *to that particular body part.*"

Tommy leaned forward and read her crotch. "Taste my honey-pot." He looked up at her with a devilish grin. "Ah sookie-sookie now!" He tore out of his clothes, laid her down and did what the note instructed. Afterwards he moved onto her breast. "Hmm, it says here to 'suck each nipple till erect…Well if I must." He said peeling off the notes.

With his lips parted and inches from her breasts Tommy was about to handle his business, when his business phone rang. He looked down at her and she rolled her eyes.

"Go on and answer it." she sighed.

With a brief peck on the lips he rolled over and picked up the receiver. The voice on the other end made Tommy snap to attention and after a few minutes she overheard Havoc say, "I'm on my way," before hanging up.

After he got off the phone he got up and robotically laid out a red turtleneck, red leather blazer, red slacks, red shoes and red accessories. He glanced at Donnie and she glared at him.

"Don't tell me you're going out." Donnie said anxious to finish what they started.

"I'm sorry babe but I have to. Next week when Tee-Tee is here I can't work. And this particular job needs my attention asap." he explained as he got dressed.

"Is it dangerous?"

"No more dangerous than any other gig." he said downplaying it and checked his guns then twirled them cowboy style and inserted them in his behind the back holsters. After he got dressed he came over and kissed Donnie. When he pulled back she looked sad. "I'm sorry baby, but this is what I do."

"Yeah, I know." Donnie pouted. "I just wanted us to spend the afternoon together."

"Yeah I know. Me too. But look, this shouldn't take too long. And when I get back we can continue where we left off cool?"

"Cool." Donnie said and kissed him.

"For real I'm out." Havoc said as his woman sucked his bottom lip and massaged his crotch.

"Seriously babe I gotta bounce. Mayhem, time to make the donuts. Hey, I'll be back before you even have a chance to miss me." Havoc promised then left out with his dog trailing behind.

After they were gone Donnie sat up cradling her pillow and said. "I already do."

The case was so widely publicized that Havoc did not even bother with doing a standardized routine background check on those involved. Seventy-five-year-old Hattie Mae Tucker of Brooklyn was patiently waiting in line at the Dime Savings Bank of Greater New York, when all of a sudden three fearsome men stormed in whipping sawed-off shotguns from their trench coats and announced they were robbing the bank. To show they meant business, they shot and killed the security guard when he went for his weapon.

Police quickly arrived on the scene, which led the bank robbers to believe that one of the tellers had secretly tipped them off. Furious, they murdered all the tellers in cold blood and kept the customers as hostages for negotiating tools. After a long standoff between the bank robbers and the police, tear gas canisters were shot through the windows and the police fought their way in. A gun battle ensued and when the smoke cleared, only one of the robbers remained, Panama Delgado, and one of the hostages, Hattie Mae Tucker.

When the case went to trial the defiant Great-great-grandmother testified before a grand jury that what began as any other day, ended in bloodshed and turmoil. With a shaky voice she recalled how Panama and two other accomplices entered the bank and brandished weapons announcing a holdup then murdered the security guard. When the police arrived, they blamed the tellers and murdered them as well then threatened to kill all of the hostages if their demands were not met. When no deal could be made between the robbers and the police, the police bum rushed the scene to rescue them. The robbers savagely kept their word and maliciously turned their weapons on the hostages. Hattie needed a moment to get herself together as the pleas and screams of the people, some she had called friend, echoed in her mind. She still was not exactly sure why she was the only hostage to survive the tragic ordeal, and although her faith in the Lord said that there was a reason for all of this, she still found herself asking why was an old woman's life spared while the lives of so many young people were cut short?

When she was asked to point out the man responsible for the brutal murders of twenty-two people Hattie rose from her seat teary-eyed and fingered the six foot three smug-faced Latin Prince with ice pick sideburns in an orange jumpsuit and shackles. For his crimes Panama was given five consecutive life sentences. With his family weeping Panama turned to Hattie and silently locked eyes with her then sadistically blew a kiss at her as he was taken away.

The media labeled Hattie Mae a hero, but not everyone seemed to agree. A week after the trial Hattie began receiving threatening phone calls and even a rock thrown through her window with a note attached threatening that snitches wind up in ditches. The police provided round the clock protection, but the stubborn old woman refused to become a prisoner in her own home and called it off after two weeks when the threats faded.

Then early one Sunday morning while at Mass, a note was found inside her Bible that said she was going to pay for dropping a dime on Panama. After that she and her family decided it would be best if she went back home to St. Petersburg, the small Virginia town where she was born. Worried that too much attention would be caused with a police escort to the airport, her grandson hired Havoc and Mayhem to accompany her incognito instead.

Havoc got out of his car in front of the secret location he was to meet Hattie at. A young man in his early twenties, who was showing off a shiny new gold Nissan Maxima to a group of impressed teens, came over.

"Havoc?" the young man asked. Havoc nodded a reply. "Troy Tucker. I'm the one who called you about my Grandmother, Hattie Mae Tucker."

"Oh hey, how you doing young brother?" Havoc said exchanging a soul brother handshake.

"Best as can be, under the circumstances." Troy said pushing the frames on his nose back. "I want to apologize about the short notice but after the latest threat we felt we needed to get my Grandmother out of Brooklyn asap!"

"Understood," Havoc nodded sympathetically. Dressed in a button-down shirt and khakis, Troy's preppy style of dress reminded him of a younger Corbin except Troy seemed cool. "So where's she at?"

"Inside saying her good-byes."

"Then lead the way." Havoc said and followed Troy inside of a quaint two-family brick house that rocked with Pastor led prayers and Church hymns as a great many people young and old knelt around a silver-haired gracious old woman bouncing one baby on her knee while

271

calling to another running in circles. From the huge amount of people in attendance it was obvious that Hattie Mae Tucker was greatly loved.

"Havoc, I'd like for you to meet a very important person in my life, my Grandmother Mrs. Hattie Mae Tucker." Troy proudly said.

Havoc bowed. "Hello Mrs. Tucker, it is very nice to meet you." he said extending his hand.

"Sweetie what's with the formalities? Put that hand away." the kindly old woman said rising out of her seat with her arms extended. Havoc softened his hard dark eyes under her own gentle soft stare and embraced Hattie with a gentle squeeze. "Now that's more like it. I never shake hands, because to me handshakes are only hugs for fraidy-cats. I like the real thing. So, you're the one my grandbaby got to take me to the airport?" she asked settling back into her chair while at the same time turning down assistance from her family.

"Yes ma'am'. I'll be escorting you." Havoc nodded with the all business intensity of a Secret Service agent. He was impressed with how Hattie was so vital looking and unbroken by age in lieu of the bad hand she was recently dealt. In a way she reminded him of his own Nana and he could picture them becoming fast friends.

"My grandbaby said your name's Havoc?"

"Yes that's right." Havoc said.

Hattie looked at him oddly. "Chile' your mama done named you Havoc?" she asked.

Havoc chuckled, "Um, no ma'am. It's the name I go by when I'm, working."

"Oh, I see." Hattie said sizing the big man up and down then smiled warmly and turned to Troy. "I like him, he makes me feel safe already. Well Havoc if my grandson says I'd be safe with you then I believe him. You know he's a college man? He's going to Columbia University. Pre-med. As a reward for all his hard work the whole family chipped in and bought him a car." she said blushing with pride.

"Word-up? That's good man. We can use more Black Doctors." He nodded at Troy.

"But I am just as equally proud of all my babies." Hattie continued. "This here is my very first great-great grandbaby Dominique Simone Tucker and I got at least six more great grandchiren, eleven more grandchiren, five sons, three daughters and a host of other nieces, nephews, kin-folks and close friends to say my good byes to before we is going anywhere. So, Havoc what I'd do if I was you is go on over to the table and see my sister Emma Jean 'bout fixin you a plate of food. And you better hurry, cause Pastor Harvey is already on his third."

"You don't have to ask me twice." Havoc smiled and left Hattie to spending time with her family. After getting a heaping plate of candied yams, turnip greens, macaroni and cheese, ham, potato salad, southern-fried chicken, peach cobbler and cornbread made from scratch he found a seat and ate until his arm got tired. Between bites and finger licking, Havoc watched Hattie enjoy what may very well be the last time she would spend time with all of her immediate family under the same roof. Havoc was not going to be naïve and ask how someone could threaten, much less harm this sweet old woman. He had come across folks so evil who did things so cruel that nothing surprised him any longer. But one thing was for certain. Nothing was going to happen to Hattie Mae Tucker!

# Chapter 20

It was a little after 5 p.m. but since it was January the sky was already dark. Befitting the time of the year, it was a bone-chilling 28 degrees and the streets were covered with a nasty concoction of salt, slush, black ice and dirty snow. Scrolling past his favorite rap stations, Havoc stopped at Bill Withers singing 'Grandma's Hands' then avoided the slow-moving throughway by taking the scenic route. But he didn't mind the extra time at all. Hattie was a joy to ride with, and Mayhem loved the attention.

"Baby you was a hit at my send off. All my grand-daughter's and nieces was smitten with you. Even a couple of the older choir sisters too." Hattie teased as she scratched Mayhem behind the ears.

"Oh really? I hadn't noticed." Havoc fibbed recalling uncomfortably eating under the starry-eyed stares from the women in Hattie's family.

"Oh yes. Dem' girls was seriously checking you out. My seventeen-year-old granddaughter Octavia who was just accepted to Spellman to study engineering, said to me, 'Grandma, that fine man taking you to the airport is da' bomb.' Now I knows what fine means but I'm assuming that da' bomb is also a good thing." Hattie said making Havoc nod and chuckle to himself.

"You have a beautiful family. Mrs. Tucker. And while we're on the topic, if they're all here, who are you going to stay with in Virginia?"

"Oh no, baby this isn't all'a my family. I'm gonna live with my sister Emma's daughter Beulah, and her family. She's a pediatrician with her own practice, and also the one who inspired my Troy to study medicine. I also have another grandbaby named Todd who's married with four boys in Richmond, then there's my Brother Leon over in DC which ain't too far. Plus, I have oodles of childhood friends I ain't seen in ages. Shoot, if you think this was a party you should see what they got planned for me back home once I get there. They say Virginia is for lovers but I guess we Tuckers took that saying to heart, cause there sure is a lot of us." Hattie said causing Havoc to laugh.

"Well with all that family, you'll be just fine."

"Yes, I've been blessed with a big loving family."

"Speaking of family, I've been going on and on about mines. Tell me something 'bout yourself Havoc."

"What would you like to know?"

Mayhem rested her huge her head between their head rests and whimpered until she got another affectionate scratch from Hattie. "Well I won't waste time asking about what you and this big ol' sweet puppy dog of yours do for a living besides chauffer old ladies to the airport. Cause I'm sure you can't tell me much. So, I'll ask something you can answer. Do you have a special lady in your life?"

"Yes ma'am." Havoc answered as he got on the Belt Parkway. Acknowledging he was in a relationship was going to take some getting used to.

"What am I thinking? Of course you do. A big handsome young man like you. Dresses nicely and drives a fancy car. Probably has lots of girlfriends."

"Nah, that's not my style. If I'm single that's one thing. But if I'm in a relationship it's one on one."

"Now that's rare but good to hear. So, about your friend, I'll bet she's very pretty."

Havoc smiled. "Helen of Troy ain't got nothing on my Donnie. Her beauty could start wars."

"My! Now that is pretty. But is she smart, nice, got a good head on her shoulders? Those things are just as important as beauty you know. It's like I always tell my babies, don't just go for looks, they can deceive. Don't go for wealth, even that fades away. Go for someone who makes you smile because it only takes a smile to make a dark day seem bright."

Havoc glanced over at his wise passenger with a grin. "You described my Donnie to a tee. She's very smart. And very sweet. In fact, she's the kind of person that if you met her you'd be asking yourself, 'Now what is that nice young lady doing with that big mean guy?'"

275

"No. I'd be more inclined to say, now there goes a beautiful black-she is black ain't she?"

"Definitely."

"Okay cause nowadays you can't be too sure. Not that I have anything against dating outside of your race, cause I'm a firm believer that love chooses you. Not the other way around. But what I'd say is, 'Now there goes a beautiful young black couple that complete one another.' Baby I don't know why you think I'd say anything different. You ain't mean. Not at all. In fact, I think you are the opposite, a perfect gentleman. In fact, you remind me of my late husband Ernest."

"Oh, how so?"

"Well like you and your lady-friend, we was one on one for sixty-three glorious years until the man above called him home. He was a big man like you and also a looker. Folks would automatically assume he was mean because of his size until they spoke to him. But afterwards they realized he was hard on the outside and soft on the inside. Like you Sweetie." She rationalized.

From anyone else he would have taken that as an insult. *'Havoc, soft on the inside?' His name rang bells all over Brooklyn!* But coming from Mrs. Hattie Mae Tucker it was a compliment. Her description of him made him reflect on how similar it was to Donnie's and he felt a special kinship with the sweet old woman.

"Tommy." He said.

"Who's Tommy?" Hattie asked.

"I am. It's what my Mamma named me." He grinned.

Hattie looked at him and smiled. "And your last name?"

"It's Strong."

"Tommy Strong. It has a real nice masculine ring to it."

Havoc nodded graciously at a red light and glanced at the rear-view mirror. His eyes did a double take. The black Mercedes with the tinted windows he would only see after he had been smoking weed was sitting behind him, and this time he was not high! His heart accelerated as Hattie rambled away. Havoc reached behind his back and pulled his gun halfway out of its holster while pretending to pay attention to whatever she was saying. Mayhem's posture instinctively tightened and she too was ready for whatever. When the light turned green the black car made a huge U-turn upsetting traffic and disappeared down the block.

"Wake up honey. The light's green." Hattie said.

"Huh? -Oh yeah right," Havoc said and smiled at Hattie then continued driving ever so often cutting his eyes in the mirror. Obviously someone was playing games and sooner or later it would come to an end.

Unfortunately for Mayhem, dogs her size were not allowed inside of JFK Airport so she had to wait in the car along with Havoc's weapons. After checking Hattie's luggage, Havoc and Hattie made their way through the jam-packed airport to the gate her plane was departing from. As he walked his eyes darted everywhere at once, over every face keeping a look out for depraved looking types that would harm an old woman. When someone got too close to Hattie they were rudely shoved aside.

"Now baby, be nice." She scolded after Havoc bumped a man into a magazine rack who was not watching where he was walking.

"I'm not taking any chances Mrs. Tucker. So, your flight doesn't depart for another half an hour. How's a cup of coffee sound?"

"Add a slice of cherry cobbler to the offer and you've got yourself a date." Hattie winked. A moment later they were seated in a nearby restaurant attached to the food court. After being in there for less than ten minutes the sweet old woman had won the hearts of all the waitresses and received her pie on the house. "People who don't live here are quick to say that New York is unfriendly, but I beg to differ. I'm really gonna miss it." Hattie sighed. "Petersburg is nice but it's sooo slow. I'm a tough old bird, used to the hustle and bustle."

"Yeah it will be a big culture shock for you going back. But you'll be safe, and that's what's important." Havoc said.

"Still I wish I could stay. But the man up above has other plans for me." Hattie said then sipped her coffee. Havoc nodded and smiled at a toy poodle peeking at him from inside of its cage by its master's feet. "I see you have a special bond with that precious puppy-dog of yours."

"Oh yeah. Mayhem's saved my life more times than I can remember. She's my best friend."

"So, you have your best friend and your best girl. Sounds like I'm not the only one who's blessed." Hattie winked.

"Yeah I guess you're ri-" From where Havoc was seated he had a perfect view of whoever entered the small establishment and was glad that he chosen that seat because he was immediately concerned with the three men in dark trench coats and shades that walked in. Hattie noticed something catch his eye and turned around. When she saw the darkly dressed men take one step after another towards her, she caught a flashback to the bank holdup and clutched her chest as her heart palpitated. Hattie's reaction was all Havoc needed and he punched his time clock and went to work! He abruptly stood as one of the men reached inside of his jacket. Before he could get whatever it was out, Havoc plowed into him like a linebacker and sent him crashing into a dessert cart. Customers ducked for cover as the Trouble Consultant connected his fist with the second man's jaw who was frozen with shock and sent him spinning. The third man was lifted above Havoc's head and tossed over the counter.

"You idiot! What the hell's your problem?" The first man Havoc knocked down demanded covered with cake and ice cream.

"You're the one with a problem if you think I'm gonna let you harm this sweet lady because she helped put away your low-life piece of shit buddy!" Havoc snarled standing protectively before Hattie.

"What the hell are you talking about! Harm who? I don't even know this woman, do you Frank?"

"Never seen her before in my life Terry." Frank said groggily from behind the counter. "Ray?" asked his buddy. Ray couldn't speak through a mouth full of loose teeth and shook his head in pain. "See, we've never seen her before!"

Havoc studied the men he just worked over more closely. All three were in their late mid to late forties, early fifties, out of shape and wore business suits. Not exactly hit-man material. He looked back at Hattie and realized for the first time in his career, he fucked up-royally.

"Oh crap! I'm really sorry about this fellas, my bad. I thought you were trying to harm Mrs. Tucker over there." Havoc explained.

"Now why in the hell would you think that?" the man covered in dessert demanded.

"Too long to go into. But when I saw you reach inside your jacket I assumed that you were reaching for-"

"For this?" Terry said in a raised voice holding up his asthma pump.

"Christ," Havoc sighed. "Here, let me help you." he said offering the man on the floor his hand.

"No thank you! I can manage. Just stay the hell away from me!" The man said and angrily pulled away. As Havoc tried to apologize to the men that were in town on business and the rest of the restaurant as well, he failed to notice the slim Spanish woman with her head down who followed them into the food court and took a seat close by.

Grateful for the coincidental distraction and foolishly assuming it was a sign, the woman who was dressed in all white like an angel of death nodded at the nervous-faced custodian drenched in sweat. He emptied the waste receptacle, wiped the station clean then nodded back and quickly exited the scene. She then nonchalantly got up from her table and carried her tray of uneaten food over to throw out. While shaking her tray inside the receptacle she glanced around then slyly reached inside and removed something wrapped in plastic.

As Hattie patiently stood by while her bodyguard tried to resolve the situation by offering to pay for their dry cleaning, the businessmen argued a lot good that would do since they were on their way to an important meeting. With everything going on no one saw the Angel walked up behind Hattie and unwrap the shiny 22 caliber she took from the waste receptacle.

"You think you can just put my man away and fly the coop? I don't think so, you dime dropping old bitch!" the Angel swore pointing her gun.

Hattie turned around slowly and her eyes stretched wide. She remembered how everyday Mrs. Delgado sat in court in the same seat with her eyes locked on her like she wanted to leap out of her seat and strangle her for testifying against her husband and putting him away for life. Now she had her chance.

Suddenly Hattie grabbed for the gun and the two women struggled. Over the shoulder of the man he was apologizing to, Havoc spotted Hattie was in danger and shoved him aside grabbing a metal napkin dispenser from a nearby table and rushing forward. Mrs. Delgado overpowered and pushed Hattie to the floor then smiled wickedly and aimed her weapon. Havoc launched the napkin dispenser like a spiral missile, striking her in the head. But his heroic quick-thinking act wasn't quick enough, as the woman holding the gun grabbed her face and blindly fired.

**BLAM!**

The loud sound made everyone duck for cover except for Havoc who fearlessly dived on top of the shooter and wrestled away her gun. Once she was no longer a threat he frantically turned to Hattie who was face down on the floor.

"Oh-no! NO!" Havoc said kneeling over Hattie then looked up at the woman responsible with fire in his eyes. Mrs. Delgado stared at Hattie unsympathetically.

Airport security rushed on the scene with guns drawn and Mrs. Delgado was arrested. Proud of what she did because it was for true love, the scorned woman with the swollen face smiled feeling vindicated and complied with the officers' commands. Then her eyes widened and her lips parted into a gasp. Havoc turned to see what had her dumbfounded and a sigh of relief came over him. Hattie looked up at him with only a slight bullet graze on her head.

The old woman winked, "Told ya I'm a tough old bird!"

<hr>

"Now you needn't worry about me baby. Those nice paramedics have checked me from head to toe and given me a clean bill of health. They even gave me a pretty pink bandage to match my dress." Hattie said pointing at her head wrap from her wheel chair as Havoc pushed her through the airport with a police escort in tow. He learned that Mrs. Delgado threatened to call Immigration on her cousin who worked at the airport as a custodian unless he smuggled the gun she used to almost kill Hattie into the airport. After what seemed like an eternity of answering questions and receiving medical attention for her non-life-threatening injuries, she refused to miss yet another plane and was determined to board the next one departing.

"You sure about this Mrs. Tucker? You can always catch a later flight."

"Baby I done already missed three later flights dealing with all this craziness."

"At least call your family and explain what really happened."

"No, they'll only worry. Besides the worse is over. As far as they know my flight was delayed and I'll be arriving a little later is all."

"Hey you know what? I can buy a roundtrip ticket and fly down with you. I'll pay for it myself."

"No, that's sweet but I'm fine really. And those nice officers assured me there would be a Federal Air Marshal on the plane. Now I know he ain't you but he'll do." Hattie smiled as Havoc personally escorted her safely to her plane then made sure she got a window seat.

"You have a safe flight and good luck." Havoc sighed remorsefully and handed her an envelope.

"What's this?"

"The payment Troy gave me. I sure didn't earn it."

"Don't be silly. You did earn that money. If it weren't for you I wouldn't be here. Even the police called you a hero. Now I see why my grandbaby hired you. You are da' bomb." Hattie winked and Havoc smiled for the first time since the ordeal. "So, you keep that and I won't take no for an answer."

"Yes ma'am." Havoc nodded with a final hug and as he exited the airport he made the day for a couple of Nuns asking for donations for their Church.

# Chapter 21

Havoc viewed Trouble Consulting as one big cowboy movie where he was the dark stranger that rode into town, the brother with the fast burners, brave enough to take on the baddest motherfucker then after busting a couple of caps in their ass rode off into sunset in a phat whip. An urban legend in his own time. That's the way it was supposed to be until someone badder beat him to the draw.

Tommy entered his loft and looked around for Donnie. She wasn't there. He collapsed in a chair then used the toe of one boot to lever against the heel of the other until he pulled his foot free. After removing the other boot, he laid back. "Today was so bad, I couldn't fuck it away," he sighed thinking Trouble Consulting was really starting to become really whack; Big Time!

He wished Donnie was there to rub the hurt away. The time they were spending together was spoiling him and he was starting to like the idea of her being around more and more. Mayhem suddenly yanked her head out of her bowl and rushed over to the door barking as it opened. Tommy sat up as Donnie walked in with packages in her arms. As soon as they saw each other their eyes lit up like Christmas lights.

"You're back." she said cheerfully. "I wanted to surprise you with a home cooked meal." Donnie said carrying the bags into the kitchen. "Oh, check it out. I also stopped by the toy store. I figured instead of playing mindless video games maybe Tee-Tee would like to play something that involves interaction between you two so I got Operation." As she spoke Tommy sat there staring at her with a huge grin. "Are you alright? Did everything go Okay today?" Donnie asked concerned.

Tommy held out his arms like an infant that wanted to be held and Donnie came over and wrapped her arms around him then kissed him on top of his shaved head. As they hugged he could feel her positive vibes enter his body and do away with all the negative energy he carried home from today's fiasco. He looked into her eyes paused for a second, woke out of the daze from darker days of being alone and returned to his brighter present, with a huge smile. The fact that she was there with him right now in his time of need meant the world to him. This was why he didn't juggle women. A quick lay would not be there right now holding him down. Having his back. He realized this and felt something powerful at that very moment.

The words to describe it were on the tip of his tongue. He opened his mouth. "Donnie I-" He began.

"Yes baby." She whispered.

"I-I" Tommy stuttered. "I-I" Donnie leaned forward and gestured for him to spit it out. "I-wanted to know if you wanted to go out for dinner instead of cooking." He was certain of what he felt in his heart but he wanted to parlay just a little longer because once he said it, there would be no turning back.

"Fine by me." Donnie said then shot him a suspicious glare. "Are you sure you're alright? Everything went Okay with you and Mayhem?"

"Let's talk about it later. Right now, I wanna take the finest lady in Brooklyn out for a delicious meal."

"Okay but I'm ordering Lobster." Donnie said zipping her jacket back up.

"Fine by me, just remember to speak directly into the clown's mouth."

"I thought I was." Donnie said giggling then jumped when Tommy popped her on her butt on the way out the door.

Stacy Latisaw and Johnny Gill's duet 'Perfect Combination' drifted throughout the Lennox Lounge. The establishment was packed with ghetto-elite dressed in expensive jewelry and upmarket brands like Fendi, Louis Vuitton and Gucci.

Seated across from Donnie, Tommy looked smooth in black Wallabees and a freshly pressed Pierre Cardin silk suit. On the tip of his broad nose sat a pair of Gucci frames with tinted lenses. The diamond in his gold pinky ring sparkled as did his gold Gucci link chain that laid comfortably across his bulging pectorals matching the shiny bracelet on his wrist.

Donnie was equally impressive. Her long black hair was pulled tightly into a French braid and she was rocking a pink cashmere v-neck sweater with a slim fitting Gucci skirt and matching Mary Jane Gucci shoes. The diamonds decorating her ears, wrists and neck sparkled like glass and she looked like an Urban princess. In the immortal words of Johnny and Stacy, they were a Perfect Combination.

"Tell me another weak ass line that brothers have tried on you." Tommy asked as he devoured his T-bone steak and baked potato, still laughing at the past three she already laid on him.

Pausing between bites of her lobster scampi she pondered, "Um let me see, oh yeah just the other day I was on my lunchbreak and this one guy says to me, "Hi, I'm new in town, what are the directions to your house?" Donnie recalled in a deep voice mimicking the guy's husky voice.

Tommy cracked up. "Aw man that is so whack."

"Then there was the time this guy licked his finger, wiped my shirt and said, 'Let's get you out those wet clothes.' But homeboy got smacked for that."

"I swear most men don't even know how to talk to a woman. They throw lame line after lame line just trying to get some ass. But me personally I never use lines when I step to women." Tommy pointed out.

"Use?" Donnie leaned forward.

"Used. Past tense baby, past tense. I just talked to them straight up because it's all in the approach." He said on the borderline of cockiness and confidence.

"See that's what I'm talking about. Women don't want brother's that are trying to be all debonair and suave saying what they think we want to hear. Now earlier when you told me how I reminded you of a honeybee that was real."

"Aw don't even try it. You was ready to flip until I broke it down to you what I meant." Tommy reminded her with a wink then washed down a bite of steak with Johnnie Walker BLACK.

Donnie laughed so wide her gold filings shined in the light. "True dat. But I'm saying, all that fake premeditated stuff is mad corny. I want to hear what's in your heart not some whack line that I heard six minutes ago from some other Herb. The other type of guys that turn me off are the wimps. When it comes to men, for me, it's all about confidence. That's sexy. I've met brothers who told me they liked me but were afraid of me rejecting them because I was too pretty and that's why they didn't approach me. I can't stand guys like that with no confidence or backbone. Give me your number, make me think if I call I'm the lucky one."

"Yeah but Donnie in these guys defense, it's not easy to approach a woman like you."

"And what's a woman like me?" Donnie wanted to know.

"A woman that's fresh to def, fine and pushes a **Bob Marley Wagon**. That's some intimidating shit for most men."

"Well *you* don't seem intimidated by my looks or car." Donnie said coyly.

"I'm not most men and if you don't know, you'd better ask somebody." he said cocky. "I'm sick of waiting for our waiter. I'm headed to the bar for a refill. You want another glass of champagne?"

"That'll work." Donnie smiled.

"Be right back." Tommy said and proceeded towards the bar.

'I shot the Sherriff' by the hot rap duo, EMPD bounced off the walls as a slim curly haired Puerto Rican man strolled in flanked by an entourage of screw-faced goons. He was dressed from head to toe in a Dapper Dan Gucci original. On his hand he wore a gaudy money sign symbolled two-fingered ring. A huge flashy dookey rope chain with an obese diamond encrusted medallion that spelled-out MI$TER PAPER$ swung perilously from his neck courtesy of Jacob the Jeweler. When the sexy scantily dressed gold diggers spotted him they flocked over like seagulls, for a different type of bread. Enjoying the attention while surveying the scene, the ghetto-celebrity spotted Tommy and came over.

"Yo, yo, yo! What's the dilly-O?" The Hispanic man asked gleefully like he hadn't a care in the world, displaying a gold encrusted smile that afforded him an expensive conversation. He held out his hand for a pound.

Tommy rolled his eyes already annoyed but still showed him respect and shook it like it pained him to do so. "Hello Papers."

"No need to get an attitude brother man. I come in peace."

"Is that right?"

"Yeah. I just want to rap a taste with you,"

"About?"

"Your future, working for me as my number one enforcer."

"Good bye Papers," Tommy growled and gave him his back.

"Come on man. Hear me out," the flashy drug kingpin pressed Tommy as the bartender handed him his drinks. When Tommy reached for his wallet, Mister Papers pulled out a fat bankroll, peeled off a crumbled fifty-dollar bill and told the bartender to keep the change. "Think of me as a guidance counselor. Let's take your chosen field. Bad choice. I recommend against it."

"Who asked you?" Tommy snapped.

"Nobody, but man I gotta tell you, you're making peanuts dealing with these welfare cases. You and I both know, the hood ain't no good. But it can be extremely profitable if you come play ball for my team. Hell, I'll sweeten the deal and pay your partner in Alpo. What do you say?"

Tommy pulled out a bank teller crisp one-hundred-dollar bill. Paid for his own drinks and left an even bigger tip, carving a huge grin onto the bartender's face. "Enjoy the rest of the evening."

After making it clear he was not interested in what Mister Papers was offering, Tommy took his drinks and headed back to his table. A large man with a scowl permanently tattooed on his face stepped up beside the Hispanic man. "You want me to go persuade him to rethink your offer?" the thug asked.

Mister Papers looked at him like he was crazy. "If you could do that, then why would I need him? Besides he's not the kinda guy you can persuade. He's the kinda guy who does the persuading!"

"What was that all about back there?" Donnie asked as Tommy presented her with her drink.

Tommy shrugged. "Oh that? Nothing. Just a local street pharmacist who wants me to come and work for him as his personal bodyguard. He figures it'd increase his street cred, which it would, if he could persuade me to join the dark side. I've gotten offers like that from practically every kingpin real or aspiring all over the city. Some even out of state."

"Okay there's something I still don't get about you and this whole Trouble Consulting thing." Donnie said.

"Which is?"

"Some people refer to you as Tommy, and other's as Havoc."

"Right-so." he said eating his meal.

"So, at first, I thought it was a situation where when you wore red clothing you were Havoc, hero of the hood and when you wore anything else you were Tommy Strong, mild-mannered homeboy from BK. But that guy just recognized you as Havoc yet you don't have any red on."

Tommy grinned. "What, you thought that my wearing red was like a superhero costume or something? When I'm in red I'm Brooklyn's Black Batman and when I'm laying low I'm Bruce Wayne?"

"Batman has Robin. Havoc has Mayhem." Donnie reasoned over a mouthful of lobster and pasta.

"Wow, you learn something new every day. I had no idea you were such a big fan of comic books." Tommy shook his head amused.

"I'm not. But I once wrote a term paper on the subject of modern day superheroes in college. It was all about the similar traits between super heroes in the pages of comic books and in real life. Their homogenous mindsets and what makes them do the things they do. The father who's up at 4am to take the train to a job he loathes to support his family versus the guy who dons a cape and mask to protect the weak and innocent because he suffered a tragic loss in life. That sorta' thing. Had I known you back then you could've saved me from all the hours I spent at the local comic book shop reading comics and being drooled on by nerds. I could've interviewed you instead and we could've drooled on each other."

"And all you would have gotten outta me is that I am nobody's superhero. Trust me there's no noble cause here. I do this strictly for the loot." Tommy promised but Donnie's look wasn't buying it. "But I guess I could see why you'd think that, cause red is my signature trademark. Even though it's definitely not the image I was going for."

"Ok, then why the red? Inquiring minds want to know."

"Because it's the color of danger. A fear tactic. And it's what I want these fools to know they're in when they see me and Mayhem coming for them! Plus, it's great at hiding blood stains." Tommy explained with a shrug and removed a piece of steak from his fork. "But to answer your question, yes, some people know me as Tommy and others as Havoc and some as both. It basically comes down to the nature of our relationship."

"Oh, I see. So if we would have never surpassed our one-time business relationship, I'd only know you as Havoc because I hired you."

"And here I thought college was a complete waste of time." Tommy winked.

Donnie stuck her tongue out then sipped on her drink. "Now something else is odd to me. Your mother doesn't know what you do, how is that?"

"Hell no! My mom would trip if she found out. Probably pull off her belt and commence to beating my ass." He snickered on the outside but wouldn't put it past her. "It makes my life a helluva' lot easier if she thinks I'm a construction worker with a dog named May."

"Secret identity, check." She giggled continuing the superhero comparisons.

"And that's where the corny similarities end because my Pop knows. As well as my cousin." He said.

"Well Batman does have Alfred."

"At the end of the day I'm just an ordinary guy who does extraordinary things."

"You're a lot of things baby. But ordinary isn't one of them."

In an attempt to move past what he felt was a ridiculous notion of him being a superhero. Tommy beckoned her with his finger then stuck his tongue in her ear hitting her spot. Donnie smiled enjoying herself as she watched two boneless kids battle it out on the dance floor with back flips, handstands and intricate pop locking moves. Then suddenly everything paused like E.F. Hutton had something to say as a tall long-legged modern-day Amazon with long Shirley Temple curls and a big butt in stiletto-heel boots, squeezed into a barely there dress tight enough to crack the shell of an armadillo sashayed in.

Heading past the eye rolls and adoration of gawking men, she went over and put her curves on display at the bar then ordered a whisky sour. Ignoring the desperados and cheap pickup lines she set her sights on Tommy and hungrily stared him down.

"Having fun, beautiful one?" Tommy asked Donnie.

"I was-a minute ago." Donnie rolled her eyes and sucked her teeth in the direction of the Amazon staring down her man. "Take a picture sweetie, it'll last longer!" she growled at the vixen.

Tommy glanced over his shoulder just as Miss Thing was showing off her oral skills by tying a cherry stem into a knot with her tongue. And he immediately set out to rectify the situation. He cupped Donnie's chin and twisted her pissed off face towards his, "Hey, did I tell you how fine you look tonight?"

"As a matter a fact, no you didn't." Donnie said looking into Tommy's magnetic hazel eyes.

"Well you do. Damn fine. Finest woman up in here." Tommy said staring directly back into her alluring green eyes causing the Amazon to suck her teeth, toss in the towel and turn her back.

Donnie blushed. None of the guys she dated ever gave her compliments because they figured since she was pretty everyone else tells her that. But not Tommy. He knew that regardless of how beautiful a woman was, she needed to be told so every once in a while. "You're looking good yourself, and you smell nice. What is that anyway?" Donnie asked sniffing Tommy's neck. "I've never smelled that fragrance before."

"You really wanna know?" Tommy asked.

"I wouldn't ask if I didn't,"

Tommy looked around then leaned in close, "It's dog cologne. One time I ran out of Polo and it smelled so good on Mayhem that I said fuck it and decided to use some myself and have been doing it ever since."

"Hilarious. Smells good though." Donnie said after sniffing Tommy's neck again and planting a kiss there.

The music lowered and a chubby black man in a tight seersucker suit strutted like George Jefferson on stage getting giggles from the audience. "Good Evening Ladies and Gentlemen my name is Tracy Morgan. How's everyone doing tonight? I see there's a lot of beautiful happy couples in the house. Me and my wife were perfectly happy for 28 years…and then we met each other." he said getting laughs from the audience. "So, I thought I'd come out and warm up the crowd with a few quick jokes before the main event if that's alright with you. How do fish get high?"

"How?" Tommy yelled out.

"Seaweed!" the comedian replied as Tommy and Donnie cracked up with everyone else. "What is Michael Jackson's favorite pants?...Billie Jeans!" the crowd erupted into laughter and applauded as the up and coming comedian took a bow. "So, are you ready to keep the party going? Then please show some love and give a warm round of applause for Champaign as they perform their chart-topping hit, How Bout Us!"

The light's dimmed as the attractive looking septet took the stage Tommy emptied his glass in one gulp then offered Donnie his hand. "My lady, would you do me the honor of accompanying me on the dance floor?" he asked.

Donnie stared at Tommy with dreamy eyes. He looked so good, so confident, so *strong* like Billy Dee Williams did in her all-time favorite movie, 'Lady Sings the Blues.' She imagined she was Diana Ross as she placed her hand inside his. She would have gone anywhere, done anything he asked.

As the baby making melody kicked in, the pair slowly swayed to the beat on the dance floor surrounded by other couples. Then after whispering some choice sweet nothings in each other's ears, they tenderly kissed.

"After the day I've had, words can't describe how good this feels." Tommy said with a grin as Donnie squeezed him tight and rubbed his back. His eyes opened when she stopped. "Hey why'd you stop?"

"Oh so I'm just supposed to stand here in the middle of the dance floor massaging you all night?" Donnie giggled. "I'll tell you what, if you want me to continue rubbing your back, then beg."

Tommy laughed. "Beg. Oh see now you're tripping. Just because I love you doesn't mean I-" he paused, "Aw shit!"

"Excuse me?" Donnie asked then pulled back overwhelmed and looked at Tommy. He stared back at her uncomfortably. It was time to either shit or get off the pot.

He laughed inwardly, "I'm Teflon. Practically invulnerable to pain. After being beaten, knifed, shot, tortured I can eat it like candy. But there's one type of pain I can't tolerate."

"And what's that?" Donnie asked.

"Heartache."

"Tommy, I would never cause you any heartache, don't you know that?" Donnie said.

"Yes I do. But it wasn't my heartache I was talking about." Donnie looked confused. "Baby there's something you don't know about my marriage. Nicky never wanted to divorce me, but I gave her no choice. I could not leave the streets alone and she could no longer deal with being awakened in the middle of the night to let in a bruised and bloodied man. So as much as it hurt her, she filed for divorce."

Donnie's feet still moved to the music but Tommy had her undivided attention. "After our divorce a part inside me died and I thought it could never come alive again. But I was wrong. That part I thought was dead is alive again, thanks to you. I don't know how you wiggled your way into my life. Or I yours, but here we are slow dancing in each other's arms. But I can't do you like this baby. I care about you too much to put you through this."

"Tommy I'm a big girl who knows what she's getting herself into. I love you and that's all that counts. Everything else, what you do, what may be, is secondary to me."

By now Tommy had stopped dancing and looked deep into her eyes. Into her soul. The time was right. The mood was right. And above all, it felt right. "We had our first date here. I remember that we sat over there and the band performed that Roberta Flack joint from that Richard Pryor movie." he pointed at a booth occupied by another blissful couple.

"Just When I needed you. Yeah, I remember. I was there too," Donnie smiled joining him down memory lane. "Fun fact. I got here earlier and paid the band to perform that song.

"Word?"

Donnie nodded. "It described how I felt when we met. I never told you because, I dunno, I thought you might think it was cheesy."

Tommy smiled shaking his head. "Quite the contrary. See, it's stuff like that, that's why I knew the moment we meant. I just refused to admit it."

"What did you know Tommy? What are you trying to say?" Donnie asked.

"That if battling poverty and crime has taught me anything, it's you have to take your pleasure where you can find it. So, I guess what I'm trying to say is that, I love you."

A smile cracked Donnie's face and developed into a big wide grin. She wished she could freeze this moment and hold onto it forever. After all this time the man she loved finally admitted what she knew in her heart all along. That he loved her back. She wrapped her arms around Tommy's neck and squeezed tightly. He smiled and kissed his woman on the dance floor, staring at her longingly.

"Let's get out of here." Tommy insisted.

"Batcave, check."

Fifteen minutes later they were in Tommy's Jeep headed for Williamsburg Brooklyn. "I don't know about you but, I'm still hungry. The food was decent, but the portions are so damn small. When we get back to my crib I'm heating up those leftover collard greens my mom left in my freezer. What about you gorgeous? You still hungry?" He said.

"No, I'm stuffed." Donnie said and slyly cut an eye over at Tommy, "I was thinking, how about we go back to my crib for a change? I mean if you're still hungry all I have is lean cuisines and Tab in the fridge but if you're really hungry I have something hot you can ea-hcy, are listening? You-hoo, Tommy?" She called but Tommy didn't respond. He was too preoccupied with the black Mercedes Benz that seemed to boldly taunt him as it slowly cruised past him, paused for a second then vanished around the corner. Was this really a coincidence or paranoia? "Way to make a sister feel special!" she complained.

"Oh, I'm sorry Princess. My mind wandered."

"I'll say. And what could possibly take your mind off of all of this?" Donnie asked, waving a hand over her curves. "It had better not be that chick with the huge calves that was clocking you from the bar. Bet you that bitch was a man anyway." She said teasingly.

"Huh-who? Oh no way. Not even. But how's this for an idea, let's stop off at the liquor store and get a bottle of Dom P. so that I can get you drunk and take advantage of your luscious body?" he said rubbing her thigh while shooting an eye in the side view mirror. If he wasn't tripping and someone was following them, he would rather that they knew his address, not Donnie's.

"Tommy, how many times do I have to tell you? You don't have to get me drunk. I'm a sure thing." Donnie stuck out her bottom lip and pouted. "And why do we always go to your place? We never go to mines."

"Aw baby that's not true." Tommy said.

"Oh really? Then what color is my bedroom?" She demanded to know. Tommy couldn't answer because frankly, he couldn't remember. "Now how fair is that? Don't you think if we're going to start a relationship then shouldn't we begin by meeting each other half way?"

Tommy sighed, she was right, they always crashed at his loft or hotels but never at her place. She looked determined and two identical cars that passed him on the street weren't going to change her mind. "Okay ya big baby, let's go to your crib." he said reluctantly giving in.

"Really?" Donnie perked up.

"Yeah. Point taken."

"I love you baby." Donnie kissed him overjoyed she was getting her way while Tommy had a bad feeling about this.

"Yeah, me too." he said with a concerned look in his eyes.

# Chapter 22

Tommy's eyes popped open at a quarter past two in the am. He looked over at Donnie. She was sleeping peacefully with her arm wrapped around him and her head nuzzled deep in the nook of his chest. He watched her sleep and liked the feeling of her smooth, warm skin against his body and contemplated on waking her up for more sex, but she looked so comfortable he let her rest. He got up without disturbing her and caught a glimpse of the hickeys on his chest in the mirror.

"This relationship shit's getting to be painful." he grinned then wrapped himself up in a lavender comforter, grabbed the half empty bottle of champagne and a spliff from his coat pocket then went out on the terrace. "Shit it's cold out here." Tommy said as the frosty cold whipped around his legs and torso. He took a swig of champagne before sparking up his spliff then leaned his six-foot-three frame into Donnie's whicker lounge chair then maxed and just relaxed.

"So, I take it you're Donnie's latest?" A voice asked out of the darkness.

Tommy sprang up and looked around. "Whoa!" he said wondering how in the hell he could have missed the thick-thighed sista' squeezed into a pair of size 6 canary yellow hip huggers on the terrace directly across from him.

"I don't know about latest. But yes, I am her man!" Tommy answered full of self-assuredness.

"My my! Ballsy, aren't we? And speaking of balls..." she giggled with big roving eyes forcing Tommy to do a better job of covering himself with the comforter. "I'm Onetta Jackson, Donnie's neighbor." She smiled and came closer to the railing. "And you are?"

"Tommy Strong." he said feeling awkward.

"Oh yes-you-are." Onetta said digging into her finger waves with a long 14k gold fingernail. "So, where's Miss Donnie at anyways?" she asked nosily.

"Around." Tommy said wrinkling his nose at her questions.

"I see you like to smoke a little weed after getting busy. So do I." Onetta confessed with a wide toothy smile.

*"Then I guess you don't smoke that often."* Tommy mumbled under his breath while flicking ashes from the spliff. He caught Onetta trying to steal a peek under his comforter and tucked the corner underneath his thigh as her slightly crooked white teeth bit into the fullness of her bottom lip. When she realized she was caught she smiled unashamed.

"Can I offer you a drink? I got some of everything over here. Beer, wine, rum a King-Sized bed."

"Nah that's aight. Besides, my moms told me not to take candy from strangers." Tommy said. He was about sick of Onetta sticking her mammoth-sized 46 triple D's where they did not belong. All he wanted to do was smoke his bud and sip his drink in peace.

"Cute and witty. Some girls got all the luck." Onetta shrugged then spun on her heels and looked over her shoulder, "Remember if you wanna feel the heat then you gots to have the meat," she cracked herself up and continued inside.

"I'll keep that in mind." Tommy said and stood up stretching and headed back inside. He was surprised to find Donnie sitting up in bed.

"So I see you met my uncouth neighbor." She said reaching over for the bottle of champagne and taking a swig.

Tommy looked over at her and chuckled. "Yo, home girl's butt's so big if somebody told her to haul ass she'd have to make two trips."

Donnie slapped her hand over her mouth so as not to spit out champagne. "You're so crazy. But on the real she needs to go find, buy or rent a man of her own instead of trying to push-up on every guy standing on my terrace." Donnie said shaking her head.

Tommy cut an eye at her while getting back in bed, "And just how many guys do you have standing on your terrace?"

Donnie rolled over on top of her big strong man and kissed him laughing. "Aw look at you getting all jealous. Okay I'm not gonna lie and say none of the guys were old boyfriends. But mostly they were my brothers and cousins and the ones that were boyfriends are ancient history."

"Yeah, I'll let you tell it." Tommy said semi suspiciously. He trusted her but being a man that was falling in love with someone as beautiful and unique as the woman he was in bed with, he could not help but be a little wary. "So baby I have to tell you something."

"What is it baby?" Donnie asked basking in the afterglow of sex.

"I know the timing sucks but, I have to go back to my crib."

"What you're leaving now?" She checked her alarm clock. "But it's after two."

"Yeah I know but I have to be home to walk Mayhem and I'm not exactly sure what time my folks are coming to drop Tee-Tee off today."

"Then leave at seven. They're not dropping her off that early, I'm certain." She reasoned.

"Nah, I'm already up so I'm gonna just bounce."

Donnie rolled her eyes, sighed, then sat up and reached for her robe. "O-kay fine. Give me a sec to get dressed."

Tommy appreciated how she was willing to get out of a warm bed and drive all the way over to his place. And the fact that Donnie had his back one hundred and one percent gave him a good feeling. God, he pitied the fool that tried to harm a hair on her pretty little head! "But you're already in bed why don't you come tomorrow."

"You don't want me to come with you?" Donnie asked.

"It's not that, I just don't think it makes any sense for the both of us getting up."

Donnie suddenly cut her eyes at him and twitched her lips like something had occurred to her. "You think I'm dumb don't cha?"

"Huh? What are you talking about?"

"I'm talking about you going out on another Trouble Consulting assignment, aren't you?"

"Well I uh, uh-" Tommy said.

"You don't have to lie Tommy" Donnie said, already convinced where he was going. What other reason would there be to leave her bed?

"Well what can I say? You got me dead to rights." Tommy grinned and held out his wrists like he was about to be cuffed.

"Can't I write you a doctor's note?"

"Sorry babe. Duty calls,"

Donnie rolled her eyes. "This is the second time today. Don't make this a habit." She said then laid back down.

After getting dressed Tommy twirled his guns cowboy style and placed them in their holsters. He stared long and hard at Donnie as she slept and did not want to leave. Between almost failing today's mission and leaving Donnie's bed, Trouble Consulting was most definitely becoming played out. Word up!

# Chapter 23

Ever since he saw that black Mercedes Benz for the second time Tommy couldn't shake the feeling it was hiding somewhere in the shadows. He also couldn't shake the feeling that this wasn't a coincidence. Which is why he had to get away from where Donnie lived. After driving through his borough, he found himself sitting at a light beneath the elevated three train in a rough looking area. He glanced over and was surprised to see Nicky get out of a gypsy cab alone and enter a seedy after-hours club called 'The Future.'

"What the hell is she doing going in there?" Tommy asked aloud and boldly made a sudden u-turn, pulled into a parking spot and shut off his car. "As if I don't have enough on my plate!" he complained as he got out and headed towards the dangerous looking building that should have a sign hanging over it that warned patrons to, enter at your ow risk!

There's a rumor that whenever the rallying cry, 'Brooklyn's in da house,' was heard in sold-out jams and seedy after hour nightspots, that was the cue to clutch one's pocketbook and tuck in gold chains before they were taxed. That bit of scuttlebutt held true inside 'The Future.' Bleakly nicknamed, 'The Grim Reaper's favorite hangout', it was smack dab in the middle of an area so rough cabs would not go there without combat pay. The Future was a den of iniquity, drab with filthy walls, a weathered bar and a number of small worn booths with taped up cushions. But the crowd that was primarily made up of stone cold Brooklynites didn't care. All that mattered to them was two things, who could they take advantage of and who they were winding up with at the end of the night.

A spicy beat pumped from the loud sound system as bodies pressed together on the dance floor bumping ironically to Whodini's 'Freaks Come Out at Night'. Liquor and beer poured from the bar while who knows what else slid from people's pockets to juice up the patrons. Women sexily swayed their curvy hips to the beat fronting like they had no idea that the guys trying to look cool were clocking them.

Back in his Mister Fix-it days Tommy was a regular fixture like Norm was in Cheers and it all came back as he slid through a murky blue haze of blazing weed and cigarette smoke receiving hugs from the honeys and pounds from the roughnecks. Every move he made was executed with the same precision the Trouble Consultant would use to disarm a thug in an alley. Suddenly a fistfight broke out and Tommy watched with mild interest as one drunk tried to knock the chin off the other. Once the bouncers broke it up he headed towards the bar looking for Nicky. After a brief catching up, he was informed by the bartender that a woman who fit his ex-wife's description had just went into the lady's room moments ago.

Three minutes later, Nicky exited the restroom dressed stylishly in heels, a denim skirt and a black leather crop jacket. Hiding behind a pair of dark don't-notice-me shades she made her way to the bar and immediately felt someone's hand circle her waist. She turned to show the drunk pushy guy a brown-eyed, I'm not interested look. But instead of taking the hint and going on about his merry drunken way, he turned on the charm even more.

"Say baby how you doin?' You got a name, or can I call you mines?" the hot breath lush asked cracking himself up.

"Do yourself a favor-give up!" Nicky sucked her teeth and wrenched her arm away.

The lush glared at her. "Oh so it's like that? And here I was trying to make your day. You ain't even all that anyway! You uppity stank ass bi-"

The diss died in his throat as Tommy appeared out of nowhere and put a beefy arm around the drunk's neck hemming him up tight. "You ok?" He asked his ex-wife and she replied with a wide-eyed nod. He then turned to the bartender. "Yo Hank, the lady'll have a white wine spritzer. Put it on my tab."

"Now you know your money's no good here. Handle your business Black man." Hank said.

"Respect." Tommy nodded then turned to Nicky, "Meet me in the back by the pool table. But take your time. Me and-" he looked down angrily at the man struggling helplessly in his hold. "Yo Poo-Putt, what's your name?"

"Junebug," the punk meekly replied.

"Of course it is." Tommy shook his head at him pitifully then turned back to Nicky. "Junebug and I have some things to discuss, like how to talk to a lady." Nicky felt her head nod. "Ain't that right?" he said like he wasn't asking and the pair disappeared into the crowd.

Five minutes later Junebug reappeared with his tail between his legs wide-eyed and very sober looking like he had just been to hell and back. "Puh-pardon me Miss. I-um, I just wanted to apologize for disrespecting you like that. I know it's not much of an excuse, but I can say some really stupid things when I've had too much to drink."

Nicky glared at him and this time he caught the hint and wisely moved on.

DJ Hollywood's hit 'Um Tang-Um Tang' ricocheted off the walls as Nicky placed her empty glass down on the bar, pushed her glasses back on her head then headed towards the rear of the packed bar where she observed Tommy engrossed in a game of pool. Briefly pausing, she ran her hand through her mane then came over.

"Well hello." Nicky said

"Give me a sec. I'm about ta' take this chump's scrilla right quick." Tommy said with the ut most confidence then leaned over the table with his cue-stick.

"You got that backwards!" the man Tommy was playing hissed.

Tommy looked up at his opponent with a tight-lipped poker face then predicted the eight ball in the side pocket by pointing it out with his cue-stick and glided it back and forth between his fingers. He glanced up at the nervous man and taunted him with a bold wink, took careful aim, let the cue-stick fly and sank the bank shot. The loser swore under his breath and tossed a fat wad of money on the pool table.

"Even pool sharks get bit." Tommy informed his opponent as he ran his fingers over his newly acquired wealth. Afterwards he turned to Nicky. "Drinks on him. So, wa'sup?"

"Chilling. And you?"

"No complaints." Tommy said feeling fresh off his victory. "You wanna grab a booth?" Nicky nodded and as he walked by she shook her head with a smile.

"Still wearing Mayhem's cologne huh?"

"Some things never change." Tommy said.

"Yeah, like you jumping up in every guy's face I have a confrontation with. You know I could have handled that jerk back there myself." Nicky said settling into her seat.

Tommy grinned. "Now you know I can't just idly sit by and not do nothing when I see you've got beef."

"Actually 'not do nothing' is a double negative and it means you did do something, which is true, because you did."

"You and my mom." Tommy rolled his eyes. "You're like the friggin' grammar police."

"I see you remembered my drink," Nicky said impressed. Tommy shrugged like it was no biggie. "So, this is a surprise my bumping into you here."

"Actually, I was on the way home from a-um-*friend's* house when I saw you come in here. So I thought I'd stop in to check on you."

"A *friend's* house hmm?" Nicky said cutting her eyes with pursed lips.

"So you're not expecting anyone are you?"

Nicky shook her head and had to laugh at Tommy trying to be coy. "No Tommy I not expecting anyone."

"What's so funny? I just don't wanna assume that's all."

"If you're so concerned about me meeting someone then why'd you buy me a drink?" Nicky asked.

"I didn't see the harm in that. We're still friends, aren't we?"

"Considering our tumultuous history, surprisingly yes,"

Tommy smiled mischievously then signaled for the waitress and ordered a double shot of Johnnie Walker BLACK while keeping an eye on the door.

"For what it's worth I should be asking you if you're expecting somebody." Nicky commented.

"I told you I was on the way home when I spotted you." Tommy explained. Even though there was no way Donnie could even know where he was, he still felt paranoid like she was going to walk through the door any second and bust him.

"If you say so." Nicky shrugged and twirled the stirrer in her drink before taking a sip after which she licked her full glossy lips and let out a sexy sounding, *"Umm, this is sooo good."*

Tommy caught a flashback to when she used to make that same exact sound, but under different circumstances and quickly pushed the old memories out of his head. "So what's the deal with you taking a cab at night to the most dangerous spot in Brooklyn?" he asked.

"I needed to get out of the house and this was the only place I knew that would be open this late." Nicky said in a frustrated voice.

"A cold night like this, I would think you'd be home chillin' with Cornflake." Tommy said snickering as he thought of yet another insulting tag to diss Corbin with.

"Actually, he's the reason I needed to get out. Maybe I shouldn't tell you this because all you're gonna do is say I told you so but that night after Tee-Tee's party, I broke up with him. I just couldn't see myself being with someone who's such a a " Nicky made circling hand gestures trying to find the right words.

"Boring, empty, vapid, piss-ant, lil schmuck?" Tommy said helping her out.

"Yeah, something like that." Nicky said with raised eyebrows. "He's been calling me around the clock ever since. Showing up outside unannounced, begging for a second chance, sending bouquets of flowers. It looks like a goddamn F.T.D. threw up in my living room!"

Tommy snickered, not so much at her joke, but at the fact Corbin was outta' there like last year. He knew a salutary woman like Nicky could not be with a brother who was straight up whack. "You want me to talk to him? I wouldn't mind." he asked.

"Yeah I bet you wouldn't. But no, that's alright, I can take care of this myself."

"Aight' but I'm saying, if you need me, let me know."

"Thanks…So, go ahead."

"Go ahead what?" Tommy asked.

"Go ahead and say I told you so."

Tommy shook his head with a slight cackle. "I'm not perfect so how am I gonna call somebody out when they mess up. I know one thing, homegirl is taking way too long with my drink!" he said darting his eyes everywhere.

"Tommy the place is packed and I am sure we aren't her only customers. You never did have any patience-look see, here she comes now." Nicky said as the waitress came over and placed Tommy's drink before him.

"What the hell's this a Johnnie Walker Junior?" Tommy asked turning his nose up at the skimpy little glass. "Hold up Princess don't go nowhere." After emptying the glass with one big gulp he turned to the waitress handed her back the glass politely and said, "Give me a double, double shot."

"So what's been up with you?" Nicky asked.

"The usual. Oh, I got a bit of gossip for you. My folks are trying for a second chance at love, can you believe that."

"Get out of town! Your mom never said anything to me."

"You know her and her superstitions. She was probably worried she might jinx it. But yeah, they leave for New Orleans Sunday."

"That's great. Tell your mother and father I hope that they have a wonderful trip. So are they taking Tee-Tee with them?"

"Nope. She's going to stay with me." Tommy said.

"You?" Nicky asked with raised eyebrows.

"Yes me. What?"

"Oh nothing, it's just that won't Tee-Tee be in the way while you and Mayhem are out running the streets?"

"Well yeah she would be. If I planned on working while she was visiting. Which I don't. Tee-Tee and I are going to spend the week doing sister and brother stuff. The museum, Prospect Park, Coney Island. I'm looking forward to it." Tommy said as the waitress returned with a glass of his favorite alcohol filled to the brim.

"That's great. So how's Donnie doing?" Nicky asked suddenly.

Tommy's cocky smirk dropped on the floor. When he heard Donnie's name it felt like he was flooring a DeLorean then suddenly slammed on the brakes without a seatbelt! "She's fine. I just left her place."

Nicky shook her head. "I see. So, that's who your friend was."

"See it ain't even like that." Tommy said and turned up his glass. Nicky who had not even put a dent in her own drink noticed how Tommy was tossing them back like there was no tomorrow. The only time he drank like that was when he was edgy and trying to calm his nerves.

"Okay what's up? The last time I saw you like this was when Drago killed Apollo Creed in Rocky four." Nicky said.

"Ok, **still** a touchy subject. And what do you mean? Nothing's up!" Tommy asked avoiding Nicky's gaze.

"What, you think just because we're no longer married that I don't know when something's bothering you? How you'll turn up your drink to take the edge off. The way you drum your fingers on the table." Tommy looked down at his fingers and immediately stopped tapping. "So what is it?" Nicky asked genuinely concerned.

Tommy shrugged and stared at the bottom of his glass. "I used to compare Trouble Consulting to watching the coming attractions to an action movie. But just like those movies, it turned out to be a rip-off. Between all the good parts is the shit you don't see until you've already paid for your large popcorn and Coke. That's when you discover it's not as good as you thought it'd be."

"O-kay I know you're making an analogy here, but I'm lost. So you mind telling me what you're talking about, in layman terms?" Nicky asked.

Tommy looked up from his drink. "Today for the first time, I messed up a consulting gig. Big time!"

Nicky's eyes stretched. "What? Oh my goodness! Are you Okay?"

Tommy nodded and his throat constricted a little as he spoke. "I'm fine but the dear sweet old woman I promised to protect…she almost died."

"Oh honey, I'm really sorry. But she's going to be okay right?"

Tommy nodded with a frown. "Yes but the fact remains I almost blew it. Then on top of that I find out Bug-Out's got AIDS."

"No!" Nicky gasped a second time. "But how?"

"He was weak to the streets. He's been shooting that garbage into his veins for a while and it caught up with him." Tommy said and rubbed his face wearily. Nicky was speechless. All she could do was shake her head in disbelief. She had known Bug-Out almost as long as she had known Tommy and even set him up with a few of her girlfriends when they were younger and he was a different person. The tragic news was definitely a shocker.

"What about Laquita, and little AJ?"

"Laquita's smoking base." Tommy growled.

"No way! Not Laquita! Oh God, poor little AJ." Nicky was in shock and couldn't close her mouth.

"I had to go and get him outta' there. He's with his grandmother now."

"I am so sorry to hear that Tommy."

Someone fed the jukebox and it began to croon 'Misty Blue' by Dorothy Moore. Art imitated life as Nicky swayed along while reminiscing to the deep-rooted lyrics that had a lot of pain and joy at the same time.

♫*Oh it's been such a long-long time. Look like I'd get you off of my mind. But I can't. Just the thought of you, turns my whole world misty blue. Oh honey, just the mention of your name. Turns the flicker to a flame.* ♫

She must have heard that song a hundred times, at least. In the car. On the radio. Singing in the shower. But right here, right now, it was much more than a mere song in the background. It was her failed marriage and feelings set to a slow groove.

♫*Listen to me good baby. I think of the things we used to do. And my whole world turns misty blue. Baby, baby, baby, baby when I said that I'm glad we are through deep in my heart I know I lied.* ♫

Tommy looked sad sitting across from Nicky and it wasn't hard to tell that his relationship with the streets of Brooklyn was more complicated than just being a Trouble Consultant. Nicky felt guilty because she was getting that familiar warm feeling that began in her head and rolled down to her toes as she remembered past lovemaking. And more importantly, love. Her eyes traveled to his full lips as he talked and all she could think about was champagne on ice, candlelight's flickering, rose petals scattered at her feet, divine music and her giving him a full-body massage. She couldn't help it, Tommy was a shining example of Black masculinity. And it had been so long since she made love.

"Tommy what happened to us? I thought we were supposed to be together, forever." Nicky quickly asked before the logical side of her brain could stop her.

♫*I know I lied, I know I lied, I can't forget you-heaven knows I tried.* ♫

Tommy shrugged. "We were…I guess we lived too long." he winked and reached for her pack of cigarettes and removed one. He could see she was expecting a serious answer and lit his cigarette before giving it to her. "C'mon Nic you know what happened. Things I felt were important, you didn't. And things you felt were important, I didn't."

Oh so you're saying our marriage wasn't important?" Nicky asked.

"Don't go twisting around what I said." Tommy sighed.

"I'm not twisting around anything. I simply repeated what you said."

"Yeah but you're taking it all out of context."

"Am I?"

Tommy wondered why they were even having this conversation then shrugged and took a slow drag.

"I think I will have that second drink now." Nicky said and raised her arm to signaled the waitress.

After their brief encounter in the kitchen at Tee-Tee's party, Nicky dreamt about Tommy every night since. She wanted him to make mad passionate toe-curling love to her. She told herself she was no longer in love with him over and over again. But still she didn't want to be with anyone else. Every time she closed her eyes she dreamt about her ex-husband touching and kissing her. It wasn't infatuation. She missed Tommy like crazy. Vixen and soul. And she wanted him back.

"Tommy…come home with me." Nicky said once again beating her brain to the punch.

"Say what now?" Tommy looked up at her, eyes glossy from the alcohol.

Nicky shook her head. "Let's forget about our problems. At least temporarily." She whispered with a smoldering glare.

"Yeah well, the problem with temporary is that it ain't forever."

"It could if we wanted it to be…let's make it-permanent." She said and placed her hands over his and squeezed. The invitation was clean, crisp and straight to the point. Just like Nicky's no-nonsense style.

Tommy stared into his ex-wife's eyes catching the white flash of her nervous smile against her ebony skin and it suddenly occurred to him what she was asking him.

"Are you saying what I think you're saying?" Tommy asked not wanting to assume.

The waitress came over and Nicky ordered another white wine spritzer before answering Tommy. She couldn't believe she was even having these feelings about him. She could have sworn he got those in the divorce settlement. "Well if you think I'm saying I want to give us another try, and if that is what you want too- then...yes."

Tommy could see the heartfelt love she still had for him. Corbin's clown ass never had a chance. Nicky began to look worried when she did not see the same look of passion in Tommy's eyes.

Tommy thought carefully before he spoke. "You know six months ago hearing you say that would have made me the happiest man in the world...But things have changed, now-"

Nicky touched Tommy's lips with a finger to silence him. "It's Donnie, right?" she asked. Tommy nodded silently. Nicky sat back and exhaled then fronted a bogus smile when the waitress placed her drink before her. "I wasn't wrong for making you choose between me and Havoc. You were wrong for choosing Havoc over me." Tommy sighed heavily dropping his eyes. "So I guess you got the perfect woman now. She's beautiful and successful and she doesn't have a problem with you playing Russian Roulette with your life. It's a match made in heaven." Nicky said bitterly.

"I never said she was cool with me doing what I do." Tommy said regretting the words as soon as they left his mouth.

Nicky's eyebrows raised. "So then she does have a problem with you Trouble Consulting?" Tommy turned up his drink and Nicky's mouth hung open. "Wow! It's like that Tommy? So what's next you're going to retire all together? Go legit?"

Tommy tried to look Nicky in the eyes but couldn't. They both looked down at Tommy's fingers rapping on the table. She wasn't lying when she said that she still knew his ways. Tommy stopped rapping his digits and looked up annoyed and tired of fussing. "Why are we even going through this? I just told you how I almost let somebody die I was supposed to protect and-" he realized how loud he was and lowered his voice to a rough whisper. "And how my cousin's got AIDS! And all you can do is carry on like a naïve girl strung out over some high school crush!"

The moment morphed from energy-charged to awkward, to hostile as Nicky's lips parted enough to gasp when Tommy's attitude cut her to the core. "Fuck you Tommy! For years I tolerated-no supported what you did! The danger, the inordinate hours!" she paused and regained her composure. "Look I am sorry about what happened today and especially about Bug-Out. But after what you just said, how do you expect me to react? Our marriage dissolved because I wanted you to stop running the streets, risking your life and then along comes this woman who says the exact same things I've been saying for years. And **now** you're ready to quit!" she stood up, threw on her coat and spun around towards the door.

"Nicky wait a minute, I never said Donnie told me to quit."

"You didn't have to!" Nicky said and continued outside. Tommy tossed some money on the table and grabbed his coat chasing out behind her.

"So, explain to me how you figure women have super powers," The gold toothed black man behind the steering wheel asked Pumpkin then took a long pull on the marijuana filled cigar they were sharing and passed it back to her.

"We get wet without water. Bleed without injury. Make boneless meat hard and can make a man eat without cooking," Pumpkin comically explained then brought the blunt to her lips inhaled and handed it back.

"Well damn Sexy. When you put it like that I guess you're right, Wonder Woman." He laughed, then took a deep pull and began coughing violently as the weed hit his lungs hard.

Pumpkin twitched her lips unconcerned watching Lenny's coughing frenzy like 'whatever'. All she cared about was the assortment of shoeboxes and shopping bags piled high in the back seat that he bought her.

"Damn! That's some primo shit! You ok?" he asked Pumpkin.

"I'm fine." She said ending the blunt in one long toke.

"O-k. So, you ready to go inside and get our party on?" Lenny asked wondering if she did have super powers because although they were smoking the same blunt it affected them differently.

"Sure," Pumpkin nodded with a scheming grin and eye on his wallet when she noticed the man her best friend was crazy about arguing with another woman outside The Future and her jaw dropped. "Wait-not yet! I want to see something."

Nicky flagged down a cab and Tommy pushed the door closed and barked at the driver to keep it moving who obeyed and peeled off. Nicky shrugged and raised her hand to flag another.

"Nicky c'mon back inside so we can talk about this." Tommy pleaded.

"Talk about what?" Nicky said still visibly pained by the topic.

"About you, me, our divorce. Everything."

Nicky had to laugh to keep from exploding. "Give me a break Tommy. We got married for a reason. And we got divorced for a reason. And that reason was you wanted out."

Tommy's jaw hit the floor. After all that had gone down today, her telling him that was the biggest blow. "You know damn well I never wanted any such thing!"

"Then why'd you give up on our marriage so easily? We could have gone to marriage counseling Tommy."

Tommy rolled his eyes. "Because you wanted us to be something that we could never be."

"And what's that?"

"A normal couple. C'mon Nicky look at what I do for a living. How could I go in there and explain that to some shrink?" Tommy pointed out emphatically.

"We didn't have to be explicit about what you do for a living Tommy, just that your job was coming between us."

"It wouldn't have worked Nicky. I mean quiet as it's kept, you've never accepted me for who I was anyway."

Nicky sucked her teeth deeply insulted. "How soon do we forget! If I didn't accept you then why on earth did my stupid ass patch you up every time you staggered in bleeding? How about all the times I rubbed your torn muscles down with alcohol? Snapped bones back into place, stuffed bleeding holes with gauze pads because you didn't want to go to the hospital and explain how you got your injuries? Accept a dog you never discussed with me about first and just brought home? So don't you dare stand there accusing me of not being there for you! And to think how many times I begged you to stop before you were killed and you refused. God, how many times I considered turning you in for your own good! But perfect little Princess Donnie comes along and complains and now you want to undergo a metamorphic-type change. Obviously you did not want to be married so you chose any opportunity to end it." Nicky said fighting back tears.

Tommy blew smoke averting her hurt eyes. "Okay I'll admit, when you put it like that it does sound messed up. But you've got it all wrong. Donnie had nothing to do with my decision to overhaul my shit. A sweet old lady named Hattie Mae Tucker did when a bullet missed killing her by a fraction of an inch. A bullet I was supposed to protect her from. It was an alarm clock for me and I realized for the first time the risks I take with other people's lives."

"And you're just realizing that now after I told you that you were living on borrowed time? That sooner or later something was gonna give and when it did, you'd be the one doing the giving, until it hurt?"

"I guess I had to find out the hard way."

"You and me both. So are you and Donnie totally honest about everything?"

"Well yeah." Tommy answered.

"Then you told her about you and me all over each other while she was in the very next room during Tee-Tee's party?"

312

Tommy stood there totally unprepared for that one. "About that, I think I confused you."

"Excuse me?"

"Well maybe not confused, but what had happened was a mistake. There was an attraction, old feelings got stirred up. Nothing more. And because that's all it was, I didn't think it was worth bringing up."

"A mistake huh? And to think what you called a mistake I called fate and thought it repeated itself twice when you walked into the bar tonight and saw me." Nicky said. Tommy had nothing. "So I guess having an alter ego provides you with an excuse for being a jerk!" Nicky said then turned her head so Tommy could not see the hurt on her face. "I'm going to leave. I need to be alone."

"You sure?" Tommy asked.

Nicky nodded her head, "It's a lot less painful than being alone with you," she said and flagged another cab. Before closing the door, she glared at her ex-husband. "I'd wish you the best. But I was yours." And she was gone.

Tommy stood there staring at Nicky's cab grow smaller, reflecting on the positive elements he might have embraced from life had he chosen his marriage to her over Trouble Consulting. Basic but practical things like stability and starting a family. Those were the things he sacrificed to operate as a Trouble Consultant and even though his earnings afforded him a sweet life, he still wondered what kind of man he would have become if things had been different. "I'm way to fucking sober for this." he said aloud then went back inside to soak his liver in Scotch.

Across the street Pumpkin sat inside Lenny's baby blue Maxima processing what just went down with a livid expression. "I've got to buy me a vowel, because O-my-God!"

"What do you care what that man is doing? You're supposed to be out on a date with me!" Lenny asked.

"Because that so-called man is dating my best friend that's why!"

"Not that redbone chick with the bourgeois attitude that you set my cousin Ray-Ray up with?" Lenny snickered. "Miss Prissy's dating him? Dude looks straight street!"

"Look Lenny, just take me home!"

"But baby I thought you said you wanted to have a drink then keep it moving over to Willie's Burgers."

"We were, but now we're not!"

Lenny muttered something under his breath about never dating 'project chicks' with kids again and started his car then his expression changed. "Oh snap! Pumpkin, peep that Benzo. Now that's a flyy ass whip! Trust me, whoever's driving that is a bad mother fucker!" He said referring to the black Mercedes Benz that drove off in the same direction as Nicky's cab.

## Chapter 24

The sunlight stabbed through Tommy's eyelids way too soon. He had barely slept after stumbling in at 5 forty-five am. And when he did drift off he kept seeing Nicky's hurt face. With a stretch and yawn, he lay in bed sporting Buddha-red eyes under a just-woke-up stocking cap rubbing bleary eyes trying to focus. He stared up at the ceiling with a slight hangover as the bitter funk of last night's countless cocktails seeped from his pores. He was so tired that he didn't want to do anything-except nothing. He sat up and rubbed his throbbing temples, thirsty as hell. He wanted to go back to sleep but he couldn't. He looked over at the phone debating over whether or not to call his ex-wife. But for all intents and purposes he decided it would be best to leave things alone. Tommy sat up and yawned then fanned the air with a frown when he caught a whiff of his breath. After brushing away the dragon and walking Mayhem, he worked out for an hour and a half pushing himself to the limits of human endurance with his daily workout routine that consisted of 500 pushups, 10 sets of wide pull-ups, 6 sets of fingertip pushups, 10 sets of dips and 8 sets of crunches. After he was done he put a new message on his business line explaining to his potential clients that 'due to personal matters,' he would not be taking on any new consulting gigs until further notice and to check back to see when he was back in operation. His mother had phoned to say she and his father would be by around one to drop off his sister and he jumped in the shower. At exactly one on the dot Tommy's doorbell rang. Since his family's flight was not scheduled to leave until four, they had plenty of time to visit.

"Carla look at our boy with his six-pack." Smitty said staring proudly at his son as he buttoned a shirt down his washboard stomach then stuffed the tail in his pants. "He gets that from me you know?"

"Sure, you're right." Carla teased patting Smitty's paunch.

"Hey I don't need a dynamite physique when I got a firecracker, c'mere." Smitty said pulling Carla into his lap and planting a kiss on her cheek.

"Get a room," Tommy shook his head smiling, he couldn't get over his parents patching things up.

"So what's up with that rag you've got tied on your head?" Smitty asked his son.

"It's a wave cap,"

Smitty and Carla traded smirks, "But you ain't got no hair son. What're you trying to wave up, your thoughts?"

"Da ha-ha-ha," Tommy laughed sarcastically.

"Honey I gave you the number to the hotel?" Carla asked.

"Yeah Ma I wrote it down somewhere." Tommy said preoccupied with Tee-Tee's electronic Simon game. "Aw damn!" he swore when the buzzing noise indicated he lost.

"Hey-language!" Carla scolded her son.

"A-ha you lose!" Tee-Tee teased. "My turn-my turn."

"No do over!" Tommy said.

"Nah-uh, no do overs!" Tee-Tee said and snatched the game.

"Somewhere, where?" Carla asked.

"On a piece of paper somewhere." Tommy shrugged.

"I'm leaving you some money for food and whatever. Tommy are you listening?"

"Ma relax. I have money. This is supposed to be a vacation remember?" He said trying to cover his sister's eyes so she'd mess up and lose the game.

"I know Tommy and I will enjoy it as long as I know that if anything happens you will be able to contact us at the hotel."

"You worry too much Ma. Nothing's going to happen."

"You worry too much Ma. Nothing's gonna happen." Tee-Tee repeated.

"Cut it out brat." Tommy said.

"Cut it out brat." Tee-Tee giggled.

"Ma, talk to your child." Tommy complained.

"Ma, talk to your child."

"Supercalifragilisticexpialidocious."

"Huh?" Tee-Tee said baffled as her brother grinned smugly. Carla shook her head smiling at her babies and tore a sheet of paper from a notebook on the table. "For the second time here's the flight number and the phone number you can reach me. We should arrive there at eight-fifteen and we're staying at the Berkley Manor Inn. I also included the number for the agency I sometimes use that sends over home care attendants to care for Tee-Tee when I'm busy. You can call them around the clock and they will send someone over. If you do have to use them ask for Beverly, your sister adores her and make sure it's an emergency because that place is very expensive even with the deduction from my medical coverage." She said scribbling everything she said down on a piece of paper and handing it to her son.

"Won't need it." Tommy said confidently and tossed the note on the table and continued wrestling with his sister.

Carla turned to Smitty, "Can you think of anything else honey?"

"Not a thing." Smitty said.

Suddenly Mayhem jumped up barking and made a mad dash for the door. The door unlocked and Donnie came in looking lovely as usual. Tee-Tee smiled and rushed over to greet her. "Hello everyone." Donnie cheerfully greeted.

"Sup babe." Tommy winked with a warm smile that made Donnie blush. Carla raised her eyebrows and shot her son a peculiar look.

"Donnie it's good to see you again. Isn't it Carla?" Smitty said nudging her.

"Huh? Oh sure, hello Donnie. Nice to see you." Carla said with a plastic smile wishing her son lived in an apartment instead of a loft so she could ask him to step into the next room and ask what was up with his new girlfriend already having her own key to his place.

"So are you guys ready for your trip? Wow New Orleans. I went there for Mardi Gras with some of my girls two summers ago. Let me tell you, Bourbon Street is one big non-stop party and the bayou is beautiful, but you have to take a tour of the old estates. Then there's the food and the people with their Southern hospitality. You two are going to have so much fun." Donnie said enthusiastically.

"I know and we don't plan on wasting a moment's time. Truth be told, this is my first trip anywhere. I haven't been out of Brooklyn since I came here as a child." Smitty admitted proudly.

"Now you see where I got my love for Brooklyn from. Cause it definitely wasn't from my mother she loves to travel, in fact come to think of it, you two have something in common. You've both visited Egypt." Tommy said.

The two women looked at each other stunned. "You've been to Egypt?" Carla asked Donnie.

Donnie looked over at Tommy oddly. Ever since they met Carla made her feel a little uncomfortable and it was pretty obvious that Tommy's ex-wife was the reason. She never mentioned it to Tommy because she knew from the bond between her own brothers and mother that the way through a man's heart was not his stomach, it was his mother.

"Really? When'd you go?" Carla asked. Donnie's mouth opened but she didn't say anything looking as though she was trying to remember.

"She visited Cairo a few years back. Ain't that right?" Tommy said placing his hands on Donnie's shoulders.

Donnie smiled uncomfortably. "Um-yeah like he said."

Carla's features softened and she came over. "Ah Cairo, what a beautiful and enchanting place. I learned all about Egypt while doing a term paper on the Pharaohs of Egypt in college and became fascinated with their beautiful culture. After graduation my family sent me there as a gift."

"Really, you are so lucky. Did you visit the Pharaoh's temples and the Sphinx?"

"That's a given. But what about the boat ride down the Nile River?" Carla asked.

"Words can't describe it." Donnie said.

"I'm trying to get certain people who shall remain nameless to travel and see the world and show them there's more to the world than Brooklyn." Carla said gesturing towards her son. "Maybe you can help me."

"While I can't promise miracles, I will try." Donnie winked and soon she and Carla were chatting openly about century old mummies, relics, art and pyramids the whole time becoming more and more acquainted with one another.

At two o'clock Tommy's parents called a cab and prepared to leave. They showered their daughter with kisses and promised to call her every day. Carla had a difficult time leaving her baby girl behind and tried not to cry but did anyway. Tee-Tee was more concerned with them bringing her back a souvenir. Carla went over her list of hotel numbers and important information with Tommy one more time and forced him to take an envelope containing one hundred dollars.

Smitty pulled his son to the side and reminded him about what the two of them discussed the other day. "No Havoc and Mayhem business while your sister is visiting! And the home care attendant is not a get out of jail free card either!"

Donnie hugged Smitty goodbye and was as surprised as everyone else when Carla gave her a hug and asked her to check in on her babies for her. Donnie promised she would and Carla said that when she got back they would make plans to visit the Brooklyn Museum of Natural History's Egypt exhibit. After they were gone Donnie spun at Tommy with narrow eyes and her hands on her hips.

"What's the matter?" He asked cluelessly.

Donnie was so pissed she couldn't speak and smacked Tommy hard on the arm. "Ow!" he yelled.

"What if I didn't know anything about Egypt?" Donnie asked.

"Hold up. What are you saying, that you've never been to Egypt?" Tommy asked rubbing his arm and trying his best to keep a straight face. Donnie shook her head not finding anything funny as Tommy began snickering. "Tee-Tee Muppet Babies is on." He informed his sister. Once she was out of ear-range he turned back to his lady. "Now come on baby. There isn't a topic under the sun that you don't know something about. My mom visited Egypt years ago but still talks about it like she was there yesterday. I figured this would be the perfect opportunity to bring you two closer together. As far as you not knowing anything about the land, I wasn't worried. You're a walking, talking Britannica, with curvy bookends." He said and threw his arms around Donnie's waist and tried to steal a kiss.

Donnie pushed him away. This time one of his toe-curling kisses was not going to cut it. She was pissed. "What if your mother saw through the charade? She isn't all that thrilled with me to begin with and if she discovered I was lying-I don't even want to think about it."

"Okay maybe I did take a risk by telling my mom that you visited Egypt when you hadn't. And I'm sorry. I just wanted you two to get along." Tommy said.

"I get along with her fine. It's she who has a problem with me." Donnie frowned.

"Yeah well not that I'm defending her but my mom is from the ol' school. She believes in the sanctity of marriage and all that jazz. Plus she and my ex have a lot in common because they both went to the same college and are both teachers. That was another reason why I said you had been to Egypt."

"Look Tommy I understand that you want your mother and me to get along. And I would like it as well, but if your mother is ever going to accept me, it has to be me, not a brand new version of your ex-wife." Donnie said

Tommy took Donnie's hand then kissed it. "I'm sorry babe that's not what I was trying to do. But I felt I had to do something. I can't have two of the most important women in my life not getting along."

Donnie smiled and kissed her man. She could not stay upset after being put in the same league with his mother. Not to mention his confidence in her wisdom about all things under the sun.

"Tommy and Donnie sitting in a tree. K-I-S-S-I-N-G!" Tee-Tee teased using her Barbie and Ken dolls to simulate her brother and his girl smooching.

"You hungry brat?"

"Uh-huh."

"Dinner and a movie?" Tommy offered.

"Tommy can we go to Pizza Hut?" Tee-Tee asked.

"Sure." Tommy smiled and turned to his lady. "What movies are playing?"

"I hear Coming to America is pretty good." Donnie said. Just then her pager beeped and she checked the number. "Now what does Pumpkin want that's so important she's paging me 911?" She asked aloud and reached for the phone. Tommy opened his mouth. "Don't say it." Donnie cut him off.

"Don't say what?" Tommy asked innocently.

"Whatever it was that you were going to say insulting about my friend."

"Look at you, thinking the worst. Now I'm insulted!"

"I'm so sure." After speaking briefly with her friend, Donnie hung up the phone frowning. "Bad news guys, I'm gonna have to take a rain check on the pizza and movie, my girl needs me. She sounds pretty upset. I think Mike, her daughter's father is tripping. She still calls him the one who got away."

"How'd he do it, by gnawing off his own arm?" Tommy laughed.

"Tommy show some compassion."

"My bad. I guess I'm just disappointed that you're not coming."

"I know. So am I. But I promise I'll make it up to the both of you."

"You better." After Donnie left Tommy turned to his kid sister, "Well brat, it's just you and me. Wanna grab a pizza and make it a Blockbusters night instead?"

"Can we rent Annie?" Tee-Tee asked.

Tommy sighed heavily. "Come on Brat, don't you have that movie on VHS?" Tommy asked frowning at the thought of sitting through a musical that his sister knew all the songs and dialogue to.

"Uh-huh, but Mommy forgot to pack it in my bag,"

Tommy sighed. "Isn't there something else you want to see?"

"Annie!"

"Ok, fine…Annie."

"Yaaayyyy!!!!"

After standing in line at Blockbusters to rent his sister's favorite movie, the siblings arrived arm in arm at Pizza Hut. The place was jam-packed so Tommy handed over all the quarters in his pocket to his sister to play video games then patiently waited in line to order their meals. The family friendly peaceful scene was interrupted by a posse of loud unruly young men five deep. An attractive voluptuous Puerto Rican woman in painted on Gloria Vanderbilt jeans sashayed past them and the young men shook their heads in awe.

"Whoa! That bitch's ass look like it's pregnant, with another ass!" one of the men in a Black Bart Simpson t-shirt pointed between sips of his 40 ounce.

"Damn she got a fat culo! It's hard to believe shit comes out of something that pretty!" another one of the punks said to his crew. "Yo mami!" he called out getting the shapely woman's attention. "Lindo tresero Vamos a hacerlo de perrito?" Offended by what he said she glared at him with detest, sucked her teeth and stomped away.

"Yo Fuego what did you say to that skeezer?" the man nursing the 40 asked.

"I told her she had a nice ass then asked if she wanted to do it doggy style." Fuego laughed sinisterly while thrusting his hips back and forth simulating the sexual act. As the crew of thugs cracked up handing out hi-fives, the mouthy hot-blooded teen peeped a fair-skinned dime-piece in a dope denim jacket with her picture and 'Tee-

Tee' spray painted on the back. He tossed his friend some crumbled bills. "Yo Divine, order me a slice with pepperoni and a large Mellow Yellow. I think I see my next baby momma." He hissed smoothing down his eyebrows and headed towards the videogames as his homeboy Louis tagged behind.

The line to play her favorite video game Dig-Dug was too long so Tee-Tee grabbed a seat where she could see her brother. She was about to yell out to remind him what special topping she wanted on her pizza when her view was blocked by two men staring at her oddly.

"Hola beautiful. I see from your jacket that your name is Tee-Tee?" the dark eyed teen asked. Tee-Tee nodded innocently with a shy smile. "My name is Fuego. And this here is my buddy Louis." His sidekick nodded returning his own creepy smile. "Nice to meet you,"

On the other side of the establishment Divine and another young man with a bouncer's build named Champ stood in line behind Tommy to order food for their crew. "Quiet as kept Fuego needs to take a break from the ladies. That fool got so many kids he just drives through the hood and waves." Divine said. He was tall with a head full of what Southern black grandmothers referred to as, 'bad hair.'

Champ laughed over a massive belch, "You want some of dis?" he asked offering Divine his forty-ounce.

Divine looked at his buddy like he was insulted, "Hell no I don't want none! I ain't drinking yo back-wash. Especially after I heard how you get down, eating bitches' asses."

"I'm a freak so what? You don't like to get your freak on?"

"Hell yeah I like to get my freak on but I don't be out here eating random bitches' asses. And then you out here smoking blunts with the guys and passing 40s around and shit. Negro I eat buttermilk biscuits. You eat butt off of bitches! There's a difference."

"Now I know you ain't trying to diss me when you're dating Muriel." Champ frowned.

"So?" Divine shrugged.

"So, that bitch is fat. Not p-h-a-t but f-a-t! And everybody knows fat girls are like mopeds. They're fun to ride. But you ain't trying to get caught riding one. You chubby chasing motherfucker!"

Tommy snickered to himself ear hustling as the two amateur comedians entertained him while he stood in the slow-moving line. Louis came back over and handed Divine more money.

"Yo, Fuego said to get an extra slice with pineapple and a grape soda." Louis said.

"Pineapple?" Champ repeated. "Who the hell puts pineapple on their pizza?" he asked. Tommy wondered the same thing since there was only one person he knew who liked that strange request.

Louis shook his head smiling sinisterly. "It ain't for him. It's for-" He paused when he noticed half the line was staring down his throat. "Dang, welcome to my business, may I take your order please!" He sucked his teeth then said, "Uegofay aggedbay upyay isthay inefay irlgay, utbay e'sshay owslay."

People in line traded odd looks upon hearing the curious sounding patois of mangled English that sounded like a backwards-playing record. Tommy immediately recognized the foreign dialect as 'Pig Latin', a secret language created and spoken by and for kids where the initial consonant cluster is moved to the end of the word and 'ay' is added. But if the word in question begins with a vowel 'yay' is added to the end.

"Owslay ikelay owhay?" Divine asked also speaking Pig Latin.

"Isyay eshay etartedray?" Champ asked.

Louis shrugged. "Iyay inkthay osay. Ouyay ottagay eesay erhay. E'sshay otgay otay ebay, atyay eastlay enty-fivetway utbay eshay actsyay ikelay e'sshay ivefay. Uegofay's aboutyay otay etgay ethay antiespay."

Tommy glared over his shoulder with clenched teeth. Up until now they were harmless court jesters there for his amusement, but after what he just overheard, they were far more dangerous. He got out of line and headed over to find his ittlelay istersay.

Tee-Tee's smile was reminiscent of a little girl's, cute and bright with a pink tint of gums showing. As a rule, she could not talk to boys without her mother's presence because Carla knew that they only saw a very pretty young woman who was mentally challenged and wanted to take advantage. But regardless of how young Tee-Tee was mentally, there was still a part of her that found boys attractive. Boys that looked like Fuego and she was curious.

"Hey you're pretty good at that," Fuego complemented Tee-Tee on her Kerbanger skills, a toy that consisted of two large acrylic balls connected to a string that was attached to a plastic handle.

"Thank you," she blushed, as she held the plastic handle and quickly moved her wrist up and down setting the balls in motion causing them to make an ear splitting 'click clack' sound.

"So Tee-Tee where'd you get your jacket made, it's real def!" Fuego pretended to care.

"I dunno. My brother gave it to me." Tee-Tee gushed modeling her new jacket.

"So, I was thinking this place is whack. How about we leave and go back to my place."

"And do what?"

"We could play some games," he said licking his lips.

"But its games here." She said pointing to the line of arcade games gobbling up quarters.

"Yeah but those are for kids. We could play, grown up games,"

"What kind of grown up games?"

"We could…" Fuego whispered something into Tee-Tee's ear and she looked at him with her face scrunched up.

"Huh? You wanna put what where?" She asked perplexed. Fuego sighed at her cluelessness and whispered something else in her ear that made her giggle. "How do you play that?" She asked curiously.

"Come with me and I'll show you." He hissed like a serpent saying and promising whatever it took to get the beautiful but seemingly slow-witted woman to come home with him. Tee-Tee smiled with eyes as innocent as her love for Smurfs and cotton candy. As far as she was concerned Fuego would make the perfect boyfriend and her feeble mind could not begin to comprehend the freaky things he had in store for her. "So, you *cumming* to my house?" he asked again.

"Ok," she said. And the pervert envisioned her naked on his filthy pull out couch.

"But can my brother Tommy come along too?"

Fuego's eyes widened. He was so busy trying to get busy that it never occurred to him someone like her should have a chaperone to protect her from the degenerate creeps and scumbags, like himself.

"Um your brother huh? So-where's he at?" He asked nervously looking all around.

"Ehindbay ouyay othermay uckerfay!" Tommy growled.

Fuego's heart skipped a beat and he turned around in slow motion then swallowed hard at the massive angry black man.

"Tee-Tee, here, go on out to the car and wait for me." Tommy ordered as he handed over the keys to his Jeep Cherokee. The entire time his eyes were locked on Fuego who dropped his vision to the floor.

"We're not eating here?" Tee-Tee asked.

"No."

"But why not?" Tee-Tee whined.

"Tee-Tee do as I say!"

"But Tom-meee, Fuego invited us over to his place to play um, what's that game again?" Fuego shrugged with a nervous grin like he had no idea what she was talking about. "Oh I remember. 'Hide the pickle.'" She laughed naively.

Tommy's teeth grinded together.

"Whoa-whoa! It's not like it sounds big man." Fuego took a step back and his eyes stretched as Tommy's chest began to heave and his eyes narrowed to dark slits. It was taking him every ounce of restraint not to circle the punk's scrawny neck with his hands and squeeze until his head was on backwards.

"I said to go!" Tommy ordered his sister.

"Okay-Okay, Mister Meanie!" Tee-Tee huffed spinning on her heels.

Tommy glared at the man who planned on taking advantage of his little sister. "I'm sure you noticed that my little sister is different." Fuego was too scared to respond. "And yet, you still were trying to take her back to your crib." He cracked his knuckles then noticed his misspelled tattoo on his forearm that read, 'Too cool for scool.' And realized the mentality he was dealing with. "Motherfucker, I don't know whether to beat you with my fists or a dictionary!"

Fuego's fright-mask suddenly transformed into a relaxed confident glare and he looked Tommy up and down unconcerned. "So, it's my fault your Special-Ed sister wants deez nuts?"

Tommy could feel someone breathing down the back of his neck and was certain that it had everything to do with Fuego's sudden boost in courage. He looked over his shoulder. Standing behind him were Fuego's friends looking eager for a fight.

"Hey. Wait a damn second. Don't I know you?" Louis said getting up in Tommy's face and squinting his eyes. He had a chocolate muscular physique and wore his hair in a greasy jheri curl that had the collar of his shirt drenched.

"Nah, I don't think so." Tommy replied sizing him up and down unconcerned.

"Naw I'm positive I know you...Hold up!" Louis said then paused and removed the lid from his fruit punch and splashed it on Tommy's white shirt.

"What the fuck!" Tommy snarled lifting Louis into the air by his collar and pulled back a fist.

"Tommy is you Okay?" Tee-Tee asked worriedly walking back over.

Tommy wanted to stuff his fist down the young man's throat so bad the nerve over his left eye began to twitch, but now was not the time. "Yeah everything's fine. Let's go Tee-Tee." He said dropping Louis on his ass then leaned in close to Fuego, "You've been touched by an Angel! Tonight, get on your knees and thank the man upstairs." he said then walked away leaving Fuego and his crew stunned.

Outside a light snow flurry began to fall and Tommy stopped his sister to make sure she was buttoned up. "So where we gonna eat then?" Tee-Tee asked her brother as they trekked through the parking lot.

"We can stop at Burger King on the way home." Tommy grumbled. He hated walking away from a fight. It was bad for business. He toyed with the idea of driving back later for a little payback. Jerks like that always hung around to gloat.

"But McDonald's has better happy meals." she insisted.

"Fine, then we'll go to McDonalds." Tommy said like he could care less.

"But I wanted pizza." she whined. Tommy sighed. He was not in the mood for his sister's spoiled ways. Suddenly the hairs on the back of his neck stood up straight and he spun around to see the four-man-threat from Pizza Hut headed his way breathing cold like a multi-headed dragon with ill intentions and balled-up fists. Tommy shook his head. Like his Nana would say, 'The Devil's always working.'

"A-yo Pendejo, where're you running off to?" Fuego called out.

"Tee-Tee go on to the car, get in lock the door and wait for me." Tommy said handing her his keys. His sister opened her mouth to defy him and he ordered, "Now!" As she stormed off mumbling how he made her sick, Tommy approached the problem head on. "Aight' fellas if you're looking for a good time, I suggest you look elsewhere!"

Fuego stepped forward and eyed Tommy up and down then looked back at his crew. "So, you're the man, the myth, the fucking legend?" he asked sounding heartbroken. "After all the astounding, larger than life stories I heard about you. I expected some 300-lb. cock-diesel dude, fresh off a jail bid, decorated with all kinds of tattoos and battle scars. Not some Herb who hangs out with his cute but slow sister at Pizza Hut."

"Sorry to disappoint you." Tommy said condescendingly.

"My man Lou tells me that you're the one that got him locked up on New Year's at Smitty's."

"Yeah. So?" Tommy casually stated. He did not want to have an altercation in front of his sister. Unfortunately, from the look of things these punks weren't giving him much of a choice

"So, it looks to me like your past has finally caught up with you homeboy." Fuego said eyeing the expensive gold around Tommy's neck. "But I think I know a way you can fix all this."

"Oh really?"

"Yup. Ante-up that phat ass rope!" he ordered and lunged for Tommy's gold chain.

Tommy dipped back and snuffed him in the face with a punch that was like a rattlesnake's bite. Blindingly swift and deadly accurate. In fact, the blow was so fast Fuego didn't even realize he was hit until the wannabe chain snatcher was on the floor tasting his own blood. "Everybody's got a plan, until they get punched in the mouth!" the bald man said with detest then spun to face the other goons.

With a roar of outrage, Champ rushed Tommy, swinging an impressive combo of punches…left jab, right jab, left roundhouse, right haymaker. But not a single one connected and to add insult to injury Tommy didn't even back away. He just twisted this way, that way and leaned all the way back as if he were a limbo dancer evading the attack. In comparison to Tommy, Champ was moving in slow motion. Frustrated he lunged at Tommy who ducked the incoming cross and rolled back onto his attacker with a reverse elbow. The hit was brutal and sent him spinning into a parked car. It was at that time another of the punks diverted Tommy's attention as Fuego back on his feet came up from behind, reached into his pocket, pulled out a roll of quarters, squeezed them tightly and smashed his fist into Tommy's face doubling the impact of the punch. Tommy was dazed as the men closed in on him. They made a game of it shoving him from one person to the other, their faces leering like jack-o-lanterns.

"Tommy!" Tee-Tee screamed and ran back to her brother.

Tommy looked up trying to shake off unconsciousness and saw Champ coming. The big man plowed into him like a runaway freight train and sent him slamming into the ground with the wind knocked out of him.

"No stop it! Leave my brother alone!" Tee-Tee screamed as Fuego used his knee to pin down Tommy's chest while his posse wickedly punched and stomped all over him. "I said stop it!" Tee-Tee screamed and swung her Kerbangers like a nun chuck and cracked him upside his head. Fuego swore in pain clutching the quickly rising speed-knot on his face and spun at Tee-Tee pissed then pushed her to the ground.

Inside the Jeep Cherokee Mayhem saw her master and Tee-Tee in trouble and went ballistic attempting to get out and protect her family. She tried in vain but was unable to get the door open because Tee-Tee had unknowingly locked it earlier. Tommy curled up in a fetal position trying to protect himself from the furious assault of arms and legs. A boot kicked his jaw and he tasted a mixture of his blood and salt from the snow. He tried to stand and was knocked back down. With the pain from his eye and the beating he was enduring, Tommy was beginning to black out. He reached for the gun in his ankle holster but the blows prevented him from pulling it out. Through the confusion he saw his dog and had an even better idea.

"The orange button on the key chain Tee-Tee! Aim it at the truck and press the orange button!" Tommy shouted.

Tee-Tee nodded and spun around on her stomach. Champ saw the savage dog spinning inside the truck like the Tasmanian Devil howling to be freed and tackled Tee-Tee knocking the keys from her hands. Mayhem became so angry she rammed her head into the door and rocked the entire vehicle.

Tee-Tee screamed. She was horrified as she struggled on the ground to get away from Champ and get the car keys. Then she remembered what her brother had once told her to do if a man attacked her, *'Knee him hard in the private parts!'* at the time she thought it was the funniest thing in the world and Tommy had to get firm with her to make her listen. But right now, she didn't find anything funny. Tee-Tee turned over on her back clenched her teeth and just like Tommy instructed, buried her knee in Champ's crotch making him fold like lawn furniture. Without a moment to spare she pushed him to the side and scooped up the keys, spun at Tommy's Jeep Cherokee and mashed the orange button. There was a quick '**Boop-Beep-Boop**' followed by the unlocking of the car doors.

A toothy grin outlined Mayhem's muzzle and she smacked the door open then poured out onto the battlefield all-business. With fangs bared and exhaling cold air, she sized up the punks then let out a deep-throated growl. All sounds within earshot were absorbed by the falling snow as Fuego and his boys frozen with fear waited, shaking, not knowing what was going to happen next.

Then someone moved. And all hell broke loose.

Mayhem charged forward to help her master. Tommy was on the ground sandwiched between Divine and Fuego. He raised his head and brought it down fast, busting Divine's nose then crashed the side of Fuego's face with his fist.

"No Mayhem help Tee-Tee!" He commanded bouncing to his feet then commenced to fighting like four people in one. He lifted Divine with a punch in the gut and he folded like a tent with a collapsed pole. Louis got his head put to bed and Fuego was dropped from a buckle punch. Someone screamed and Tommy spun around. "That's enough Mayhem!" Tommy yelled at his dog as she viciously tore the clothes from Champ's body proving her bite was far worse than her bark! Tommy had to intervene and pull her off the screaming boy, trying to hold her back as she jerked at him attempting to reach Champ. Dragging his gnarling dog by her collar Tommy pushed past Fuego and his crew of losers, put his dog in the back seat and climbed behind the wheel of his ride.

"You Okay?" He asked his sister as she got in.

"Uh-huh." Tee-Tee nodded. She looked a little shaken up but otherwise fine.

"Mayhem?" Tommy asked looking through the rearview mirror. She barked a 'yes' and returned her attention outside to the punks stirring on the ground.

"Tommy?" Tee-Tee called. Tommy turned to his sister and braced himself for her question. "I changed my mind. I do want to go to Mickey D's."

"Oh, Okay. Whatever you want." Tommy said exhaling. And with that said he twisted the key in the ignition and pulled out the parking lot.

After they were long gone a black Mercedes Benz pulled up on the scene. The door opened and a dark figure got out and walked over to the men lying all over the ground. Fuego looked up speechless praying his night wasn't about to get worse.

# Chapter 25

"Beat it! Beat it! Beat it! Nobody is deleted! Show him you funky hmm-hmm-hmm fight! It doesn't' matter ooh, cause I'm right! So beat it-so beat it!" Tee-Tee sang loud, incorrectly and off-key along with Michael Jackson courtesy of her Sony Walkman ever since they pulled out of Mickey D's drive through. "So beat it!"

"Hey brat. Eat your fries. Before I beat you," Tommy jokingly ordered partially pulling off his sister's headphones.

"But you said not to eat in your car."

"Don't worry about it-cat," he said preferring to clean up a mess over another ear-splitting chorus.

"Big brother?"

"Yes?"

"Is it true that if you say Bloody Mary in the bathroom mirror three times she'll appear behind you?"

"No," he replied, massaging his aching head.

"Is it true that if you eat pop-rocks and drink Pepsi at the same time your stomach explodes?"

Tommy looked over at his sister, "Who told you this stuff?"

"Cousin Gus."

"Sweetie don't listen to your cousin Gus, he's so dumb he got locked in Key Food." Tommy shook his head at the urban legends and sighed then sat forward in his seat, "Is that Donnie's ride?" He asked himself as he pulled onto his block.

Tommy strained at her car and was curious why she was sitting outside when she had a key to his place. When he pulled up alongside of her car and saw Pumpkin seated beside his girlfriend he sucked his teeth. He lowered the passenger window automatically then honked his horn. Donnie sat behind the wheel of her car staring straight ahead with an angry pout on her face and lowered her window.

"Hey you." Tommy called out to her.

"Hey." She replied with less enthusiasm drumming her nails on the steering wheel without turning her head towards his direction.

Tommy wasn't sure where the attitude was coming from, but he was certain that her pain-in-the-ass friend had everything to do with it. "Is everything alright?" He asked. Donnie and Pumpkin traded all-knowing glances but she never said a word. Tommy remembered that earlier Donnie mentioned something about her girlfriend having man problems and assumed that was the reason for her foul mood. But why take it out on him? If anything, she should be glad that she was not in the same predicament and had a good man that did not put her through the same bullshit!

"Hi Donnie." Tee-Tee said a little too bright and cheerfully for a woman her age causing Pumpkin's eyebrows to rise perplexed.

*'Oh snap! Donnie wasn't bullshitting. Tommy really does have a twenty-five-year-old sister with the mental capacity of a child.'* Pumpkin thought to herself but pretended not to notice. As it was once he found out what she had done, she might have to get an order of protection against him.

"Hi Tee-Tee. Tommy! What happened to your face?" Donnie said turning her head to say hello then saw Tommy's face all bruised and pulpy. She rushed out her car and coming over as Pumpkin sucked her teeth and shook her head at her friend's sudden change of heart.

"I look like something Chef Boy-ar-dee makes," Tommy said with a mangled smile.

"Tommy got into a fight with these boys at Pizza Hut. And one of them wanted me to play with his pickle." Tee-Tee reported.

"What?" Donnie said.

"It's cool." Tommy assured Donnie and she gently held his face in her hands as he flinched licking his sore lips. Even though his injuries hurt like hell right now he was almost grateful for them because of the reaction that they got out of Donnie. "This punk was trying to take advantage of my sister, *if you know what I mean.*"

Donnie shook her head catching what he implied. "Is she Okay?"

"She's fine."

"Ahem, Donnie ain't there something you want to ask your man?" Pumpkin asked busting up the mood.

Donnie's posture immediately tightened and her hands dropped from his face. She looked at him upset and Tommy knew none of this had anything to do with Pumpkin's trivial ghetto drama.

"We need to talk." she said in a serious voice.

"You want to go upstairs?" Tommy suggested.

"No need. I'm not staying long."

For the first time tonight, Tommy was nervous. "Aight, let me take Tee-Tee and my dog upstairs. I'll be right back." Donnie nodded and got back into her car. Tommy glared at Pumpkin causing her to shiver then pulled into his driveway.

"So, after a couple of minutes of the wackest sex I've ever had in my entire life, this fool Lenny rolls over smiling and got the nerve to ask me, 'Baby you came?' I looked him dead in the eye and said, yeah, I came over here and wasted my time wit your sorry ass!" Pumpkin said retelling Donnie her latest saga while Stacy Lattisaw and Johnny Gill sang 'Where Do We Go From Here' in the background.

Donnie stared silently at the wipers removing the falling snow like she had something on her mind. "Pumpkin, are you really sure it was him?" she asked sounding desperate.

"As sure as government cheese is hard." Pumpkin said. Donnie sighed and Pumpkin rubbed her friend's shoulder. "I'm sorry sis, but it's better you found this out now before you became too emotionally involved."

"Too late for that." Donnie frowned.

"Look, I know you're upset but you've got to be strong. And above all don't let him sweet-talk you. Because trust me he'll try to give you some bogus ass reason for his skeezing. They all do-Oh here he comes. Now Donnie remember, Do-not-let-him-sweet-talk-you!" Pumpkin advised squeezing her hand.

"Okay, Okay!" Donnie said vexed with her friend's advice. She got out her car and came over to Tommy. He had changed out of his wet shirt into a warm turtleneck and long green overcoat. When he leaned in to kiss Donnie she backed away.

"So what's going on baby? Why are we standing out here in the snow? And why'd you bring Anita the beast with you?" Tommy asked pretending that he did not just get dissed trying to steal a kiss.

"She's here for moral support." Donnie said straight-faced.

"I'm confused. Why would you need moral support from her, when according to you she was the one having problems in her relationship?"

Donnie sucked her teeth at the irony of his question then inhaled deeply and exhaled, "Refresh my memory Tommy, where'd you go when you left my house late last night?" she asked in complete earnestness.

"Last night?" he repeated wide-eyed.

Donnie folded her arms across her chest and cocked her head. "It's not a difficult question. Where did you go after you left my place? And more importantly, whom did you go see?"

Tommy realized she knew where he was and blew steam, then placed his hands on Donnie's shoulders. "Now baby before you start jumping to conclusions, let me explain-"

Donnie snatched back like he was burning to the touch. "Explain? You don't have to explain I already know! After you left me you went to be with another woman! Now I see why you didn't want me to come with you."

"No it's not like that. The woman I was with was my ex-wife,"

"It gets better."

"No it's not like that-" Tommy paused and lowered his voice speaking almost in a whisper so Pumpkin who was all ears could not hear. "For the past week or so I've been followed around town by somebody in a black Mercedes with tinted windows. I don't know who it is. All I know is whenever I look over my shoulder there's this damn car! Close enough to be threatening, yet far enough that I cannot see who's behind the wheel. It could be out here right now. Watching in the shadows." Donnie folded her arms across her chest and twisted her lips like she was not buying it. "Look at my eyes. I got this a couple of hours ago from some other unrelated beef. That's why I left last night. I didn't want to bring this type of shit to your doorstep. Trust me I never wanted to leave you. I swear it."

"Trust you? You lied about where you were going. And why didn't you tell me about this Mercedes before? And how does your ex-wife fit into all of this?"

"I didn't tell you because I don't have all the facts yet. Not even a driver behind the wheel. Just a car."

"And your ex?" Donnie repeated.

"On the way home, I saw Nicky heading into this little dive. I went in to check on her because it's a rough neighborhood."

"How convenient!"

"Nothing happened I swear-wait a second. How'd you even know where I-" Tommy spun at Donnie's car and his eyes went dark. "YOU!" He growled.

Pumpkin's eyes bugged out as Tommy angrily stormed her way. "Oh shit!" she screamed then quickly locked the doors. Not that he would have actually used his guns. But he was glad he left them upstairs.

"Fucking instigator! What'd you tell her?" Tommy demanded.

"The fucking truth!" Pumpkin yelled back.

"What do you know about the truth? You lie so damn much you could uncork a bottle of wine with that tongue of yours!"

"Whatever Tommy! Your problem is that you fail to recognize that my home girl Donnie is an educated black woman! She ain't stupid!" Pumpkin boldly shouted back safely behind locked doors and raised windows.

"I don't need you to tell me that!" Tommy based.

"Look at you perpetrating the fraud. You talk about me but you can't even keep your own lies straight!" Pumpkin snapped with a head roll.

Tommy turned to Donnie. "C'mon baby she doesn't want to see us together. Think about it, she wants you to be alone. Bitter and miserable just like her!"

Pumpkin gasped. "So Tommy is you saying that it wasn't you I saw last night outside of The Future, arguing with some Pocahontas looking girl?" Donnie turned to Tommy hoping he would say something to vindicate himself. But his normal jovial manner turned quiet. "This ain't Jeopardy. Answer the question!" Pumpkin snapped spitefully. Tommy could have strangled Pumpkin until her eyes popped out their sockets but instead let out his frustration by roaring to the top of his lungs and slamming his hands down on the roof of Donnie's car. "You see this mess here Donnie? Do you need another Sam? An emotional violent liar in your life? Instead of beating up on your car he should'a beat up whoever it was that gave him that eye-jammie!"

"Would the both of you just chill-out for a second! God, I'm getting a damn migraine!" Donnie stressed, massaging her temples. "Tommy would you come here please."

Tommy came back over and met the hurt gaze of his beloved. Unsure of what to say he raised both eyebrows, which then seemed to fall under their own weight with a sigh. "I feel like the guy in the movies who has to cut either the red or the blue wire on the bomb," he smiled attempting to lighten the mood.

"Why don't you cut the crap wire," Donnie snapped.

"Ouch," Tommy flinched.

"So it's true?" she asked.

"Of course not! -Well the part about me seeing Nicky is true. But there's nothing going on."

Donnie shook her head feeling stupid as Stacy and Johnny fittingly asked her where do they go from here or do they keep on trying? "Why is it men always want the unattainable and are willing to sacrifice what they have to get it." she said then dug into her pocket. "Here."

338

Tommy let out an exasperated sigh and frowned at the keys to his crib. "Aw c'mon babe don't do this."

"Tommy I've always known you had a lot of nerve but you proved it by leaving me to meet your ex-wife. I am well aware of the fact that I have not exactly tried to stop you and to some degree I have encouraged this selfish behavior."

"But Donnie-"

"No buts. I have distanced myself from people for far less than what you've been doing. I don't have the time or the energy to deal with your bullshit any longer. Fucking with my head and emotions will no longer be your favorite past time. Tommy, I love you dearly but I need to be free of this farce of a relationship. We're both wasting our time and have nothing to gain by continuing."

"I disagree." Tommy whispered.

"That's on you. I've said far more than I needed to and I truly wish you the best and hope you have no worries...Now can I have my key back?"

"Donnie I'm not a perfect man and I've made my share of mistakes. Perhaps it was a bad judgment call but I sincerely thought I was doing the right thing." Tommy said, but the look on Donnie's face told him he was only talking and not saying anything. Reluctantly he handed Donnie her apartment key.

"Thank you." Donnie said.

"C'mon baby we can get through this, I love you and you love me." Tommy pleaded folding her in his arms and kissing her forehead. Donnie caught herself feeling weak and pushed him away.

"No! There's a time to admit failure and a time to keep on trying. I'm tired of trying." Donnie said then leaned in and kissed Tommy. "Take care of yourself."

Tommy took her hand making one last attempt to get her to rethink this. The awful pain in his face from his fight in the parking lot, was replaced by the awful pain in his heart when he looked deep into Donnie's hurt eyes. She got into her car before the tears building could fall.

"Don't do this baby." Tommy banged on the window. Donnie ignored him and keyed the ignition and began to drive off as Tommy kept up with the car. "Donnie please!"

By now the tears were rolling down Donnie's cheeks. When she got to the corner she pulled off into the night. "Not one word." She sniffled as Pumpkin opened her mouth. Pumpkin respected her wishes nodding and kept her comments to herself as she glanced at Tommy in her side view mirror standing in the street and a smile formed in the side of her mouth.

Tommy stood there in the snow watching Donnie's car drive away as the taillights grew smaller and smaller missing her already. He sagged like a puppet with its strings severed. After a few moments had passed he was about to head upstairs when he heard a car horn and looked to see where it came from.

He couldn't believe his eyes. "Son-of-a-bitch!" he said at the sight of the infamous black Mercedes Benz with its illegally completely covered, tinted windows that was responsible for all his woes as it boldly cruised down his block mocking him.

Without a thought Tommy took off like lightning. "Hey Asshole!" he shouted chasing after the car. "Yo you hear me Jack-off? Pull over! Where are you going? Here I am!" The car continued at an even pace. Slow enough so that he could keep up, but fast enough that he had to work to do it. Tommy began to tire of the cat and mouse shit and stopped to catch his breath as the car continued on down the street. "Yeah that's right, keep booking! You'd better stay in your bitch mobile if you know what's good for you! Cause if you come back, I'll flyy that head coward!" Tommy threatened in between gulps of air.

Suddenly the car hit the brakes grinding skid marks into the street as if to say, 'Oh really?' Tommy stood in the middle of the street stooped over resting on his knees as the car sat there idly with its motor humming. The abrupt screeching of tires startled him as the car peeled off backward coming directly at him! "Oh shit!" Tommy shouted and tumbled off to the side into a pile of slush and ice before he was run over. Back on his feet he squinted as the car's high beams cut the darkness of the night while its engine roared ferociously. Tommy dipped back onto the sidewalk as the out-of-control Mercedes jumped the curb accelerating at him like a land shark intent on mashing him into road kill. Running frantically, he spotted a half-lowered fire escape ladder outside a faded two-story brick building on the edge of the block and went for it. With the Benz hot on his heels, he leap-frogged up to the ladder and tucked his legs into his chest as the car missed his legs by a fraction of an inch and collided head-on with a garbage dumpster. Dangling above the car, Tommy observed the dumpster's mangled handles were twisted around the car's fender. He let go of the ladder and his boots dented the hood. With a twisted snarl he looked back at the dumpster and snatched out a long metal pipe and began bashing the windshield with it. As he went to work, the car's back tires furiously spun out of control trying to free itself from the dumpster's hold.

"Your timing's impeccable! Where the hell were you fifteen minutes ago huh motherfucker?" Tommy shouted at whomever was inside as his wild swings decorated the glass with cracked marks. "So who are you? A pimp? A drug dealer? A pedophile? Or some other piece of shit low-life whose ass I stomped into a mudhole and now you want revenge? Well come and get it tough guy! Stop hiding and get out the car pussy!" he said as he switched to kicking and stomping on the glass while the car continued its tug of war with the garbage dumpster. Tommy's heated efforts were beginning to take their toll as the windshield began to collapse and he held the pipe up and stabbed it through the window. Exactly where the driver would be sitting. The back wheels suddenly came to a dead halt and the car calmed down. He squinted at the black tinted window wondering if he struck oil, in the driver's head. He kicked at the windshield. Nothing. "Hello? Hey asshole! You dead in there?" he called out. Nothing. He clenched his teeth and placed shaky hands on the pipe then yanked it out and studied it. There was some blood on the end. Suddenly the car roared back to life! "Oh shit!" he yelled startled as the cars back tires grinded black stripes into the asphalt struggling furiously until the fender finally ripped free and the ebony car flew backwards. Tommy's feet were snatched out from under him and he slammed hard onto his back like a safe tossed out of a six-story window. The Benz flew backwards into the street spinning into a screeching 360 and made a hasty retreat into the night.

The snow stopped but his problems were just beginning. Tommy sat up and sighed. "...Well, at least my Mama still loves me." he told himself then climbed to his feet and limped across the street. Brawling with a pack of vicious street punks in a parking lot, being dumped by the love of your life and nearly being the victim of a hit and run all in the same night might be Earth shattering to most. But for the Trouble Consultant, it was a regular Sunday night.

Tommy staggered in his front door, visibly spent, to find his sister lying beneath a makeshift tent she made out of a sheet and two chairs, snuggled up with his dog watching Annie.

"Tommy come get under the tent with us," Tee-Tee asked as she playfully dressed the dog in her brother's Kangol hat and Gazelle shades.

"Maybe later." Her brother said solemnly as he emptied a tray of ice cubes into a dishrag then applied the cold compress to his head and collapsed on the couch.

"Where's Donnie at?"

"She left," Tommy said.

"When is she coming back?"

"She's not."

"How come?" Tee-Tee asked.

"She's just not." Tommy repeated with a bit of sorrow in his voice.

"But she said she was gonna go out with us." Tee-Tee's harmless prying was beginning to seriously get on her brother's nerves.

Tommy sat up. "Tee-Tee pack some clothes and your toothbrush and whatever else you might need. We're spending the night out."

"Yay!" Tee-Tee cheered then calmed down and asked, "Where we going?"

*"That's a good question."* Tommy asked under his breath. He had no idea where they were going, but he knew they could not stay there with a potential hit and run killer waiting outside.

"Mommy always packs my bag." Tee-Tee said interrupting his thoughts.

"Mommy does way too much for you Tee-Tee. You're a big girl."

"But Tom-"

"Dammit Tee-Tee! I don't have time for this!" Tommy yelled regretting the words and tone as it came out. There was as uncomfortable silence as his sister's eyes welled with tears. She'd never seen this side of her brother, much less directed at her. "Aw geez. I'm sorry for yelling at you." He apologized hugging her as the tears flowed from her eyes. "I just have a lot on my mind. But I should have never spoken to you like that. You forgive me sis?"

Tee-Tee nodded wiping her eyes and kissed his cheek. "It's ok I still love you,"

"Now you're gonna make me cry. How about you pack an overnight bag with a couple of jeans and shirts, underwear, socks and after you're done I'll make you a cup of hot chocolate?" Tommy said feeling guilty for allowing the mad cap crazy hijinks of his wild life to beset his sister's cheerful mood.

"With marshmallows?"

"Sure. Whatever you want."

Tee-Tee nodded and proceeded to pack her bag. Tommy checked the pulse in his neck, it was beating like a racehorse. He went into the bathroom and looked into his medicine cabinet wishing he could pop a couple of sleeping pills and snooze away his troubles. Instead he opted for splashing cold water in his face. Pondering his next move, he spotted the Ocean Pacific pin-striped men's button-down shirt he replaced three years ago after forgetting the old one when he moved on his own, hanging on a hook and it came to him.

# Chapter 26

Sitting on the edge of her couch in a baby blue terrycloth robe with cotton balls placed in between her toes as her toe nails dried, Nicky sipped on a white wine spritzer while singing along with The Force MDs.

Emptying then refilling her glass, she fondly remembered her days as Mrs. Nicky Strong while flipping through her old wedding photo album. A warm smile came over her face as she looked over the pictures of friends and family celebrating her day of happiness. Between two pages she found an old wedding invitation.

"With joyful hearts, we ask your presence at the ceremony uniting Nicolette Hunter and Thomas Strong on Saturday July Nineteenth at six o'clock in the evening. Concord Baptist Church..." she read aloud then sucked her teeth and proceeded to flip past more pictures. She stopped at a picture of the bride and groom taken on a small wooden bridge overlooking a babbling brook at Prospect Park and sighed. She looked absolutely stunning in a vintage gown for a modern-day princess. Tommy looked handsome in his white tuxedo with matching cummerbund but like a completely different person because of his long curly faded hairstyle. As she remembered their honeymoon in the Poconos she beamed recalling how Tommy would pamper her and treat her like a queen for no special reason except that he loved her.

"Ah perfect." Nicky said smiling approvingly at the neat job she had done on her toes. Although it wasn't as thorough as when Tommy used to do it, it still looked like she had them done professionally. The phone rang. "Hello?...Hel-lo?" she repeated when no one answered. She could tell someone was listening on the other end. "Hello?"

Nicky hung the phone back up and picked up the Virginia Slim burning in the ashtray on the coffee table and took a drag. She was beginning to get good at blowing smoke rings and tossed one in the direction of the giant Benetton teddy bear piled up in the corner. She put out the cigarette and sighed disgustedly at the 'I-know-I-fucked-up-but-baby-please-give-me-another-chance' gifts that Corbin sent. Nicky rolled her eyes. It was beginning to get annoying that Corbin could not accept the fact that what they once had was over. She got up and went over to her stereo then ran a long thin finger down the collection of costly CDs and came across one that put a smile on her face. She removed the shiny thin round disc from its jewel case and inserted it into the CD player, hit play and went back to the couch. Prince started singing 'Do Me Baby' and she opened her robe and began to rub down her body with cocoa butter. As she listened to the romantic melody that was both resonant and hauntingly beautiful, she thought back to the days when she and Tommy would make passionate love. Always the one to go the extra mile to get the job done, Tommy would never stop at foreplay and proceeded on to five, six, seven, eight play. Treating her body like a temple, making her feel like every part of her was lovely and delicious.

The more Nicky thought about her ex-husband's big strong hands groping her, the hornier she became. It had been a long time since she had sex and her body was screaming out to be pleasured. It was especially hard to deal because when she was married she got laid on a regular basis and now, nothing. She felt like she had gone from being a millionaire to the poor house in the blink of an eye.

When she and Corbin started dating she thought that her drought was finally over, but after they attempted to have sex she knew it would not work out. After being married to a man who was the perfect package, with an incredible libido to boot, she could not see herself getting with someone who ejaculated prematurely as soon as he got a glimpse of her breasts, then had the audacity to not maintain another erection for the remainder of the night. As Nicky massaged her inner thighs she could feel her desire growing stronger. Unable to resist the urge any longer she pushed her photo album on the floor and gave in to her body's demands and leaned back, closed her eyes and slid her hand down her flat stomach and inside her panties. As she caressed herself she fanaticized that it was Tommy's big hands fondling her breasts and causing her juices to flow. Seven minutes into it she was so moist she could slide out of her seat, when the phone rang again. She cut her eyes over at the phone then squeezed them shut and tried to block out the annoying ringing and concentrate on achieving an orgasm. Success was in her grasp as her body began to spasm and she could feel herself cumming when the answering machine inappropriately came on.

*'This is Nicky, you know what to do.'* - BEEP

"Hello Nicolette-oops I mean Nicky. Sorry, I apologize, I know you don't like me calling you Nicolette. In any event, it's me

345

Corbin. Hello? Please Nicolette, ugh I've said it again. Please pick up the phone, I know you are home. The lights are on."

"Shit!" Nicky gritted her teeth and tried to hurry up and cum. She felt like getting up and picking up then slamming down the receiver but she feared that if she did she would lose the moment.

"Nicky? Come on Nicky. I'm certain we can get past this. For heaven's sake, we are two mature adults here."

Nicky sat up pissed and swore loudly. She had lost the moment. She snatched up the receiver. "What?" she hissed.

"Nico-Nicky! Hi. How are you." Corbin stuttered.

"I **was** fine! What do you want?"

"Only to talk."

Nicky snatched her robe closed and went over and smacked the power button on the CD player. When she plopped back down she realized that she had smeared a toenail. "Shit!" Now she was really livid. "Corbin we've said everything that needed to be said to one another the other night. And while we are on the topic I want you to stop leaving bears and candy and flowers outside my door. Oh, and just so you know, I know it was you that called here a little while ago and hung up."

"Nicky I haven't the foggiest idea what you are talking about. This is my first time calling you. I swear it."

"You really expect me to believe that?"

"Yes, I do. Just like I expect you to believe that I am sorry for saying those things about you and Tommy. Nicky I love you."

"Well get over it. I did!" Nicky hissed void of emotions.

"Why you-you…cold-hearted bitch!"

Nicky was slack-jawed. Her eyes became balls of pure fire. "What did you just call me?"

"Oh, so that you heard huh? Typical. Here I am spilling my heart and soul out and I might as well be talking to the blasted wall for what it's worth! But I call you out of your name and that you hear. I guess it's safe to say tha-"

"Listen up you weak, pathetic little man! If you ever call my house or come by again, so help me I'll-"

"You'll what?" Corbin said almost daring her, like he was above the law.

"I'll get Tommy to kick your punk ass! Test me if you think I'm bullshitting!" Nicky threatened.

There was a long pause on the other end as Corbin pictured Tommy doing the moonwalk on his chest. "Sweetheart listen to me I-"

**KLICK!**

Once Corbin disrespected her there was nothing else left to say. In all the years she was married to Tommy things were not always like his Nana would say, 'peachy-keen.' Like regular couples they had their share of fights. But no matter how angry and upset they got with one another, he never raised his hands to her and never under any circumstances did he ever call her out of her name. And how she saw it, if she did not receive that kind of verbal abuse from her own husband, then she damn sure was not about to take it from this loser.

Nicky was so angry she entertained the idea of still telling Tommy to kick his ass. Even if his heart now belonged to Donnie she knew she could still count on him to have her back. But there was no way she'd do something like that. She was about to head into the kitchen when suddenly the doorbell rang. She approached the door with caution then glanced at the phone. If that was Corbin she was going to have Tommy reach out and touch someone!

"Who is it?" she called out.

"It's me, Tee-Tee." A shy voice replied.

"Tee-Tee?" Nicky repeated. "What are you doing here?" she unlocked the door and was surprised to find Tee-Tee was standing outside her doorway by herself smiling and lugging a Hello Kitty traveling bag. "Tee-Tee what on Earth are you doing here? Where's Tommy?"

"He just left but he's coming back later."

"Later?" she looked past Tee-Tee and spotted her brother's Jeep drive off.

"Uh-huh, he said to give you this." Tee-Tee explained and handed Nicky a folded note.

Nicky took the note and opened it. *"I apologize if we are imposing, but you know I would not do this unless it was a life or death situation! You two sit tight and I will explain everything when I get there. —Tommy"* After reading the note she was even more confused.

Nicky decided to wait until Tommy got there to ask what in the hell was going on. "Are you hungry?"

"Nah-uh. I already ate McDonalds." Tee-Tee said fascinated with Nicky's aquarium. "Nicky your fishies is pretty. Can I feed them?"

"Huh? Oh, sure you can, sweetie." Nicky said. She almost did not hear her because she was deep in thought wondering, 'What in the hell was Tommy thinking? Dropping Tee-Tee over at her place unannounced. Then pulling off like that?' Then it all made perfect sense. Havoc had a consulting gig and he needed a babysitter. This did not set well with her and she planned to let him know it, whenever he showed up.

# Chapter 27

The sky was the color of ink and the moon was a pearly crescent as Tommy pulled up onto the curb of a silent block. He eased out and pulled his sweatshirt's hood tightly over his head. Before taking a step, he looked everywhere at once checking to make sure he wasn't being followed then sprinted around the corner to Donnie's building. He was about to ring her bell when he spotted Donnie's busybody neighbor, Onetta Jackson, standing in the lobby sorting her mail. Suddenly the little Yorkshire terrier at her feet began yapping at the top of its lungs.

"What's wrong with my wittle Schnoogie-Woogie?" Onetta asked smiling at her baby pooch Miss Thing. She looked up and her eyes went wide. She scooped up her dog and was about to run upstairs when the menacing looking man outside her co-op pounded on the window.

"Wait Onetta, hold up! It's me Tommy. Donnie's man." He said pulling back his hood.

Onetta caught her breath and calmed down once she recognized Tommy and let him in. "Tommy?

"Yeah. Why're you treating me like a Jehovah Witness?"

"Cause you almost gave me a heart attack! -Damn! What happened to your eye man?" she asked pointing in his face.

"I ran into a door."

Onetta twitched her lips. "Umm-hmm. And I'm a size six."

"Anyway-have you seen Donnie?"

"Yeah she's upstairs," she said then blocked his path. "But hold on there Hulk. I wouldn't go up there if I was you."

"Why not?"

"As if you didn't know, Mister sneaking around with his ex-wife on the down-low." Onetta smirked nudging him in the ribs.

"She told you huh?"

"She ain't have to. I could hear her and her loud ass friends from my terrace cause they got the door wide open. Not like I was eavesdropping or nothing mind you. The building's super has the heat turned up too high." she said making excuses.

"Friends?" Tommy said concerned.

"Uh-huh, a whole bunch of 'em are over there having a 'Pity-party. And guess who for?"

"Can this night possibly get any worse?" Tommy groaned smacking himself in the head. "So do you think I have a chance?"

"With me, in a heartbeat Stud muffin. With her weelll-I dunno. She sounded pretty pissed."

Tommy paced the lobby for a minute then took Onetta by the shoulders looking desperate. "Let's go up to your place."

"Oh baby, I thought you'd never ask!" Onetta grinned from ear to ear.

"See Donnie what you need to do is cook Tommy a delicious meal like some paella, empanadas or arroz con pollo and put a tiny drop of your period blood in it. My cousin Marisol did that to her baby daddy Miguel and he stopped going out hoeing and started coming straight home after work. Just like that." Nelda said snapping her stylishly manicured fingers to demonstrate the instant change in the roaming Romeo. She was a pretty Latina with an olive complexion who wore her hair with one side shaved and the other swooped over one of her heavily eyelined eyes.

Pumpkin rolled her eyes, "Ain't nobody trying to do that nasty Santa Maria voodoo shit. Look Dee, hear a sister out, I been around the block of romance a few times and picked up a few things along the way."

"Girl please, the only thing you picked up along the way was some questionable rashes." Nelda said instigating laughs as Pumpkin rolled her eyes at her Macy's co-worker.

"Whateva low-budget Lisa-Lisa! Ain't nobody trying to get lost in your emotions. Anyway Dee, the best way to get over a man is to get under a new one," Pumpkin advised as Nelda hissed, *'Ay dios mio'* through sucked teeth.

Donnie shook her head frustrated with the bad advice from her friends and poured herself a shot of Smirnoff straight, no chaser. "To hell with Tommy Strong! I don't want him if I have to resort to taboo and trickery to make him love me. I'm an independent, confident, secure, strong black woman who can face adversity head on! Check it out. I have a wonderful career. My girls!" Donnie said as the room filled with her closest homegirls held up their glasses in unison saying, *'Here! Here!'* "Although I'm no threat to Beverly Johnson's modeling career, nobody's going to hold up my picture to frighten away crows either. I'm beautiful inside and more importantly, outside. Shit, I deserve better!" she said with a head roll before chugging the remainder of her glass.

"I know that's right! Because once you've got heartbreak, disloyalty, distrust, aggravation-once you've gone down those avenues and you end up at the corner of redemption, you have to redeem yourself. And let me tell you something, it is not worth going back down avenues. Especially over some two-timing, lying no good dog of a man! I should know. I tolerated enough crap for every woman in this room over my daughter's no good father!" Sonia, Donnie's Delta Sigma Theta sorority sister and old college roommate said pouring herself her third drink. She was stunning with a deep dark complexion and briefly modeled on the runways of Paris before giving it up to become a mother and lawyer.

"See Dee that's why when it comes to relationships, I'm out for self." Pumpkin said slightly tipsy tossing an arm around her best friend's neck. "My motto iz, get what you can! I swear, guys be killin' me knowing good and damn well that they be doing it too. But let a sister try and get her groove on and suddenly I'm the slut, the hoe, the bitch! Well if I'm a bitch then I'm a **B**eautiful, **I**ntelligent, **T**houghtful, **C**harming, **H**uman being who knows what she wants, and knows how to use what she's got to get what she wants."

"And what's that?" Donnie asked.

"Clothes, furs, money, jewels and expensive dinners. Duh." Pumpkin winked.

"See it's because of women like you that there will never be a Madam President." Said Solange, the passive and docile one of the crew who fit the description of her accountant profession to a tee. Owl-wide lens glasses, hair pulled back in an unflattering style and a plain floor length dress.

"What do you mean women 'like me' little Miss Prima Donna?" Pumpkin rolled her eyes insulted.

"I think she's just trying to say to be careful because all that glitters ain't gold." Nelda said trying to prevent a catfight.

"Yeah but that's okay. Cause I also accept diamonds, pearls and other sparkling jewelry!" Pumpkin said bouncing in her chair.

Solange shook her head pitifully. It bothered her how Pumpkin perpetuated the gold-digging, trifling, highly sexualized image. "Pumpkin, having it all is being completely on your own. A man is the icing on the cake to the life you've created for yourself." When she saw she was not getting through to Pumpkin she turned to Donnie who was much more levelheaded. "Dee it's not about that. Trust me, Tommy's doing you a favor. You deserve a man that will love you and treat you right. Just like my-"

*"A-lon-zo!"* The entire room chimed in sync cutting Solange off in mid-sentence then laughed. Even Donnie smiled for the first time all night.

"We all know how perfect you *think* yo man is." Pumpkin rolled her eyes.

"Well he is!" Solange defensively snapped back.

"Let me ask you something Solange, if Alonzo is all of that and a dime sack, then how come he ain't asked you to marry his ass yet?" Pumpkin inquired.

"Oh see we already discussed that."

"Is that right?" Pumpkin asked skeptically nudging Donnie.

"That's right, and Alonzo said that since we've been living together for over eight years, we don't need to get married because we are already married by common law. He said we know what we have is real and we don't need no piece of paper to prove it." Solange explained snootily and proceeded to sip on her non-alcoholic beverage. Pumpkin looked at Donnie and the two burst out laughing. "And what's so darn funny?" Solange demanded to know.

"That you fell for that load of horse shit!" Pumpkin laughed.

Donnie made a face at Pumpkin to stop being so mean then went back to Solange. "Honey New York is not a common wealth state."

"So?"

"So SIS-ta-girl even I know common law marriage is not recognized here in the Big Apple. It don't exist." Pumpkin said laughing vindictively. She and Solange were cool, but the dowdy looking young woman who let her man control everything could be a bit annoying at times.

"I'm sure he didn't know!" Solange rolled her eyes as she held out her glass to be filled with vodka and orange juice then emptied it in one sip.

Donnie's cousin Mecca shook her head with a sigh as her Ankh earrings angrily swung back and forth. Out of the sisterhood, she was the one most in tune with her Afrocentricity and always sported seashell jewelry and colorful T-shirts with righteous afro-isms boasting Black Pride while reading conscious literature like the Isis Papers. Tall and unassumingly pretty, she was brown skinned with a dancer's body and shoulder-length dread-locks. "I hate how brotha's always say that we are the ones who be illin' when nine times out of ten, it's them! All we want is respect, kindness and the love of a good Black Man. Shoot-any man that will produce strong healthy children and stick around to help raise them, for that matter!" Mecca said.

"Whoa back up! I know that ain't Miss Angela Davis Power-to-the-People over there talking about dating outside of her race. I was feeling you for a second there, but you lost me when you started talking about that swirl business. Cause there's just something about black men that's, universal, O-K?" Pumpkin spoke up receiving an approving head nod from Donnie.

"My sister you're taking what I said way out of context." Mecca said refilling her glass with mango juice. "I am by no means saying to abandon our Kings...Even though many of them have no qualms about doing it to us once they reach a certain class status or sign a seven-figure sports deal. But you know like I do that our men are spoiled. They are too damn comfortable knowing that we will remain loyal to them. I agree they are the desired race but there are plenty of suitable non-black men begging sistas for a date and we refuse because of our loyalty or because we are ashamed to go there."

"Shoot I ain't ashamed!" Sonia spoke up in a tipsy drawl. She was attractive with an athletic form from teaching West African dance at the Alvin Ailey American Dance Theater and thanks to the cute mole over her right eyebrow and similar bone structure, she often received complimentary comparisons to Thelma on 'Good Times.'

"Not you too Sonia." Pumpkin said disappointedly.

"And why the hell not? I'm sick and tired of trifling ass brotha's dogging me out. Either I'm too dark skin, too independent, too opinionated, too that, too this! My grandmother used to say, man's rejection is God's protection. Maybe it's time to heed her sapience and explore other options too! There's this white guy Owen that owns a quaint little book store in my neighborhood and whenever I come in he drops what he's doing and gives me his personal undivided attention, following me around making certain I got everything I need.

"Girl please, Owen's just making sure your black ass don't steal shit!" Pumpkin said making the room laugh.

"Sonia I'm not telling you how to lead your life, but to label all our black Kings as dogs is wrong. And please remember, a dog knows no color, he can be black, white, red, yellow or brown and he still ain't shit." Mecca said, "Now like I was saying, we have always been the backbone of Black Men. We've always understood that our men need our support and understanding because of how hard they have it. And we've always been there for them. That's why it burns me up when we do everything we are supposed to and still get dogged-out."

"I hear you girl and some of what you say does make sense, but I swear when my girls get older they're not gonna repeat my mistakes. Number one college is a must! It may be too late for me but not them." Pumpkin said adamantly.

"You still can go," Mecca said encouragingly.

"No, in High School I wasted my time on sports. You know, the football team, the basketball team." Pumpkin said sadly staring at the bottom of her glass. "But I want them to know that they do not have to be dependent on a man for anything! Cause I don't want them caught up in the situation I'm in." she paused and sighed wearily. "Before sex, you help each other get naked. After sex you dress yourself. Moral of the story, in life no one helps you once you're fucked." Pumpkin said and wiped a tear with her sleeve. Donnie threw an arm around her best friend. Pumpkin shook her head laughing at herself for getting drunk and emotional. "Look at me. I'm supposed to be cheering you up and you are the one who's consoling me." Pumpkin said through one big sob.

"Ok, time to lighten the mood," Mecca said and pulled a cassette out of her Walkman then jumped up and went over to the stereo and put it in. As soon as Bobby Brown's, 'My Prerogative' started to play tears were wiped away and the women danced and sang along. With the help of her neo Soul Sisters, Donnie was laughing and feeling a whole lot better and Tommy Strong was becoming a distant memory. Word up!

"I'm so fucked!" Tommy sighed while eavesdropping from Onetta's terrace. He rubbed his face in frustration wondering how in the hell was he supposed to persuade Donnie to listen to anything he had to say after what he just heard.

"Hungry?" Onetta asked sashaying out on the terrace carrying a steaming tray of La Choy Chinese egg rolls.

"Nah this'll do." Tommy huffed and polished off his Heineken before walking back inside.

The Cosby Show was on and it was the episode where Theo paid Denise to make him a knock-off Gordon Gartrell designer shirt. As Onetta howled with laughter Tommy picked his brain for a solution to his Donnie dilemma but came up blank. He picked up a small plastic container of Sea-Monkeys off the coffee table and stared at the odd looking tiny swimming creatures then placed it back down and got up to pace the floor.

Onetta's place was a pop culture explosion. Classic blaxploitation movie posters of The Mack, Truck Turner, Superfly and

Foxy Brown decorated the walls. On the table was a lava lamp. In the corner was a yellow beanbag chair. A huge floor model television that no longer work was used as a stand for a smaller television and figurines. Tommy went over to the wall unit and looked at the framed certificate surprised to discover that his horny, hefty, host was a registered nurse at Kings County Hospital. He was about mention that he was born there but figured it would lead into a discussion that he was not in the mood to have and kept his mouth shut. He picked up a Magic Eight-Ball and asked it if he had a chance of getting Donnie to listen. It replied, 'Outlook Not So Good.' He plopped on the couch. Then something caught his eye.

"Say Onetta, does that thing work?" Tommy asked pointing at the dusty box containing a karaoke machine in the corner by a tall potted plant.

"It should. I only used it once." Onetta said.

Tommy went over to the large wooden cassette rack mounted on the wall and ran a finger over Onetta's vast collection, hoping she had the tape that might turn everything around for him. When he found it, he grinned. "Now where's the mike-ah never mind I got it." he said snatching it from the coffee table.

"Um-Tommy-that ain't no microphone." Onetta giggled.

Tommy looked at the thick long black object in his hands. He switched it on and when it began vibrating and humming he tossed it on the couch then turned to her dumbfounded.

"Hey sometimes a girl's got to do, what a girl's got to do." Onetta shrugged unashamed. Tommy shook his head as she handed him the real microphone.

"I can't help but feel sort of responsible for all of this." Pumpkin said feeling guilty about hooking her best friend up with the Trouble Consultant.

"Don't be ridiculous. You had no idea that we would hook up. And he did take care of Sam." Donnie said.

"That may be but I for one am glad you and Tommy are no longer together." Mecca said. "He's nice and all but let's not forget what he does for a living. In fact, a lot of us felt that way."

"Is this true?" Donnie asked the room, and most of her friends either nodded or said yes.

"C'mon Dee, Tommy deals with thugs and low lives for a living. Not exactly a stellar resume." Nelda said.

"Well with all his faults, I liked him." Solange admitted and received stares from the room. "What? He's got that je ne sais quoi."

Donnie smiled at her friend for not judging, "Look guys, I know Tommy leads a somewhat perilous life and I admit in the beginning I was attracted to his quiet danger. And that it was exhilarating dating the guy your mother warned you about but somewhere between the fantasy and reality I discovered there was more to him. He's unlike any other guy I've ever known. When I was with him I felt like the safest person in the world. He has this cute boyish side that watches Saturday morning cartoons with a bowl of Captain Crunch in his lap. Then there's the charming romantic side that would feed me, undress me, bathe me and make body-rocking love to me for hours upon end. And believe it or not he's extremely smart and business savvy. He's like gravity and I was pulled towards him. That's why it hurts so much because I thought he was the one." she paused and twirled her chain between her fingers then let out a heartfelt sigh. "When relationships failed in the past I'd think it was my fault. That it was because I did or didn't do something that messed everything up."

"That's crazy talk." Mecca spoke up.

"I know it sounds foolish but I blamed myself when the walls came tumbling down. Then along comes Tommy Strong and he renewed my faith in relationships. It was like all the things I liked about him and even the things I disliked about him I couldn't live without, because I loved him. Like Pumpkin said, the pickings out there are mighty slim. Most brothers are either married, involved, in jail or gay. And the ones who aren't know that they are a commodity and take full advantage." She paused to sip her drink. "As the saying goes when you hit rock bottom there's nowhere to go but up." She said sounding defeated.

Suddenly a romantic tune began playing so loud it sounded as if it was coming through the walls of her neighbor's home. Pumpkin turned to Donnie with an annoyed expression. "How much are you paying to finally have a piece of the pie? Cause I got inconsiderate neighbors in the projects for a lot cheaper." she asked sarcastically.

The familiar melody, not the level of it made Donnie go out on her terrace to investigate. What she saw made her knees weak. Standing directly across from her on Onetta's terrace was Tommy holding a microphone and dancing in place to the song. But it wasn't just any song, this song was special. It was 'How Bout Us', the song they danced to the night he confessed his love for her.

"Tommy what do you think you're doing?" Donnie asked taken by surprise as her girls came out onto the terrace to be nosy.

Tommy signaled to Onetta to lower the music. "Whatever it takes to get you back." he said into the microphone as his voice boomed through Onetta's speakers.

Donnie was both flattered and embarrassed at the same time. She looked back at her girls who by their expressions were waiting to see what Juliet was going to say to her Romeo. "Tommy it's late. You're going to wake my neighbors!" she said.

"I'm not going anywhere until you listen." Tommy said showing no signs of backing down determined to get his woman back.

"My girl doesn't want anything to do with you. So build a bridge and get over it!" Pumpkin barked.

"Then let me hear her say that!" Tommy said.

Pumpkin turned to her homegirl eyebrows raised, certain after their man bashing session that she'd send Tommy's no good bald ass packing. "Go on, tell him you're no longer addicted to his love drug."

Donnie sighed knowing she was going to get it for what she was about to say. But she didn't care. It wasn't about what Pumpkin or anyone thought. It was about her feelings for him. "What is it you want to say?" Donnie asked Tommy ignoring Pumpkin's tantrum.

"I want you to know that there's nothing going on between me and my ex. That until you came along, I had no idea how alone I was. And that I love you very much." Tommy said.

"I don't know. You hurt me Tommy."

"Yeah…I know." he replied meekly. His posture told he was aching too.

"Not once, but twice!"

"Donnie, baby I didn't mean to. Hurting you is the last thing I would ever want to do." He said. Donnie glanced over at her sistas for advice. Solange's face said, 'go on honey give him a chance,' while Pumpkin's said, 'girl don't be crazy, he'll only hurt you again.' But she knew ultimately, she would have to make this decision on her own. "Coming from your brother, I can give you a hundred reasons why you shouldn't take the guy standing on the terrace across from you back. Coming from the guy standing on the terrace across from you…Donnie, please take me back." Tommy pleaded and he looked like he would collapse and die if she turned him down.

Admittedly, Tommy was saying all the right things, and the music was a nice touch, like something straight out of a Daniele Steel novel. But it was not enough for her to take him back. Not this time. Tommy was fine, but not that fine! This time she needed more.

Donnie folded her arms across her chest. "Okay Tommy, I'll take you back, if you can answer me one simple question. Why me? Why all of this?" she asked using big gestures to describe his grand performance.

Tommy handed Onetta the microphone and walked over to the railing. He looked deeply into Donnie's eyes praying his nervousness did not show. He only had one shot to convince her to give him another chance. But he was unsure how. Then he asked himself, what would his father say or do to his mother to win her back? And that's when he stopped overthinking and spoke from the heart. "That old adage is true. We don't know what we've got until we lose it. But you know something else? It's also true that we don't know what we've been missing, until it arrives." Donnie blushed and Solange muttered, *'Damn Money is good!* "You want to know why I'm doing all of this stuff baby? It's because when I look at you, I see the other half of me. And I need my half back, so I can feel whole again."

Donnie pondered it over then after a moment smiled. "I'm gonna hold you to that." she said.

Tommy was so happy he wanted to hold Donnie in his arms, and he did not want to wait until he left Onetta's apartment to do it. "Stay right there. I'm coming over." Tommy said then climbed off Onetta's terrace. All the women were both amazed and daunted by Tommy as he bravely scooted along the narrow four-foot railing connecting Onetta and Donnie's terraces disregarding the twelve-story drop. When he made it safely to the other side he threw his leg over the railing of Donnie's terrace. All her friends where envious because they couldn't get their men to leave the toilet seat down much less go to such great lengths to prove his love to them.

"You better mean what you say," Donnie warned in a trembling voice staring deeply into Tommy's eyes.

"Scout's honor" Tommy promised and wrapped his arms around her and lifted her off her feet moving in for a kiss.

"Woo-hoo! Hey An Officer and a Gentleman just remember, if she don't want you, you can always bring your fine ass back over here. I got egg rolls." Onetta said jokingly, breaking the silence and pausing the lover's lips inches apart.

Donnie shook her head and wrapped her arms around Tommy's neck then responded to her neighbor's offer by passionately kissing her man. Pumpkin looked like she wanted to say something when Mecca put her hand on her shoulder, "Just let it go. She's in love. And you know what? So is he."

Pumpkin rolled her eyes and sucked her teeth. She hated to admit it but Donnie was right, Tommy Strong was not like other men. He was a man's man.

# Chapter 28

Donnie's homegirls left so that the lovebirds could be get reacquainted. Pumpkin needed more convincing about Tommy's feelings and felt he needed to do more than put on some cheesy lip-sync daredevil show to prove his love. But there was nothing anyone could do. Donnie was in love.

As the couple sat on the couch wrapped up tight, Tommy brought her up to speed on what happened after she left. She felt an insurmountable amount of guilt but Tommy assured her she had nothing to apologize about.

"I have an idea, why don't you go get Tee-Tee and you stay here with me until your folks return? And then why don't you stay here, indefinitely?"

Tommy turned to her stunned, he was not expecting that. "I don't know Donnie. Whoever this is, they mean business. I don't want to risk bringing my problems to your doorstep." Tommy said and kissed the back of her hand. Part of him couldn't help wondering if the fact that his sister was at his ex-wife's place had anything to do with the offer. But he would just have to wonder because he was not about to go there.

"Your problem, is our problem. Besides nobody knows where I live." Donnie said.

Tommy looked at his beautiful woman thinking maybe his mother was right, maybe it was time to stop living like a kid and settle down. He considered her offer and it made sense. "Okay. Let's do it. I'll go over to Nicky's and get my sister and bring her back here." he said praying that he was making the right decision. "Are you sure because it's going to be awfully crowded in here with the three of us and a dog."

"Just go get her and we'll figure it out when you get back. But what about my other offer?"

"Guess we have a lot to figure out when I get back." He said wrapping his arms around her.

"Be careful." Donnie said and kissed him.

"It's the only way I know how to be." Tommy said confidently with a wink and left.

As Tommy rode the elevator down to the lobby he was in such good spirits about Donnie and him patching things up that he felt compelled to sing along with the cheesy Milli Vanilli elevator music. When he reached the lobby, there was a soft ping as the elevator doors slid open to reveal a chest almost as wide as the width of the elevator doors. He looked up and gulped audibly when he found himself standing before a feral-faced seven-foot something nightmare.

Every inch of the brute's face was covered with scarification patterns and tribal tattoos. Around his neck was a charm necklace made out of animal's teeth. He had long thick black dreadlocks with sandy blonde tips, huge bulging muscles with fists like bowling balls and eyes that looked like glinting black pools of evil.

"Jesus Christ!" Tommy jumped back startled.

"No-but I am flattered by da' compliment!" the Man-beast replied.

Not the type of man who wasted time yammering away with tough talk, Tommy threw his hands up like liquor on an empty stomach and began swinging on his adversary who looked as though he leaped off of the pages of National Geographic magazine. Bobbing and weaving every blow as if he were psychic, the Man-beast evaded Tommy's punches and knocked him back into the elevator where he crashed into the wall. Showcasing a gleaming set of gold encrusted dagger sharp canine teeth, the Man-beast stepped inside the elevator shaking it with his weight. He grabbed Tommy by his collar then sent him spinning with an open smack that rocked his head on his shoulders. Tommy whirled back around and cold-cocked the Man-beast in the jaw making his knees buckle.

"You big ugly Predator looking motherfucker! So what you wanna do? Cause there ain't nothing but space and opportunity between us!" Tommy shouted with clenched fists in the cramped quarters. The Man-beast wiped the trickle of blood from his mouth then charged into Tommy headfirst.

Tussling in the elevator was like being in a steel cage match with a rabid wolverine. A brutal uppercut to the chin sent Tommy slamming back against the wall where he sunk to the ground with a dizzying moan. His body shook the elevator walls so severe that it loosened a fire extinguisher hanging overhead that dropped into his lap. Dazed, Tommy was snatched to his feet as the dread locked gargantuan drew back a sharp knuckled fist but before he could land another blow the door slid open. An old woman dressed in a pink fuzzy robe with matching slippers stood there holding a fat tabby cat, shocked-face.

"You may wanna catch the next elevator," The Man-beast suggested. The old woman nodded weakly looking like she was about to faint.

The door closed and the Man-beast went back to Tommy. "Now, where were we?" He asked and was promptly answered as Tommy brought the fire extinguisher down hard against his head with a loud bone crunching smack. He then followed up with a shot that snapped the Man-beast's head back like a Pez dispenser and he stumbled out into the lobby dazed as the door opened.

Tommy was exhausted but saw his enemy was on the ropes and charged at his attacker then taking to the air he planted both feet hard in his chest sending him crashing through lobby's plate glass window. The sound of crunching glass under his boots could be heard as Tommy walked over and stood defiantly over his foe.

"Not so tough now are you, asshole?" He asked sucking wind. Then he felt a tap on the shoulder. He spun around and was hit with a powerful blow that sent him slamming to the ground chin-first. Tommy's vision swam as he looked up and was startled by the alarming presence of the person who sucker-punched him. Dressed in a dark hooded leather outfit reminiscent of Clive Barker's Hell raiser, was a lanky figure whose face was hidden beneath a white porcelain mask. "What the hell's your problem Doll face?" Tommy asked as he clambered to his feet more dazed from his attacker's blow than he thought. He wondered who this weirdo was, then looked over his shoulder and his eyes widened. Parked outside was the same black Mercedes Benz that had almost succeeded in running him down earlier that evening. "Son of a bitch!" he said no longer concerned with Doll face's identity. He swung then yelled out in pain shaking his aching hand after punching what felt like solid granite. A pair of eyes cold, dark and calculating with no emotion behind them stared at him through the mask's eyeholes and Tommy was sent flying like a rag doll with a backhanded smack.

Tommy realized he was up against something far more complicated than he could handle and got up and went for his Glocks but before he could get a shot off they were knocked from his hands and he was lifted into the air kicking and wiggling in the Man-beast's viselike grip.

Doll face watched Tommy struggling for air then realized what his cohort was attempting.

"Just what do you think you're doing?" Doll face demanded.

"Fuck's it look like? I'm breaking this sorry bastard's neck!" The Man-beast replied struggling to keep Havoc at bay.

"Don't you dare! I've worked far too hard to let him get off so easily. He must suffer…The way I have! The way we all have! Besides, when the time's right, I want to be the one to kill him! Now release him," the masked figure ordered.

The Man-beast played deaf and tightened his grip around Tommy's throat that is until he felt the cold piece of steel pressed against his right temple.

"Don't," Doll face warned.

The Man-beast grunted like a hibernating bear then as much as it pained him only squeezed tight enough to put Tommy to sleep then dropped him to the floor and stormed out. Doll face kneeled beside Tommy and stared at his limp body. "I swear before this is over you'll be wishing I would've let Nature snap your sorry neck!" Afterwards Doll face and the Man-beast exited the lobby.

# Chapter 29

*'Hey! Where's the Beef?'*

As soon as Tommy's eyes opened he felt pain all over his body. Although his vision was blurry he could make out the Wendy's commercial playing on the television across the room. He was lying down on someone's couch. But whose? He shut his eyes and tried to recall what happened to him. The last thing he remembered was leaving Donnie's crib and heading home then suddenly he was attacked by an old enemy. They fought, he was getting the best of him and that's when the lunatic wearing the freaky doll facemask and weird clothes jumped him from behind. It was also around that time he recognized the identical black Mercedes Benz that tried to run him down parked out front. He put two and two together and came up with drama!

He hit Doll face in the chest and it was hard like a rock. Whoever was beneath that mask wasn't human! It hurt to swallow and he remembered hands, big hands come up from behind. Choking him, killing him-and everything went black! Tommy opened his eyes and a pair of big hands came at him! To finish him! He freaked. Not again! No way was he going out like that! He grabbed a hand and twisted it with every intention of tearing the arm out of the monster's socket!

"Ow! Donnie get yo man offa' me! This crazy fool's gonna break my arm!" Onetta screamed dropping the cold compress she was using to keep the swelling on Tommy's face down.

"Tommy! What's wrong with you? Stop it!" Donnie shouted pulling Tommy back as he had Onetta down on one knee with her arm twisted behind her back. Left no choice she slapped Tommy hard across the face and he snapped out of the trance. When realized what he was doing he immediately calmed down.

"Oh geeez! Onetta I am so sorry. I thought you-were somebody else." Tommy apologized.

Donnie went back to Tommy. "How are you feeling baby?" she asked with intense sincerity, lightly touching his face.

Tommy shook his head grimacing a painful response and lay back down feeling safe in familiar surroundings. "Not sure."

"Here. Onetta brought you some painkillers." Donnie said handing him some pills and a glass water.

"It's the good stuff from the hospital. Not over the counter." Onetta said.

Tommy nodded 'thanks' and washed down the jock style doses of pain medication with some water. He looked up at Donnie, her eyes were red and her cheeks were stained with tears. He rubbed her hand to assure her he was all right. "How did I wind up here?"

"My neighbor Misses Goldsmith called me and said that she saw two men fighting in the elevator. I immediately thought of you and ran out. Onetta saw me in the hall and rode down with me." Donnie explained. Tommy nodded recalling the old woman in fuzzy slippers holding the cat.

"That's when we found you in the lobby all jacked up." Onetta said then twisted to Donnie with a huge plastic cup. "Hey gurl you got any more red Kool-Aid? My throat's a bit parched after carrying yo man up here."

"No sorry. But-Onetta, thanks for your help. I can take it from here, okay?" Donnie said giving her the hint it was time to exit stage right.

"Um okay but if you need me for anything remember I am right across the hall."

"I'll keep that in mind." Donnie said practically pushing her out the door.

"So did big Mama really carry me up here by herself?" Tommy asked.

"Over her shoulder, caveman style." Donnie nodded. Tommy shook his head at the image then began patting himself down. When he didn't find what he was looking for he jumped up and started looking everywhere at once. "They're in the drawer." she said.

Tommy reached over and opened the drawer to the small end table and took out his Glocks.

"I grabbed them before Onetta noticed."

366

Tommy nodded 'thanks' then got up and went over to the hanging mirror in a daze. He did not recognize the man staring back at him and reached out a hand towards his reflection and sighed as their fingers met. His neck had purple bruises and one side of his face was red and swollen. He poked his tongue around and flinched tasting his blood then went back over to the couch and plopped down with a defeated look.

"You want to tell me what happened?" Donnie asked as she began massaging his shoulders.

"I stepped off the elevator and an old buddy of mines is in your lobby waiting on me."

"A buddy did this to you?"

"Figure of speech. Anyway, we danced a few rounds and I get the drop on him. That's when this other jerk-off wearing a freaky mask sucker punches me from behind."

"Hold up. You mean you fought two men? Downstairs in my lobby? After you left-here?" she asked in disbelief.

"Please. I've dealt with as many as six heads at once." Tommy said like it was nothing. "But are you ready for the shocker?" Donnie nodded like she was unsure she wanted to hear any more. "This guy, with the mask wasn't like anybody I've ever faced before. It was like-I dunno, like fighting a brick wall or punching the ground. I don't care how much iron you pump or steroids you take, muscles just don't get that hard!"

Donnie glanced at Tommy oddly. "I'm not saying I doubt you, but baby do you know what you're saying?"

Tommy nodded slowly staring at the floor. "That I'm basically up shit's creek without a paddle." Feeling the need to comfort him, Donnie wrapped her arms around her man and rocked him slowly. He suddenly sprang forward. "Oh no!"

"What-what is it?"

"They know you're my girl. And where you live. It's not safe for you here. Is there somewhere you could go? Pumpkin's? A relative's?"

Donnie screwed up her face. "You think I'd leave your side baby? You know me better than that."

"Sweetheart I'm really touched that you got my back and all but we're talking about some major life and death shit here!"

"You just said that whoever is after you knows where I live. So wherever I went who's to say that I might not be followed? I'd never bring that kind of drama to friends and families."

"Like I've done to you," Tommy said angry with himself. "Fuck!"

"I didn't mean it like that. Look I knew what I was getting involved in by dating you. But when it comes down to it I wouldn't leave you because like I told you before, your beef, is our beef."

"Sorry, but you must be this big to ride this problem." Havoc said holding up his hand to demonstrate the height of the situation.

Donnie folded her arms across her chest like she wasn't trying to hear it. "Tommy look at me!" she demanded. Tommy looked wearily into his woman's eyes. She had the face of an Angel and the heart of a warrior. "Do you love me?"

"Of course I do baby but-"

"No ifs ands or buts. Do-you-love-me?"

"You know I do." Tommy said and planted a kiss on her lips.

"And if the situation was reversed and someone was trying to harm me, would you be there for me?"

"In a heartbeat!"

"Then there's nothing left to discuss. So what's the plan?"

Tommy sighed, "First my place. I need to check on a hunch. I might have an idea who's behind all of this. Then pick up my sister and go somewhere safe."

Donnie tossed on a jacket. "Then let's go!"

Tommy exhaled. He really had no choice since he could not leave her there by herself and she refused to go to a friend's house. He stuffed his guns in their holsters, looked up at the ceiling for strength and shook his head then followed Donnie out thinking perhaps there was something to the square life. At least it was safer!

# Chapter 30

Mayhem was excited to see her master and Donnie walk through the front door. Tommy gave her a pat on the head then proceeded over to where two double-decker aluminum file cabinets stood. He unlocked the drawers and inside were files on every trouble consulting job he had ever taken since day one. Each file was color coded and arranged in perfect military order.

"I keep records on all my clients with their pictures and those I consult attached in case I ever have to revisit them or the case, I'm prepared."

Donnie looked over his shoulder and frowned. "Written files? Babe, this is the 80s. You really need to invest in a Commodore 64 home computer and store all of that information on a floppy disk."

As he flipped through the files he paused to look over the countless pictures of men and women who hired him as well as the intimidating-looking thugs he was hired to consult. He glanced up and noticed that both his phone's answering machines were blinking and sped past the greeting on his personal line first.

BEEP! *'Hi, this is your momma. Your father and I arrived here in New Orleans and checked into our room, at the hotel. I was hoping you were home so you could talk some sense into your father. During the entire flight he insisted he saw some young men back in New York following us through the airport.'*

*'I'm not crazy Carla. I know what I saw. Them boys was following us! Right up till we boarded. Then they disappeared."*

*'You hear your paranoid father? Anyway, we're about to go have dinner. You two have fun. I love you.'*

BEEP! *'Hello, this message is for Tommy Strong. Mister Strong this is Andrew Carmichael, the detox counselor over at Brooklyn Hospital. I am calling about your cousin Alonzo. We allowed him to leave on Friday January eighth for a relative's party with the understanding that he would return the following morning but we have not heard from him since. If you know where he is please inform him that this kind of behavior will not be tolerated and if he does not contact me soon he will lose his bed to someone who wants to be helped, thank you.'*

Tommy sucked his teeth and shrugged.

BEEP! *'Tommy this is Nicky! What in the hell were you thinking dropping Tee-Tee over here without checking with me? What could have been so important? At first I thought you abandoned Tee-Tee for a job but I quickly nixed that theory since you are quitting for your new **girl-friend**!'* Donnie snapped her head at the answering machine. *'Look you call me as soon as you get this message!'*

"I-think I'll wait until she's calmed down." Tommy said.

"Good idea." Donnie agreed.

BEEP! *'My goodness you guys are still out? You must be having fun. This is your mom again. Well your father finally calmed down and we are about to have dinner then take a tour through the French Quarter. You have the number. We are going to go out and get some Cajun food. Your dad is trying to get me to eat alligator and crawfish. Maybe I'll try the crawfish because they look like tiny lobsters, but I don't know about the alligator-Oh hold on, your father wants to say something.'*

*'Hey son, hey baby girl and if you're there hey to you too Donnie.'* Donnie glanced up from the kitchen table blushing. *'Son I see you are still not home and I just wanted to remind you about what we discussed. Your mother and I are about to go and we'll talk to you-huh, what's that?...Okay. Tommy your mother says not to have your sister out too late. Okay son, call us when you get in. Talk to you later.'*

"What did your father want to remind you about?" Donnie asked.

"Not to take on any consulting gigs while Tee-Tee is visiting." Tommy answered. He stopped flipping and pulled out two files, opened one and studied it with great interest.

"What?" Donnie asked.

"Remember the story I told you about the guy I was chasing who fell through a skylight?"

"The one who proposed to his girlfriend then got busted by his mistress and started harassing her when she left him?"

Tommy nodded. "After meeting Doll Face that job came back to me. Read this and you'll see the connection between the two."

Donnie took the file. Stapled to it were three pictures, one of an attractive blonde woman labeled 'Lisa Greenstein' leaning against a chain link fence in jeans and a midriff top smiling. The second picture was of a tall handsome Caucasian man with stoic features labeled 'Nathan Owens' and the third was of Lisa and a chubby smiling black man in a romantic embrace labeled, 'Tide Carter' all three looked no older than thirty. Donnie brushed over Lisa's information skimming past the info about her living in Clinton Hills and being an art curator for a gallery in Soho and found the date she first contacted Tommy. "December third, nineteen eighty- five." She looked at him for a link between this and a guy who celebrates Halloween in January.

"Keep reading and peep the date." Tommy instructed.

"Tide Carter is no longer a threat to clients Lisa Greenstein and her fiancé, Nathan Owens. Assignment carried out on...January tenth, nineteen eighty-six." She looked up at Tommy wide-eyed. "Today's the tenth!"

"Precisely. I'm thinking that Tide's looking for a little payback on the anniversary of his accident with me." Tommy said and picked up the phone.

"Who are you calling?"

"Lisa Greenstein. I know it's a long shot but I'm hoping she'll be able to provide me with some answers."

"Such as?"

"Well for starters back when I paid her a visit at her gallery she had all these fancy masks hanging on the walls. I'm thinking Tide might have a scar or three from the fall and she might be missing a mask or two." Tommy said. Donnie looked at the picture of Tide and Lisa skeptically. "What?"

"I don't know. I mean looking at this tubby unassuming guy, I find it hard to believe he could take you on even if he made a complete transformation. It's also highly unlikely that she kept tabs on him after all this time."

"That's why it's called a long shot-" Tommy hung up. "I hit a brick wall. The number's disconnected. But I got another idea."

"Now who are you calling?" Donnie asked.

"That night everything went down I called an ambulance and I distinctly remember that it came from Brookdale Hospital. I have a connect there who works in the records department. Maybe he can give me some info on this guy...Hello...Yeah hi-lemme' speak to Drake Baltimore in records please.... Drake what's crack-a-lacking?... That's right, the one and only...Taking it one day at a time...Mayhem's fine, yeah listen I need a favor. I need any info you can give me on a guy that was admitted there on January tenth, a couple years back named Tide Carter...Yeah that's right Tide, like the laundry detergent...What?...He dropped through a skylight and got diced up pretty bad...It's not important how. The less you know the better off you are. So can you help me?" Tommy asked then smiled. "...My man fifty-grand. I knew I could count on you...Ok, I'll be here waiting...Yeah, the number's the same. Aight, peace." After Tommy hung up he turned to Donnie. "Drake's gonna check it out and get right back at me." he said then stared off into space blankly.

"Hey-are you Okay?"

Tommy exhaled and shook his head. "Too much is coming at me at once. I need a drink, you want one?"

"No thanks. So what's in the other file you've got?" she asked pointing at the folder in Tommy's hand.

Tommy looked at the folder and huffed. "Ever heard of a bunch of ruthless sons of bitches who call themselves the Decepticons?" Donnie nodded recalling the notorious gang who stole their name from the bad guys on the Transformers cartoon, and their violent antics that got mentions on the front page of the Daily News. "Well they kicked this guy out for being too rough." he said handing her a folder then went over to the kitchenette and poured out some Johnnie Walker Black into a glass.

Donnie frowned at the snapshot of the man with biceps bigger than most human torsos and lots of piercings and tribal tattoos. He kind of resembled a lion with his matted bright blonde dreads, thick ridge of bone that jutted out above his eyes, wide nose, prognathous jaw and protrusive lips.

"That's what you fought in my building?" Donnie grimaced in disbelief and began flipping through his file. She could not believe the information on the paper and read it aloud. "Ras Grazmatch a.k.a. Nature, Height about seven-foot one, Weight around three-hundred and fifty pounds, Age unknown but presumably early to mid-forties, Nationality African. Enormously big and powerful with dynamite agility and speed, a master at murder and known for his lethal hand-to-hand combat skills, sheer cunning, savagery and animalistic ruthlessness. He is also very knowledgeable of various types of instruments of death and practically every handgun imaginable. He's a force of Nature and was branded as such." She paused and looked up at Tommy skeptically.

"Look all I know for certain is that Nature came here to the U.S. four years ago to bring back the wife of a powerful modern day monarch who heads the left wing regime of the Ethiopian People's Republic. Evidentially she fled the country because she saw her husband involved in something she should not have that could have toppled their government. When she contacted me, she was hiding out with relatives in Flatbush. The poor woman was more terrified of Nature than of whatever it was she saw that forced her to run in the first place. Not that I blame her, he's one spooky son of a bitch. Supposedly he wears the bones of his enemies as souvenirs around his neck and has even drank their blood." Donnie raised an eyebrow at Tommy with twitched lips. "Yeah, even I'm not buying that one. But still I protected her, and even helped her relocate to a place where he'd never find her. But because he never completed his mission he can't return home a failure and blames me for being stuck here. To make a living he hires himself out to loan sharks, drug dealers and other scum."

"Kinda' the opposite of you." Donnie said

"I suppose." Tommy paused, reflecting, "We only fought once but it didn't last long. The cops showed up on the scene and he took off. But it in brief moments it was like fighting a machine that doesn't have an off switch. I've fought a lot of hardcore dudes in my time, but I'd have to say that out of everyone I've ever fought, Nature's been my toughest fight to date."

A chill ran down Tommy's spine at the thought of having to do battle with him again. He shrugged then picked up the phone then began dialing. "-Hello, yeah-let me speak to Andrew Carmichael please…Hello Andrew it's me Tommy Strong, Alonzo's cousin…Yeah Bug-Out. Listen I got your call and I doubt if my cousin will be coming back...yeah, I'm sorry too. But the truth of the matter is, after receiving the news that he's got AIDS he just didn't feel the need to-huh? AIDS.... What do you mean who told him? You did...WHAT?" Tommy shouted and made both Donnie and Mayhem jump. "...Yeah this comes as a surprise to me too...I have no idea why...Right-right. Listen, if I see him I'll let him know but I wouldn't worry about it too much. There are others who are more deserving that can use that bed...Okay man thanks for all you've done...Yeah, I'm sorry too. Take care." Tommy hung up the phone and turned to his girlfriend stressed. "There are some days where my life seems absolutely unlikely. So unlikely that when I live that day in question, I have to pinch myself to realize that it is true."

"What are you talking about?"

"Bug-Out doesn't have AIDS. He fucking lied!"

"What? But why would he lie about something like that?"

"I don't know but I'm about to find out now! That's if he actually got his phone turned back on." Tommy said angrily and dialed Bug-Out up. To his shock it rang and as soon as his cousin answered the phone Tommy proceeded to curse him out, calling him every name in the book. After a few weak lies Bug-Out admitted that he did not have AIDS and the reason he said he did was so that he could do his drugs in peace and be left alone. He said he appreciated everything his cousin had done for him but it was time to face the truth, he was and would always be an addict. Bug-Out apologized to Tommy from the bottom of his heart and said that he would tell his mother the truth and ask her to keep his son. Then with that said he hung up so he could continue getting high. Tommy sat there holding the phone in his hands. "Fuck!"

"Are you okay?" she asked.

Tommy shook his head no. "Bug-Out was the big brother I never had. True he may have been small in size but he was huge in heart. He wasn't scared of anybody and as kids, when shit went down, he always had my back and I had his."

Tommy's second line rang and he looked at Donnie then ran his hand from the top of his head to his chin in a frustrated sweep. With everything heavily weighing down on his shoulders, he did not need more density to his problems.

375

"Hello…" Suddenly Tommy's face contorted into a snarl. "Listen up you demented motherfucker if you think your puny threats scare me then you obviously don't-Whoa!…What did you just say to me?…" Tommy's jaw swung open when the contemptuous voice on the other end repeated what he was hoping-praying he didn't just hear. His mind reeled and he was overcome with a sickening feeling in his stomach that enveloped his entire body. He dropped the phone. "This can't be happening! It can't!"

"Tommy?" Donnie called to him.

Tommy opened his mouth to answer, but nothing came out. He dragged his feet over to the couch and collapsed. Donnie was panic-stricken. Her heart was beating so rapidly that it felt like it would jump out her chest. Tommy was the bravest man she had ever known and if the words he was told over the phone could instill such fear and trepidation on his face, then it must mean the end of the world. Tommy turned to Donnie slowly wide-eyed, still in shock.

"Who was that?" she asked apprehensively.

"Doll face."

"What did he want?"

"To tell me the flight number of the plane my parents were on. Even what they were wearing and how easy it would be to arrange an accident to befall them." Tommy said struggling to get the words out.

"Oh my God!" Donnie cupped her hand over her mouth.

"I need to think," He said massaging his temples with the tips of his fingers. "Tee-Tee! I need to go and get my sister. I need to get Nicky and stash them in a hotel." he spun at her. "You too! God I can't think straight. I don't know how long this sick fuck's been clocking me. A week, a month, a year, two years. I was so sure that I had everything under control. How could I have been so stupid?" He shouted pounding his head with his fists. "My Pop's tried to tell me, Nicky-even you dropped hints about how everything I did would come full circle and bite me in the ass. But did I listen? And now everyone's involved." he paused and squeezed his eyes. He was prepared for whatever came his way but what about the people he loved? "If anything were to happen to-God I don't even want to think about it."

"Honey calm down." Donnie said stroking his back.

"How the hell am I supposed to calm down? This asshole just threatened my parents! I don't know what to do! It's too much!" Tommy fussed overwhelmed with stress as he collapsed on his bed.

Donnie folded her arms and stared at him shaking her head. "I never saw a Trouble Consultant feel sorry for himself before, mind if I watch?" She said. Tommy sat up glaring with glassy eyes. "Now you listen to me Tommy Strong, from the moment I met you, you have proven that you are at your best when things are at their worst. Have you forgotten all the fights, the shootings, the trials and tribulations that you overcame? Now you may not be invincible but, you are strong! And yes, it looks bad. But God is on your side. And so am I. And together we can handle this. Now get it together!" Tommy listened quietly. "Now, once again. Are you Okay?"

He nodded. For a minute he had forgotten who he was but Donnie didn't. "Yeah-I'm Okay." He smiled and caressed her face feeling damn lucky.

Tommy's business line rang and he scooped it up on the first ring. "Havoc...Yo Drake talk to me. What do you have on Carter...Uh-huh...a living autopsy huh?...Uh-huh ...Word?...Yeah I'm still here." he said after a few moments of silence. "So, how'd they die?...This is exactly why I said the less you know the better off you are. By the way, how's that little problem I took care of for you? Everything copacetic?...Good...Who me?...Naw, I'm retiring from all this insanity...Well believe it. Back when I started doing this psychos, criminals and derelicts had more consideration for their fellow man...I dunno, maybe I'll open up a nightclub." Tommy said and winked at Donnie causing her to smile in spite of the serious situation facing them. "Listen man I gotta' bounce. Thanks again, it's been an education."

Tommy hung up and exhaled then got up and went over to his closet in a daze and started pulling out clothes leaving Donnie hanging on the edge of her seat.

"Well, what'd he say?" Donnie asked zealously.

"Oh, I'm sorry babe. I'm just tripping off of what Drake told me."

"Which was?"

"He said that Carter was so messed up when he was admitted the staff in ER dubbed him the human Autopsy. After only two weeks he checked out of the hospital against doctor's orders. As Carter stormed out wrapped in bandages from head to toe, he shouted and carried on like a madman swearing to get even with Lisa, her fiancé and especially me for destroying his life. And that was the last anybody's ever heard from him.

"A year later Detectives visited the hospital asking a whole bunch of questions about Carter after Lisa disappeared without a trace. Because of the threats and frame of mind Carter was in when he checked out, they were operating on the presumption that Lisa was in danger and Carter was their primary focus. But he fell off the radar and they couldn't locate his whereabouts. Then Detectives found her body on the roof of an abandoned building.

"Even though the hospital staff was not much help the first time, Detectives repaid them a visit last year after the body of Nathan Owens, Lisa's fiancé and the man she left Carter for, washed ashore in Queens bloated and badly decomposed. Medical examiners determined the cause of death was multiple lacerations, from a jagged instrument. Just like Lisa." Tommy paused and turned to Donnie with a look of seriousness. "It's all starting to add up. First Carter checks himself out the hospital making threats against his girl, her fiancé and me. The following year she turns up dead, exactly one year later he's found dead, now I'm hassled by a weirdo in a mask."

"And if Carter was left disfigured from his accident to the point people were calling him a living Autopsy, of course he would want to cover his scars with a mask." Donnie said.

Tommy pointed at her as if to say, 'precisely'. "Follow the pattern. I'm last on his 'to-do' list." he said.

"Like the saying, death comes, in threes." Donnie whispered. "So then your gut feeling was right." she said worriedly.

Tommy blew frustratedly. "I don't know. I mean it all points to Carter but in my line of work you quickly learn that things are not always what they seem. The only thing my gut is right about is the guy I fought with was not a man. He was not human." he said rubbing his sore ribs.

Donnie felt a shiver shoot up her spine. "I feel like I'm in camp before an open fire listening to one of those scary camp stories."

"Yeah but the problem is, there ain't no campfire and we ain't in camp." Havoc came back over to the bed dressed in a red T-shirt, red bomber jacket, a pair of red cargo pants and matching Doc Martens.

He stood on top of the ottoman and slid back a hidden compartment in the ceiling and pulled down a large red duffel bag. He reached into the bag and removed a Dillinger then stared at the gun smiling. It was the very first piece he used to keep in his quarter field coat back when he was Mister Fix-It, running up on fools in the projects. It was a reliable weapon but not strong enough so he put it to the side and dug deeper past an assortment of other weapons. While searching for something with a stronger kick he discovered a red handled double barrel sawed-off shotgun that he slid into his hip holster. He looked down at Donnie and sighed, "It's about to get real ugly. Why don't you-"

"No! I told you before, I'm coming." She said stubbornly.

Havoc nodded hopping down and placed a red full leather body harness on his dog with specially made pouches on either side, courtesy of Dapper Dan. Then he shoved a gun into one pouch and an extra clip into the other.

"Can she shoot?" Donnie asked.

"We've suckered some cats into believing she can but no, it's only a backup piece. But we're working on it right girl?" he grinned scratching her head then rose to his feet and handed Donnie his four-fingered HAVOC ring. "Hold on to this for me."

"Anything smaller?" She said putting it on her dainty hand.

"It's not for you to wear. That ring has always brought me luck. And we can use some tonight. So, for the last time, you sure about this?" he asked pulling his red Kangol on.

"I'm sure." Donnie nodded placing his lucky charm in her jacket pocket.

"Aight, then let's bounce." Havoc said then paused in the doorway and prayed everything would be alright.

After they were gone, Havoc's business phone rang again and the answering machine picked up, "Yo Havoc! It's me Drake. Hello? Yo, I got a bit of the info mixed up. Evidentially it wasn't Tide they called the living Autopsy. It's-" Filled to the capacity of messages the machine ended.

# Chapter 31

The only space Havoc could find was under a street lamp around the corner from Nicky's. At this point it was pointless to sneak around and play the shadows. Whoever the mystery man with the steel hide was, he was probably out there somewhere watching him at that very moment. Havoc turned off his car and paused feeling very uneasy about all of this. Usually he was in control of the situation.

"Maybe I should wait here in the car." Donnie said suddenly.

"There's no way I'm letting you out of my sight! Nature and that masked freakazoid are probably out there, somewhere watching us as we speak." Havoc said.

"But I don't think your ex wants me in her home, much less you. You heard her on the phone."

Havoc twisted at her like she was insane. "You're kidding me right? We've got bigger issues to deal with than Nicky's beef with me. Girl if you don't come on!"

Nicky opened the door, folded her arms across her chest and stared at him with a denouncing look. "So I was right, you did send Tee-Tee here so you could work." She said sucking her teeth.

"And hello to you too." Havoc said.

"Don't be coy with me. Do you have any idea how utterly selfish what you did was?" Nicky argued.

"Can we talk about this inside?" Havoc asked calmly.

"Why what's the matter-embarrassed? Well you should be! Tell me, does your new girlfriend know what kind of man you are?"

"As a matter-a-fact, I do." Donnie said stepping into the light. Nicky's eyes stretched from astonishment then just as quickly narrowed to fine slits. "Nicky you've got it all wrong. It's not what you think." she was going to stay in the background and let her man handle it, but the more Nicky screamed on him without knowing the full story, the more difficult it became to stand there silently.

Nicky shot Donnie a catty look that telepathically said, *"Bitch what the hell are you doing in front of my house?"* then turned to Havoc with a look of disgust.

═══════════════════════════

"So that was you who called here then hung up? I thought it was Corbin playing games." Nicky said shaking her head but still felt no remorse about blaming him.

"Like I said I didn't have time to go into it. I called from a pay phone. Once I knew you were home I brought Tee-Tee over and when you answered I went to get Donnie." Havoc explained.

"Okay so let me make sure I got this right. For the past week or so you've noticed that a black Benz has been following you all over town." Nicky asked. Havoc nodded with a slight grimace. "Then tonight you narrowly escape getting run over by the same car outside of your place."

"That's right." Havoc said.

"Then while coming out of *her* building," Nicky cut her eyes in Donnie's direction, "Two people attack you. One you've fought before and the other you don't know because they're wearing a mask and have seemingly impenetrable skin like a rock. During the fight you spot the same car that almost hit you, but before you can react, you are knocked unconscious. Later on, you get a call from this Doll face person who threatens your parents and messes with your head and you have no idea who this person is or why any of this is happening?"

Havoc shook his head cluelessly. "No,"

"Hello, Mc Fly. You beat people up for a living. Made countless enemies. This masked person could be anybody!" Nicky collapsed on her couch with a defeated look. "I warned you that something like this would happen one day didn't I? That one day you'd get blood on your hands and it won't wash off in the sink!" Havoc rolled his eyes. Now was not the time for, 'I told you so's.' "Look I am sorry for all the crap going on in your life, really. But this is no longer my problem. It's hers." she said pointing at Donnie. "Now if you don't mind, its late and I have to finish grading papers, I have lesson plans to write and I have to prep for my meeting with the UFT and the

Superintendent later this week to discuss my ideas for the special education department."

"Nicky you don't get it. This guy's been watching me for a while. Watching all my moves. Where I live and where my people live."

"I don't know why you're acting like this is the first time something like this has happened! Or did you forget why we got divorced?" Nicky sharply reminded Havoc to which he replied with a frustrated sigh. She then turned to the woman sitting on the edge of her couch. "So, Donnie you've been very quiet. How do you feel about all of this?"

Donnie shrugged. "Well I'd be lying if I didn't admit it's a lot to swallow. But I knew what I was getting into when we first started dating." she said not sounding very convincing.

Nicky looked like she was two seconds from laughing. "Take it from someone who knows, after he starts coming home late and leaving early and the only trace of him being there is blood in the sink, you will get tired of all his bullshit." Nicky said rolling her eyes and turned back to Havoc dissatisfied with Donnie's aloof attitude about all of this. She thought Donnie was weak for being so understanding and wanted her to be as upset with her ex-husband as she was. "And as for you, do you realize what you're asking me? I'm supposed to just up and go into hiding like some kind'a fugitive."

"It's only for a few days. A week tops." Havoc reasoned.

"A week? Do you even know if this masked person is even after me?"

"No I don't." Havoc admitted.

"You don't know much do you?" Nicky sucked her teeth.

Havoc could not blame her for being upset. When she divorced him, she divorced all the headaches that went along with being the wife of a Trouble Consultant as well. She didn't deserve this drama. Nicky folded her arms over her chest and mumbled something to herself.

Havoc tossed his hands in the air in defeat. "Look I came to get my sister out of here and take her somewhere safe. I was hoping you'd understand and come too. You said she's asleep upstairs?" he asked. Nicky moodily nodded. "Fine, I'll be right-"

Mayhem suddenly fixed her eyes on the front door and let out an angry growl from deep within. Havoc was half-way up the stairs and turned back to see what had his dog so riled up. He traced her vision to the door.

"You expecting company?" Havoc asked Nicky in a low voice. She promptly shook her head. "Hush Mayhem!" Havoc commanded his dog. "You two get behind Mayhem!" he ordered Donnie and Nicky, then he crept over to the door.

Without making a sound Havoc listened and heard movement on the other side of the door. He unlocked the door then with the other hand he removed a gun and glanced back at the women. They were scared shitless. Uncertain of who or what was on the opposite side of the door he took a deep breath and snatched open the door then lunged his gun out.

"Don't shoot! Don't shoot!" Corbin begged holding his hands up in the air.

Havoc gritted his teeth and let his gun drop to his side. "Son-of-a-Man get your ass in here before I...!" he said yanking Corbin in the door by his jacket. Mayhem snarled taking Havoc's sudden move as her cue to attack.

"Get that beast away from me!" Corbin screamed and jumped into Havoc's arms.

"Mayhem chill!" Havoc commanded and his dog froze in place. "And you, get off of me!" Havoc said and mushed Corbin to the floor.

"Corbin! What were you doing lurking outside of my house?" Nicky complained.

"Don't flatter yourself, I'm not here to see you Nicolette." Corbin stood rubbing his behind from where he landed and turned to Havoc with a stern face. "I'm here to see, you."

"Look homeboy, I'ma give it to ya' straight, no chaser. Nicky and I are over! Understand?" Havoc said causing Corbin to nod and

Nicky to roll her eyes in her ex-husband's direction. "But that has nothing to do with you two splitting up. So stop sneaking around her home and stalking her because she doesn't like it."

"Nicolette has made it very clear what her true feelings for me are." Corbin said shooting Nicky a dirty look.

"Then why are you here?" Nicky asked in a jaded tone.

"To save your ex-husband's life."

"Whoa. My life?" Havoc asked noticing for the first time how bad Corbin looked. There was a raw purple bruise over his right eye. There was also some dried blood on his collar. He was about to ask what happened when Nicky's phone rang.

"It's your mother. And she sounds pretty upset." Nicky said covering the phone and holding it out to Havoc.

"Shit! I forgot to call her back. Does she sound mad?"

Nicky shook her head like he was a goner. "Put it like this, she didn't even say hello. All she said was, 'Is my son there?' and when I said yes she was like, 'Put him on the phone now!'"

Havoc clenched his teeth and sucked wind like he was already stinging from the verbal spanking he was going to get, then took the receiver. "I must have really been one evil son-of-a-bitch in a past life to deserve all this in one night." He said as Nicky muttered something under her breath to the effect of agreeing with him. The Trouble Consultant exhaled then spoke. "Hey Mommy-O, how's New Orleans? Did Pop get you to try alligator yet?" He immediately rolled his eyes at the ceiling for strength. "...Yeah I got your message...I know but...Okay...but if you'll just let me explain...but...but-but...Christ Ma why are you illin? We went to rent a movie and then for pizza and lost track of time. What's the big deal?...Huh?-What am I doing here at Nicky's? Um see what had happened was, Nicky called after you and Pop left and said Tee-Tee left one of her gifts behind after the party so I stopped by to get it...Huh?-Where's Tee-Tee? She's, at my place-with Donnie...Oh well they must've went to the store, that's why nobody answered my phone. Yes, I trust her to watch after Tee-Tee." he looked at Donnie and shrugged his shoulders. "Look Ma I'm sorry if you were worried but maybe if you didn't treat her like a baby-" He held the phone away from his ear and everyone in the room could hear his mother's loud angry voice coming out the other end. Even Corbin pitied him. After several more minutes of squirming uncomfortably he hung up.

"Well, that went well." Havoc said sarcastically then turned to Corbin. "Corn-dog we're sorta' in the middle of a little major catastrophe. So if you have something you want to say then say it."

Corbin shook his head like he was disgusted. "From the moment we've met you've done nothing but insult me, purposely mispronounce my name, ridicule me and accuse me of being a sellout. So, you can imagine my surprise and utter disbelief when I discovered that in fact you've been the sell out all along. Havoc, the infamous hit man of Brooklyn who beats up his own people for a living."

"What are you talking about? I'm nobody's hit man!"

"Oh really?" Corbin smiled. "I know all about your little-or should I say major catastrophe. The black Mercedes following you. Long forgotten enemies attacking you. And let's not forget the masked orchestrator with a horror movie fetish." Havoc's lips parted incredulously. "Your mystery stalker paid me a visit." Havoc stood there dumbfounded. "I thought that would change your attitude. So, still claiming that you're a simple blue-collar worker?" Corbin asked flashing his trademark pompous grin. "I thought not."

Havoc inhaled then exhaled deeply. "For the record, I'm not a hit-man, I'm a Trouble Consultant."

"Oh, and there's a difference?" Corbin smirked.

"Breaking down Trouble Consulting to a clown like you, would be like talking astrophysics to a wino. Now tell me what you know!"

"Now is that any way to ask?" Corbin said derisively.

"No," Havoc roughly shoved Corbin down on the couch and got up in his face. "This is!"

"You know what? I think coming here was a huge mistake." Corbin said rising up and was immediately forced back down by Havoc. "Excuse me!"

"Look Corbin I ain't kissing your pompous ass but keep fucking with me and I will put my size thirteen up in it!" Havoc warned.

Corbin looked around the room and shuddered. If looks could kill Nicky would be charged with manslaughter and Donnie looked like she was two minutes off his ass as well. What he wouldn't give to just have one of those beautiful women that concerned for his own welfare. How he envied Havoc. "So, you can pronounce my name." Havoc gave no reaction. "Fine. That night after your sister's party Nicolette and I decided it would be best for both of us to part ways amicably-"

"HA!" Nicky blurted melodramatically.

Corbin shot her a venomous look and continued. "On the way home, I stopped by the office to take care of some pending matters. While seated at my desk the door suddenly creaked open and a dreadful sounding voice spoke to me from the darkness. That was my first meeting with our masked friend."

"I just call him Doll face." Havoc corrected.

"Doll face? Oh, I get it-the porcelain mask. How witty." Corbin said. "Now I don't know the history between you two because details of the matter were not discussed. But whatever happened must have been horrendous because that warped individual is fueled by a bottomless hatred for you and would like nothing better than to see you die a horrible, painful most despicable death!" Havoc glared at Corbin and he dropped his smirk, "Doll face's words. Not mines."

A noise came from upstairs. "Nicky check on my sister for me." Havoc asked.

"Alright but keep in mind, I still have to get up early tomorrow." Nicky said and headed upstairs. As far as she was concerned every one of her unwelcomed guests except for Tee-Tee could get the hell out!

"So, you were saying." Havoc said to Corbin.

"I was saying how this Doll face character offered me a lot of money if I would help him execute some maniacal plan devised for you."

"Plan, what plan?" Donnie asked before Havoc could.

"I have no idea. I guess he's waiting for me to accept before I am filled in." Havoc leaned forward awaiting his answer. "Which I of course turned down! Why do you think I'm here? To beg **her** for another chance?" Corbin asked pointing his chin in Nicky's direction. Havoc pursed his lips like he wasn't buying that. "Okay-I'll admit you're not my most favorite person in the world, but I couldn't live with myself if any harm befell you and it was my fault. What's odd is how he knew so much about you. Even me for that matter. It was his whole basis for even approaching me. He was trying to convince me that it was all your fault that Nicolette and I were having problems." He said and stared at Havoc like he believed it was.

"So you said that was your first encounter with Doll face, when was your next?" he asked.

"About an hour ago. This Black Mercedes pulls up alongside me and the window comes partially down. I couldn't see inside on account of the tinted windows but I could tell it was him right away because of that God-awful voice of his, so he asks me a second time to help him get even with you and again I refused. That's when two of his enforcers jumped out. They dragged me from my car and started beating me severely then left me there and warned me to rethink their offer. Afterwards I got myself together I hurried over here."

Havoc stared at Corbin long and hard trying to look through him and spot the truth. He had an awful hard time believing that this man would suffer a vicious beating to protect him regardless of what he said or how bad of shape he was in physically. How he saw it things just do not happen in a black and white situation. There are always shades of gray.

"Tragic. So, where'd you park at?"

"Huh? A block away? Why?"

"No reason. Why didn't you warn me after your first meeting?" Havoc asked doing his best not to sound accusing.

"Honestly? When Nicolette broke up with me I was devastated. This Doll face character showed up at the right time. I was intoxicated and he whispered poison into my ear like an evil conscience sitting on my shoulder, how everything was all your fault and if you were out of the picture she and I could get back together. He was offering me the perfect opportunity to get even. It sounded good. But in the end, I just couldn't go through with it. I guess my moral compass pointed to good."

Havoc stood and came over to Corbin. He sighed before extending his hand. "Thanks Corbin. I guess, I owe you one."

"You're welcome." Corbin replied with a smile hearing his name pronounced correctly. With respect.

Havoc suddenly jerked his head at Corbin and his grip tightened. "Why'd you park a block away?"

"Ow! -Huh? Why'd I what?" Corbin said snatching his hand back from Havoc and shaking the feeling back into it.

"You said you were parked a block away."

"Yeah so."

"So if I was trying to deliver life or death news I wouldn't take the time to find a parking space a block away then walk the distance to deliver said news. I'd pull up out front."

"This is preposterous!"

"Ok then take me to your car."

"Why on earth would you want to see my car?" Corbin asked. Even Donnie was wondering why Havoc was playing twenty questions after Corbin obviously put his life on the line for him.

"Because I want to see the car that you drove here!"

"You're being paranoid. But under the circumstances it's understandable. I'll admit were the roles were reversed-"

"You'd be dead! Now walk me through this Kumquat. You claim Doll face's men beat you after you refused to join them, right?" Corbin nodded. "So I guess that would explain why you have those bruises?"

"Obviously."

"Because obviously, you'd be such a valuable asset to this Legion of Doom Doll face is organizing and they can't pull it off without you."

"I don't know. Maybe they saw me as the brains of their operation. Maybe they were worried I'd come back and warn you. Which let's not forget, I did."

"Which brings me to my next question. Don't you find that just a little strange these criminals let you in on their plans then allow you to think it over? Allowed you to live? Cause I sure as hell do. You know what else I find strange Corby? You claimed to have danced a few rounds with a couple of these guys and walked away. And let's be honest, we both know you can't dance!" Havoc said nonchalantly then suddenly grabbed Corbin by the collar and ripped his shirt open. A purple horizontal welt stretched across his shoulder and chest. Havoc's eyes went dark and Mayhem sprang to her feet. "You son of a bitch! You were the one who tried to mow me down outside my place! That's where those bruises came from! You're not here to warn me about Doll face! You're working for him!" Havoc accused lifting Corbin with one hand. "Mayhem chill! Donnie hold her!" he ordered as his dog tried to get at Corbin.

"You damned ingrate! I was beat within an inch of my life protecting you!" he protested struggling in Havoc's grasp.

Nicky came running down stairs. "What the hell is going on down here?"

"Your boy Corbin's full of shit! He's not here to warn me. He's here to set me up!" Havoc blasted tossing Corbin to the floor.

"What?"

"Nicolette don't listen to him, he's crazy!" Corbin said standing.

"Am I? The car that almost hit me crashed into a garbage dumpster and it's no coincidence that you have the exact same mark across your chest that a victim of car accident would have that was saved by a seatbelt! I've been in several car crashes so I know! And then there's the bruise that looks like you got hit with a pipe. The pipe I stabbed through the windshield!" Havoc said. Corbin turned to Nicky panic stricken shaking his head no. "Go on Nicky ask him where his

390

precious Porsche is. If it's parked a block close by like he said then I will climb the highest mountain and apologize for doubting him, but if you ask me he's hiding it because I'm right."

"Corbin is it true?" Nicky asked.

"The claim that I would even stoop to such levels is pathetic in its ignorance, and…" Corbin paused tired of the charade then flashed a lecherous smile. "In life you do the things you can live with and try and avoid the things you cannot. Like disregarding that mask wearing sociopath's strict policy about not trying to kill your ex-husband with the souped-up bulletproof car he so graciously provided me with."

"Son of a bitch! I knew it!" Havoc advanced.

Corbin frantically dug into his jacket pocket and clumsily came out with a handgun. "Stay the hell back!" he shouted waving the handgun all over the room like Barney Fife. Havoc hit the brakes and held up his hands. Mayhem struggled to get at Corbin. "Let that mutt go and so help me I'll shoot it!"

"What the hell's wrong with you Corbin have you lost your damn mind?" Nicky shouted.

"Oh I did, the day I met you and was stricken with a severe case of selective amnesia, causing me to forfeit my personal philosophy which has always served me well in the past. Trust no one! It's your only defense against being betrayed. But I've since regained my sanity and then some!" Corbin said then turned back to the Trouble Consultant. "Now Havoc-I can call you Havoc right?" he asked. Havoc clenched his teeth glaring at him. "Please remove your guns and put them on the floor. Slowly! And don't try any funny stuff." Corbin threatened with a shaky gun.

"What the hell do you want from me?" Havoc demanded.

"Oh, lots of things, my woman back, your head on a platter. But let's start with an easy one. Since our first encounter you have never given me an ounce of respect."

"You never earned it." Havoc said.

"Fine. Then I'll take your guns!" Corbin glared.

"You're gonna have to!" Havoc said.

Corbin shot Havoc a, 'Dirty Harry' glare then turned his gun upon Mayhem and the Trouble Consultant huffed as he removed his weapons. "Now place them on the floor. And kick them over here," Corbin instructed. Havoc obeyed with furious eyes. "Good boy." he said catching them under his foot.

"Now I see why your last name's Ramses, you're a real scumbag!" Havoc snapped.

"Sticks and stones my friend. Sticks and stones." Corbin replied unscathed.

"Corbin do you honestly believe that doing this will get me to take you back?" Nicky asked.

"Take you back? Surely you jest! Every time I think about your vaudevillian performance pretending to care for me while secretly pining over him I become incensed all over again! No, my dear, I figure if I hand Ram-Bro here over to his nightmare nemesis and apologize for my malevolence, I can undo the mess I've created for myself and walk away from all of this and you for good." Corbin said then faced Havoc.

"You honestly think by bringing me to them you'll be spared? Think again. You betrayed them. Go back and you're as good as dead. But you can still walk away from this if you let me go and-" Havoc reasoned.

"No deal! If trust is a two-way street right now you're lying in a ditch at the side of the road! Now come along. We have a party to attend."

"No!" Donnie said worriedly.

"It'll be alright." Havoc promised with a hopeful grin then dropped his smile when he turned to Corbin. "So, you ready to go?"

"I must say you're taking this quite well. Perhaps if you behaved civilly like this when we first met then we wouldn't be going through all of this right now." Corbin said.

Havoc eyed his dog, communicating with her in secret sign language behind his back. Mayhem immediately calmed down and arched her back as Donnie looked at the dog and wondered just what in the hell was going on. "Perhaps-or perhaps not!" Havoc said with an arched eyebrow then turned to his dog and they locked eyes communicating on levels far more comprehensive and subtler than speech. "HAMMER TIME!" Mayhem let out a sharp knowing bark then just like they practiced so many times before, she twisted her head and grabbed the butt of the gun out of her harness and flung it at Havoc. In one perfectly choreographed slick move he snatched it out of the air spun around and shoved it in Corbin's face. The two stood there pointing their weapons at each other in a Mexican standoff neither one showing any sign of backing down. "Drop the piece." Havoc said, an old hand at poker-faced machismo. Corbin wildly shook his head no.

"Corbin, don't be an idiot! Put your gun down!" Nicky shouted.

"Why should I drop mines? See Nicolette this is exactly the kind of disloyalty which has led us to the moment at hand."

It was a tense moment by all in the room especially for Nicky who prayed it would not end with a dead body on her living room floor.

"I gotta be honest with you Cream corn, by sticking that Roscoe in my mug you're only leaving me with two options, kill or be killed. And if I have to choose between you and me, guess who I'm betting on?" Havoc asked straight-up.

Corbin stared down the barrel of the high-powered pistol, wide-eyed and trembling with fear. What in the hell was he doing? He wasn't built for this. He killed competition behind a desk not a gun. After giving it careful thought, he handed Havoc his peashooter.

"Good boy." Havoc said accepting the gun. Then in a flash he dropped Corbin like a bottle of milk on the floor then stood over him defiantly. "You said you wanted to know the difference between a Trouble Consultant and a hit man? Well the fact you're still breathing is your goddamn answer because a hit man would have smoked yo bitch ass!"

# Chapter 32

"Go on, get out of my sight!" Havoc snarled at Corbin outside Nicky's house as Donnie, Nicky, Mayhem and a clueless Tee-Tee looked on.

"Just like that, I'm free to go?" Corbin asked surprised.

"That's what I said ain't it?" Havoc said aggravated.

"Gosh!"

"That's all you can say is gosh? And here I thought playing Scrabble expanded your vocabulary,"

Corbin shook his head perplexed. "Were the roles reversed I would not have reacted the same way."

"Tell me something I don't know."

"Just when I think I have you figured out you go and do the opposite."

"Well what can I say? I'm trying to be the kind of person my dog thinks I am." Havoc shrugged.

"Well whatever your reasons, I am embarrassingly grateful."

Tee-Tee covered a yawn then tapped her brother on the shoulder. "I'm still sleepy. Can I go sit in your car?"

Havoc handed his keys to Donnie. "It's right around the corner. I'll be there in a sec."

Corbin met Havoc's exhausted stare and felt a sense of admiration for the man multi-tasking things that would have him in a fetal position. "You once said to me to be careful of the toes you step on today, because they might be connected to the ass you have to kiss tomorrow," he shook his head embarrassed with himself. "Fate, it would seem, is not without a sense of irony."

Havoc rolled his eyes like, *'Now I know this sorry ass bastard ain't expecting sympathy from me.'* "Well as much as I'd like to stand here and kick it with you on some Kumbaya shit I have to be going."

"Wait. There's something you need to know. About the one you refer to as Doll face." Corbin said.

Havoc's face scrunched up into a 'whateva' look as the tinted window of a dark Camaro parked a few feet away slowly lowered.

"Now why in the hell should I believe anything you have to say?" The Trouble Consulted asked.

"Under the circumstances, you shouldn't. But I feel I owe you the truth. He isn't who you think he is."

"What the hell's that supposed to mean?" Havoc asked.

Corbin nervously darted his vision around. "The reason Doll face hates you is because-"

**BLAM! BLAM! BLAM! BLAM! BLAM! BLAM!**

Bullets pumped into Corbin's body zapping him like volts of lightning keeping him on his feet as he danced with soul for the first time in his life.

"Get down!" Havoc shouted tackling a screaming Corbin behind a parked car.

The car that the bullets came from sprang to life and wildly pulled out into the street. Havoc looked sympathetically down at Corbin's lifeless body then scrambled to his feet. He had to get to the women but the car the shots came from sat there patiently waiting for him to step into the light.

Stealing a peek at the killer car Havoc armed his shotgun, pushed his ruby red shades back on the bridge of his nose then rose to his feet. It was on, like Donkey Kong!

"What's up MOTHER FUCKER?!!" The Trouble Consultant shouted and began blasting at the car.

**BOOM! BOOM! BOOM!**

The Lights of neighboring houses came on and curtains pulled back slightly. It sounded like World War III was going down in the middle of Canarsie as Havoc's weapon ripped gaping holes in the car's exterior. Arms holding guns reached out the car and returned fire but couldn't get a decent bead on the man in red ducking behind cars. Havoc's heart pounded like waves against the seashore as he ducked behind a mailbox. He counted to three jumped up and flattened the front tire then boldly ran out into the street and fired another blast into the on-coming car's hood. Sparks and smoke erupted out of the engine as the driver lost control and swerved past him plowing into a parked car. Instantly flames engulfed the car then in a flash it exploded.

After the worst was over Havoc walked up to the flaming wreck cautiously. He looked inside grimacingly at the grotesquely twisted charred shapes trying to figure out who they were. Then it hit him as his eyes widened. He darted around the corner and spotted Corbin's wrecked loaner up the block then snatched open his car door and was met with screams from Nicky and Donnie. He looked in the backseat relieved to find his sister fast asleep and Mayhem protectively on guard. He hopped behind the wheel.

"Time to go!" Havoc announced.

"Are you ok? We heard gunfire" Donnie asked frantically.

"Yeah I'm fine but…" He looked sadly at Nicky and she instantly knew.

"Take me to him." Nicky insisted. Havoc sighed and nodded.

Nicky stared at Corbin's lifeless body and began to cry consumed with guilt and paralyzed with emotions. "Who did it?" she asked.

Pretty sure it was the same group of punks me and Tee-Tee had it out with earlier at Pizza Hut."

"Pretty sure?"

"I'm sure." He said positively after spotting the misspelled tattoo on Fuego's crispy forearm. "Bastards must've tailed me back here looking for payback. Their kind always does."

"Their kind?" She hissed sarcastically.

Havoc flinched at the remark. "Nicky come on, there's nothing we can do for him anymore. Besides the police'll be here any minute." He said as the approaching sirens blared in the background.

"Fine then we'll explain what happened. You wanted to walk away from this right? This is your out."

"And while I'm at the precinct wasting time explaining everything from the beginning, the ones responsible are getting away in the end."

"You've helped cops in the past. Can't they help now?"

"Perhaps. But I started this. And I have to finish it. Myself!"

"And there it is!" Nicky pointed out.

"We really don't have time for this."

"Then go. But I'm staying!"

"What do you mean you're staying?"

"You still don't you get it do you? This is why we got divorced! I am no longer a part of this. If this is what you want fine but count me out…Besides you don't need me." Nicky was speaking to Havoc but indirectly to Donnie seated in the car fidgeting uncomfortably.

"You sure?" he asked making one last attempt.

Nicky looked up from Corbin into her ex-husband's eyes. "I am."

Havoc recognized that look inhaled and blew frustrated. It was the same look she gave him when he begged her to reconsider divorcing him. He couldn't sway her then and he couldn't do it now. With a heavy heart he got behind the wheel. Keyed the ignition and slipped the gearshift into first. The engine roared to life belching fumes through the dual exhaust then screeched off into the night.

After they were gone Nicky sat there as the bright lights came closer. She stood and she dried her eyes and prepared for the worst when she realized it wasn't the police!

# Chapter 33

Tee-Tee sat up yawning and tapped her brother's shoulder as he drove, breaking his concentration. He turned to her expressionless.

"What happened to Nicky?" she innocently asked.

"She decided not to come."

"Aww. How com-"

A loud horn blared in the background. Havoc twisted his head to the right and observed a large truck execute a daring backward curve, tires screaming as it accelerated, cutting across two lanes, heading straight for them. Mayhem lifted her head and growled.

"What the hell!" Havoc said locked on the 4x4's headlights arcing at his car, as if taking aim. Suddenly it sped forward showing no signs of slowing down. His eyes bulged. "OH SHIT! Tee-Tee sit back! Donnie, brace yourself! Mayhem, down on the floor now!" Havoc spit out orders as he planted his forearm into Donnie's chest pinning her back into her seat, popped his car into reverse and stomped on the gas pedal making the rear wheels grind into the street.

"Oh-my-God!" Donnie screamed as they swerved wide. There was a frozen instant of silence as the hulking mass of metal descended on them. They almost avoided being hit altogether but weren't quick enough and took some front-end damage as the truck clipped them then struck a lamp post jumping a curb and smashed into a brick wall.

Code Red spun out of control stopping in the middle of the street. Havoc checked on his passengers, everyone was shaken but thankfully appeared unscathed. He peeked past the hood and swore at the ugly twisted fender. Stroking the dashboard gently he pleaded, "Hold it together for me baby." Suddenly the dark was cut in half and Havoc squinted under the bright hi-beams of a fleet of cars. The black tinted out Mercedes Benz he had become well acquainted with led the convoy. That offer his father made to run his own club was sounding real good right about now.

Havoc sat quietly transfixed on the cars. His left hand was tight on the steering wheel, knuckles turned toward him the right was wrapped around the gearshift. He glanced in the rear-view mirror at his wide-eyed sister and winked then yanked the gearshift into third.

Mayhem sighed as if to say, 'Here we go, again' then laid down on the floor and placed her paws over her eyes.

Donnie's eyes bulged and she swallowed hard. "Um, you're not going to do, what I think you're going to do...are you?" she asked leaning forward.

Havoc shrugged in the face of disaster. He looked so cool and laid-back Donnie wondered if he was on tranquilizers. He turned to her with a saucy grin, "Shit's about to get real hectic!" he said then Donnie put her hand on his knee. He put his foot on the gas. They almost got whiplash, they took off so fast!

Donnie was so frightened she couldn't utter a sound. Havoc clenched his teeth as he flew directly at the line of cars. When the drivers realized he wasn't backing down they swerved onto the sidewalk as Havoc flew past them and disappeared into the night. His insane actions prompted all the cars to make skidding U-turns and chase after them.

Reaching speeds of up to 110 miles per hour, Havoc ignored the traffic laws that protect pedestrians as he led a hi-speed chase through the streets of downtown Brooklyn. Donnie's stomach churned with fear. They were going so fast it felt like they were hovering a few feet off the road, and she could feel the vibration of the car as it pushed the very limits of factory installed standards.

"You ok back there Tee-Tee?" Havoc asked darting his eyes into the rearview mirror at his sister.

"Uh-uh," She shook her head nervously. "You're going too fast! Slow down please."

He glanced into the sideview mirror and knew he couldn't do that. "You like Knight Rider?" he asked. She nodded her head timidly. "Me too. Let's pretend we're Knight Rider." He said doing his best to distract her. Unfortunately, he knew that wouldn't work on Donnie who looked absolutely terrified.

"Where are we going?" Donnie asked fighting back the nausea.

"Somewhere we can lay low." Havoc replied hugging the corner like a slow dance on a Saturday night. "But first, I've gotta lose my fans!" Havoc said racing through a stop sign. Weaving in and out of traffic, he made a U-turn and switched lanes as the cars behind him made the same maneuver. From seemingly out of nowhere a police cruiser joined in the chase with cherries flashing.

'PULL OVER NOW!' the cruiser demanded.

"Oh great, just what I need. More agrafuckingvation!" he growled as sirens echoed behind him. He twisted to Donnie with a look of panic. "Too much is happening at once! I-I can't focus!" he said swerving in and out of danger and almost lost control of the car. Unsure of what to do or how to help, Donnie leaned forward and fiddled with the buttons on the car's tape deck. Suddenly the rollercoaster ride was made a touch more surreal by the pulsing beat of Kurtis Blow's 'White Lines' on the stereo at full blast and Havoc turned to her and nodded approvingly. He squeezed his eyes shut and exhaled blowing out the negative energy and tension. His eyes popped open and he calmly blocked out everything and let his situational-awareness take control.

Driving like a devil behind the wheel, Havoc floored it through a red light and in an attempt to lose his pursuers made a hard right into a side street. Dodging dumpsters, he exited the narrow street with the cop car gaining, when from out of nowhere a dark van swerved into the police cruiser and caused it to flip over, bumping off cars like a pinball machine. The van swerved up on Havoc's right side and its door slid open to reveal Johnny Hop's pets Dun-Deal and Musk armed with machine guns.

"Everybody down!" Havoc shouted as rapid gunfire ate away his car's rear exterior. Tee-Tee screamed and Donnie hit the deck as her heart pounded at a rate only matched by the car's RPMs. Havoc's palms were sweaty and his face twisted into a contemptuous sneer as he yanked the steering wheel and made a sudden turn under an overpass.

Trying to keep up, the van misjudged the angle and slammed through a row of newspaper boxes sending unsold papers flying and lost Musk as he tumbled out into the street and was grinded into road kill. Determined to even the score with the Trouble Consultant, Done-Deal leaned out of the van and continued blasting away. Havoc sneered swerving away then lowered his window and stuck his shotgun out. While darting his eyes between the road and the van, he aimed his weapon low then fired tearing out a chunk of the van's front wheel.

Sparks flew as the driver lost control then flipped over, crumbling into a ball of twisted metal and bursting into flames.

Glancing in the sideview mirror, a smile of satisfaction formed in the corner of Havoc's mouth which quickly vanished as an uzi toting motorcyclist swerved on the scene spitting hot lead. The side mirror was blown off causing Havoc to drop his weapon in the street. "Dammit!" Havoc hissed then mashed the gas pedal all the way to the floor thrusting ahead. Not letting them escape that easily, the cyclist caught up and swooped in on Havoc's side like a Tron bike. His dark helmet twisted at him then the cyclist raised the visor. Havoc immediately recognized Johnny Hop's cloudy white eye staring back at him as he raised his gun. The Trouble Consultant winked then calmly pointed straight ahead. Johnny Hop turned to see what in the hell he was pointing at then held up his arms screaming before ramming hard into the rear of a double-parked car. "Asshole!" Havoc smiled watching the destruction in his dust.

"Watch where you're driving!" Donnie shouted pointing wildly.

Havoc turned to see a big orange sign coming up fast that said, 'CONSTRUCTION WORK AHEAD' and his pulse accelerated. "Oh crap!" he shouted as he maneuvered his car through the barricades, pieces of wood, debris and flying plastic orange cones that bounced off the hood and windshield. When he reached the end of the trajectory he hit a flatbed and jumped a five-foot fence then charged right into the street and did a screeching 360. After the crippling landing, he threw the gearshift into fifth and stomped on the gas pedal leaving all the other cars eating dust like he made the jump to lightspeed.

# Chapter 34

As Havoc sped through the barren streets Donnie played Bonnie to his Clyde, keeping an eye out for danger, down for her man. Smitty once told his son that you can judge a man's power by the actions of his woman, and right now Havoc felt like one of the most powerful men alive.

Suddenly a funny sound erupted from underneath the hood along with a hiss and a cloud of thick smoke. The music died and the engine followed.

"No-no-no! Don't do this to me baby! Please, not now!" Havoc begged as his crash-damaged engine overheated and seized up coming to a slow halt and stranding them in the middle of a shapeless grotesque neighborhood filled with crumbling tenements and 24/7 bodegas.

"What's going on, why are we stopping here?" Donnie asked darting her eyes everywhere at what appeared to be the bleakest part of Brooklyn.

"This can't be." Havoc said shaking his head dumbfounded at the dashboard.

"What's wrong?"

"Not sure, but for one we're losing gas. Practically on 'E'. But that's impossible. I keep a full tank in her at all times. Just what the hell is going on?" Havoc asked opening his door then immediately got his answer when he stepped into a noxious puddle trailing from underneath his car and out into the street. "Shit! The fuel tank is ruptured."

"But how?" Donnie asked.

Havoc shrugged. "I'm no mechanic, but she's an old car that's taken a lot of abuse. Bullets, a tractor trailer slamming into us. Jumping that flatbed and crash landing so hard. Could be any of those things or all of them. But it doesn't matter. What does is that we're-" he paused when something shinny flickered in the rearview mirror and he spotted a multitude of car's headlights approaching in the not so far distance. "Everybody out, NOW!" he shouted tearing off his sister's seatbelt.

Everyone scrambled out into the street that was so narrow two cars could barely travel down it side by side. The hum of car engines sounding like hundreds of angry hornets grew dangerously close and Havoc spun at Donnie.

"Take Tee-Tee and keep heading up the block. I'll catch up in a sec." he said trying his best to keep his wits.

"But what're you going to do?" Donnie asked worriedly.

"...Say goodbye, to an old friend." Havoc said sadly. She had no idea what that meant but trusted he would take care of things and left with Tee-Tee flanked by Mayhem. After they were gone he pulled out a Newport and placed it between his teeth.

Speeding like a crazed banshee, the black Mercedes Benz led a procession of cars racing wildly towards Havoc. Disregarding them he calmly sparked up and blew a thick white billow of smoke through his nostrils. He gently stroked his car's mangled hood reminiscing about how many times Code Red saved his ass in a lot of daring situations.

When Donnie, Tee-Tee and Mayhem reached the end of the block Donnie looked back and gasped. "Why the hell is he just standing there?" she asked aloud. "What are you doing? Come on!" she shouted frantically but Havoc ignored her. Even Mayhem barked concerned.

"Well baby, looks like we've come to the end of the road." The Trouble Consultant said choked up like he was breaking up with a lover. Then with a heavy heart he dropped his cigarette onto the ground and it quickly ignited the puddle of gas. Unable to watch, Havoc turned his back and jogged away as Code Red became engulfed in flames.

The procession was closing in fast, seemingly hell-bent on mowing Havoc down when suddenly a thunderous ground-shaking explosion occurred. Havoc was knocked off his feet and the black Benz hit the brakes. Cars crashed into each other creating a chain reaction of accidents and rear end collisions as Code Red created a flaming roadblock. The timing was so perfect it almost seemed as if Havoc's beloved automobile saved his ass one last time.

Havoc reached Donnie and Tee-Tee then looked over his shoulder as the black Benz and remaining cars circled back and disappeared around the corner. "Dammit!" he said. Any minute they would be coming up the opposite block. With his car up in flames, he had no way of transporting them to safety. Tee-Tee asked her brother a question and he stifled her trying to think then noticed for the first time, the dull smell of salt water off the Atlantic shore. He studied his surroundings and recognized where he was at, and what he was near.

Havoc checked the clips in both guns. "Come on!" he said grabbing his sister's arm and running. "I know a place where we can go!"

Coney Island, the eighth wonder of the world. Brooklyn's playground by the sea was so dark it looked as if someone had forgotten to pay the Con Ed bill. Rides such as the world-famous roller coaster the Cyclone and the bright and blinking 'Wonder Wheel' which in the summer could be seen for miles around were on hiatus until the end of spring turning the usually active park into an abandoned ghost town.

Havoc sat crouched behind a dumpster keeping an eye out for the cars that were after him. After leading the way through a series of back alleys and vacant lots, he, his sister, his girlfriend and dog found themselves before the desolate amusement park. Tee-Tee amused herself by doing cartwheels and handstands in the background.

"Ooh big brother 'member how sometimes you me and Nicky used to come here in the summer and ride the Himalaya on Friday nights? It'd be so many people outside dancing and playing music." Tee-Tee asked her brother.

"Yes I remember honey, now please chill with the cartwheels." Havoc said. All that hyper energy was making him nervous.

"Are we going on rides? I wanna go on the Himalaya." Tee-Tee asked enthusiastically.

"Shhh! Lower your voice Tee-Tee. Christ, where'd you learn how to whisper in a helicopter?" her brother asked.

"But I wanna go on the Himalaya." she whined.

"Not now Tee-Tee. Now shush." Havoc said darting his eyes everywhere.

"So, what's the plan fearless leader?" Donnie asked red-eyed and low on energy.

"I figure we can hang out here for a few hours till dusk."

"Then what?"

"Then hopefully the cars after us will pass and we'll go from there."

"Go where? We don't have a car."

"I dunno, I'll get us a car. If not there's a train station nearby."

Donnie looked at him worried. "You don't know?"

"What is this Donnie, twenty questions? What the hell is your problem?" Havoc growled.

"What's **my** problem? Hello-people have been killed in front of me. Cars have been chasing us all over Brooklyn trying to run us off the road. Bullets are flying over my head, I'd say there were quite a few problems!"

Tee-Tee yanked on her big brother's arm to get his attention. "I said I wanna go on the Himalaya!"

Havoc looked up at the sky for strength. "Tee-Tee, honey-baby-light of my life, I told you, we can't go on the rides, the park's closed. Now chill-out Okay?" he pleaded with her. Tee-Tee crossed her arms and pouted. Between his sister plucking his nerves and Donnie getting on them, he was running out of patience. He glanced over at his lady. She looked upset and worried and scared. He sighed and squeezed her arm. "Sorry." he said.

"No, I'm sorry. You have enough to deal with without me adding to everything that's going on. It's just that I'm tired and scared and it's making me a little cranky." Donnie said and leaned against the wall.

"I understand," Havoc said and softly touched her face. "Baby I won't let anything happen to you. I'll protect you from harm. I'll protect all of you." He said assuredly bringing a sad smile to her face.

"I know." Donnie said and leaned in for a brief kiss. She suddenly paused inches from his lips and looked around worriedly. "Where's Tee-Tee?"

"What do you mean-she's right-" Havoc paused and frantically darted his eyes everywhere. "What the hell! But she was just-" Mayhem was sitting on the ground waging her tail but his sister was nowhere to be seen. He stood and scanned the area then slumped to the ground. "Shit!"

Donnie was practically walking on the back of Havoc's heels as they inched down a narrow path between two brick buildings with only the dim moonlight to guide them.

"C'mon girl find Tee-Tee." Havoc begged his dog as she sniffed the ground picking up what he hoped was his sister's scent. They rounded a corner and Havoc's eyes widened to the size of golf balls when they came upon a man standing beside his car taking a leak.

"Oh shit-Reef Hustle!" Havoc whispered quickly pushing Donnie back into the shadows before they could be spotted.

"Who's he?" Donnie asked.

"Gangster. Drug dealer. Murderer. Somebody you don't want on your ass. But what's he doing out here?"

"I don't know. But let's not stick around to find out." Donnie advised.

Havoc agreed and they made an about-face. Reef Hustle was shaking his Jimmy dry when he spun around then squinted at what looked like people sneaking off into the night.

"Son of a-Hey-Freeze! Mothafucka I said freeze!" Reef Hustle shouted and whipped out a gun and began firing in their direction.

Havoc spun around with veins full of adrenaline, Glocks in both hands, arms crossed left over right and let loose painting Reef red with powerful bullets that hurled him back onto the hood of his car.

As Reef moaned in a puddle of his blood. A dark-colored Cadillac screeched up on the scene and Havoc watched as more angry familiar faces jumped out. One man in particular shouted obscenities and rushed at Havoc. Havoc ducked under a swing and miss then knocked out his attacker.

"Mayhem go find Tee-Tee!" Havoc commanded to which his dog replied with an indulgent bark and galloped off into the night. Havoc grabbed Donnie's wrist, "C'mon!" he said and took off in the opposite direction. They rounded a corner and hit a dead-end. "Oh Damn!" At the opposite end more cars pulled into the alley. Havoc stood protectively in front of Donnie and raised his guns prepared to go all out.

"No-no! Look that way!" Donnie shouted pointing at a nearby fence and Havoc boosted Donnie over it then cleared it with one jump. On the other side they found themselves in a narrow alley. At the end of the court was a frighteningly detailed mural of a psychotic clown smiling with fiery orange hair, yellow demonic eyes and jagged teeth that took up the entire brick wall. Between its scary grin was a door. Havoc yanked his head right then left. There was another extending alley and cars were getting closer.

No time to think!

Havoc ran for the door between the clown's teeth. It was locked so he blasted the locks to pieces then kicked the clown's teeth open and immediately began firing at the approaching cars behind him.

"Inside now!" he ordered his woman as bullets whistled past his head. Once Donnie was safely inside he ran inside too.

As Havoc and Donnie quickly moved down a seemingly endless twisted long dark corridor they kept bumping into walls. After a minute of walking blind, Donnie walked into yet another glossy wall.

"Ow!" Donnie said.

"You Okay?" Havoc asked.

"Yeah I'm Okay. But what's the deal with the walls popping out of nowhere? I feel claustrophobic, like I'm inside of one of those lab rat mazes."

"I know what you mean."

Donnie could hear Havoc pat himself down in the dark then suck his teeth and swear. "What're you doing?"

"Trying to get my lighter to work. We need to see where we're going,"

"Let me try. Just keep talking so I can hear where you are."

"I'm right here."

"Is that you?"

"Well if it ain't you're in a handful of trouble." Havoc said removing Donnie's hand from his crotch and placing his lighter inside of it.

Donnie shook the lighter, held it upside down, shook it some more then flicked it. A spark lit and she tried it again. This time a flame came on.

"Never send a man to do a woman's jo-Oh God!" Donnie screamed when she found herself having a close encounter of the worst kind with what looked like an alien. The screaming creature that was just as startled by Donnie's appearance had huge saucer eyes a long neck and huge head. But what was even freakier was aside from its deformities, the alien and Donnie looked identical and could pass for twins.

Havoc scooped up the lighter Donnie dropped and was startled by his own bald extraterrestrial twin except his was fat with a tiny head and mimicked his every move. As soon as he saw his twin also owned a lighter exactly like his, Havoc realized this was no coincidence.

"Donnie-baby calm down. It's one of them funhouse shape-shifting mirrors see?" Havoc said contorting his reflection in the mirror.

"Where the hell are we?" Donnie asked clinging on to Havoc for dear life.

Havoc waved around the lighter and although it was hard to see he could make out they were inside a maze of infinite mirrors. "The world's biggest science project."

# Chapter 35

It looked like something out of the movie The Warriors. As various crews of rough hoodlums, hard rocks and three-time jail bidders climbed out of their rides exchanging pounds and "Wa'sup my nigga's?"

Nature stepped out of his vehicle with a Mac-10 strapped to his chest and a necklace made of animal teeth and bones around his neck. "So dat's where he's hiding?" he asked staring at the creeping dark that slowly spilled out of the hole between the clown's teeth then turned to the group of men. "Anybody saw what happened to the dog?"

"Yeah-me and my boys chased it." A stout tracksuit wearing kid from Bensonhurst with his hair pulled back into a ponytail named Joey T. said in between puffs on a Marlboro. The Italian had a score to settle with Havoc after he humiliated him and his crew when the Trouble Consultant was hired to stop them from shaking down small businesses for protection money in their neighborhood.

"And?"

"We almost ran it down, but the friggin' mutt hopped a fence and hi-tailed it outta' here."

Nature grinded his molars in frustration thinking they'd definitely encounter the hell hound again. "Okay listen up everyone. How I see it, if Havoc can bust his way in on this side. I'm more than certain he can bust his way out on the other side, making our job much harder than it has to be."

"Then we need to go up in there and get dat son-of-a-bitch before he does just that!" Lights-Out suggested eager to get some payback for the face full of ugly burn scars Havoc gave him. Not to mention the 'HAVOC' shaped scar.

"Simmer down Fire Marshall Bill. We **read** you loud and clear!" Diamond Ken said causing others to laugh, "Now by a show of hands who else thinks it's a stupid idea to go running inside Bozo's mouth? Huh? Anybody?" no one raised their hands. "C'mon guys think! Havoc's probably waiting for us in there with a loaded cannon ready to blow us to bits as soon as we set foot inside." Diamond Ken whined.

Nature frowned. "You big scary ass punk! He's one man. We are many!"

A slim man with shady features and a top lip wide as a push broom went over to his car and popped the trunk then tossed the pimp a flashlight. "Ay y'all, don't even trip. I've got plenty of flashlights for everybody."

Diamond Ken peered over his shoulder. Inside of the trunk was everything needed to pull off the perfect caper, rope, masking tape, shiny weapons and plenty of flashlights. "Damn what the hell are you doing with all that shit in your trunk?"

"I don't ask you about your shady dealings. Don't ask me about mines." Shady said.

"Enough chatter, let's get ready." Nature said.

"What about him?" Diamond Ken asked motioning towards Reef Hustle who was leaned up against a car bleeding profusely from his wounds.

Nature looked at Reef unemotionally, "He falls under the category of, not my fucking problem!"

"Number one fuck you! Number two don't worry about my mother's son!" Reef snarled, barely able to stand as his thoughts raced faster than his mouth could catch on. "I'm good" he groaned unconvincingly.

"Dang yo, maybe we should take him to Brookdale Hospital. Money-grip's all messed up." The pimp said to Nature out the corner of his mouth.

"He's already dead. His brain just don't know it yet!" Nature said turning on his heels.

"Ay nigga I said I'm fine! Now stop sweatin me!" Reef Hustle barked.

Nature turned and faced Reef, "Look my friend, and I call you my friend only because we have similar interests, namely offing Havoc and getting paid in the process. You have to face reality. Havoc has ripped you a new asshole. We can't take you in there with us. You'll slow us down. Now I understand that you are upset but-"

"Upset? Screw you Magilla! I got just as much right to go up in there and put two in that bald bastard's dome as you do! What, you think you're special cause Havoc's got your monkey ass stuck here civilized in America instead'a back in the jungle swinging from vines and shit?" Reef dissed unmercifully.

The men traded uncertain looks as Nature looked at Reef Hustle for a moment like a fierce creature whose emotion can explode unpredictably at any minute. Suddenly Nature grabbed hold of Reef's hair put the barrel of his Mac-10 to his temple and sprayed the hood of the car with his brains. Then in an even bolder move Nature helped himself to the cable around the dead man's neck and the fat wad of ducats in his black leather goose. Everyone watched in disbelief. For all their knowledge of hard knocks, pure homicidal mania and corruption there were still areas of evil where they were equal in virginity to the world's biggest Herbs.

Nature looked up under a sea of shocked stares and smiled flashing his pointy bicuspids. "Let his mistake be a lesson to you all. I'm like AIDS. Fuck wit me, and you die!"

The horn from the black Mercedes Benz honked and Nature bopped over. Behind the steering wheel sat Havoc's masked enemy he liked to refer to as Doll face. "Guess some men are born with a conscious." Doll face said.

Nature shrugged unconcerned then glanced at the back seat. "So what's dat one's problem?" he asked pointing to the passenger occupying the back seat.

"Never you mind. Let me worry about that. You just tell those imbeciles to get ready." After Nature was gone the masked man turned to face his silent passenger. "You've been awfully quiet. You ok?" he asked. There was no answer just light sobbing. "What the hell? I know you aren't crying over that sorry bastard! Especially after how he tossed you to the side. How I see it, out of all of us here you're the only one besides myself who has a legitimate reason to hate Havoc. Between you and me these other low-lives deserved what our mutual enemy did to them. So are you ready for some payback?" the passenger failed to respond and continued sobbing. "I don't know what I was even thinking bringing you along! But I have a sneaky suspicion that if you sit there for a while and think about exactly what he did to you, you'll change your mind." With that said Doll face exited the car and stormed over to where a group of hard-faced men stood.

Doll face's mask and creepy appearance was so intimidating that everyone stopped breathing until he passed by. "Man I thought I'd seen it all until this freaky mutha' came on the scene." One thug whispered to another.

"So, what's Spooky's deal anyway?"

"Man, all I know is that a month ago a black Benz was parked outside of Sing-Sing waiting on me the day I came off my bid with the promise of two things. Enough money that I could start my life over and revenge against the asshole responsible for ruining it!"

"I asked around and everybody's story is pretty much the same. Havoc messed them over and Trick O' Treat offered them money and payback. One thing's for certain, whoever or whatever the fuck our mutual benefactor is, their hate for Havoc must be stronger than all of ours combined to set all this shit up."

The punk nodded in agreement. "Well just make sure you don't try and go off on your own personal payback mission. I heard some fool tried to kill Havoc for self and it didn't turn out too well for him. The Mask had him turned into swiss cheese!"

"Damn!"

Doll Face's twisted voice addressed the crowd and interrupted their conversation. "Just so there are no misunderstandings, I kill Havoc! You can beat him. Bite him. Wound him whatever. But I and I alone get to put the final bullet in his bald head. Are we clear?" Everyone nodded intimidated as Nature walked up and cleared his throat for emphasis, "Good, because I've sacrificed and lost way too much putting this together and do not want or need any more surprises from someone who thinks their hate for Havoc supersedes mines. Play stupid games win stupid prizes!" The masked menace said referring to Corbin's rogue actions that got him killed. "Now that we all understand one another, smiles, everyone. Smiles. It's time for what we've all been waiting for. Let's go kill ourselves a Trouble Consultant!"

# Chapter 36

Havoc and Donnie continued feeling their way through the glass maze as best they could, using his lighter as a makeshift torch until they came upon a door at the bottom of a short ramp. Havoc unlocked it then with a breath of uncertainty opened the door. To his surprise they were back outside on the opposite side of the building in the cold air amongst other shut down rides and attractions. Angry voices and footsteps in the background made them jump outside and pull the door closed behind them. Donnie alerted Havoc to a port-o-potty and they ducked inside.

Havoc peeked out at the front of the colorful building. "Death row huh?" He read the name on the sign hanging over the attraction, "Fitting."

"How many of them do you think are in there?" Donnie asked worriedly.

"I'm not sure. More than ten, less than a hundred." Havoc shrugged indifferently. "Went to bed last night and all was right with the world. I get up this morning my enemies have joined forces and are gunning for me."

"What are we going to do?"

Havoc turned to Donnie. "We ain't doing nothing. But you're going to sit tight and be cool."

"And you?" Donnie's voice trembled.

Havoc smacked a full magazine into his Glock then turned to Donnie. "I'm gonna inside and do some subtraction!"

"But you're out gunned and outnumbered."

"Then I guess I'll have to outsmart them won't I?" Havoc said confidentially.

"What is it with you? Do you have a death wish or something? You can't go back in there! And what about your sister? Or have you forgotten about her?"

"Of course I haven't forgotten about my sister. But I've got to go back in there and stick it to em'!" Havoc snarled. Donnie looked at him trying to understand why in the hell would he walk back into a burning building if he were lucky enough to escape without getting scorched. "That place may be huge, but it's only but so huge. Eventually those clowns are going to realize that I'm no longer in there and come looking for us."

"There has to be another way."

"Look, I don't like it any more than you do baby. But my chances are a helluva lot better if I deal with them in there. Out here in the open. We're as good as dead." Havoc said and slapped another clip into his second Glock. "You ever shoot a gun before?"

"No never." Donnie said.

Havoc snorted derisively. "And you claim to be from the PJ's. Okay safety's off, the round's already in the chamber." he said using his thumb to drop the clip and show her it was full then smacked it back in. "Real simple. All you have to do is point the end with the hole at the bad guy and pull the trigger. But remember if you point it at someone-then make sure you shoot them."

"Is that all?" Donnie asked sarcastically.

Havoc shook his head, "What you wanna do is breathe out before you shoot because if you pull in air, it can cause the barrel to jump, and you miss the target." He said and handed her the weapon.

"Anything else?"

"Yes," Havoc said and bowed his head and closed his eyes. Donnie was taken aback. She didn't think her man was an atheist but at the same time she didn't picture him as the praying type either. She said nothing and bowed her head. As Havoc asked God to protect them against whatever danger lie ahead as well as watch over his sister and dog, Donnie stared at the overwhelming piece of steel in her tiny hands with a look of uncertainty. After he was done praying Havoc looked at Donnie. He realized this was a lot for her to deal with but at the same time he did not have time to hold her hand through this. "Donnie, no matter what you hear in there under no circumstances are you to come inside looking for me. Are we clear?" He asked. Donnie looked emotional. She was unable to answer and nodded. "Hang in there babe. It's almost over. And remember, I've kicked all their asses before."

"Individually-but not all at once." Donnie said with uneasiness and concern in her voice.

Havoc nodded at her valid point then smiled. "First time for everything." he said confidentially then leaned in for a kiss and headed back into Death row.

# Chapter 37

"One, Two Freddy's coming for you!" Lights-Out called out in the dark getting a laugh from the others.

"Quit prolonging the inevitable Havoc and bring your punk ass!" Nature yelled out shining his flashlight all over.

"Yeah court's in session chump! And we're your judge, jury and executioners!" Diamond Ken said and snap cocked an uzi.

Nature noticed a series of light switches on the far wall of the booth. "Hello, what have we here?" he said and hit a switch. Suddenly strobe lights flashed on and off.

"This should help flush out our little fish." Doll face said.

Nature stopped in his tracks and began inhaling deeply like a bloodhound. "It has already. Our fish is close."

"How close?" the masked man asked as people in the huddle traded shocked looks at the fact Nature could actually sniff out a man like his given namesake.

"I ain't feeling this!" Lights-Out confessed looking like he was going to piss in his pants. "Damn these mirrors! Anybody even remember where the entrance is?"

"Shhh!" Joey T. said pressing the barrel of his gun to his lips. "I heard something." Out the corner of his eye he spotted a red blur dart around a corner. "There!" the brawny Italian's voice rang like a trumpet-call as he opened fire shattering mirrors to bits and forcing a tall Jamaican named Ronald Perry to dance out of harm's way almost being shot.

"What the bumbaclot chu' shootin' at bwoy?" the Rude Boy angrily protested in a thick yardy accent.

"Havoc! It was friggin Havoc!" Joey T. said frantically sucking wind.

"Me no see dat rasclot Havoc 'round 'ere! When you see 'im point 'im out, don't shoot!"

Joey T. looked all around and felt like an idiot. There was no sign of Havoc anywhere. "Look I'm telling you that friggin moolie was there one minute and gone the next...like a ghost. Or in his case, like a spook." The Italian wisecracked getting a laugh out of his crew.

"Fuck ya say grape stompa, ya wan die today? Say one more ting out ya rude mout' an-"

"You'll what eggplant?" Joey T. asked swelling up.

The Jamaican gritted his teeth then let his fists do the talking and gave Joey T. the back of his hand knocking him to the ground. Simultaneously Joey T's boys pulled out on Perry while Perry's boys drew on them.

"Hey if you idiots wanna kill each other do it on your own time!" Doll face riffed. "Right now you're on my clock so fan out and keep your eyes open."

"You heard the man move it...move it!" Nature ordered giving people an extra push. The men inched down the maze guns extended, scared to death. Over their beating hearts they heard heavy footsteps running outside and amongst them. Strobe lights played across the house of mirrors interior, elongating shadows, throwing false targets.

A red blur flashed in a mirror and a thug whirled around blazing but no one was there. The red blur made another brief appearance and a sharp kick was tossed lifting a thug off his feet.

"Oh snap, Steven Segal was right! It is him!" a thug shouted and killed Havoc's reflection in a mirror.

"No there!" another man shouted destroying another mirror. When he realized his mistake he nervously backed away into something hard. When he turned around he realized he had backed smack dab into Havoc's brick wall of a chest. Havoc connected with the man's arm sending his gun clattering across the floor then sent him hurtling through a mirror.

Diamond Ken raised his gun and Havoc took off running, "You can run but you can't hide!" the pimp shouted locked on the moving target and sprayed his Uzi chopping a ragged line through glass and sheet rock.

Havoc moved as if every object in the room had a million volts running through it then dived on the floor and tumbled while firing back. He caught another punk in the shoulder then flew around the corner like a skipping stone. Immediately his instincts and reflexes saved him from losing his head to the wild swing of a machete toting man awaiting him. He raised his gun but the machete blade smacked it out of his hand. The man swung the machete again and Havoc ducked the blow and threw a kick into the man's knee breaking it. Havoc immediately scooped up his gun and grabbed his screaming attacker by his jacket. At that moment the others came around the corner like a pack of hungry wolves. Clutching the punk to his chest, Havoc spun around and opened fire dropping men like arcade ducks. Diamond Ken was the first to fire back and the others followed suit setting off a shootout in motion and the human shield in Havoc's arms took the punishment meant for him.

"No stop! Don't shoot!" a man in the group of shooters screamed frantically and began pushing men shooting at Havoc out of his way.

When everyone stopped firing, Havoc let the man in his arms drop to the floor then vanished around the corner. The other man who was frantically screaming rushed to the fallen man's side.

Diamond Ken came over. "What y'all related or something?"

The man kneeled over the dead boy nodded silently, "He was my kid brother."

"Word? Damn, that's fucked up!" the pimp said unremorsefully.

Heartbroken, the man pushed his baby brother's eyes closed, then hand gestured a cross over him and pulled his gun. "And so's this!" he said turning on the pimp then squeezed the trigger.

**BOOM!**

Diamond Ken took a bullet in the stomach and his finger hit the trigger of the Uzi spraying the man back in the face. Clutching his stomach in an attempt to keep the contents from spilling out, the pimp stumbled woozily into the center of the blinking room where everybody was staring at him. He looked at Doll face and a sinister

418

smile came over him. Then without justification or pretext he raised his gun.

"Fuck Havoc! Fuck his dog! Fuck your money and fuck you!" the pimp shouted and pointed his weapon in Doll Face's direction. In a flash Nature moved like a cheetah knocking Doll Face to safety as Diamond Ken sprayed gunfire all over the room dropping men like apples in autumn.

Doll face's mask twisted at Nature. Even with no emotions, Doll face was amazed that he saved him. "You only paid us half!" Nature explained.

Once the shooting happened, it was every man for himself. Diamond Ken lifted his Uzi but was met with the spit of another punk's gun. Joey T. blew Ronald Perry away. One of Ronald's boys put two in the back of Joey T's head forcing his crew to retaliate. Then they killed some people, who killed some people and so on and so on.

A man crept up behind Doll face with a gun and Nature blew a hole the size of a bowling ball through his chest. "Get outta here! We'll regroup later!" Nature shouted. Doll face nodded and disappeared.

With bullets flying this way and that way no one had time to do anything. It was practically impossible to see under the flashing lights. There was screaming, panicking, cursing, bullets flying and more screaming. Squibs exploded out the backs of men leaving smears on the walls behind them. Then above the shouting and tumult there was a loud blood-curdling scream followed by deadly silence.

All this time Havoc remained hidden in the shadows waiting for the right time to move. When everything stopped he stumbled warily out gun drawn into the main open area. What he saw gave him grim satisfaction. Everywhere the bodies of his enemies lay strewn about like discarded sacks torn, broken and lifeless.

"I knew there was no way in hell these idiots could work together." Havoc hissed. As he made his way through the aftermath of the carnage he had to remind himself that it was okay to be nervous. Suddenly a bloody hand reached out and grabbed his ankle. It was Diamond Ken. The pimp looked up at him and opened his mouth but nothing came out. He was dead.

After prying the dead pimp's cold grip from his calve Havoc bent over to catch his breath and noticed Nature's lifeless body. He went over and moved him with his foot. Nothing. When he turned to leave, Nature's eyes opened. Havoc got that feeling that something was behind him and when he turned around, Nature was standing there.

"The possum ain't dead til it's scraped off the road!" Nature said then smacked Havoc's gun across the room and hit him in the jaw so hard the fillings in his teeth rattled. Havoc raised his fists and Nature pointed his gun in his face, "Give me a reason!" he begged but Havoc kept his cool and didn't. Nature paused and looked around sniffing the air, "Tell your bitch to step out where I can see her."

At first Havoc didn't know what Nature was talking about. Then he closed his eyes and blew exasperated. "Donnie. If you're out there hiding please come out."

Nature grabbed Havoc in a chokehold and placed the barrel of his gun to the side of Havoc's head. "Your perfume gave you up so listen to your boyfriend Donnie, or I'll splatter his brains."

After a minute Donnie stepped out looking disheveled and ghostly pale with Havoc's gun in a shaky grasp. When she saw all the dead bodies she fought the urge to vomit and almost dropped the gun.

"What are you doing here? I told you stay put!" Havoc demanded.

"I-I know but I was worried about you." Donnie reasoned.

Nature found the whole thing amusing. "Don't tell me Annie Oakley's your new partner? Man, if I were you I'd call Mayhem back in a hurry. This one here doesn't have the stomach for this line of work. I will say this much, you have good taste when it comes to broads."

"Look just let us go. Nobody else has to die." Donnie begged pointing her weapon at Nature while trying not to show how afraid she was.

Nature smiled, "Hey Donnie, have you ever killed somebody before?" Donnie's bottom lip trembled like she wanted to answer but nothing came out. Nature was amused. "It's okay. Me, I've killed so many I lost count years ago. The only one I do remember is the very

420

first. His face is etched in my brain permanently. That's because you never forget your first."

"Don't listen to him Donnie! He's trying to fuck with your head! Just squeeze the trigger and bust a cap in his ass!" Havoc cautioned under Nature's vice grip.

Nature didn't even bother to deny what he was up to. "Think about it. If you do this Donnie, are you prepared to carry around my face in your head for the rest of your life?"

A chill ran down Donnie's spine. The thought of Nature's ghastly mug haunting her forever in her dreams was too heavy to bear! She asked herself, was she prepared to kill a man? Even one as vile and despicable as Nature who would kill her without blinking twice, given the chance? Someone stepped out of the shadows. In the background Donnie could hear Havoc's voice warning her to 'Look behind her!' Her finger curled around the trigger but she couldn't bring herself to pull it. Suddenly the gun was snatched from her grasp and a pair of clammy hands circled her waist.

"Havoc you should take better care of your woman, or should I say **my** woman." The tall fiendish man smirked and Havoc's eyes narrowed at the man who was responsible for he and Donnie meeting. Her ex-boyfriend Sam. "Hey Donnie, you missed me?" Sam asked then licked Donnie's cheek making her cringe. Infuriated, Havoc broke from Nature's grip then dropped to his knee from a sharp blow behind the head.

"Wha-what are you doing here Sam?" Donnie managed to ask.

"The same as everyone else baby. To see your boyfriend die. And reclaim what's mines! You should have never left me Donnie."

"No, she should have just stayed with you and allowed you to continue beating up on her!" Havoc snarled.

"Shut up! If I want your opinion I'll beat it out of you! Matter'a fact why ain't that son-of-a-bitch dead?" Sam asked Nature.

Havoc spun at Nature. "So now what? You gonna kill me?"

Nature cut an eye at Sam but continued speaking to Havoc, "No…him!" he raised his gun and blew Sam's brains out. Donnie screamed hysterically as Sam's head exploded and she was doused with blood and brains. "Oh for Crying out loud! He's dead!" Nature said to Donnie then shot Sam's twitching corpse again causing it to stop moving. "See? He's dead!" the Shaman shouted this time shooting another lifeless body. "And so's he!" Nature said and shot a dead body playing possum that screamed then writhed and twisted before expiring for real. Nature looked up at Donnie and Havoc, "…Well the mothafucka's dead now!"

# Chapter 38

"This a'way!" Nature directed with the hand that held his gun as they headed past a boarded-up Nathan's restaurant.

Donnie walked quietly wishing she had listened to Havoc when he told her to shoot Nature. But she knew there was no way she could have done that. She wasn't a killer. Perhaps Havoc knew that as well, which is why he shot her a warm smile that told her he wasn't upset with her.

"Where the hell are you taking us?" Havoc stopped and demanded to know.

"All in due time." Nature said waving his gun for emphasis.

Havoc began walking again and kept a worried eye out for his sister and dog but neither was anywhere to be found. He looked over at Donnie and cursed himself for bringing her into his problems.

"Stop!" Nature said when they reached the boardwalk. He blasted the lock off of the ticket booth of a children's roller coaster then waved at Donnie. "You-inside."

Donnie looked at Havoc who nodded for her to go ahead and assured her that everything would be okay. Keeping his gun drawn on Havoc, Nature tipped over the large ten-foot smiling caterpillar statue outside of the booth's ride and barricaded Donnie inside.

"Proceed." Nature instructed as he led Havoc down a long flight of stairs towards the beach.

After walking a short distance Nature stopped. "This is far enough. So, you're probably wondering why I brought you all the way down here."

"The thought crossed my mind." Havoc said.

Nature yanked off his jacket to display a beautifully designed shirt with green, yellow and red horizontal stripes of equal size across his chest. At the center was a mighty gold lion marching east carrying a cross and wearing a gold crown.

"You see this? This is the Imperial Flag of Ethiopia. Inside is The Lion of Judah, which symbolizes the Emperor of Ethiopia and represents the king of kings." Nature said proudly then paused and let out a heartfelt sigh. "I am the son of a tribal chief. A great leader who sat in a circle with other elders at tribal meetings and because his opinion mattered most, was always the last to speak! I'm a descendant of royalty! But, whenever I look at this I do not think about all the power and greatness this emblem represents. All I see is your face mocking me! Because thanks to you, the closest I will ever come to my homeland again is this blasted shirt!"

"Cheer up Buttercup. At least you're not stuck in Jersey" Havoc smiled

"Funny guy," Nature bared his sharp teeth with disdain. "The first time we fought, Trouble Consultant, Po Po interrupted us. The second time, we were disrupted once again before we could learn who between us is the superior fighter. I've been in countless combative situations. All effortless victories. But you my bloody dressed friend are the only opponent who's ever made me ask myself, what the fuck, if we would have gone the distance. So, I think it's high time we separated the men from the boys and find out who truly is the baddest. Just you and me. No dogs," he said then held up his gun and flung it over the boardwalk. "And no weapons."

"Works for me," Havoc said calmly as he removed his hat and stripped down to a red wife-beater. Nature's eyes instinctively widened at the Ashanti tribal tattoos on his muscular arms.

"Those fraudulent markings won't help you here boy. Not today!" Nature laughed.

"Let's find out!" Havoc said jumping into a fighting stance fists raised.

With hands raised combatively and eyes locked, the two circled one another like hungry wolves looking for an opportunity to strike. Nature's nostrils flared and his eyes winced as he set off the match with dirty tactics by kicking sand into Havoc's face and pouncing onto his back, digging his claws into his back like a wild dog. Havoc tossed him off and the two went at each other like a couple of alley cats, almost like a hockey fight, not aiming punches, just keeping them fast and furious.

Nature hauled off and belted Havoc hard in the jaw. The Trouble Consultant took a couple of steps back and shook it off then bounced right back with four-and five-punch combinations making Nature a staggering wreck and he collapsed forward onto Havoc clutching him into the fold. As the two wrestled, Nature reached behind his back then in a flash something sharp raked across Havoc's chest cutting him deep. Havoc jumped back clutching his chest and strained at what appeared to be a claw-like apparatus with four razor sharp talons in Nature's grasp.

"First rule of the beast, always strike when you see an opening!" Nature said with a devilish leer then rushed Havoc slashing at him from all angles.

Havoc moved like lightning, flipping, dipping, dodging every razor-sharp swing by a fraction of an inch then lifted Nature four feet into the air with an awesome uppercut putting him on his back in the sand.

"And the second rule, Dance with the Devil and you pay for the tunes!" Havoc smugly retorted.

With an embarrassed snort, Nature rolled his knees into his chest then performed a kip up and landed on his feet. He spit blood onto the sand then smiled at Havoc impressed. "I see you are well trained in the art of hand to hand combat and quite disciplined. Excellent! This means I'll have to earn my victory. But fighting out here in the open is for amateurs, which it appears neither of us are, so let's make this interesting." He said then spun on his heels, yanked open a rusted gate and disappeared beneath the boardwalk.

Havoc reached the entrance and stared into the pitch black beneath it. He was about to step in when his logical side asked, *"Man are you crazy? I know you ain't about to step foot under there where that deranged lunatic went. Just look at what he did to your chest!"*

Havoc looked down at his wounds. They weren't life threatening, but they were deep enough that he'd have more ugly scars to add to his collection. *"Imagine what that freak'll do to you under there where its cramped, dark and hard to maneuver!"* His illogical side quickly reminded him that if he didn't go after Nature now he'd have to face him later and with his sister still missing, it might be too late. After a few moments of debating, he listened to his logical side removed his dog whistle from his shirt and blew into it hard then he pushed open the creaky gate sighed and entered the dark unknown.

Beneath the boardwalk the air was musty, thick and damp. Havoc could hardly see his own hand in front of his face because the only sources of light was the moonlight faintly peeking through the wooden slats overhead. Remembering his trusty lighter, he flicked it on then creeped past old splintered beams covered in seaweed. As he moved cautiously, herky-jerky movements reached out from the dark looking as though something would jump out and grab him at any minute.

"Yea, though I walk through the valley in the shadow of death I shall fear no evil…cause I'm the meanest son-of-a-bitch in the motherfucking valley!" Havoc muttered to himself then something moved behind him and he spun around and smashed his fist into a wooden beam weak and pulpy from sea water, shattering it into matchsticks. He cursed out in pain then froze as diabolical laughter echoed over the distant roar of the crashing waves.

"This country, what a joke it is!" Nature's voice cut through silence and darkness. Havoc waved the lighter all around unable to locate the source. "Here, rites of passage mean having your first underage drink of alcohol then passing out intoxicated in a puddle of your own waste only to wake up next to a woman whose name you can't recall much less the events of the night before. But in my country that phrase takes on a far more significant meaning. At sixteen the chief of your clan chooses 3 rituals for you to undergo that test your mind, body and courage before you can truly be considered a man. The first test was based on my studies, understanding and comprehension of my beloved homeland and ancestors to instill self-pride and knowledge of thyself. The second was trial by combat which I had been preparing for since birth, training in multiple fighting styles like Musangwe, a South African form of bare fist fighting and Nuba Wrestling, popular in South Sudan. Both trials I breezed through with ease, as I was the best and brightest student and most fiercest fighter in my age group. But for my final task I had to go out into the underbrush alone for three days and nights without any supplies, weapons or food to track down and kill a lion. The killing of the beast signifies the final test of manhood and by drinking its blood it is said that you are endowed with supernatural qualities of the beast itself. Of course, it is always customary to bring back a souvenir."

Havoc rubbed the fresh claw marks on his chest courtesy of Nature's souvenir as he listened trying to pinpoint the source of his voice. His eyes flashed around the shadowed space where every corner of darkness held lethal promise. "Damn, all that by sixteen? I guess they don't have social services where you're from huh? Well my story's a tad bit different. I honed my skills and earned my stripes on the streets of Brooklyn where we do things a helluva' lot different. Cause in case you didn't realize this ain't the jungle," The Trouble Consultant called out as he moved about in the darkness.

"No, but it is the concrete jungle. So the same rules apply!"

Something wet dripped on top of Havoc's head and he paused to wipe it off. He held his lighter to his hand and winced at his palm. It was red. It was blood. Blood that didn't belong to him. Blood that dropped down, from up above. *'Shit!'* Another drop hit his shoulder then ran down his arm. And slowly, he lifted his lighter. Looking directly up, he strained at the darkness. "What the fuck?" he whispered. Something was up there. Hiding. Something large and scary. And it was staring back at him. Was it smiling? He squinted then his eyes stretched wide in astonishment as he made out Nature hanging directly overhead from the wooden beams. But before Havoc could react, three hundred and fifty-three pounds of solid muscle fell out of the sky and washed over him like a tidal wave. Then two extremely different fighting styles collided!

The two enemies wrestled like wild animals, struggling, growling, snarling and roaring as lethal hand to hand techniques and spinning kicks were viciously traded. Throughout the barbaric exchange the fight escalated further beneath the boardwalk, resuming at a visually better location near the shoreline and beneath the moon. All the while, Havoc mindfully remained calm breathing deeply through his nose and exhaling from his mouth so as not to tire out unlike Nature who was sucking wind and already in the early stages of fatigue.

Havoc bobbed and weaved a tremendous punch and followed up with his own making Nature's knees buckle. Nature snarled then charged forward slamming Havoc's spine against a beam. Refusing to give him a chance to recuperate he angrily headbutted Havoc stunning him then followed up with two powerful face numbing right and left hooks. Taking advantage of the moment he threw back his head, jaws stretching wide and sunk his sharp teeth deep into Havoc's shoulder blade. The Trouble Consultant yelled out in pain then moved Nature off of him with a stinging punch to the ear. Havoc slid halfway down a beam and grabbed his wound then looked on in disbelief as his enemy licked his blood from his lips.

"I've tasted the flesh and blood of many foes. Man, and beast. But yours Trouble Consultant, is by far the tastiest." Nature said with a lascivious red grin.

"You sick fucking bastard!" Havoc shouted repulsed clutching the bite mark on his shoulder while using the beam behind him to help keep him on his feet.

"Never a truer word spoken." Nature taunted and laughed.

Havoc suddenly felt off balance and slid to the floor. He looked at his wet red palm through blurred vision. Then at Nature for answers. "What the hell?"

"No, my fangs aren't poisonous. But there is a mild tranquilizer drop in each I'm immune to, that'll temporarily take the Trouble out of the Consultant." He laughed pointing.

Havoc struggled to stand and stumbled forward tossing feeble punches as his enemy taunted and mocked him. Underestimating his foe and overestimating himself, Nature got too close and was socked in the face. Furious he grabbed Havoc's shoulders and pulled him towards him kneeing him in the gut then began raining punches into his ribs and kidneys. When he was done punishing him he hoisted Havoc into the air and body slammed him onto his back. When the Trouble Consultant fought to get up a sharp knee was planted in the center of his chest pausing him.

"Look at you, you're as pathetic as a band-aid on cancer." Nature shook his head then leaned forward and brandished his lion's claw. Holding its razor-sharp talons inches from Havoc's face he sneered. "Tell me, do the ladies dig those hazel eyes of yours? I bet they do." Feeling the effects of Nature's fang toxin coursing through his veins, Havoc squirmed trying to escape but felt helpless.

"You...said...no weapons!" Havoc whispered struggling beneath his weight.

"I say lots of things. Few are true." Nature said and grabbed Havoc's face forcefully holding his head still. "Now calm down. I'm not greedy. I only want one eye. For a souvenir."

"No!"

The sudden creak of a gate being pushed open ceased everything and was followed by a nightmarish snarling growl. Nature and Havoc both turned then observed a pair of glowing yellow eyes staring back at them floating in the darkness. Havoc let out a sigh of relief as Mayhem stepped out of the shadows, erect, legs bowed and feet widened in a muscular development patiently awaiting the four words that would set her off.

Havoc smiled at a shock-faced Nature, "You've got your weapons and I've got mines." he then turned to his dog and shouted, "ALL-BETS-ARE-OFF!"

When his devoted dog heard the in case of emergency-break-glass command, eyes winced and teeth dripped saliva as something snapped and there was only one thing on her astute mind, attack! And don't hold back! Then in a flash, Havoc and Mayhem were all over Nature attacking from every angle as a powerful team.

In a blurred ballet of lethal moves Nature used the amazing abilities and fighting skills he was force fed since exiting the womb to successfully defend himself against the furious man and his dog. A round housed kick caught Havoc high on the chest lifting him cleanly off his feet. Mayhem picked up the slack and leaped onto Nature's chest biting him about the shoulders and arm. Exhausted and strained to the limit Havoc laid in the sand as Mayhem and his enemy tussled. Nature fell onto his back then forced an elbow against Mayhem's throat trying to keep her at bay then with his other hand he reached back furtively and pulled his lion's claw and buried it deep inside of her rib cage.

"Mayhem!" Havoc yelled as Mayhem let out a painful yelp.

Nature stood laughing sinisterly and maliciously kicked her through the air with a metal-toed boot. Havoc stared at his dog writhing in the sand then looked at Nature and literally saw RED. His face twisted with hate and he felt a charge in his belly as he was engulfed by total and complete rage. He sprang to his feet like a man possessed, no longer under the influence of the toxin and charged.

Nature met Havoc head-on, dropping into a low kick and sweeping the Trouble Consultant's legs out from under him then opened fresh claw marks across Havoc's back. Havoc was so high off of vengeance that he felt nothing. Gritting his teeth, he proceeded to paint Nature with powerful punches and combos. A devastating overhand left fractured his enemy's jaw. A bone crushing right cross loosened his teeth. Then the Trouble Consultant moved downtown and unleashed rib shattering blows to painfully remind Nature that regardless of how much agony he was already in, it was possible to experience so much more.

Bloody, bruised and swollen with starry vision, Nature turned to run. "Oh no you don't!" Havoc shouted as he grabbed the coward's dreadlocks wrapping them around his fist. He then snatched him back and swung him wildly through the air crashing into a wooden beam face first. Down on his back defeated, Nature twitched in the sand, his nose a geyser of blood. Havoc tossed the fistful of dreadlocks ripped from his enemy's skull to the sand and rushed to his dog's side.

"Thank you for having my back." He said and kissed her on the head stroking her head as she made a whining sound managing to wag her tail. A few feet away Nature sat up woozy with a concussion. He spotted Havoc and remembered he had one last trick up his sleeve. He reached into the small of his back removing something that would work. Havoc was nurturing Mayhem when she began growling and the Trouble Consultant looked up to find himself staring into the black muzzle of Nature's semi-automatic. "You never planned on us fighting a fair one, did you?"

"What I never planned on was you being that damn good. I tip my dreads to you Trouble Consultant. You are without a doubt, the best damn opponent I've ever fought."

"Don't you mean cheated?" Havoc snarled.

"Tsk, tsk, tsk. Don't ruin the moment with petty technicalities. Instead graciously accept your death with the comfort of knowing you've earned my respect. Now with that said, duces." Nature said then pointed and squeezed the trigger as Havoc flinched in anticipation. Except nothing happened. It jammed. Nature's eyes went wide and he squeezed again and again. Each time he got a click instead of a bang! He couldn't believe it and shook his head in utter disbelief, then grinned. "What is bad luck for one man, is good luck for another."

"You damn skippy!" Havoc said then lunged forward and grabbed his legs. Cold, sore and exhausted, Havoc powered through the sharp punches and pistol whipping raining down on his head, neck and shoulders as Nature attempted to free himself. Then with one mighty surge of strength combined with an ear-splitting rage induced yell, Havoc stood abruptly launching his enemy skyward where unbeknownst to him was a long curved rusty metal spike hiding in the darkness that once held the deteriorating structure in place. As he pushed with all his might, the metal spike made a horrible popping sound like it was piercing a watermelon as it drove through the top of Nature's skull and out the side of his jaw pinning him like a slab of beef in a butcher's shop. "Oh shit!" Havoc said as he backed away when he realized what he'd done. Nature began choking and flailing wildly, clawing at the hook protruding from his face. Then the Trouble Consultant stepped forward and looked Nature directly in his eyes and said, "Now you know, who's the baddest!"

Nature calmed down. His's lips parted as though he attempted to respond over a steady flow of dark blood running out both sides of his mouth. But to Havoc's surprise he smiled as the life slowly drained from his body. His arms swung to his sides as he hung there impaled, staring back at the only man on Earth he both feared and respected.

Staggering out the gate's entrance accompanied by his loyal and limping dog, Havoc found his clothes and got dressed. He looked over at Mayhem, no worse for wear. "Worst night ever huh?" he asked to which she replied with a concurring whine. Then with a brave smile the pair soldiered on.

# Chapter 39

Donnie sat on the floor of the ticket booth as her brain raced with only one thought. How could she escape and help her man?

"Donnie?" a sore voice whispered.

Donnie stood up trembling and looked around certain she heard her name called but no one was there. She turned and almost leaped out of her skin when she saw Havoc standing on the opposite side of the gate looking exhausted. "Jesus! You almost gave me a heart attack!" she said clutching her chest.

"Sorry baby. Step back from the gate." Havoc said and pushed the caterpillar statue out of the way with a deep grunt.

Donnie came out and fell into his arms. "I was so worried. I thought-" She stopped in mid-sentence and looked down at his chest, "Oh my God! Is that your blood?"

Havoc looked down at his battered torso, "Some of it."

"And Nature?" Donnie asked.

"…I sent flowers." Havoc answered with a wry look.

"Are you sure you're alright?"

"I'm fine but…" Havoc shook his head sadly then looked over at Mayhem having trouble standing from her wounds.

"Oh no!" Donnie said.

Havoc's eyes welled up. "There's a vet I have on twenty-four hour call. Once we find Tee-Tee I'll take her to him. He can fix her. My girl's a trooper. Ain't cha baby?" He asked his dog choked-up.

Mayhem climbed wearily to her feet and shunned the help offered by her master. She barked indicating she wanted him to follow then hobbled in slow motion leading them through the amusement park. After a moment she was distracted from her mission and began growling towards the edge of the pier where a lone figure in a long black robe was standing with their arms folded behind their back looking out over the ocean. They walked towards the figure when Havoc paused half way along the pier and turned to Donnie.

"Wait here. And I do mean here." he said pointing at the ground for emphasis. "And that goes for you too, stay put!" he said to his dog then with a look of uncertainty in his eyes traveled the remaining short distance of the pier stopping a few feet behind the person standing there.

"With everything going on I almost forgot all about your spooky ass." Havoc admitted.

Doll face turned around slowly, "Really? And here I was trying to make a lasting impression.

"So, care to tell me why you went through all this trouble for little ol' me?" he asked.

Doll face eerily cocked his mask at Havoc as if he should know the answer then finally asked, "Have you ever heard of Scleroderma?"

"Scleroderma-Scleroderma? Nope. Doesn't ring a bell." Havoc pondered for a moment then lit up at the realization, "Hey wait a second. I think I do know her. Doesn't she live in Fort Greene projects and got two baby daddies, and three baby fathers?"

Doll face shook his head, "No Scleroderma is not the name of one of your little hood rats. It's an extremely rare chronic autoimmune disease that translates to 'hard skin.' Sclero meaning hard, derma meaning skin in which the body's immune system mistakenly attacks its own connective tissue and organs."

"And this rare genetic disorder, I take it you were the one in a zillion to get it?"

Doll face began with an exasperated sigh, "It came without warning. Unannounced, like a thief in the night, robbing me of my identity and integrity. Imagine for me if you would that you're living a normal life then one day out of the clear blue your skin begins to thicken and harden, turning shinny and discolored. Then on top of this you have a painful sensitivity to cold, frequent heartburn and stiff and swollen joints. You see one clueless doctor after the next and they all tell you the same thing. That it's a chronic ailment and the cause for this is unknown. Treatment can help somewhat but unfortunately, there is no cure." Havoc frowned and took a cautious step back. "Oh don't worry handsome, it's not contagious. Cause believe me if it were, I

433

would have infected you a long time ago. But even then, you're more than likely not to have caught it since it afflicts primarily women." Havoc frowned confused wondering what that was supposed to mean, "There are two categories of this disease. Localized and systemic. I guess if you absolutely had to contract Scleroderma, localized is the version you'd want to catch because it is relatively mild and while it affects the skin it's only in the lower arms and legs and it does not affect the organs. Now Systemic is a bitch. Not only does it harden both your skin and blood vessels, your internal organs as well."

"And I take it you've got Systemic?" Havoc asked.

"Guess I was born under a lousy zodiac sign because not only was I blessed with a rare incurable disease, I have both forms of it, merged into one souped-up monstrosity on steroids."

"Di-zamn, sucks to be you."

"That it does. Doctors said the odds are so great, the probability so inconceivable, that my condition is unbelievable. Unbelievable, has to be the stupidest word in the dictionary. It shouldn't ever come out of our mouths. It happened. I witnessed it. I'm living it. Believe it. But there's the other side of unbelievable, for instance certain parts of my body are damn near impenetrable. And because of all the anti-inflammatory medications, corticosteroid shots and a host of experimental drugs I've taken to combat muscle pain and deterioration, as a result I have increased strength equivalent to that of a small army."

"Well that explains a lot He-Man." Havoc said.

"Of, course those costly experiments came at a much bigger price. Cancer! But luckily, if you want to call it that. Pounds of flesh were hacked off in time. Still the negatives far outweigh the positives. Every waking moment feels like my bones are being scorched and my essence is being torn away by the fiercest hounds of hell, even now I suffer. I've just learned to tolerate it. Movement of my tongue is greatly impaired which is why my voice sounds like tumbling boulders. Alopecia, a skin condition common with Scleroderma, caused most of my hair to fall out and my face...my face..." Doll face paused, "well in just under a year and a half of being diagnosed, I went from attracting the opposite sex, to making them run in pure horror!"

"Ok, I get it. You were dealt a shitty hand…and a shitty face. But life's not easy. It never was. It isn't now, and it won't ever be. We've all got our problems. But what the fuck do yours have to do with me?" Havoc asked.

"Because while this godforsaken disease has made my life a living hell. You took away from me the one last thing I had worth living for!"

"Sounds like you have a lot of misdirected anger…Mister Carter."

Doll face twisted at Havoc eerily, "What did you call me?"

"Your name. Nice try Tide but losing a ton of weight and dressing like an extra from Hellraiser can't hide who you are."

"So you have it all figured out?"

"I did a little investigating. Word on the street is after our brief tussle, you left the hospital badly disfigured and vowing revenge. Then the back to back deaths of Lisa Greenstein and her boyfriend Nathan Owens followed each a year apart. And if we connect the dots to your diabolical plan, I'm the last thing on your to-do-list."

"Brief tussle huh? I love how you just neatly explained away all the damage you caused." Doll Face's head shook. "Regarding your detective work, I have to agree with you. Little effort was put into it"

"So, what are you trying to say?"

"I'm not trying to say anything! I'm flat out saying it!" Doll face shouted. Havoc looked back at Donnie who was just as confused. "That day in the hospital, I could hear those insensitive bastards. I just chose to ignore them because I had bigger issues to deal with, namely my little brother losing his sanity because of what you and your dog did to him. But over his ranting and raving I could hear the guards on staff gasping, whispering things about me. Calling me a living Autopsy."

"Hold up. You're not Tide? But you're Autopsy?" Havoc asked confused, recalling what his informant Drake told him. The mask nodded a response. "So then you and Tide are…brothers?"

"No, siblings."

"But you just said he was your brother."

"Yes he is."

"How the hell can Tide be your brother but you're not his, yet you just said the two of you are siblings?" Havoc suddenly paused and his eyes widened at the same time Donnie realized it too, "Unless you're his...Sister?"

"Boy George, I think he's got it." Doll face said then removed the porcelain mask, shattering it as it fell, revealing a leather hood underneath. But unlike the first mask that was a handcrafted work of art, this one was gnarled and ugly and made of patchwork leather sewn and riveted together covering Doll face's entire head.

"What the fuck, Ben Cooper's running a sale on shitty looking masks?"

"But wait. There's more!" Doll Face said and grabbed a piece of stitching hanging from the leather mask and pulled unraveling it. Long stringy patches of silver hair spilled out as the mask split in half and dropped to the floor. "Ta-dah!"

Donnie's eyes bulged and her lips parted into a gasp as she fought the urge not to faint. Havoc flinched shock-faced and his mind overloaded as reality hit him. Never in all of his clamorous years as a Trouble Consultant had he ever seen something so frighteningly appalling. The hospital security guards were ruthless in their name calling, but spot on. For lack for a better word, the only way to describe Tide's sister was Autopsy. A skin-crawling-awful, nightmare come chillingly to life. A living breathing mummified corpse with leathery skin, twisted lips that drooped down her face like melting candle wax and gnarled teeth that were unequal to a jack o' lantern's. But what was most alarming was her eyes. There weren't any. She didn't have irises, just huge, soul-less, deep, black-pool pupils.

"Yea I know. It's pretty bad. But I didn't always look like this. Once upon a time I was a successful business owner. Undeniably pretty. Men literally lined up around the corner to date me. Can you believe that this was once the face that promoted Jan's luxury car and limousine service on billboards all over the city?" Autopsy paused to reflect on happier days.

"Funny. You don't look like a Jan. I'm getting more of a Marsha-Marsha-Marsha vibe from you," The Trouble Consultant said literally smiling in the face of danger.

"That is funny. But you know, what's even funnier? Is when the Doctor told me he had to remove my breasts due to the cancer. I actually protested. Like it still mattered. Guess it was the last thing left that still made me feel like a woman. Unbelievable? I don't think so."

"There's somebody out there for everybody." Havoc said cynically.

Autopsy saddled up to Havoc and got disturbingly close. "So pretty-boy you really think I still got it?" she asked then licked her lips with a nauseating smile.

Havoc returned a half-cringed smile as a chill ran down his spine. "Totally. Hell, I'd ask you out if I wasn't already seeing someone."

"Aw, isn't that sweet? But unfortunately, you ain't my type!" she said with a crooked sneer and dazed Havoc with a backhanded smack. "I like my men with a little more flavor than you have to offer!" she hissed swinging.

Since Havoc had already become painfully aware to Autopsy's power, he avoided the granite fists at all costs. While returning blows that only seemed to hurt his hands, he discovered that various places on Autopsy's body were brick hard while other body parts were soft and fleshy as he deflected a well-executed punch. He then followed up with a kidney shot that got a reaction, as the monster staggered back clutching her side.

"You felt that?" Havoc said in an a-ha like voice then dipped under a wild swing and followed up with what he was certain was the problem solving-knockout punch across his adversary's jaw. "Fuck!" he snarled in pain rubbing his throbbing fist. A spinning round house kick from Autopsy put the Trouble Consultant on his back and he looked up in disbelief at the most bizarre foe he ever had the displeasure of coming into contact with.

"You felt that? Tae Bo!" Autopsy bragged.

Mayhem could no longer stand watching her master hurt and let out a bark showing there was a bit of fight left in her then protectively charged at Autopsy. Unable to sink her teeth into the ghoul's iron hide she was easily swatted aside and overwhelmed from pain and fatigue, collapsed when she tried to stand.

Donnie moved in breaking a bottle over Autopsy's head which did nothing but piss her off! She shook her disfigured head in utter disbelief and grabbed Donnie by the throat and lifted her into the air.

"Let go of me you ugly bitch!" Donnie demanded struggling in Autopsy's grasp as she began to squeeze the life out of her.

"Let her go!" Havoc shouted tackling them to the ground and freed Donnie from her grasp. He then climbed on top of the monster and hit her in the face, inadvertently hurting his own hand.

"Good luck trying to hurt me." Autopsy laughed.

Something occurred to Donnie and she reached into her pocket, "Baby!" she called out. Havoc turned to Donnie and she was holding his lucky four-fingered HAVOC ring. "Here!" she said and tossed it to him.

Havoc snatched it out of the air, slid it on grinned and began viciously pounding Autopsy's stone face and torso with profanity laced vengeful haymakers! When he landed one jackhammer punch too many, the ring split in two and she made a sound like a wounded animal. With his fist drawn back he froze then looked down at her. Regardless of how vicious natured she was or how hideous she looked, underneath it all was still a woman. And here he was striking her with everything he had. His momma raised him better. He momentarily forgot who he was and dropped his head in shame.

Autopsy began to shake while making a demonic noise that resembled a witch's cackle, "Aw, what's wrong Dudley Do Right? Moral code won't allow you to hit a lady?"

Havoc shook his head and removed the broken ring pieces then jammed them back into his pocket. "Not even one that's batshit crazy and looks like a bowl of burning diarrhea." The Trouble Consultant said and was violently forced off of her with a sudden groin punch.

"What's the matter Havoc? You don't look so good. Can I get you something? Water? A transfusion perhaps?" Autopsy laughed trailing behind him as he crawled around on all fours deliriously. She planted a sharp rib cracking boot in his side causing him to twist on his back in agony. "So this is the man you love? This killer?" she asked Donnie who crawled to her man's side.

"I didn't kill your brother!" Havoc said in a pain-filled voice clutching his sides.

"That's right, I forgot. You only tussled with him!" Autopsy snarled facetiously. "Believe it or not Havoc there was a time I would have never been capable of such brutal acts. But sometimes it takes a major tragedy like an incurable disease and the death of a loved one for you to find out who and what you really are capable of. As my condition intensified and my appearance worsened, my boyfriend dumped me. Friends stopped calling. The world abandoned me. But not Tide. He was there for me from the start. Selflessly accompanying me to doctor's appointments, and anywhere else I needed to go. I wished I was dead. People were frightened by the way I looked. Especially children. It was very difficult for me to deal, so isolation was ideal. But that meant I could no longer run my business, so he quit his job and took it over. I would have taken my life if it wasn't for my brother. But as a result, he didn't have a life. All he did was run the business and come home to tend to my needs. I became totally dependent on him. And he selflessly put my needs before his own. Then all that changed when he met Lisa. She was pretty, free-spirited eccentric, educated and a successful entrepreneur. Like I used to be. And I despised her. It's not like he neglected me now that he had found love. He just didn't have as much time for me like he used to and I lived for our time together. Sometimes he'd bring her around and she seemed cordial but then I'd catch her staring at me with the same pity and disgust like everyone else. I didn't trust her. Tide had managed to turn my company into an even bigger success. I was convinced she saw dollar signs. Why else would she spend so much time with an overweight reclusive and his hideously deformed sister? So, I hired a private investigator to do a background check on her. Get something, anything I could use against her. And do you know what I found out?"

"That, she wasn't after his money?" Havoc said.

Autopsy sighed and shook her head, "Not only wasn't she after his money. She came from wealth and had her own. In fact, she loved my brother as much as I did. So, you can imagine my concern when he told me he was going to propose. I was at my wits end. What would happen to me? So even though it was not an easy decision, I had to end it between them. I hired an escort from an agency to pose as Tide's scorned lover and provided her with information that only the woman who was having an affair with my brother would know. Then I sent her to the restaurant that he planned on proposing to Lisa at to throw a monkey wrench in his plans. It worked perfectly. Too perfectly. Heartbroken, Lisa left him and ran back to her ex Nathan. But I never imagined that Tide would react the way he did. Do the things he did. Then Lisa hired you and things were too far gone to fix. After you caused him to fall through the window. Doctor's said it would take years of plastic surgery just to make him look semi normal again. Upon hearing this he checked himself out of the hospital and ironically the roles in our relationship had reversed. Now I was the nursemaid taking care of him. At first things were fine. I sold my business to the competition and we had plenty of money. But all Tide would do was whine and complain about Lisa and how she would never want him now that he looked like he did. Eventually he fell into a deep dark depression and one morning I woke up to find he had committed suicide by overdosing with every bottle of pills in the medicine cabinet. I lost my best friend and wanted to get even. Make the ones responsible pay! So yes, I did kill that bitch Lisa. Even helped myself to a couple of pricey masks from her fancy art collection as you can see. I laid low and a year later I tracked down and killed her idiot boyfriend as well."

"Why-" Havoc began.

"Why you ask? Because, hurt people, **hurt**-people!"

"No....Why didn't you kill yourself?" He asked causing Autopsy to recoil as if the words stung. "After all it's your fault your he's dead."

"Careful, you're treading into dangerous waters!" Autopsy warned.

"Because I'm telling the truth? It was your selfishness that killed your brother!"

"No, don't you dare say that! I cared about my brother!"

"No. Lisa cared about your brother. You only cared about yourself." Havoc said.

"Shut up." Autopsy dropped her head in shame sounding less demanding and more like pleading.

"Instead of realizing with everything terrible that happened to you, you were still blessed. That there are folks who have to deal with conditions like yours and worse but they have to go it alone. And here your kid brother goes and puts his life on hold, endures his own life changing tragedy for you but when an opportunity for him to have a little bit of happiness comes along what do you go and do? Take it away. That's what's unbelievable."

"I said shut up!" Autopsy shouted and shoved Donnie aside then grabbed Havoc up by his jacket and viciously beat him in his face. "I could easily kill you right now. But then you'd never feel my pain. You need to suffer like I have and that can only come from losing somebody you love! Like her!" She said pulling a gun from her pocket and aiming at Donnie.

"Donnie, run!" Havoc yelled struggling with Autopsy.

Donnie turned to bolt and her jaw dropped in total shock to find another gun drawn on her.

"Well, well look who finally decided to join the party," Autopsy said salaciously.

Havoc's eyes stretched wide. He thought he was dreaming from the beating he just received as he observed his ex-wife walk towards Donnie with a gun drawn and a wicked look on her face.

"Nicky? What the hell are you doing here?" Havoc asked as Autopsy pushed him to the ground.

"Oh I can answer that. See after you so nobly left your ex-wife behind with her little weasel boyfriend's corpse to face the police alone, I rolled on the scene. I've got to be honest, I've been following you around for a long time putting all of this together. Studying you. Learning your darkest secrets, paying off informants, approaching your enemies and making back-alley deals. Seems you've given a lot of people plenty of reasons to hate your guts who'd gladly accept a small fortune to hunt you down and kill you. But to my surprise the only one who didn't care about money was your ex-wife. As soon as I asked if she wanted redemption, she was on her feet and in the back seat of my car. Guess it's true what they say about a scorned woman." Autopsy said gesturing towards Donnie.

"Nicky, I know you didn't let this Crypt Keeper looking bitch brainwash you!" he said refusing to believe she could betray him like this.

Nicky ice grilled Donnie hard from head to toe with her lips twisted in disgust. Donnie was frozen not sure whether she was about to die. Then Nicky dropped the act and pointed her weapon at Autopsy. "Of course not!"

"What? But why?" Autopsy demanded.

"I just let you think I was down with the program so I could hitch a ride." Nicky said and turned to Havoc. "In case **you** needed help. And from the look of things, I can see you do."

"Why you double-crossing bitch!" the She-monster snarled and pointed her gun at Nicky and fired.

Nicky fired back. Autopsy caught the blast square in the left shoulder. The force of the bullet knocked her back a few steps but had no real effect aside from a grunt. Nicky was hit in the arm and her weapon landed at Donnie's feet. Autopsy advanced forward sending Nicky and Donnie to the floor with flashy martial arts moves. The ugly woman then kicked Nicky's gun over the pier and pointed her own weapon at the ladies. She looked back in time to see Havoc give his injured dog a consoling pat then climb wearily to his feet and limp forward.

"Good you're just in time. I was standing here trying to determine which one of these lovely young ladies to kill but I'm not sure which one. So, I'll let you decide." Havoc stopped in his tracks, taken aback by the macabre request. "Come on I don't have all day. Who means the most to you? I mean if you can't decide I could just as easily kill them both!" Autopsy threatened pushing her gun forward and causing the horrified women to react.

"No don't! Please! Take me instead," The Trouble Consultant said valiantly.

"How noble. If my tear ducts still worked I might shed one. But as I said earlier, you need to feel my pain. And I can't think of a better way than by making you choose!"

Havoc turned to the terrified women huddled together looking at him. "I can't!" He pleaded.

"You can and you will!" Autopsy insisted. Havoc shook his head. Both women meant the world to him. There was no way he could make a decision. He sighed and dropped his head bewildered as Autopsy taunted. "Your past or your present? Choose! Past or present?! Choose! Past! Or! Pre!-"

"Ok-ok! You sick evil bitch!" Havoc shouted feeling light headed. He turned to Nicky and Donnie trembling with a look of dismay. His old love and his current love. So many memories between both ladies ran through his mind. So many emotions. So many feelings with love being at the center of them all. The women were horrified, unsure of who he'd pick. His lips parted and he began to speak with shaky words, "Fine…I choose…" Autopsy leaned forward with anticipation. "Mayhem!" he yelled.

"No! Choose a different bitch! Not your-" Autopsy paused upon hearing the distinct sound of galloping on the wooden planks of the pier approaching and turned to Havoc confused.

Havoc winked then shouted the command, "UP AND AT 'EM!" as he dropped to one knee and bent forward. That's when she saw the ferocious beast, teeth bared, saliva flailing, eyes piercing, sprint her way full speed. Before she could react, Mayhem charged up the ramp of Havoc's back and launched herself at Autopsy catching her arm in her powerful jaws, clamping shut like a bear trap and pulling her down.

Autopsy screamed as she lost her gun and was viciously shaken in Mayhem's powerful grip. The dog ferociously chewed and tugged as determined teeth eventually pierced through Autopsy's hardened skin causing the deformed woman to let out a horrific blood curdling sound of pain and terror as she struggled with Mayhem. Quick thinking, she brandished a long knife from her jacket to which Mayhem let out a painful yelp releasing her. A glum silence infected the boardwalk as Autopsy noticed her arm. It was shredded like lobster meat, red and slick below the bicep. It was then she noticed Havoc and turned her attention to him. She looked like a horror movie that leaped off the screen as she maniacally approached bleeding with murder in her lifeless dead eyes and a knife in her hand. The Trouble Consultant frantically stumbled backwards and fell then crab walked until his back was against the railing with nowhere to go.

Nicky spotted Autopsy's gun but was out of commission and motioned a shock-faced Donnie to grab it. Donnie frantically stood pointing the weapon amateurish, "Bitch back away from him!" she heard herself shout. Autopsy saw her coming and immediately placed the knife to Havoc's throat freezing Donnie in place.

"On your feet! Havoc! Get up dammit!" Autopsy commanded yanking and pulling on him. With the tip of the knife dangerously close to opening his jugular vein, he reluctantly stood grimacing in pain. She cowered behind him completely blocked by his frame, pulled him back then placed the knife to his Adams apple. Feeling painted into a corner and fearing everything would soon be coming to a tragic end, there was something she had to know, "Why? Didn't you save him?" she asked Havoc. "He told me how you could have saved him, but instead you let him fall-why?"

"I had no choice," the Trouble Consultant replied.

"Bullshit! You could have saved my brother but instead you saved your damn dog!" Autopsy screamed pressing the blade hard against his skin and slightly cutting him. Havoc nervously gritted his teeth and glanced over at Donnie and Nicky then averted their inquisitive stares. "What don't your women know what kind of man you are?"

Havoc sighed as he played back the consulting job that haunted him for years. It all came back to him as if it were yesterday. After a brief scuffle he and Mayhem were hot on Tide's ass as he scampered up the staircase of his ex-girlfriend Lisa's apartment building and to the roof. When he bolted out the door he saw all the buildings were connected like an open field. He spotted Tide sprint to the far edge of the roof and dive to the next lower rooftop. Mayhem took off as Havoc ran parallel trying to keep up.

Overweight and out of breath Tide reached the edge and discovered a void waiting there where the buildings stopped connecting. He looked back and saw Mayhem's fangs about to reach him then looked back at the second building, took a step back and launched himself through the air landing on the other side. Landing perfectly, so he thought, until he heard Havoc's voice yell at Mayhem not to follow but it was too late, the dog was on the roof with him. He turned to run and his foot slipped. He looked down and through the snow he could see light below and realized he was standing on a huge sheet of glass.

Mayhem was about to pounce but Havoc called out to her to be still. That's when Tide heard something crack. And that's when things went from bad to worse!

Time was of the essence and Havoc knew if he was to save them he'd have to act quickly. Through the scattered breaks in the otherwise smooth layer of snow he could see just how dizzyingly high they were as well as how far the drop was. Looking all around he spotted a painter's ladder on a tarp and some overturned empty paint cans set before a freshly-painted white wall. In a flash he effortlessly lifted and lowered the ladder over the edge to the stranded dog and man.

"No wait!" he called out to Tide making his way over. "Let my dog go first."

"Your dog?" He repeated astounded.

"You heard me Fat-Boy. Besides she's closer and your weight might break the glass if you rush."

Tide looked at Havoc like he was speaking a foreign language. "Are you insane? I'm not going after no damn dog!" he said and continued forward then immediately stopped in his tracks when the Trouble Consultant pointed a gun at him.

"This isn't up for negotiations. I said my dog goes first!" Havoc repeated defiantly. "Mayhem. Come!" Tide who could not believe he was second in line after a dog cursed Havoc and Mayhem under his breath as he watched the dog obey its master and climb the ladder like a circus act. Once she was safely on the higher ground Havoc lowered his weapon. "Ok now you. And take your time. Slowly."

Tide nodded nervously and began to make his way towards the ladder when the unthinkable happened. Glass began to crack around him like ice on a frozen pond. With fear painted on his face Tide looked to Havoc for help. But it was too late and all Havoc could do was watch on as the sky light gave way under Tide's feet and swallowed him whole.

"So you don't feel responsible for what happened to my brother huh?" Autopsy's gnarled voice snatched Havoc abruptly from his thoughts.

"Look I made a judgment call! My road-dog who's had my back for as long as I can remember or the guy I was hired to stop terrorizing his ex-girlfriend." Havoc reasoned, "Now perhaps my decision to choose my dog was not the one that you and your brother would have liked for me to make but it's the choice I made and I can live with that decision. The question is can you live with the decision you made that caused your brother's death?"

Havoc's words penetrated Autopsy's resilient skin and impermeable demeanor when she discovered that her tear ducts did in fact still work. She was taken out of the moment and allowed the blade to slightly drop from his throat. Seizing the opportunity, Havoc brought his hands up and pulled with both arms at her wrists, cocked up his shoulder getting the knife away from his neck for a split second. Then keeping her forearm nice and close to his collarbone, he pulled it towards himself and twisted himself under her arm then plunged the blade deeply into her rib cage. It all happened so fast she didn't realize what happened to her at first. Then she felt a new pain in addition to the constant one brought on by her condition and looked down. With a hard tug and loud screech, she pulled the blade out of her side dousing the boardwalk with dark blood.

Autopsy stood there holding the bloody knife. All she could think about was what Havoc just asked her. Could she live with her decision? Could she live with what she had done to her brother? She'd been so preoccupied with plotting and scheming her revenge that it never occurred to her to ask herself that question. But now she had. And as the tears ran down her face she realized she couldn't. She looked at Donnie holding a shaky gun then at Havoc. The last thing on her 'to-do' list.

"If there's a hell I'll gladly go. But you're coming with me!" she announced then raised her knife high and screamed charging at him.

Remembering the brief lesson Havoc gave her when firing a gun, Donnie exhaled so she wouldn't jump and miss her target. Then she pointed the end with the hole at the bad guy and pulled the trigger. The bullet halted Autopsy in her tracks and she was thrown in reverse but she shrugged it off and advanced forward determined to get to him. Donnie began firing repeatedly forcing her back against the railing. Struggling to hang on, Autopsy flipped over screaming bloody murder down into a hell of her own making and disappearing into blackness below.

After she was gone Donnie dropped the gun and collapsed into Havoc's arms. Nicky came over and offered her hand, "Thank you." Donnie looked at her hand, smiled and embraced her.

Havoc helped Mayhem to her feet and she licked his face. He then cautiously crept over to the railing and peered over the edge at the long drop below and spotted a motionless Autopsy lying on jagged rocks in a twisted position. A huge wave crashed against the rocks and when it disappeared, so did she.

"Saved by my ex-wife, my girlfriend and my dog. Who would'a thunk it?" Havoc grunted hobbling over to the women. "Are you gonna be okay?" he asked Nicky.

"It's just a flesh wound. I'll be fine." She said as Donnie tied a torn piece of material over it.

He looked at his ex-wife and nodded. "Come on we still need to find Tee-Tee." Upon hearing her name Mayhem pulled on Havoc's jacket and whined like she wanted him to follow. After leading him through Luna Park, she locked steadfast and offered a weak bark staring straight ahead.

"What is it girl?" Havoc asked then looked up and realized what she was excited over. They were standing before the Himalaya, Tee-Tee's favorite ride in Coney Island.

Havoc went over to the ride and discovered his sister fast asleep in the first car. He looked back at the ladies, "She's been trying to lead us to Tee-Tee the entire time. Before I sent her over to your place Nicky, I put a sleeping pill in her Hot Chocolate. My original plan was to drive you all somewhere safe. I figured with her sleeping it'd make things easier. I guess in a way it did." he explained grateful

447

she didn't have to witness the worst parts of the night's tragic events. He then nudged his sister. "Hey sleepy head. Up and at em.'"

Tee-Tee opened her eyes stretching and looked at everyone. "Hey big brother! Where'd you go?"

"Where'd I go? Where'd you go brat?" he smiled hugging her.

"I wanted to ride the Himalaya. But I couldn't anyway, cause it's broken." She frowned oblivious to the anxiety and stress she put her brother through.

"Tee-Tee the ride's not broken. It's shut off because the park's closed."

"Oh ok." She nodded then a look of sudden dismay etched over her face. "What's wrong? Is she gonna be okay?"

Havoc glanced back at Donnie. She still looked a bit shaken up from tonight's revelries. "Donnie? Yes, she'll be fine." he hoped.

"No-no, not Donnie...her!" Tee-Tee asked pointing past everyone.

Havoc, Donnie and Nicky looked back stunned. "Oh no!"

Mayhem was lying on her side twitching with labored breathing. "Mayhem!" he rushed over to her side and dropped to his knees noticing the severity of the long gash across her under belly for the first time.

"That bitch cut you...deep." Havoc said gently stroking his dog as she whimpered. "Oh no. Don't die. Please-don't." he begged realizing his on call veterinarian was good but he wasn't a miracle worker. Mayhem looked up at her master, wagged her tail twice then licked him in the face and all the light faded out of her eyes as she slipped into oblivion. Havoc gently stroked his best friend's head then buried his face against her lifeless form slowly rocking her in his arms inconsolable.

# Chapter 40

Nicky, Donnie and Tee-Tee watched from the shoreline as Havoc carried Mayhem towards the ocean. It was on this very same beach that he used to bring her in the summer and they'd race up and down it playing, tossing sticks and having a good ol' time. The water was freezing cold but he didn't react. Once he was up to his waist he gently placed her in the water and stroked her head.

"You always seemed happiest out here. So, I figure this is where your final resting place should be." Havoc said as his bottom lip trembled. "Damn Mayhem you were the best friend a guy could ever ask for. You were loyal, loved me unconditionally, overlooked my faults and made me a better person. And for that I'll be forever indebted to you. I love you!"

Havoc did not regard crying as a sign of weakness, but it did take quite a bit to milk tears from his hard-bitten eyes. Like the car accident that stole Tee-Tee away from him and right now as he stared at his best friend's lifelessly body floating in the water. He wiped his face then said, "Goodbye girl." then kissed his dog and let her float off into the blue waters of the Atlantic.

Back on the sand all three women were waiting for him with tears in their eyes. Havoc stood before them inconsolable. A profound sadness swept his face. "She was my best friend and now she's…" he dropped to his knees struggling to come to terms with his tremendous loss.

Nicky found Havoc's coat lying in the sand and started to go to him then caught herself and gave it to Donnie. Donnie graciously mouthed 'thank you' then went over to comfort her man. Havoc felt his coat placed around his shoulders and looked up at Donnie. His eyes were red and wet. He stood and looked out on the horizon as the sun rose over the Atlantic Ocean. Seagulls began circling overhead and the sound of crashing waves played in the background. An early morning jogger could be seen running in the distance.

"We've got to get out of here. It won't be long before people and the cops'll be here and I can't do this right now. I don't have the energy. I've got to find us a car." he said.

"Take your pick. There's plenty." Nicky said referring to all the abandoned cars his enemies drove there. And would no longer be needing.

"I'm scared." Tee-Tee said.

Havoc turned to his kid sister then took a deep breath and placed his hands on her shoulders, "Tee-Tee, do you remember those bad men that were chasing us all night in their cars?" He asked her.

"Uh-huh," Tee-Tee nodded frightened.

"Well they are friends of the other bad men who attacked us at Pizza hut."

"We beat them up right?"

"That's right we did. And that's why they chased us because they wanted to get even. So, if anybody asks you about what happened tonight, Mom, Dad, the police. That's what you'll tell them. That all of this started because of the bad men at Pizza Hut okay?"

"Okay!" she nodded.

Havoc looked over at Donnie and Nicky and their faces both agreed that it was the perfect cover up to what went down tonight.

"I'm sad about Mayhem." Tee-Tee sobbed.

Havoc glanced back at the ocean in time to witness a huge wave wash over Mayhem and just like that, she was gone, forever. "Yeah, me too." he sighed and dropped his head.

Tee-Tee stepped beside her brother and took his hand then sang, "When I'm stuck in a day that's sad and mopey. I can stick out my chin and then I sinnnnng. Tomorrow-tomorrow I'll love you tomorrow. Tomorrow's a brand new day,"

Suddenly a peaceful look like that of a wanderer who had found his way home transformed his face and Havoc turned to his sister with a smile and kissed her forehead. "Thank you," he said then looked at Donnie and Nicky. "Well, it's finally over. The thing is I've been in the revenge business so long that I don't know what to do with the rest of my life."

Donnie came forward and put her arms around him and squeezed tight, "We'll figure it out-together."

Tommy Strong nodded. "Let's get out of here."

He had run his course as a paid Trouble Consultant and it was time to move on to the next chapter in his life...

# Chapter 41

On the corner between Stand and Lean, overly dressed for this season in a trench coat, Tommy plucked a half-smoked Newport onto the ground then untied the doo-rag from his head. He ran his hand from the top of his shinny wavy locks that spun 360 degrees, down to the bottom of his neatly manicured full bearded chin and crossed the street at a red light. Fittingly Nina Simone's song, 'Feeling Good' came from an idle car and he smiled at the irony of it being a new dawn and a new day. But he didn't feel so good. He continued on past the parked limousines, double parked cars and long line of people to the nightclub's entrance.

"Okay I need some order! Can everybody please step back and form a line on the opposite side of the barricade? If you don't do that then you're not coming in! And trust me, you want to come in." Julius a ridiculously swollen bouncer loudly instructed the huge multitude of partygoers anxious to pay the cover charge so they that could get their groove on inside. "No caps, scarves, doo-rags or weapons of any kind allowed inside. And fellas do us both a favor. If you pride yourself on being a troublemaker then save us both the headache and get off of the line right now! We're here to have a good time." When the doorman spotted the man who buttered his bread, he immediately unhinged the velvet rope so that he could enter. "Evening Mister Strong." Julius greeted.

"Sup Big Jay, how's everything going?" Tommy asked giving his head of security a fist bump.

"Major turnout tonight Boss. Mark my words, this spot is gonna go down in history. And you my friend are going to be a huge success! Trust me, nineteen eighty-nine is going to be your year." the doorman said energetically.

"Yeah-well, it can't be worse than eighty-eight…I hope." Tommy sighed with the apathy of a pallbearer then entered the grand opening of his new club.

Conveniently located downtown Brooklyn near every form of public transportation imaginable as well as the Brooklyn Bridge, 'The Crimson Lounge' was already being hailed as the hippest place to party in Brooklyn thanks to clever radio promotions and a snazzy street team that handed out vivid flyers from Soho to Staten Island.

Frankie Beverly and Maze's 'Before I Let You Go' bounced off the walls as scores of party goers danced like mad amid the 2,400 lights and numerous video monitors that periodically painted the room in the same color as the club's namesake. Some walls were splashed in vivid colors and others were covered from floor to ceiling with gorgeous graffiti murals. At the crowded bar, homeboys and homegirls kept the bartenders busy while up on the balcony immaculately dressed hip-hop trendsetters lounged on overstuffed black velveteen sofas sipping colorful drinks.

When random celebrities such as Mike Tyson, Naomi Campbell, Biz Markie, Roxanne Shante, Heavy Dee, Salt N Pepa, MC Lyte, R&B vocal group Levert, Queen Latifah and Fab 5 Freddy randomly came over to tell Tommy how flyy and fresh his new club was, and to wish him all the best, he'd put on a plastic smile, thank them, pose for pictures then drop it when they were gone. After briefly conferring with his staff and confirming everything was running smoothly he went downstairs to the restaurant section. His Uncle Booze was at the bar tossing back shots while his parents and Tee-Tee were dinning in the rear. As Tommy watched them he wondered if his father really bought the story about the punks from the Pizza Hut being responsible for everything that happened. But if he didn't, he never said a word.

When his mother noticed him she waved him over, but he gestured that he was busy and would be back later. His father waved his arms over the club and gave him a thumbs-up seal of approval. Tommy nodded his appreciation then headed back upstairs. On the way up, he bumped into Bug-Out coming down and the two eyed one another uncomfortably.

"Hey cuz," Bug-Out said timidly.

"Sup!" Tommy replied even toned.

"Uncle Smitty invited me. He um-told me about you and him going into business together with the club. The place looks really great." Bug-Out said squirming like he was under hot lights.

"Thanks." Tommy nodded eyeing his cousin from head to toe. Even though they had not spoken in over a year Tommy still kept tabs on him. That night when he took little AJ away from his dysfunctional drug addicted parents, was an awakening for Bug-Out and shortly afterwards he checked himself back into and completed the rehab program. When he got out Bug-Out did an amazing 360. He left the drugs alone for good and began anew with his son. He even began attending Church with his mother. And while some days were harder than others he got through them all without using. But in spite of his efforts to help his wife get on the straight path, Laquita's habit won out in the end and they parted ways.

"You put on some weight." Tommy noticed.

Bug-Out grinned. "I moved back home. And you know how my mom's is. She keeps a nig-," Tommy raised an eyebrow. "I mean she keeps a brotha full." he smiled patting his belly.

"Drug free looks good on you."

"Thanks. Coming from you, that means a helluva lot. Look Tommy, I never got a chance to apologize for what I did with the bad blood between us and all. But from the bottom of my heart, I'm really sorry cousin." Bug-Out said and offered his cousin his hand in act of contrition.

A slight smile formed at the corners of Tommy's lips and he pulled him in for a brief embrace. "We straight. So, you working yet?" he inquired.

Bug-Out shook his head and sighed. "No, not yet. I've been looking everywhere. But it seems nobody wants to hire an ex con slash ex drug addict. Go figure."

"Well, I do. Especially when it's family. I tell you what, stop by tomorrow afternoon and we'll discuss putting you on the payroll."

"Wow man for real? Thanks cousin I really appreciate the opportunity. And I promise I won't let you down." Bug-Out swore.

"I know." Tommy said then walked up the stairs.

"Hey!" Bug-Out called and his cousin looked back. "I still wanna be you when I grow up."

Tommy smiled and continued on.

Upstairs a deep voice came over the PA system asking for everyone's attention and the music died down as Tommy standing on

454

stage, thanked everyone for coming out for the opening of The Crimson Lounge. After a few choice words about the night club and a joke at his expense, about his father being pleased he finally got a real job, he said that it was an honor and privilege to have one of the founding fathers of hip-hop, DJ Kool Herc, spinning on the ones and twos. Then he demanded, that everyone give it up for the smoothest Black Man to bless a microphone and introduced Big Daddy Kane. The crowd went into overdrive as the suave rapper along with his back-up dancers Scoob and Scrap lover took the stage, gave Tommy a pound and then performed his hit song 'Set it Off' while his DJ Mister Cee put on a dazzling turntablism display. Tommy waved at the crowd then exited the stage feeling like he didn't belong there.

Dressed in a knockout spaghetti strap black dress, Donnie walked up holding a full champagne flute and greeted her man with a squeeze and a kiss. "Hey bay-bee."

"Hey," Tommy turned with a half-smile.

"Come, I have a spot set up for us over here," she said leading him over to a table with a large basket adorned with a Purple bow sitting in a chair. He took a seat. "Everything looks wonderful." she said sitting beside him.

"Yeah-thanks." Tommy said unenthused.

Donnie spotted her girlfriends enter the club and bit her bottom lip. "Ok, don't be mad but I invited Pumpkin and my girls." she said cringing expecting an argument.

Tommy shrugged unfazed. "It's cool." He said and called over his hostess and instructed her to set Donnie's friends up with a VIP table and free drinks and appetizers.

Donnie smiled relieved. "Thanks baby. That was so nice. And I still can't get over the new look. Got a sister feeling sea sick from all those waves." She teased running her hand over his thick wavy hair do.

"Yeah-well, I felt it was time for some changes." Tommy muttered like he was distracted with something on his mind.

She detected his sullen mood but assumed he was just nervous about the club's opening and let it go. "O-kay. But honey, what's up with the Inspector Gadget trench coat?" Tommy shrugged with no explanation. "Are you coming down with something?"

"I'm fine." Tommy said and stopped a passing waiter and ordered a double shot of Johnnie Walker RED.

Concerned about her man Donnie placed her head over his forehead and face. "You don't feel warm."

"Would you stop already Donnie, I said I'm fine!"

"What is your problem?"

"Nothing!" He snapped then realized he was out of line and eased up, "Nothing really-sorry baby. It's just the club opening and you know, stuff."

"Well never fear, Donnie is here. And together we can get through the opening and your stuff." Donnie smiled and Tommy nodded returning her smile with one of his own as the waiter came back with his drink.

"So, what's in the basket?" he inquired changing the subject.

"One of two major surprises that I am certain will cheer you up."

"Oh?"

"Uh-huh, here." Donnie smiled and struggled to lift the gift basket and place it in his lap.

Something inside of the basket moved and Tommy looked up at Donnie bewildered. "What the hell!" he said then pulled back the purple ribbon and an adorable black and sandy-brown dog with pointy ears pushed its head out the top. It was so cute it looked like a stuffed animal come to life. Tommy perked up instantly and removed the small dog from the basket. "Whoa well would you looka' here! A mini German Shepherd. Hey little guy,"

"Actually, he's a Belgian Malinois. A Shepherd look-alike." Donnie informed.

"Not familiar with the breed. What is he a year old?"

"Try three months old."

"Wait a minute, this is a three-month-old puppy and he's already this big?" Tommy asked amazed at the puppy's size. "I thought he was a small dog. Look at his paws for crying out loud. They're huge!"

"Well you ain't seen nothing yet. The man at the pet store told me that this breed of dog can grow pretty big."

"Say word? Hey there-big guy. How's it going?" Tommy laughed at the feisty pup as it playfully growled nibbling on his finger. "Wow look at him. He's a tough little son a gun."

"I'm glad you like him. I was worried you might not be ready because, well you know." Donnie said.

Tommy nodded sadly but immediately smiled at the puppy. "You were right. This is a major surprise. Thank you." He said.

"The first of two remember?"

"So, what's the other one?"

She checked her watch. "Later. When the time is right." she said then leaned in for a kiss. When she pulled back he looked troubled.

"What is it?" She asked,

He tossed back his double shot of liquid courage then turned to his woman. "We need to talk,"

"Yes, we do." She agreed.

Outside in the back alley of 'The Crimson Lounge' at the bottom of a flight of stairs, Donnie watched as Tommy was down on one knee using the belt on his coat to play tug-of-war with his new puppy.

"I'm so proud of you honey. Your club is already a huge success and who knows, after a year or two maybe you can expand. Pretty soon you'd have your own chain of clubs all over the map. Wouldn't that be something?"

"Yes, that would be something all right." Tommy shrugged unenthusiastic.

"Okay I gotta' ask. What's up with the gloomy face? This should be the happiest night of your life. Aside from the day we met of course." Donnie smiled. "Hey I bet my other surprise will put a smile on your face."

"I have something to say as well." Tommy mumbled avoiding eye contact.

"Ok you first." Donnie said.

Tommy nodded and rose to his feet. He cut his eyes up at the exit door of his club. "I tried, but I can't do this any longer."

"Can't, lives on won't street. I mean are you sure? All that work for nothing? And besides if you don't want the club what else are you going to-" Donnie paused when something suddenly occurred to her, "You weren't talking about the club, were you?" she asked nervously and Tommy shook his head no. "Are you breaking up with me?"

"No, it's not that. But you might want to break up with me after I tell you what's really going on." Tommy frowned and slowly unbuttoned his trench coat allowing it to fall to the floor. A moment later Donnie realized what was eating Tommy as Havoc the Trouble Consultant stepped forward reborn dressed in a tailored red silk outfit that complimented his physique. Donnie shook her head ruefully and sipped from her champagne glass that she brought outside with her.

"Aren't you at least going to comment?" Havoc asked.

"You want me to comment? Okay, go to hell!"

"That wasn't exactly the comment I was looking for."

"What is it you want me to say Tomm-oh silly me. You're wearing red. So I should be calling you Havoc right?" Donnie snapped.

"This isn't easy for me either." Havoc explained as Donnie glared at him. "Do you remember who I was?"

"Do you remember what you promised me?"

458

"Yes." he said ruefully.

"After Coney Island you said you were done. Have you forgotten how lucky you were? How we all were?" she sharply reminded him.

"No. Of course I haven't." Havoc replied remembering how thanks to Detective Fisk keeping his word about returning a favor, the worst night of his life was neatly squared away with a secret all-knowing wink and fist bump.

"Then why the hell are we having this conversation?"

"Because it's high time I was real with you and myself. Donnie I'm not the guy who comes home to his woman every night after a long day at the office. I've been in these streets for far too long, living off of my wits and primal instincts. I can't turn that around and acclimate a new lifestyle just because we've fallen in love. And another thing I can't do is drag you back into it and put your life in danger again." Havoc said.

Donnie's lips parted to say something when her thoughts were ambushed by the sound of a phone ringing. After a moment Havoc realized it was coming from him looked down and drew the clumsy object from the gun holster on his hip like a gunslinger would a pistol. Her eyes widened.

"Just give me a sec." Havoc said and pressed a button then brought the phone to his ear. "Who dis? … Whoa-whoa, calm down Ma'am I can barely hear you…What?...Yes this is he…Am I back in business?" he looked over at Donnie who was hanging on to his every word, praying he would say the right thing. Havoc knew his next response would change the dynamics of his relationship and everything else, forever then sighed heavily and said, "…Yes Ma'am it's true-I'm back." At that instant Donnie felt her heart drop to her feet and she closed her eyes disappointedly. "So how can I be of service?...They did what?! Where can I find these sons of a bitches?...Yes, I know exactly where that is. I can meet you there in an hour…What?...No, don't worry about payment Ma'am. If your story checks out then **they** will pay, with interest!"

Havoc shut off his phone sliding it back into its holster and looked over at Donnie. She stood there expressionless. "I thought you were allergic to portable phones and beepers." she said dumbfounded as she noticed in addition to the phone, a pager clipped on to his holster as well.

"I was…still am. Originally Pop insisted I get one because of the nightclub and seeing as I retired from-" He stopped short realizing he was digging himself into a deeper hole as Donnie angrily folded her arms across her chest. "Then I realized the benefits." He quickly deflected. Donnie shook her head adding the cellular brick phone to his growing list of betrayal. "Babe I-" he began.

"An hour ago, I was on cloud nine celebrating your club and our future together." She cut him off speaking as if she was talking to herself. "And now, thanks to one stupid phone call I lost it all!" She said glaring at him.

"Don't say that. You haven't lost me,"

Donnie shook her head smiling but finding absolutely nothing amusing. "You're right. Because I never really had you. To begin with."

"Donnie I-"

"I want to get married." she said and Havoc's eyebrows raised perplexed. "I mean not tonight or even to you necessarily. Look, I know when we first got together it was a method of convenience that eventually led to more. And we never spoke about taking it this far. But that's what I want. I want a family and I want to live in a little house with a garden with a tree for the kids to climb on. And I want to go to sleep every night with the same person by my side and wake up next to him in the morning. Every morning. For the rest of our lives."

"But I thought you didn't want the 'American Dream.'"

"I didn't…until I met you."

"I-um," Havoc tried to find the words and she placed her hand on his chest.

"Don't. You made a choice. And it wasn't…us." she said looking down. Deep down she always knew they were living on borrowed time. That he'd never completely betray his masochistic devotion to the streets. But a girl can dream.

Havoc cupped her chin to make eye contact. "Donnie you know that's not true. There's not another soul on this whole planet I'd rather be with except for you. Hanging out with you has been an absolute slice of heaven."

Donnie recoiled from his hand like his touch burned. "Wow. Is that what we've been doing all this time? Hanging out?" She asked. Her voice flushed with anger and pain.

"No of course not. It's just after what happened, I threw myself into this club, and us, and I left my past in the past."

"And look at everything you've accomplished for your future." Donnie reminded him.

"Look baby I honestly tried to let it go and move on. And for a while there I had. But for the past month or so I've been fighting a tug of war in my head. Debating whether I should or shouldn't go back. Then a couple of days ago fate decided for me when I happened upon Barbara Jean Holliday and her daughter Mercedes." Donnie looked at Havoc as if he expected her to know who they were. "My first consulting job last year. Barbara hired me after Mercedes got caught up in the street life and was being forced into prostitution. The cops wouldn't do anything. But I did. And now she's back home with her family. Safe. Registered in college and has a future. But I keep asking myself, what if I hadn't taken the job? What if I don't take the next job? What'll happen to the next Mercedes?"

"But why does it have to be you who takes on the burden? The responsibility?" Donnie argued.

Havoc let her question hang in the air for a moment while pondering it over. *'Why him?'* he asked himself, as he recalled that night in The Lennox Lounge when she jokingly referred to him as hero of the hood. Back then he shrugged it off as utter nonsense and insisted she was wrong. He was no hero. But was she right? Was he wrong? His father's wise words replayed in in his head, *'it's never too late to be what you might have been.'* Detective Fisk telling him, *'You're needed right where you are, Trouble Consulting! Doing what we can't that needs to be done!'* He inhaled deeply and released a long-winded breath as the answer to her million-dollar question came to him then turned to the woman he loved hoping she'd understand. "Because if I don't, who will?"

Champaign's 'How 'Bout Us' began to pour out of the nightclub and Havoc looked at Donnie stunned by the ironic twist of fate. She shook her head sadly, "I asked the DJ to play it at midnight. I thought it'd be romantic. The two of us dancing, celebrating a future...together." she explained feeling silly due to the recent change of events.

The Trouble Consultant moved closer and opened his arms invitingly. "My lady, would you do me the honor of accompanying me on the dance floor?" he asked. Donnie sighed allowing herself to be engulfed in his embrace.

Havoc could see the disappointment and hurt in Donnie's face and wrapped his arms around her then began moving slowly to the music. At first, she resisted but gave in and nuzzled her head inside of his chest and the two began to move in sync. As she danced she stopped a tear that tried to escape.

*'Ooh short and sweet. No sense in draggin on past our needs. Let's don't keep it hangin on. If the fire's out we should both be gone,'*

She heard that ballad so many times before it officially became their love theme, that she lost count. And each and every time it always described the beginning of the perfect relationship, with the perfect man. But, at that moment slow dancing and really listening to the words for the first time, it described the end of the perfect relationship. With the perfect man.

*'Some people are made for each other. Some people are made for another for life, how bout us? Some people can hold it together. Last through all kinds of weather tell me, can we?'*

When the music was over she looked up at him forcing a smile holding back tears. Havoc pulled her close and gave her a tight squeeze and passionate kiss that felt final. He removed a set of car keys and aimed the remote at the far end of the dark alley and pressed a button. Suddenly a pair of bright headlights belonging to a shiny candy red Ferrari F40 too flyy for words with a license plate the read CODE RED2 blinked on illuminating the alley followed by the deep growl of its engine.

Havoc moved towards the vehicle then stopped and snapped his fingers, "You said you had another other surprise?" he asked.

"Huh? Oh yeah, I was offered a promotion, if I want it." Donnie said somberly staring at his car.

"Congratulations. But why are you saying a good thing like it's a bad thing? Don't you want it?" he asked.

"I'm not sure because it's in the California office. And I'd have to relocate there."

"Wow, that's a big decision. What are you going to do?"

"You're right it is a big decision, that I was hoping to make with you. But apparently you don't want to include me in on your big decisions. So, this may be a decision I have to make on my own."

"Babe I can't tell you what to do. But I'll support whatever you do."

Donnie sighed. It wasn't what she wanted to hear. But it was what she needed to hear. "Take care of yourself, Tommy." She said refusing to acknowledge the Trouble Consultant.

"You do the same," Havoc nodded. "Does this mean we're good?"

"Yes...we're good." she lied through a phony smile.

And with a nod, Havoc continued towards his whip. He got in behind the wheel then heard the sound of whimpering. He looked down on the ground, sighed then placed the whimpering puppy in the seat beside him. Glancing over at the puppy happily wagging its tail, The Trouble Consultant thought to himself he had some big paws to fill.

"So, I've given it some thought. What do you think about the name Major?" Havoc asked the feisty pup who replied with a zesty yelp. A slight smile formed in the corner of his mouth as he scratched behind newly dubbed Major's ear, "Then it's settled." He said eyeing the thin gold dog whistle hanging on the rear-view mirror. Havoc glanced up at Donnie who hadn't taken her eyes off of him and thought how rare it was to find mind, body and soul wrapped up in the same beautiful package. Yet he did it twice. And he threw it away, twice. He pushed the guilt out of his head. He had a job to do. "Aight listen up partner. This is a simple job. Piece of cake. I don't anticipate on needing any back up. So keep your overzealous ass in the car. If I need you, I'll call you. Are we clear?" Havoc asked his new partner in training. Major barked excitedly bouncing around in his seat like he understood. Just like his old partner used to do, right before a job. Feeling déjà vu, he smiled and inserted a CD in the dashboard player then nodded his head to the hypnotic hip-hop beat pounding from the BOSE speakers as LL Cool J's hit, 'I'm Bad' fittingly played. "Well, time to make the doughnuts," he said and Major-Havoc burst out of the alley like a rocket on wheels.

Donnie watched the car disappear into the night then raised her glass, "A toast, to the dumbest man alive. And the woman who's even dumber." She said emptying it with one swallow.

"You're not dumb." A voice behind Donnie said. She looked back to find Nicky standing at the top of the steps dressed for a night of celebrating.

"If you're going to say, 'I told you so', then save your breath." Donnie hissed too angry and upset to be embarrassed.

Nicky came down the stairs smiling empathetically, "I would never play you like that Sista' girl. Not after the shit we've been through. Besides, I understand what you're feeling. Because he did the same exact thing to me."

Donnie did a confused double take, "But I thought that **you** asked him for a divorce."

Nicky shook her head. "He probably told you that because he wanted to make me look like the stronger person. But no, it was the other way around. I was never okay with what my husband, correction, ex-husband did but I was willing to accept it because I loved him. And, as much I hate to admit it even though we've both moved on respectively, I guess a small part of me always will. Because truth be told, we both know that Thomas Oliver Strong is not an easy man to get over."

"Amen," Donnie agreed and wiped her tears.

"I never asked him for a divorce. He asked me…on our anniversary. We were out celebrating when one of his enemies attacked him. I swear if I didn't stop him he would have killed that man." As Donnie listened she now realized what Tommy was referring to when he told her how he once almost killed someone and lost everything in the process. Nicky continued, "Later on, that night after I patched him up, he turned to me and said it would kill him if anything were to ever happen to me. I thought for sure the next thing he was going to say was that he was walking away from being a Trouble Consultant. Get his old construction job back. And things would go back to the way they were. But instead he said the opposite. I was devastated and refused to speak to him even when he moved out but continued paying off the mortgage on our house. On the day I graduated from college he signed it over to me as a gift. Some gift. All I ever wanted was my husband. All he ever wanted was a way to provide. Even if that way, kept him from me." She said in a sad voice revealing that she still hadn't completely healed. "But I will say this though, he's changing."

"How so?"

"You heard him yourself, 'Don't worry about payment?' The old Havoc would have never taken on a Consulting job without discussing payment first. He's different. He has a new agenda." Nicky said. Donnie nodded in agreement but her sad expression said she didn't care about the new and improved Havoc coming full circle and finally accepting who he was. All she knew was her man was gone. Nicky tossed an arm around her shoulder. "The sooner you realize that Tommy has these fierce principles and will stand up to them without apology, regardless of consequences, the better off you'll be." Nicky said but Donnie didn't look like she was ready to realize anything. "Hey gurl, what do you say we head back inside and party like it's 1999. But tomorrow you and I throw on our baddest outfits and hit this place I know where we can meet some actual committed men."

"Oh really and where's this?" Donnie asked with a sniffle.

"The mental hospital." Nicky said with a wink. The two burst into laughter and although Donnie's heart was nowhere near mended, Nicky's cheesy joke did scotch tape it together temporarily. "C'mon let's get you another drink."

"Okay, but just so you know, I don't drink alcohol." Donnie said.

"Since when? The last five minutes? Unless my eyes are deceiving me weren't you and that champagne glass just lip locking?"

"Ginger ale. And I'm gonna have to take a raincheck on the double date. I'm gonna be out of town for a while." Donnie said.

Nicky tossed a comforting arm around Donnie's shoulder, "Well then before you go, I'll treat you to a double-shot of Ginger Ale."

Donnie nodded then followed her, pausing at the top of the stairs to rub her belly. She had it all planned out perfectly. With their song asking 'How bout us?' in the background she was going to reveal her life changing second secret. But after Havoc revealed his, she decided to keep hers to herself and instead tell him about the job promotion she originally planned on turning down. Besides, had she told him he was about to be a father, all he would have done was stay with her out of guilt and obligation. And she didn't want that. How she saw it, he was free and if or when he came back, it was meant to be. She needed to get away to think and California was the perfect escape.

And with that the two women went back inside as the man they both had a soft spot in their hearts for cruised the streets of Brooklyn, AKA the borough that's thorough, to settle beef, but no longer for a fee.

# Dedication

For the past 14 years I worked at a job that provided me with a decent salary and benefits to support my family. The problem was I was miserable because it wasn't what I wanted to do or who I wanted to be. One day after a particularly stressful day at work I came home and collapsed on the couch. While channel surfing I stopped at Tracy Morgan a popular successful comedian from my hometown of Brooklyn who was on a talk show promoting his latest project. I listened as he spoke about how overcoming rough patches in life, believing in his God given talent and never giving up led him to where he is today. Then he looked directly into the camera and said, "Without no struggle there is no progress. But hey, I'm just a regular kid from Brooklyn who had a dream and if I can make mines come true, then so can YOU."

I swear it felt like Tracy was speaking directly to me because the next thing I knew I was up on my feet and turning on my computer. I located and dusted off the file containing the manuscript I'd given up on trying to get published over twenty years ago. I opened it up and was reintroduced to characters I hadn't thought about in decades. To my surprise my book still captivated me. Still made me laugh. Still told a story I knew that people would love to read. And still made me want to become a published author. That's when I made two phone calls. The first was to my wife. The second to my best friend. I explained to them how the thought of working another eleven years until I could retire at a job I didn't want to work another eleven minutes depressed me. How this comedian's story inspired me. And most importantly, how I was ready to get back on the saddle and publish my novel. Both of them said the same thing, "Well It's about time. Let's get to work!"

So, here's to the incredible people in my life who without their love, devotion and hard work I could not have done this.

First to my beautiful supportive, perfect wife of 10 years; web page builder, t-shirt designer, copy editor slash book-keeper and fact-finder, Charon. From our very first date when I told you how I'd written two books and dreamed of becoming a successful novelist but it never came to fruition, you constantly encouraged me to never stop trying. Time went by, we got married and started a beautiful family. Throughout the years not a week had gone by that you didn't remind me of how talented of a writer I am and to get back into it. But how I saw it, if it hadn't happened already, it was never going to. So I gave up on my dream. But you didn't give up on it, or me and told me, *"it's never too late to become what you might have been"*. Then you unselfishly insisted I use the money we had saved up for our ten-year wedding anniversary trip to Vegas to instead self-publish my book. Thank you Baby-ths.

To the other special lady in my life, my mother. Thank you for always supporting and believing in me. And thank you for raising me to believe that I could do anything I set my mind to. Then reminding me, when I forgot.

I also want to thank my brother from another mother, one-man advertising and promotions team, Kevin C. Meggett. Back in 1994 when we first met at that soul-sucking mailroom job and you asked why I was constantly scribbling things down on pieces of scrap paper during our lunch break, I said I had a great idea for a novel. You were the only person who didn't laugh or brush it off as delusions of grandeur. Instead you believed in me and even used your own money to help me get my first book Alley-Katt self-published and start Books N' Beats our old publishing company. And when I decided to walk away from it against your advice, you still promised it would someday happen. Well this time I promise we're going to see this to the end.

A special shout out to my play-play cousin, talented artist and graphic designer, Veronique Meggett creator of www.veryuniques.com who designed the front and back cover for both my novels.

To my sons, my pride and joys the Bonner Brothers D.A.B. & D.L.B. who I also did this for. I want you guys to grow up living life to the fullest and following your dreams. And how can I expect you to if I don't? Oh, and Dad promises to write a book without bad words that you can read. I believe in you.

Thank you to my fellow Brooklynite the extremely talented Tracy Morgan for sharing your amazing story and inspiring me when I REALLY needed to hear it.

And last but certainly not least thank you to YOU whomever you are who just finished reading my novel. I hope you enjoyed reading it as much as I enjoyed writing it and that you want to read more of my stories. And if you do, you're in luck because I have plenty more to tell so stay tuned.

Coming soon, MAJOR HAVOC.

# Author's Bio

 Derrick A. Bonner was born and bred in Brooklyn New York and is the author of 2 outstanding novels, Alley Katt and Havoc and Mayhem. He self-published his first novel Alley Katt back in 1998, and even though he had decent success for a first-time author, he discontinued writing and shelved his second novel Havoc and Mayhem. Twenty years later at the request of his wife he decided to resurrect his writing career and finally put out Havoc and Mayhem. Set in the 80's, the lead character Havoc is a combination of the strong and influential men he grew up idolizing in his East New York neighborhood, as well as the lead characters from his all-time favorite television shows growing up. A Man Called Hawk, an impeccably dressed jack-of-all-trades, renaissance man who helped out desperate people in trouble who had nowhere to turn. And ROC, a traditional family man who believed in an honest day's work and went out of his way to help his neighbors, often confronting racism, gangs and drug dealers head on, to protect his community.

*"The thing about my lead characters is they are people we all know. We've seen them in the neighborhood doing good, and giving back to the community. You ever knew someone who was ordinary but did extraordinary things and you were like wow? They seemed like they had super powers, but the truth is they were just good individuals, who cared. That is Havoc and Mayhem....That is Alley Katt."*

Derrick currently lives in Hudson Valley New York with his wife and two sons. And although he no longer resides in the borough that's thorough, he still shouts 'BROOKLYN!' at concerts & still considers himself a Brooklynite. Because as he puts it, *'You can take me outta Brooklyn. But, you can't take Brooklyn outta me!"*